Carol O'Connell is the *New York Times* bestselling creator of Kathy Mallory, and the author of thirteen books, eleven featuring her acclaimed detective, most recently IT HAPPENS IN THE DARK, as well as the stand-alone thrillers JUDAS CHILD and BONE BY BONE. She lives in New York City.

Acclaim for Carol O'Connell and the Mallory series of novels:

'If any writer could make me break my New Year's resolution to avoid serial killer novels, it's the brilliant Carol O'Connell . . . her books are moving as well as thrilling' *Daily Telegraph*

'Mallory is one of the most original and intriguing detectives you'll ever meet . . . Wild, sly and breathless – all things a good thriller ought to be' Carl Hiaasen

'Mallory grips us like a hand on the throat' *The Times*

'Readers, beware! That sly (and oh so gifted) Carol O'Connell is just as cunning as her beautiful, near-sociopathic heroine, Kathy Mallory, creeping up on unsuspecting readers with softly caressing words and languidly flowing sentences, then sucker-punching them with shockingly explicit violence that's as vivid as it is grisly' *Booklist*

'As I read *Mallory's Oracle*, I kept wanting to hug both Kathy Mallory and Carol O'Connell, and that is the mark of a story and an author who really involve you, and make you care – and that is so rare!' James Patterson

'A smart, skilful practitioner of the mystery-writing arts, O'Connell writes discreetly dazzling books' *New York Times*

'O'Connell is a consummate storyteller – a unique talent who deserves to be a household name' Val McDermid

'Memorable characters and blazingly original prose. Once again, O'Connell transcends the genre

Carol O'Connell

WINTER HOUSE

headline

First published in the United States in 2004
by G.P. PUTNAM & SONS, an imprint of the PENGUIN GROUP

First published in Great Britain in 2005
by HUTCHINSON

First published in paperback in Great Britain in 2005
by ARROW BOOKS

This edition published in Great Britain in 2014
by HEADLINE PUBLISHING GROUP

1

Cataloguing in Publication Data is available from the British Library

ISBN 978 1 4722 1285 6

Typeset in Fournier by Avon DataSet Ltd, Bidford-on-Avon, Warwickshire

Printed and bound in Great Britain by
Clays Ltd, St Ives plc

Papers used by Headline are from well-managed forests
and other responsible sources.

MIX
Paper from
responsible sources
FSC® C104740

HEADLINE PUBLISHING GROUP
An Hachette UK Company
338 Euston Road
London NW1 3BH

www.headline.co.uk
www.hachette.co.uk

This book is dedicated to a woman who had two wedding rings. My mother's only marriage had outlasted the original gold band. On a cold day in February, I found that first ring my father had given her. It was worn until it was worn out, thin and brittle, but not broken.

And then she died.

ACKNOWLEDGEMENTS

Many thanks to researcher Dianne Burke, who answers legal and medical questions and can chart the paths of binary stars with equal facility. And thanks to Phillip Skodinski, attorney-at-law. Any errors in this novel are surely my own. And any untoward humor at the expense of the legal profession is expressed by fictional people (not me); and, said humorous, though disparaging, remarks would not have been made if they had not been important to the plot – really – no, *really*.

And thanks to my brother Bruce for the gift of time; and thanks to cousins Norman, Melinda, Camille and Noel for an eleventh-hour visit that meant the world to me.

ONE

The hour was late. The traffic was scarce. A few cars crawled by at the pace of bugs attracted by house lights, five flights of electric-yellow windows.

The narrow mansion was not a rarity in New York City, home to millionaires and billionaires. However, its nineteenth-century façade was an anachronism on this particular block of Central Park West. The steep-pitched roof was split by a skylight dome, and attendant gargoyles were carved in stone. Wedged in tight between two condominium behemoths, this dwelling was in the wrong place at the wrong time and regally unrepentant, though the police were at the door.

And in the parlor, up the stairs and down in the cellar.

So *many* police.

Nedda Winter sat quietly and watched them pass her by on their way to other rooms – and they watched her for a while. Soon they came to regard her as furniture, but she took no offense. She turned on the antique radio that stood beside her chair. No one reprimanded her, and so she turned up the volume.

White hot jazz.

Benny Goodman on the clarinet and other ghosts from the big-band era flooded the front room and infected the steps of people in and out of uniform, passing to and fro.

Lift those feet. Tap those toes.

Miss Winter repressed a smile, for that would be unseemly, but

1

she nodded in time to the music. The house was alive again, drunk on life, though the party revolved around the dead man at the center of the floor.

Miss Winter was well named. She had the countenance of that season. Her long hair was pure white, and her skin had the pallor of one who has been shut away for a long time. Even her eyes had gone pale, leached of color, bleached to the lightest tint of blue. She was so well disguised by time that the police continued to ignore her, demanding no apologies, nor any explanation for her long absence. They had even failed to recognize this house, an address that was infamous when the music on the radio was young.

Fifty-eight years earlier, in the aftermath of another violent crime, which remained unsolved, a twelve-year-old girl had vanished from this house, and now the lost child, grown up and grown old, had come back home.

The medical examiner's vehicle was parked at the curb, and behind it was another van with the CSU logo of the crime-scene technicians. The front windows of the house were all alight, and the silhouettes of men and women moved across pulled-down shades and closed drapes.

A warm October breeze of Indian summer rippled the yellow crime-scene tapes that extended down the stone steps to include a patch of the sidewalk. The tape did the restraining duty of a velvet rope for theatrical productions, though tonight's audience amounted to only three stragglers, refugees from a saloon in the hour after closing time. Happy intoxication was in their stance and in their badly sung song, which was grating on the nerves of a uniformed officer. The spinning cherry lights of police units made the officer's face alternately beet red and pale white as he waved off the drunks with a loud 'Get the hell outta here!'

Charles Butler parked his Mercedes behind a police car and stepped out into the street, unfolding and rising to a stand of six feet four. Smooth grace in motion served as compensation for his foolish face. Bulbous eyes the size of hens' eggs were half closed by heavy lids and pocked with small blue irises that gave him a look of permanent astonishment, and his hook of a nose might perch two sparrows or one fat pigeon. Otherwise, the forty-year-old man was well made from the necktie down and well turned out, though he had omitted the vest from his three-piece suit.

He had dressed in a hurry. Mallory was waiting.

Two uniformed policemen stood guard before the house, barring all comers from the short flight of stone steps leading up to the front door. As he approached these officers, Charles inadvertently smiled – a *huge* mistake. Whenever his features were gathered up into any happy expression, it gave him the look of a loon – a second cousin to the three departing drunks. Before he could be driven off, Charles pointed upward to the worst-dressed man in America, Detective Sergeant Riker, who slouched against a wrought-iron railing, cadging a light from another man, then exhaling a cloud of cigarette smoke with his conversation.

'I'm with him.'

At the sound of a familiar voice, Riker turned around with that crooked smile he saved for people he liked. 'Hey, how ya doin'?' The detective descended the short flight of steps to the sidewalk and gripped the larger man's hand. 'Thanks for coming out. I know it's late.'

Indeed it was, and Riker had the appearance of a man who had slept away most of this night in his suit. But then he always dressed that way, prewrinkled at the start of every workday. The yellow light at the top of the staircase had the flattering effect of minimizing the creases in the detective's face, making him appear somewhat younger than his fifty-five years.

'My pleasure.' Charles looked down at his friend of average height, feeling the need to apologize for looming over him.

'Did Mallory tell you anything useful?'

'No, nothing at all.'

3

'Maybe it's better that way.' Riker motioned him toward the stairs, then led the way up. 'Two women live here. One of them killed a man tonight. Simple enough?' He flicked his cigarette over the railing. 'Check 'em out. We'll talk later.'

When they passed through the open door, Charles heard music, vintage jazz, and he would not have been surprised to hear the clink of ice in cocktail glasses as they entered a din of conversation in the large foyer. They walked by a cluster of men wearing badges clipped to their suit pockets, and Detective Riker nodded to them in passing. 'Those guys are settling a little problem of jurisdiction.' He led Charles through a louder dispute between a woman in uniform and a man in a suit. Riker explained this one, too. He pointed to the young man with the folded stethoscope squeezed tightly in one raised fist. 'Now, that's one pissed off medical examiner. Mallory won't release the body. She's using it to rattle the ladies who live here.'

At the threshold of the front room, Charles had only time enough to blink once before entering a spatial paradox. The inside of the house appeared to be much larger than the exterior – a trick of cunning architecture. And some of the magic was done with a score of mirrors in elaborate silver frames ten feet tall. They created a labyrinth of rooms and flights of stairs and corridors where none existed. Thus, a dozen people were transformed into a mob, and each reflection added its own energy to the fray.

The grand staircase was the focal point, a tenuous bit of engineering that seemed to have no secure supports as it curved up to a partial vista on a floor above the cathedral ceiling. Though the rest of the stairs spiraled out of sight, in mind's eye, he was swept along with them, rushing round and upward through all the dizzying flights.

Back to earth – a corpse lay on the floor, partially obscured by upright people, and Charles Butler, unaccustomed to crime scenes, was caught in a quandary of manners: perhaps he should have admired the dead man first, and maybe he should not be tapping his feet in time to the music of a clarinet.

An even less reverent police photographer stepped over the body to speak with Detective Riker, who directed the close-up shots of the deceased. After snapping pictures in quick succession, and in time to the beat of a snare drum, the photographer departed to another room, giving Charles his first clear view of the victim.

He had been prepared for something brutal and grisly, given that this case had attracted so much attention, but the man on the floor seemed to be merely resting – if one could only discount the pair of scissors protruding from the chest. The victim did not belong in this neighborhood of wealth. His pants were shapeless and dirty, the T-shirt stained with more sweat than blood, and a pointed object lay near one open hand. Thus laid out was the simple story of an ice-pick-wielding intruder felled by a homeowner who favored shears.

What could possibly interest all of these—

Following a cue of upturned heads, his attention was drawn to the second-floor landing and the slender young woman standing there in blue jeans and an attitude of privilege. Blonde curls, cut by a virtuoso, grazed the shoulders of a tailored blazer worn over a silk T-shirt. Arms folded, she affected the pose of one who owned all that she surveyed, even the people in the room below and, most particularly, the corpse.

Mallory.

More formally, she was Detective Mallory and never Kathy anymore. She preferred the distancing surname even among those who knew her best. And, though Charles was her foremost apologist, he found the background music fitting. Louis Armstrong was belting out the lyrics of Savannah's hard-hearted Hannah.

—pouring water on a drowning man—

One cream white hand with red fingernails – call them talons – lightly touched the banister as she slowly descended the grand staircase, circling in a wide arc, her eyes fixed on one face in the crowd.

But not *his* face.

5

Two crime-scene technicians moved out of Charles's way, and now he could see the object of Mallory's fixation.

A child?

Detective Riker had told him that two women lived at this address. There had been no mention of this little girl shivering like a whippet, that nervous, tremulous breed of dog that can never quite get warm, no matter what the temperature. No – wait. This was no child, but a tiny woman with a few silver threads in her dark brown hair, someone closer to his own age. Eyes cast down, this person presented herself at the bottom of the staircase in the manner of a penitent – or a volunteer for human sacrifice.

Tall Mallory literally descended upon the smaller woman, rapidly closing the distance and causing the little householder to shrink even more. Before the small head could turtle into the cowl of a white robe, Charles noted one charming detail: the short brown hair was angled across the ears, creating the illusion that they were pointed in the elfin way.

'That's Miss Bitty Smyth.' Detective Riker raised one eyebrow, as if expecting Charles to recognize the name.

He did not.

'Bitty? That's a nickname?'

Riker shrugged and splayed one hand to say *Who knows?* 'That's how she introduced herself. If she's got another name, we can't get it out of her. We can't get *anything* out of her.'

'She might be in shock.' Charles watched on in helpless fascination as Mallory reached out to Bitty Smyth and gripped the woman's thin arm. He was about to discount the possibility that Miss Smyth was the scissor-wielding homeowner when he turned to see the other resident of the house, a woman with long white hair and a green silk robe. She was barefoot and seated beside an antique radio, the source of the music. How amazing to find this old piece in working order. By the detail on its cabinet, he could date the radio back to the middle nineteen-thirties – the woman, too. He guessed her age at seventy

6

or thereabouts. Her hand was on the dial, raising the volume.

'That's Miss Nedda Winter,' said Riker. 'She's Bitty's aunt.' Again, something in Riker's manner suggested that Charles should also know this person.

She caught Charles staring at her, and he could only describe her expression as one of curious recognition.

The old woman turned off the music. Her attention had quickly shifted to the young homicide detective who had hold of Bitty Smyth's arm. Nedda Winter rose from her chair. She was taller than many of the men in this room, and her strides were long as she rushed toward her niece with an obvious plan of rescue. Riker, moving faster than his usual mosey, headed off Miss Winter. And now Charles was treated to a display that simply did not fit the man he knew. Playing the consummate gentleman, Riker extended one arm to the lady, as if she might need his support, then dazzled her with a broad smile and smoothly led her out of the room.

Star treatment. Perhaps he *should* know that old woman.

Charles turned back to the interrogation of Bitty Smyth, who was now facing in his direction. A Bible was clutched to the tiny prisoner's breast, and her large brown eyes rolled back as her lips moved in what he took for whispers of fervent prayer.

Well, Mallory had that effect on people.

His next impression was that Miss Smyth had disconnected from the solid earth and might fly upward if not restrained. As Charles drew nearer, he heard Mallory say that, no, she had not found Jesus and had no intention of being saved. The smaller woman's head wobbled and nodded, perhaps in a fearful palsy, or maybe agreeing that this young policewoman was beyond salvation.

'Charles.' Mallory quickly dropped her hold on Bitty Smyth's arm, as if caught in the act of beating a suspect. Supporting this illusion, Miss Smyth sank to an armchair, still nodding and trembling on the verge of a smile, so greatly relieved.

The long slants of Mallory's eyes were always the first thing one

7

noticed – a strange bright shade of green not found in nature. She did not smile upon greeting him, and he had not expected that. Her expressions were usually deliberate or absent, a chilling idiosyncrasy.

She had others.

Though Charles Butler possessed a vast knowledge of abnormal psychology, Mallory sidestepped every attempt to classify her with any sense of confidence, as if she belonged to a separate species of one, a denizen of some unsentimental planet of perpetual cold weather.

'Hello,' he said, smiling and standing back a pace to take her in, as if he had expected her to have grown over the weekend.

Her hand was on his arm, and, with the lightest of pressure, she was able to drag him down a narrow hallway and into a small boxy room all decked out like a tailor's shop with the tools and machines of the trade. Racks of thread spools lined one wall, and a basket of mending sat on the floor near a dressmaker's dummy.

'A sewing room,' she said, 'without a single pair of scissors.'

'I think I noticed them back in the parlor.' And here, wisely, he stopped, for Mallory's eyes widened slightly to tell him that she did not appreciate his pointing out the obvious thing – the shears planted in the dead man's chest. And neither did she care to be interrupted. Arms folding across her chest was all the warning he would ever get.

'So,' the detective continued, 'this woman comes downstairs – in the *dark* – sees the burglar. Then she runs to the other end of the house to look for the sewing shears. And the perp just stands there in the front room, waiting for her to come back and stab him to death.'

Charles hesitated – always a good idea to tread carefully with her. There was only one logical conclusion, but he sensed a trap in the making. 'Then it's not a case of self-defense?'

'No, that's exactly what it is,' she said, somewhat impatient. 'Self-defense. That much I believe.'

'*Right.*' Charles needed no mirror to tell him that he wore the comical face of a fool who has just discovered that it was not night but day. Hands in his pockets, he stared at his shoes. 'I gathered from

Riker that you wanted a psych evaluation of those two women.'

'No, that was just an afterthought.' She closed the door, then leaned her back against it, as if to block his escape. 'What can you tell me about those people?'

He shrugged. 'Only their names. I just got here.'

She put one hand on her hip, a sign that she did not entirely believe him, but then it was her nature to be suspicious of everyone who did not carry a badge – and everyone who did. 'You've never met them before?'

'No,' said Charles, 'I don't know either of them.'

'Well, they know *you*. And they've known you for a long time.' Her eyes were asking, accusing and demanding all at once, *And how do you explain that?*

Detective Riker liked the kitchen best. Unlike the rest of the house, this room was built to human scale. The low ceiling made it cozy, almost cottagelike. He declined an offer of alcohol but allowed Nedda Winter to make him a glass of iced tea with thanks.

She selected a lemon from a bowl of fruit. Knife in hand, she stood at the butcher block and smiled at him. It was almost a tease, as if to ask – did he object to her holding this dangerously pointed object?

Riker's mouth dipped on one side to say, *Yeah, right.*

He made a cursory inventory of the room, his gaze passing over a meat cleaver, then traveling on to a cutlery block of knives. A case bolted to the far wall contained a fire extinguisher and a small ax. With all the lethal weapons in this kitchen arsenal, a pair of scissors had been an odd choice to bring down an intruder tonight.

Miss Winter made short work of the lemon, cutting a slice and draping it over the edge of a tall glass full of ice cubes. She stood at the table, pouring tea from a pitcher and saying, 'Please sit down, Detective. Don't wait on me.'

As Riker settled into a chair, the woman pulled a frosty beer from the refrigerator and uncapped it. Now he revised his ideas of society matrons, for Nedda Winter drank straight from the bottle, long swigs.

'Beer,' she said, pulling up a chair on the other side of the table. 'Nothing like it on a warm night. They go together, don't they?'

'Yeah.'

There was no false note in her voice and nothing ingratiating in her manner. He liked her style and her brand of beer. This was one of *his* people.

'Of course—' She paused to study the bottle in her hand, then flashed him a wry smile. 'If you *do* beat a confession out of me, the alcohol might argue for diminished capacity.'

'I can live with that.' Riker reached into his breast pocket and pulled out a folded sheet of yellow-lined paper. 'We've already got this statement you gave to the West Side detectives. But there's just a few . . . *inconsistencies*.' This word was a cop's euphemism for lies and more lies. 'A few things that need explaining.' In other words, *Try and talk your way out of this if you can.*

Her gray eyebrows were on the rise. They were whimsical things, stray hairs growing this way and that. How old was she? So much hung on the year of Nedda Winter's birth. The detective searched her face and found wrinkles enough to make her seventy – the right age for a legend but he could not be certain, not in this world of plastic miracles where women of sixty passed for forty. There was evidence of surgery, anomalies in the planes of her cheeks and forehead, as if she had been badly broken long ago and put back together. She withstood this intense scrutiny with smiling pale blue eyes. Their directness appealed to him and also put him on his guard. She was looking past his smile.

There was still some doubt about her identity. Or maybe he could simply not believe his own luck to find her in this house tonight. Blunt questions were not an option, not yet, and so he must go slowly with this woman. Intelligence lived in those quick blue eyes that missed nothing. As he took her measure, she measured him.

'So why are all of these people still in my house?' She set her beer bottle to one side. 'The *truth*.'

Riker settled on a half-truth. 'They're trying to reconstruct what happened here.'

'I told them what happened – several times.'

'Like I said, Miss Winter, there's a few glitches in your statement. And then there's the problem of the ice pick.'

Charles Butler followed Mallory into the front room, where the tall mirrors created an unsettling carnival effect. It was impossible to look anywhere without encountering one's own reflection repeating two and three times.

Yet Mallory managed it.

He watched reflected copies of her negotiating the ocular maze with downcast eyes. Actually, this was a familiar phenomenon. She had always avoided every looking glass, even shunning reflections in shop windows. He once had a theory to fit her early history as a homeless child: she might see something ugly or worthless when she met herself in mirrors; self-esteem issues were the sad baggage of that background. However, he had retired this idea for another one that was truly eerie and almost akin to vampirism. She raised her eyes now, and there was no way she could fail to see her own reflection walking toward her from three directions. Yet, she lacked the instant catch-eyes response of every normal person. She appeared to see nothing at all, no recognizable form or proof of her own existence, and she moved on without pause.

What a bundle of contradictions was this stunning young woman who could not enter any room unnoticed – invisible Mallory.

He climbed the spiral staircase, following her black running shoes, Italian leather imports that might cost a week's pay for the other civil servants in this house. He sometimes wondered if she did not delight in raising rumors that she might have an illegal source of income.

And, of course, this was true. She was his business partner. They were headhunters.

Halfway up the stairs, Charles discovered a design flaw. Because of the cathedral ceiling, this march of steps to the second floor was the length of more than two flights. The house had been made for appearances only and with no consideration for inhabitants of Nedda Winter's age. Did that name sound more familiar to him now? He was distracted by Mallory as she explained that there were not enough ice picks in the house.

But there had been an ice pick lying on the floor by the dead man. Surely the one was sufficient.

Enigma, thy name is Mallory.

And sometimes he wondered if she simply enjoyed sharpening her claws on his brain. He looked over the railing and down at the lavishly stocked wet bar by the foot of the stairs – and the silver ice bucket, which would so nicely complement the burglar's expensive ice pick. He could not recall when he had last found a use for his own pick. Regrettably, the day of the old-fashioned ice block delivered by horse-drawn cart was long gone. Perhaps Miss Winter, like himself, had inherited one with the family silver.

'Well,' he began, picking his words more carefully this time, 'I'm guessing – not assuming, mind you – that the ice pick near the body doesn't belong to the burglar.' So far, if he interpreted her silence correctly, he was on safe ground. 'I suppose the man found the pick *after* he broke into the house?'

'Looks that way, doesn't it?' she said.

And so, of course, his theory must be dead wrong. All right, the bedrock of logic was a bit shaky here. Mallory had already conceded self-defense, so either the pick belonged to the burglar or the man had found it in the house. One of these two things must be true – or not.

He sighed.

Mallory paused on the stairs and turned to face him. 'The dead man wasn't a burglar. He was a serial killer out on bail. I'm the one

12

who arrested him. He always used a hunting knife. I found one strapped to his leg. He never had a chance to pull it out before one of those women stabbed him. There's only one line in her statement that rings true. She said it was done in the dark. Now that part's true. If the lights had been on, she'd never have gotten close enough to kill him.'

'This serial killer was out on bail?' Dangerous, but he had to ask. 'How is that possible?'

'Bad judge, good lawyer.' Mallory glanced over the railing, looking down at the front room below and the dead man at its center. 'So that ice pick was out of character for him – and one weapon too many.' She resumed her climb.

'Well,' said Charles to Mallory's back, 'given his history with women, the very fact that he broke in with a knife strapped to his leg, that should be enough to—'

She paused on the second-floor landing to stare at him in a way that asked whose side he was on. 'Neither one of those women knew he had a knife.' Mallory turned her back on him and approached a door to the right of the stairs. 'Odds are, they still don't know.' She rested one hand on the knob. 'When Riker and I showed up, the West Side cops were still trying to get Bitty Smyth to unlock this bedroom door. I had better luck.'

Charles was not certain that he wanted more detail on this.

'I told her to open up or I'd shoot off the lock. That's when Bitty decided to come out.' Mallory opened the door and waved him into the darkness ahead of her, saying behind his back, 'And this is what she didn't want the cops to see.'

What a flair she had for drama.

The lights switched on, and, in the sudden bright light, Charles faced a wall lined with scores of photographs and saw his own face looking back at him from the picture frames.

His eyes gravitated first to a shot taken when he was a child of ten. The backdrop was a birthday party in Gramercy Park. A neighboring frame held a small portrait with the gray grain of newsprint and a companion article about the youngest student ever to matriculate at Harvard University. Next was a picture of a child in cap and gown, inches taller than his graduating class of young adults. In successive photographs, he passed through puberty, collected more academic credentials and entered a prestigious corporate think tank. The caption of an old photo cut from *Fortune* had him escaping the corporation to strike out on his own. And the rest were a collection of society-page shots from weddings and funerals.

The most recent picture of the lot was a candid photograph taken on the streets of SoHo. This one was framed in silver on the table beside Bitty's bed.

'So you have a stalker.' Mallory turned to the bureau and picked up a stack of three diaries, each with a flimsy lock that had been opened. 'Take a look at these. I need to know if she's dangerous.'

'You're joking.'

Her chin jutted forward, and an angry line appeared between her eyes, an unsubtle reminder that she had no sense of humor. Mallory held out the journals.

Charles recoiled as if she were offering something unclean. 'This can't be right, reading her personal—'

'This is a crime scene, Charles. I don't need a warrant.' And her subtext was unmistakable: she was the law; friend and business partner aside, he should not push his luck with her tonight.

A third voice chimed in to say, 'What?'

They looked over to the far corner of the room to see a bird emerge from a large cage on the floor. It was smaller than a parrot but somewhat larger than a parakeet. A comb of yellow feathers unfurled at the top of its head in a gesture of surprise.

'It's a cockatiel,' said Charles.

Mallory looked down at the bird, clearly regarding it as something that she planned to wipe off the sole of her shoe. Charles sensed that this was not their first meeting. The tiny creature was too quick to pick up on her hostility. It opened its beak wide, but not to scream. The posture reminded Charles of a baby bird begging for worms, or, in this instance, begging for its life. The cockatiel flattened its comb of yellow feathers and, head ducked low to floor, retreated behind the fringe of the bedspread.

Charles, however, had nowhere to hide. He stared at the journals as Mallory pressed them into his hands. He shook his head. 'Bitty Smyth impressed me as a very fragile personality. Reading her diaries would be rather like an assault.'

'Read fast and she'll never know.' Mallory turned away from him to rifle the contents of the closet shelves.

He sat down on the unmade bed as he took in all the items of the room. Bitty's interests were not limited to himself. His photographs shared a bit of wall space with the Virgin Mary, and small statues of saints decorated her dresser alongside lipstick tubes and other toilet articles. There was also a collection of equestrian figurines from a young girl's horse-crazy stage of life, and stuffed bears abounded here. Apart from the religious themes, the underlying decor was that of a teenage girl, who was approximately forty years old.

He opened the earliest of the diaries and read it as fast as he could turn pages. Even given his skill as a speed reader, this was a waste of time. All the famed diarists in history had written with posterity and an audience in mind, and so did damn near everyone else on the planet. Consequently, the entries were usually absent anything as embarrassing as truth. In a matter of minutes, he was reading the final page of handwriting, small and neat, and not one line to support the idea of Bitty Smyth as an obsessive stalker. 'I'm not in any of these diaries,' he said. 'Satisfied?'

'No.' Mallory stood before the open closet, holding a sheaf of papers bound in clear plastic. 'This is a Ph.D. dissertation — yours. Think she read it?' Mallory held up a worn sock with a hole in it. 'Or did she just want another souvenir like this one?' She tossed the sock into his lap. 'Your size, I think.'

Charles shrugged this off. 'Bitty moved on to another obsession two years ago.' He stacked the diaries on the bedside table. 'All she wrote about were her religious retreats on the weekends.'

His Ph.D. dissertation flew across the room to join the holey sock in his lap, and he looked down at the cover sheet of this paper authored before he was out of his teens. The subject was prodigies, his own peer group. Charles rose from the bed, drawn to the wall of framed pictures and another sort of peer group – children ganged by age and social strata. 'This one,' he said, staring at the group photograph taken at his tenth birthday party. 'This is the connection between Bitty and me.'

Mallory crossed the room to stand beside him as he pointed to the smirking face of one child in the crowd.

'That boy is Paul Smyth. Must be a relative. I don't remember meeting Bitty Smyth as a child, but I suppose she could have been at this party. Though . . . I don't see her in the picture. Odd. She has the kind of face that never changes – gamine, all eyes. Maybe she was the one with the camera. The shot angles upward, a child's point of view – a child smaller than the others.'

Mallory stepped closer to the photograph. 'There must've been fifty kids at that party.'

'At least,' said Charles.

'So you don't remember Bitty – very distinctive face – but you remember Paul Smyth, the ordinary-looking kid. He was a friend of yours?'

'Hardly.' All of his childhood friends had been adults. 'I didn't even know most of these children.' This had been a family experiment in social interaction with youngsters of normal intelligence. All such experiments had ended in disaster. Children were so good at sussing out and torturing the alien in their midst, the child with the freakish large brain. 'But I knew Paul Smyth too well. He called me Froggy all morning.'

Of course Mallory would not ask why. So obvious. His bulging eyes did call to mind a bullfrog.

'Froggy – only nickname I ever had. So *that* was memorable. It caught on with all the other children that day, and that's what he wanted. He was setting me up. I figured that out when it came time to open my presents.'

'He gave you a frog?'

'A big one.' The huge frog had leapt from the open gift box, initiating a scream from one of the mothers. For six seconds, that amphibian had been the only pet that Charles had ever owned. But then, of course, the other children had converged upon the creature and slaughtered it – slowly – smashing it out of existence under sandals and sneakers and patent-leather shoes. The frog-stomping had been the highlight of his birthday party, for normally the children were not encouraged to kill living things. Later in the day, they had turned their sights on him – froggy number two.

'All right – back to Bitty.' Mallory picked up the stack of diaries. 'She's a religious fanatic. I think I guessed that. What else can you tell me?'

Charles absently stared at the stuffed toys on the bed. The teddy bears were quite old. A child – Bitty, no doubt – had loved the small leather noses off their faces, rubbed them all away with kisses. And then there was the little bird hiding beneath the bed, a metaphor for its mistress who shared the trait of extreme timidity. 'I can't believe this woman could kill anyone.'

'Bitty? Of course not,' said Mallory, oh so casually. 'It was the old woman who did the stabbing. Nedda Winter confessed to the first cop on the scene.'

Charles turned his eyes heavenward. He was *not* praying. 'Then why—' He paused a moment to dial back the frustration. 'Why did you put me through this? Invading this woman's—'

'Because she's a stalker.'

'No, Mallory, that's not quite *it*. Try again.'

'I want you to talk to Bitty Smyth. You said you didn't know her.' Mallory stacked the journals on a closet shelf. 'Well, now you do.'

He shook his head, but denial was futile. 'You set me up!'

She raised one eyebrow in a silent acknowledgment of *Yeah? So?*

'You seriously expect me to make use of this woman's personal diaries to interrogate her?'

'She won't talk to cops. She just throws out quotations from the Bible.'

Yea, though I walk through the valley of the shadow of death? Given Mallory's effect on the woman, that might be—

'It's like biblical Tourette's,' said Mallory. 'So just go down there and talk to her. Get her to open up.'

'I have no intention of—'

'You do it, or *I* do it.'

Her tone implied a threat. No – cancel that – it was a solid promise to do some damage to that fragile little woman downstairs. Bitty Smyth was most likely in shock, and Mallory would be best described as sociopathic on a good day – not that he adored her less for that. And, even understanding that emotional blackmail was Mallory's idea of sport, he said, 'All right.'

When the door had closed on the detective, a small voice from the darkness beneath the bed said, 'What?'

Charles looked down to see the bird emerge from its hiding place. It limped badly on one leg and could not travel in a straight line, but veered in curving paths and circles. One of its wings was missing a full complement of flight feathers, and the raggedy tail feathers dragging along behind the creature were more proof of a walking bird, hence the cage on the floor to accommodate the handicap of being earthbound.

He picked up a bottle of pills, the vitamin prescription of a veterinarian. He had nearly guessed the bird's name – Rags. A second bottle of tablets carried the prescription of a doctor who catered to humans, and this one was filled with sleeping pills. He read the pharmacist's date, then shook the bottle out in his hand and counted the tablets.

All there.

For the past month, Bitty Smyth had not required a sleep aid. Or had she been afraid to sleep?

The bolt on the bedroom door was a great sturdy thing, thick as a steel cigar, and it had the shiny look of a recent installation. The woman was certainly afraid of something or someone.

Detective Riker wondered if Miss Winter knew how many mistakes she had made tonight. He decided that a few of those errors must have occurred to her, for their suspicion was mutual as they stared at one another across the kitchen table.

He smiled. And she smiled.

'Well, ma'am—'

'Call me Nedda.'

'Unusual name.' And unforgettable to Riker. His younger brother was called Ned. But Nedda was not the name that most people would know this woman by, not even those old enough to remember the lurid tabloid stories. Though given names were often passed down through generations of a family, he was certain of her identity now, and he planned to bludgeon her with it later on. 'Maybe we can straighten out some of these loose ends,' said Riker. 'Then we'll just pack up and get out of your life.'

Yeah, like that's gonna happen.

He flipped through the pages of a small notebook, as if he might need this reminder. 'You had a break-in last week. And, tonight, we find a body in your house – after another break-in. Now the ice pick next to the body – looks like he brought it with him.'

'But I shouldn't jump to that conclusion?'

More pages flipped by. 'Lucky guess.' He looked up at her smiling face. 'Did I mention that the guy on your rug was charged with three counts of murder? Now what are the odds that we wrap up three homicides and a break-in with minimal paperwork? You see, we almost never get this kind of happy ending. But we'd be willing to buy it if the guy brought that ice pick into your house. Now here's the problem. It looks expensive. The trim is real silver.'

'Doesn't really go with his ensemble, does it? The torn, sweaty T-shirt and all.'

'Where's *your* ice pick, Nedda? We checked the wet bar in the front room. No luck. Maybe you keep it in the kitchen?'

'No idea, Detective. I rarely drink hard liquor.'

'So you wouldn't know if that was his ice pick or yours?'

'It's a mystery.' She placed an ashtray on the table as an invitation for Riker to pull out the pack of cigarettes that he had been longing for all night.

Remembering his manners, he first offered the pack to the lady. 'You smoke?'

She surprised him by accepting one, then bending down to his match flame. In answer to his question, she inhaled deeply and blew a perfect smoke ring. Riker found her entirely too cool for a woman with a houseful of police and a dead body on her living-room floor. He finished his iced tea, then casually perused the written statement that Nedda Winter had signed for the West Side detectives. 'Ma'am? Does anybody else live in this house? I don't see anything here about—'

'Yes. There's my sister. Her name is Cleo Winter-Smyth.'

Riker's pen hovered over his open notebook. 'Is she one of those hyphenated people?'

'I'm afraid so. My brother, Lionel, lives here, too. But tonight they're both at the summer house in the Hamptons.'

'Why don't we give 'em a call and ask where the ice pick is?'

'You could leave a message on their machine. They never pick up the phone out there. They have privacy issues.'

Riker turned toward the sound of heavy footsteps from the hallway. He was surprised to see the head of Forensics making a personal appearance. Heller, a great bear of a man, hovered in the doorway. A baby-faced technician stood by his side, and this was a new face. A trainee? The chief crime-scene investigator had always taken great pride in the hands-on training of his crews. This might explain his presence here tonight. The man owed none of the detectives any favors that would warrant turning out for a penny-ante burglary gone wrong.

Heller remained in the hall as his new recruit entered the kitchen with a fingerprint kit. The younger man was shaking his head and muttering, 'Why elimination prints? The perp's dead.'

'Just do it, kid.' Heller's tone conveyed that he would deal with the youngster's attitude problem later. He turned his back and ambled away down the hall.

The rookie opened his kit on the table, then laid out his white cards, an ink pad and a roller. When he picked up Miss Winter's right hand, he treated it as an inanimate object. Without a word spoken, no *May I?* or *Excuse me, ma'am*, he bent over his work, inking her thumb, then rolling it across a small square on the card.

Nedda Winter looked up at the young man's face, but the technician clearly did not see her. She bowed her head in resignation, understanding that she was invisible to him, all but the fingers of her captive hand. It was a revealing moment and not the response that Riker would have predicted, not at this posh address. Ensconced in a mansion, this grande dame was accustomed to indifferent manhandling by minions. And so he needed no psychiatrist to tell him that she had spent some time in an institution – a long time.

Prison? Or the nuthouse?

As her hand was being manipulated by the technician, so carelessly, impersonally, the sleeve of her robe slipped down her right arm, exposing a long and jagged welt of old scar tissue that told a story of a body torn to the bone.

Riker rose quickly, knocking over his chair as he turned on the crime-scene technician. 'Let her alone! Tell Heller I want someone else to do it.' When the younger man only gawked at him, the detective yelled, 'Get *out!*'

* * *

21

Bitty Smyth sat alone in the dining room, waiting for someone, anyone, to give her life direction, or that was Charles Butler's impression when he sat down on the other side of the table. If he could caption the look on her face, her unspoken words would be – *at last* – as if she had been expecting him for all of the thirty years that had passed since his tenth birthday party, waiting in absolute faith that he would come.

'I'm sorry,' she said. 'The police dragging you here so late and all. It was because of the pictures in my room, wasn't it?'

His one and only stalker seemed not at all embarrassed about the shrine in her bedroom, and he wondered if this was a first warning sign. He gravitated toward the possibility of a harmless, almost magical fixation that would not interfere with the everyday function of her life. He preferred this to the darker diagnosis of an obsessive psychotic. For a moment, he was lost in her eyes, so large, so dark, the antithesis of his own small blue irises. Physically pulling away from her, he sat well back in his chair.

It was his everyday job to observe people and pass judgments upon their mental well-being before marrying them to the proper think tanks, but there was something at work here that was quite beyond him for the present.

Her face was heart shaped. He would not call it pretty, and yet he was charmed by it and leaning toward her once more without under-standing why. Perhaps magical thinking worked both ways tonight, for he was reverting to his earlier impression of a pointed-eared elf.

'I can't imagine,' she said, 'what the police must have thought of my little gallery of photographs.'

'Yes, the pictures,' he said. 'I'm sure they assumed I was a friend of the family.' He handed her a business card for Butler and Company. An earlier version of the card had borne the name Mallory and Butler, but NYPD had ordered her to dissolve the business partnership. In Mallory's version of compliance, she had removed her name from the stationery.

Bitty Smyth never glanced at the card. 'I was at your birthday party in Gramercy Park.'

'I know,' said Charles, though he still had no memory of her. Granted, she would be inclined to remember him, the tallest boy, the one with the beak of an eagle, the eyes of a frog. But he had been blessed with eidetic memory, and he wondered how he could have forgotten her. She would have been unusually small, given her camera's low point of view when she had taken the party photograph. All the other children had been normal size — at least a head smaller than himself. Gradually, he formed a portrait of a little person who did her best to blend into every wall she leaned against. And now he imagined her as a little girl watching from behind the foliage of Gramercy Park, hiding out — the shy child and perhaps the only one not to take part in the incident of the unfortunate frog.

She leaned toward him. 'Wasn't it your uncle who did the magic show?'

'No, he was my cousin, Max Candle. Old enough to be my uncle, though. So . . . how's Paul? Forgive me if I don't recall the relationship. Was Paul your—'

'My brother,' said Bitty, 'half brother. We have the same father.'

'So now you look after your aunt, is that right?' He wondered if she had forgotten to breathe for a moment. Why should her aunt's health be a touchy subject? 'I'm told there's a lot of medication in Miss Winter's room. I assumed you were—'

'Yes, you must have been talking to the medical examiner. He wanted to give me a sedative, but I can't swallow pills. Now what was I – Oh, Aunt Nedda. Yes. End-stage cancer.'

'But she appeared to be in rather good health.'

Bitty lowered her eyes with a modest smile, as if taking this as a personal compliment. 'You should have seen her six months ago. Her skin was all yellow.'

'So she had a successful surgery, something like that?'

'No.'

And now he noticed something new in her eyes: the pupils were dilating. This was the unconscious tactic of a small child anxious to curry favor with an adult, and it usually worked, enhancing the unwitting adult's concern and affection. It was a child's act of self-preservation carried into adulthood. He wondered what other tactics she might have, both instinctive and deliberate ones for negotiating her way through a forest of taller beings.

'How do you account for your aunt's recovery? A miracle? Or the wrong diagnosis?' This was a trick question, a trap, and he wondered if she had guessed that.

She was staring at her Bible, reaching toward it and its pious explanations for all things miraculous, but then she pushed it away, electing not to play the Bible-thumping zealot, not with him.

It occurred to him, in that moment, that the Bible and the journals were props for an illusion, rather like the trick of the eyes. More survival tactics? This intuition posed an ethical dilemma: either this woman was more vulnerable than anyone imagined, or she was a worthy adversary for Mallory. He decided to keep his silence. If he guessed wrong, Mallory might shred this woman into pieces.

Ah, but what if he was right about Bitty? Well, in that event, Mallory would *certainly* shred her.

Police from the West Side precinct had gone, and so had Charles Butler. After Bitty Smyth had been shepherded off to the dining room, only the CSU technicians and their boss remained at the crime scene with Mallory and the dead man.

The young detective looked past the foyer to the open door. The assistant medical examiner stood on the front steps smoking a cigarette. He looked her way, then tapped his watch to remind her that his people were still waiting to collect the corpse. She turned her back on him to make it clear that this was *her* dead body, not his.

And now, not hurrying any, she strolled over to the foot of the stairs and slowly paced out the movements of Nedda Winter and her victim, guided by the old woman's statement. Mallory ended her pantomime of a killing by hunkering down at the dead man's side and running her fingers through his hair. She waved to a technician standing by the foyer entrance. 'Kill the lights!'

He did, and now, in the etiquette of sudden darkness, no one moved or spoke. Streetlights glowed dully behind the drapes, only silhouetting the technician standing before them. All else was pitch black. She could not even see the face of the man nearest her, the dead man on the floor.

Mallory smiled.

Heller's voice boomed across the void. 'I know what you're thinking, kid. She couldn't have done it in the dark.'

'Yes, she could – and she *did*. It was dark when she stabbed him the first time, but not the second time.'

'But he was only stabbed one time.' Dr Morgan, the medical examiner, had come stealing back into the house, and there was exasperation in every word. 'There's only one entry wound, one—'

'Stabbed twice,' she said. And now they had a game. 'Lights!' yelled Mallory. And there was light.

Heller entered the kitchen carrying a fingerprint kit and settled his massive bulk into a chair beside Nedda Winter. After introducing himself, he smiled as he held out one hand for hers, asking, almost courtly, 'May I?'

Who knew that Heller was secretly a ladies' man?

She smiled, placing her veined and wrinkled hand in his, then watched absently as the head of Forensics did the grunt work of inking her index finger. Rolling it back and forth on a small white card, he said. 'Sorry about the mess. Comes off easy enough. Taking prints is routine in a case like this.'

'No, it isn't,' she said, contradicting him without any trace of rancor.

'Okay, call it a formality.' Heller gently continued to make the black impressions on his fingerprint cards. 'Nothing to worry about, ma'am.'

'Unless you've got a record.' Riker smiled to let her know that he was not serious. And she smiled, not buying into that for one minute. He exhaled a blue cloud of cigarette smoke and stared at the window. He might have been innocently inquiring about the weather outside when he asked, 'You never murdered anyone, did you, Nedda?'

'Oh, don't get me started, Detective. We'll be here all night.'

He liked sparring with this woman, and he was gradually losing his awe of her, though he had never been so close to a legend. If his father only knew who he was sitting with right now. And Granddad – how he wished that beloved old man had lived long enough to see this night.

'We always fingerprint the householders,' said Heller, as if she had never called this a lie and called it right. 'You see, this is the way we eliminate—'

'No,' she said, still smiling. 'There's no need for elimination prints. You don't care what he touched or we touched, not in a burglary with a dead suspect.' She turned to Riker. 'Sorry. I've watched entirely too much television.'

Resignation was in her face when she turned his way. She knew why the cops had come to her door and why they had stayed so long.

'Okay, you got us,' said Riker. 'We lied about the prints. But you can see why. We got problems here.' He lit another cigarette and watched the smoke curl, wondering if he could turn her suspicions around. 'Civilians have TV ideas about how this works, when a good taxpayer, like yourself, kills a criminal type – like our friend on the floor out there.' Riker nodded in the direction of the crime scene down the hall. 'You think the cops just show up as a courtesy. They take the dead body off your hands, maybe even clean up the mess for you. Then they write you an excuse note for a homicide.'

He waved this idea away with one hand. 'Naw. When we find a

body with a pair of shears stuck in the chest, we call it unnatural death. Doesn't matter if the victim is scum and, believe me, this guy would have to do some social climbing before we could call him anything as grand as scum. But he still gets a full homicide investigation. Now first we had to figure out which cophouse owns the crime scene. If the perp came to rob you, then the case goes to Robbery Homicide Division. If not, then it could go to the West Side cops. They showed up first, and it's their turf. And then there's me and Mallory. We're from Special Crimes Unit. We might get the case 'cause we had a prior interest in the dead man.'

'So how many detectives are fighting over the body?'

'Only one left standing out there.' Heller turned his eyes to the hallway. 'The body belongs to Riker's partner, Mallory.'

'And I predicted that.' Riker turned his face to Nedda's. 'She was the catching detective on your dead man's three murders. Too bad we can't turn up your ice pick.' He watched Nedda Winter's body relax as she slid back into a comfort zone, believing that she was merely suspected of homicide.

'Yes, I see the problem,' she said. 'You have to be sure the pick belonged to him before you can close out the case. As I said, I've never had any use for an ice pick.'

'Well, it's a big house,' said Riker. 'You got a maid or a house-keeper?'

'There was a live-in housekeeper. My niece, Bitty, tried to save her soul, and she ran away from home. Now my sister, Cleo, deals with an agency. They send different people every week.'

Done with the fingerprinting, Heller gently wiped the ink from her hands, then filed his print cards away in an envelope. He was working on the identifying labels when he and Riker looked up to see Bitty Smyth hovering in the doorway, asking with her eyes if she might enter.

'Come in, dear,' said Nedda. 'This is Mr Heller, and you've met Detective Riker.'

For a moment, Riker believed that Bitty might curtsy, but instead, she held out her Bible as an offering, voting him the most likely soul to be in need of religion. 'It's a gift,' she said, when he failed to take it from her. 'You *are* a Christian, are you not?'

'My church is Finnegan's.' And Riker's religion revolved around sacramental bourbon and beer. Finnegan's was the cop bar beneath his Greenwich Village apartment. Free drinks, courtesy of his new landlord and barkeep, made it a religious experience every night.

The tiny woman patted his head in the manner of rewarding a dog.

'Bitty,' said her aunt, 'do you know where the ice pick is?'

'It's on the floor beside the body.'

'No, dear. Where is *our* ice pick?'

The younger woman shook her head, uncomprehending. Suddenly, one pointing finger rose in the air as a divining rod, and she walked in a straight line to a drawer beside the sink. She pulled out an ice pick, then placed it on the table in front of Nedda and left the room. Heller followed after her, fingerprint kit in hand and calling out, 'Ma'am? Miss Smyth? A minute, please?'

Nedda Winter studied the plain ice pick on the table. Its wooden handle was cracked and worn. 'Doesn't quite go with the silver ice bucket, does it?'

'No, ma'am, it doesn't.' And he had already found this one during an earlier search of the kitchen. Riker's eyes were on the hallway when Mallory paused just outside the door, standing there in low conversation with the police photographer. She moved on down the hall, no doubt wanting pictures of a sewing room with no scissors. He turned back to face Nedda. 'We'll keep looking till we find the other ice pick – the good one.'

If she took this as a threat – and it was – she showed no outward sign. Leaning toward Riker, speaking in her dry way, she said, 'Our Bitty is a soldier in the army of the Lord – in case that escaped your notice. She's also very delicate. I hope you don't see her as a woman who fancies dangerous men, maybe lures them home so she can murder them.'

'I like your sense of humor, Nedda.' He had already surmised that if Bitty, the Christian soldier, were hanging nose to nose with a fruit fly, the fly would beat the living crap out of her.

A shriek came from the front room, and now Bitty Smyth was screaming, 'No fingerprints! No, you can't *do* this!'

Riker watched Kathy Mallory passing the kitchen doorway again, advancing on the front room with grim resolve. He was already feeling sorry for the smaller, weaker woman; the little soldier was indeed delicate in mind and body.

Oh, yes, there would be fingerprints, and *right now*.

Mallory's end of the conversation was not intelligible at this distance, but Riker could imagine the scene in the other room: his partner's attitude conjuring up a faint aroma from the sulfurs of hell and maybe a little smoke; Bitty's eyes growing wide and wild.

'No!' Bitty Smyth yelled. 'I want a *lawyer*!'

Bitty Smyth flitted about the room, staring into every face, silently begging for relief. She avoided looking at Mallory, whose eyes were green neon signs with the words *no mercy*.

Nedda Winter entered the room, followed by a more languid Riker, who hardly ever moved quite so fast as an old lady, though Mallory knew that her partner would not call this white-haired woman old; the little lost girl of the nineteen-forties would only be fifteen years his senior.

Deserting her niece, Miss Winter hurried past Mallory and disappeared into a small powder room in the foyer. Every pair of eyes was on that closing door. Dazed by this abandonment, even Bitty Smyth was quietly keeping watch.

When the old woman emerged, she held a glass of water in her hand and moved toward her niece, smiling, extending the glass, then holding it to Bitty's lips and urging her to drink. 'Big gulps, dear. Everything is all right.'

Bitty Smyth stole a glance at Mallory, then shook her head slowly from side to side to say that this could not be true.

'I've already given them my fingerprints.' Nedda Winter settled her niece on the sofa. 'There's no harm in letting them take yours.'

Heller pulled up a chair alongside the couch and gently took the tiny woman's hand and kissed it.

Well, this was new. The only one more startled than Bitty was Mallory.

The head of Forensics was not only doing the work of underlings tonight but he was also in rare diplomatic form, and Mallory disapproved. She preferred her interview subjects unhinged and easier to intimidate – less work. Before Heller had inked the third finger, Bitty Smyth's head lolled back on the upholstery and her eyes closed. Mallory turned on the older woman. 'What did you put in that water?'

'A sedative.' Miss Winter opened her hand to show the label on the bottle. 'This house almost qualifies as a pharmacy. These belong to my sister, Cleo.'

This civilian was surprisingly unruffled. Mallory decided to work on that.

While Heller finished the fingerprinting process, one of the medical examiner's underlings returned to remind the detectives that the meat wagon was still waiting for the corpse. Mallory shot him a look to tell him that he should get out of here – *now*.

Nedda Winter searched the remaining faces, then turned to Riker. 'Mr Butler is gone?'

'Yeah,' said Riker. 'It didn't take him long to check out the pictures in Bitty's room.'

'Is he going to make any trouble for my niece?'

'I wouldn't be surprised.' Mallory glanced at the small woman asleep on the sofa. 'By law, we had to warn him. We're really scrupulous about that when we find the stalker at a crime scene with a dead body.'

'My niece is harmless.'

'You really believe that?' Mallory opened her blazer, pausing a beat to display a very large gun and her authority in this room. 'I'm surprised.' Her hand passed over the weapon to dip into an inside breast pocket. She produced a wrinkled sheet of paper. 'I found this in your bedroom waste-basket. It's the same line written over and over again. "Crazy people make sane people crazy."' Mallory glanced at the small sleeper on the couch. 'Was Bitty getting on your nerves?'

The older woman looked as if she had just been slapped.

Mallory edged closer. 'Need to take a pill, Miss Winter? I saw all that medication in your room.'

'I'm fine, thank you.'

'Sit down,' said Mallory, indicating a chair close to the corpse.

Nedda Winter shook her head, defying a direct order and electing to stand. 'I've been sitting for too long.' With a slight lift of one shoulder, she said, 'You know – old bones.' And so her dignity remained intact – for the moment.

'Really?' Mallory made a wide circle around Miss Winter, forcing the woman to revolve. 'The medical examiner says you're in very good shape for your age. Good hearing and coordination. No confusion at all. Now Dr Morgan thought that was strange . . . considering all of your meds. He said the high doses should've created massive confusion bordering on dementia, but you're pretty sharp.'

'Thank you.'

Once more Mallory looked down at the sleeping niece. 'Does Bitty know that you flush all those pills every day?'

She noted just the barest inclination of Nedda Winter's head, a small gesture of congratulation. And now this old woman must understand that Riker's interrogation had been merely a friendly little warm-up.

Showtime.

31

'And your color surprised Dr Morgan, too. According to your niece, your skin turned yellow in the end stage of cancer. But now you look entirely too healthy.' Mallory stopped circling her interview subject. They stood toe-to-toe. 'Can you explain that?'

'Doctor–patient confidentiality,' said the old woman. 'The state of my health isn't open to police scrutiny.'

'Wrong.' Mallory turned her back on the older woman. 'I can ask you anything I want.' And that was true. She could legally *ask*. 'And now we'll go over the holes in your statement until I hear something believable. You might want to sit down now. This could take all night.'

And with this more polite invitation, this consideration for her comfort – *yeah, right* – Nedda Winter did sit down. But this was not the advantage that Mallory sought; she had wanted subservience, and all she got was tolerance. Miss Winter's head was level and regal; she would not strain by one bare inch to look up at her adversary.

The detective moved behind the woman, leaning down close to her ear and saying, 'I like money motives.' Mallory rounded the chair in time to catch the trace of a smile.

'I never touched the man's wallet,' said Nedda Winter.

'I did. He had a lot of cash. But you told the responding officer there was none missing from the wall safe. You were positive about that.' She signaled Riker to bring in the patrolman waiting outside on the steps. After sitting down in an armchair on the other side of the corpse, she proceeded to ignore the old woman, turning all her attention to the pages of a small notebook.

The young officer entered the front room. He smiled at Miss Winter, and one finger tapped the visor of his hat in a mock salute. Mallory caught his eye, and, with a look that promised something nasty, she put an end to all that friendliness. He stood at attention, all properly lined up on the side of Mallory and the law.

The detective turned back to her notes, saying, 'You remember Officer Brill, don't you? He shows up for all of your break-ins.'

'Yes, I remember him. But that first one was only an attempted burglary.'

Mallory kept her eyes on the notebook. 'According to Officer Brill, your relatives were out of town for that one, too. What a coincidence.' She looked up at the staircase and the small device well concealed in the woodwork. 'Oh, and the tape cassette is missing from your security camera. Another coincidence? Don't look at Officer Brill. He's not a friend of the family. He's with us.'

But not for much longer. With only a nod, she sent the man back to his post outside the front door. Nedda followed the young officer with her eyes, clearly sorry to see him go.

'We'll start over.' Mallory accepted a yellow pad from Riker, then pulled out a pen and clicked it absently. 'You said you stabbed the burglar with the scissors.'

Click, click.

'Yes.' Miss Winter pulled a pack of cigarettes from the pocket of her robe. 'This makes the fourth confession of the evening. I stabbed him with the scissors.'

'But *his* weapon,' said Mallory, 'the ice pick – that's *yours*. Don't waste my time making me prove it.'

Click, click, click, click.

'I never said it wasn't mine.' She shook a cigarette loose from the pack. 'I only said I couldn't identify it.' And now she searched her pockets for a light. 'Maybe he found it here in the house.'

'In the dark? According to your statement, the lights were off. You didn't turn the lights on until it was all over. How could he find that ice pick in a strange house in the dark?'

Click, click, click, click, click.

'I believe I saw a small flashlight on the floor by the—'

'Yeah, a penlight.' Riker stepped forward with a lit match for her cigarette. 'That was his. We found his fingerprints on the case and the batteries – the *dead* batteries.'

Mallory leaned forward. 'While you're changing your statement,

33

some advice – don't fool with the lights, okay? If the lights had been on, he would've pulled his knife, and you'd be the dead body on the floor tonight.' She leaned down to raise one pants leg of the corpse and exposed the long hunting knife in a leather holster strapped to his leg. Now the old woman was taken by surprise, but it passed quickly.

'You see the problem, Miss Winter? Too many weapons. If he had a knife, why would he waste time hunting for a—'

'All right, I lied. After I realized that he was dead – and he had no weapon – well, none that I could see – I put the ice pick in his hand. I thought it might make the police more sympathetic. But it *was* dark. I *was* afraid for my life.'

'That's the only thing you've said that I believe.'

'I'm sorry I misled you.'

Mallory looked down at her notes again, as if the next question mattered not at all to her. 'Are you sorry enough to take a polygraph exam?'

'Yes, of course, if you wish.'

'That's good,' said Riker. 'Now explain this.' He held up a small plastic bag to the light of the chandelier so that she could clearly see the key inside. 'We found dirt in the front door lock, and we found this key in the potted plant on the stairs outside. Our boy put it back after he opened the door. Didn't you wonder why the alarm went off for last week's burglary, but not tonight's?' He nodded toward the corpse. 'This guy knew the code to turn off the alarm. You know what that means?'

'We have an endless parade of temporary help. I suppose one of them set us up for a robbery.'

'No, that doesn't work for me.' Mallory nudged the corpse with the toe of her running shoe. 'Someone wants you dead, Miss Winter. This man was a murderer, not a burglar. He grabbed his victims off the street. Never broke into a house before, and he didn't break into this one, either. So tell me – who benefits from your death?'

'My death would make no difference to anyone.'

Riker stared at the little woman on the couch. Bitty Smyth had begun to snore. 'So maybe your niece is the target. Now that should make you real eager to help us out with this investigation.'

'And if you don't,' said Mallory, 'we've got you for tampering with evidence, obstruction of a homicide investigation and making false statements to the police. Does that worry you?'

'My medication causes confusion,' said Nedda Winter, throwing the young detective's own words back at her. 'And there go your charges.'

'Nice try,' said Mallory. 'But that only tells me you've got secrets that'll get you killed – you or your niece. What about your brother and sister? They were out of town for both break-ins.'

'Nothing odd about that. Lionel and Cleo spend most of their time out of town.'

Mallory left her chair to stand over the unconscious Bitty Smyth. Her long red nails grazed the sleeping woman's hair. 'Does Bitty know secrets, too? Let me put it another way. Would you trust your niece with a secret?'

Nedda Winter rose to stand beside the detective. The cigarette, tightly clutched in her hand, had gone dark and smokeless, and now she broke it in half.

Mallory never took her eyes off Bitty Smyth, her hostage in this interview. 'All the doors in this house have old-fashioned locks and keyholes, except for your niece's bedroom. She's got a dead bolt and a slide bolt. Your brother and sister are always out of town. Why?' She looked up at Nedda Winter. 'Is your whole family afraid of you?'

Riker stepped forward to deliver the blow that he had been waiting for all night long. 'Mind if I call you Red?'

Nedda Winter smiled, perhaps in relief, now that it was finally out. '*Red Winter* was the title of a painting,' she said, 'my portrait. Once my hair was red, but Red was never my name.'

* * *

Bitty Smyth woke in the night, but not in her bed. The windows of the front room were looming rectangles of dull light. There was no other detail to be seen. By touch, she recognized the knitted afghan that always draped the sofa. Her aunt must have covered her with it as she lay sleeping. Bitty pulled it up to her chin, taking a little comfort from this thin protection of wool. And now she played the childhood game of ferreting out the monsters in the shadows.

A dark silhouette passed by one window, the shadow of someone *inside* the house. She held her breath and heard whispers of a silk robe and slippered feet. It was Aunt Nedda, straight and tall, marching back and forth, an aged sentry pausing at each window to part the drapes and look outside. But the aunt's form and face were lost in the dark, and so the shadow prevailed on Bitty's imaginings.

Old monsters never died.

TWO

Chief Medical Examiner Edward Slope might have been taken for a military man as he walked down the hall to his office. He had a stride that bordered on a march, and his face had all the animation of a granite war monument.

The doctor was an early riser. Though he had minions, a small army of them, he was always the first to report for work. He cherished the quiet hours of daybreak, when the dead were content to wait until he had finished the newspaper, and the living would not intrude upon him while his coffee was still hot. If there was a God, then one of the assistant medical examiners could crack open the first corpse of the morning, and he might get caught up on a backlog of files. But first – a little solitude. He unlocked the door to his office with a plan to work on the *Times* crossword puzzle.

Or not.

Kathy Mallory was asleep in his chair.

Well, this put a lie to Detective Riker's theory that she slept hanging by her heels like a bat. While her uncivilized eyes were closed, she looked rather like a child napping after a busy tour of duty on a homicide squad – and a bit of illegal trespass. A velvet pouch, holding bright bits of metal, lay open upon his desk blotter.

Poor baby.

Apparently, sleep had overtaken her before she could put her lock picks away.

Oh, surprise number two.

Her eyes snapped open in the mechanical fashion of a doll – or a robot. There was no middle gear of rousing from sleep and dreams. She was simply awake, and this lent credence to his own theory that she had an on-off switch.

'Good morning, Kathy.'

'Mallory,' she said, reminding him of the rules. She liked the chilly distance of formality.

Well, isn't that just too bad.

He had known her as Kathy since she was ten years old, though she had insisted at the time that she was twelve. His oldest friend, Louis Markowitz, had bargained her down to the more realistic age of eleven so that he could complete the paperwork for her foster care.

Eleven, in a pig's eye.

But who could discern the true age of a homeless child who was also a gifted liar – and worse. She was the fault in the doctor's personal myth of himself as an intractable man. Upon the death of her foster father, killed in the line of duty, Edward Slope had tried to fill that void, loving her enough for two, but he was no pushover. And this business of breaking into his office – well, he was not about to let that slide. He reached across the desk to grab her lock picks, planning to use them as a show-and-tell exhibit while he lectured her on—

The lock picks were gone.

She had pocketed them in a sleight of hand, and the doctor knew this drill all too well: if he had no evidence of her illegal entry, then there had been no crime that she would own up to.

Kathy Mallory laid her hands flat on the desk, *her* desk now. How she loved these little hieratic strategies of furniture and psychological leverage. 'I need an autopsy, all the trimmings.'

'Get in line.' Slope settled into one of the visitors' chairs. 'It might take a few days.' He opened his newspaper, her cue to leave, as if that ever worked. 'I'll have Dr Morgan determine the—'

'No. It has to be *you*.' She was almost petulant. 'It has to be *now*.'

'You don't have the rank to make that kind of a request,' he said, tacking on, 'Kathy,' just for fun.

'Mallory,' she said, insistent.

She held up a stack of photographs, then fanned them like a deck of cards and dealt them out, one by one – just like her old man. Louis Markowitz had been a portly soul with hound-dog jowls and a charming way about him. Charm had never been an option for Kathy, and yet, every now and then, the doctor fancied that he found traces of Lou lingering on in his foster child, sometimes a gesture or a phrase.

Briefly put, Lou's daughter knew how to manipulate him.

Even though he was fully aware of her calculation, this deliberate and casual way she had of breaking his heart, he played along every time. The doctor leaned forward to examine the crime-scene photographs, torso shots all of them, and every camera angle showed a pair of scissors driven into the victim's chest.

'Good aim,' he said, 'no hesitation marks. Hardly any blood loss, so it was a quick death – but you already knew that.' Truly, he was intrigued by the request for a full autopsy, but he could not simply ask her a direct question. Their relationship had the strict parameters of a duel. And now, as he leaned back in his chair, he was even more generous with his sarcasm. 'So . . . you had some doubt about what killed this man?'

'No, but it wasn't the scissors.' She wore the only smile in her limited store of expression that was not forced. It was the smile that said, *Gotcha.*

In the early gray light of her bedroom, Nedda Winter lay very still, not even drawing a breath – waiting for the panic to subside. It was always alarming to open her eyes and find herself alone. And how quiet it was. She had lived too many years with constant companions, never awakening in any normal sense, but ripped from sleep with the early morning orchestra of a one-note moaner in the next bed, and beyond that one, the screamer's bed and a chorus of harpies singing an angry song of *Shut up! Shut the hell up!* or *Nursey, Nursey, I'm cold, I'm wet.* Nedda had played the audience for them, staring vacantly in the direction of their noise and wondering how she would get through another day. Her nights had been whiled away with plans for her own slow death. But that was over now. She had a new plan and something to live for.

Her heart settled into a normal rhythm, and her gaze calmly roved over the daisy pattern on the century-old wallpaper. The flowers had been yellowed with age generations before she was born. All the other bedrooms of the house had been repapered in her absence. Here, nothing had changed. The furniture was the same, just as she had left it when she was twelve years old, except for the trunk that once sat at the foot of her bed. All of the Winter children had had such trunks. By custom of the house, hers had probably been consigned to the attic when she was assumed to be dead. Otherwise, this might be like any morning from her childhood.

Only the music was missing.

She reached out to her bedside table and turned on the old radio. It was tuned to a station that played only jazz, her father's favorite music for as far back as memory would take her. When Quentin Winter was alive, trumpets and piano riffs had filled this house, day and night, loudest in the party hours. Mellow saxophones had dominated at the break of a new day, and, toward midmorning, Daddy had played the blues as background music for his hangovers.

Nedda pulled on her robe and entered the bathroom, where her eyes bypassed that strange old woman in the mirror. She looked down at the wide array of pharmacy bottles lined up on the sink. One by one, she flushed her morning doses down the toilet. The medication had been prescribed for an illness that she had never had, and now she watched the tablets swirling around the toilet bowl. What luxury this was after all the years of picking up the pills that other patients had spit out, then ingesting them, tasting other people's bile and inheriting their diseases and sundry germs. How difficult it would be to make anyone understand that this slow attempt at suicide had been the act of a sane woman. Now, in the absence of any medication, she was getting stronger every day, disappointing her brother and sister.

Barefoot, she left her room. On the other side of the door, she met her dead stepmother on the day of the massacre. In the manner of a puppeteer, memory worked Alice Winter's limbs, and the pretty woman crossed the threshold of the bedroom to rouse another version of Nedda – *young* Nedda with the long red hair. The house itself had been drowsing, running off the low batteries of nine sleepy children on a Sunday morning.

As Nedda started down the staircase, her father, with only a few more hours to live, was climbing toward her. Fifty-eight years ago, she had stood on tiptoe to kiss him in passing. Now she simply watched him go by in his silk pajamas and dressing gown. What a beautiful man he was, long fair hair like a prince from another age. He was holding a glass with the foul-smelling ingredients of his hangover cure. The disembodied voice of Billie Holiday wafted up the stairs behind him, dogging him from the phonograph below and moaning the blues to Daddy.

In the next century, Nedda completed her descent to the parlor floor, where Bitty was a child-size lump beneath the afghan on the sofa. She sat down in a chair beside her sleeping niece and waited. A few minutes passed before the younger woman sensed another presence in the room. Small hands gripped the afghan, and her eyes opened, cagey at first, only looking through slits for signs of danger. 'Aunt Nedda?'

Was there just a touch of fear in Bitty's voice? Yes, and Nedda winced.

'Good morning, dear. I was just curious. What did you do with the tape from the security camera? The police were asking about it.'

'I put it where they'd never want to look.' Bitty fumbled with the afghan then produced her Bible from the folds of wool and opened it.

Oh, not a book at all.

The Bible was a clever box, and nestled inside a rectangular compartment was the videotape.

The morgue attendant from the graveyard shift was not at his desk. The chief medical examiner was about to ask Kathy Mallory what she had done with the poor man's body, but then the double doors swung open and Ray Fallon appeared, alive if not well. He was nervous – Kathy had that effect on him – and sweating from recent exertion.

After handing a deli bag to the detective, the attendant was tipped lavishly but not thanked, not that Fallon cared, so eager was he to get away from her. 'Men's room,' he said to his boss.

And Slope knew that the man would not be back again until Kathy had left the premises. 'You sent him out for your breakfast?' The doctor affected the lecture mode that he used when he suspected her of cheating at cards. 'If you think I'm going to tolerate—'

'I had to get rid of him.' She dug into the brown paper bag and pulled out a bagel. 'I can't afford any leaks on this case, and he's the worst. You know you should've fired that weasel years ago.'

This was her very best trick – reversal of guilt, and he should have seen it coming because she was right.

Kathy Mallory bit into her bagel. With her free hand, she pulled out the metal drawer where she kept her own personal corpse. The victim was still encased in the body bag, and there was no attendant paperwork attached. None of her crime-scene photos had included any body parts above or below the torso, and now she pulled back the zipper to give the pathologist his first look at the face. 'It's Willy Roy Boyd.'

'Ah,' said Slope, 'your lady-killer. So, given his current condition – dead – I'm guessing that you lost your temper when he made bail.'

Her strip show continued downward until she had exposed the pair of scissors sticking out of the man's chest.

'Point taken,' he said. 'Not your style.' If Kathy had inflicted this wound, the scissors would have been placed more symmetrically and at a perfect right angle to the flesh. She was peculiar that way, compulsively neat.

The doctor unzipped the rest of the body. 'If I were to roll him over, would I see any other signs of trauma?'

'No,' she said. 'That's not it.'

And the game went on.

He checked the dead man's eyes and fingernails. 'No obvious indication of poison.' He stared at the chest. 'Those shears make a hell of an entry wound. I would've expected more blood.'

'Right. He was dead when the scissors went in, but Dr Morgan didn't catch that. He said the scissors contained the bleeding like a stopper in a bottle.'

In defense of his young and unseasoned, possibly incompetent, medical examiner, Dr Slope said, 'Well, that's *one* possibility.' Like hell it was. Hers was the more likely explanation. The dead man was thin, his chest concave, and the shears went deep. One did not rupture the human heart so neatly, not with a weapon of this size and thickness. 'I'll know for sure after the chest is cracked. So you don't think he was stabbed to death.'

'Of *course* he was stabbed to death.' The perverse brat paused a moment to relish this small win, the look of surprise in his eyes. She pointed to the chest. 'And that's the only entry wound.'

Edward Slope had to smile. He was the one who had taught her this twisted game. The student was surpassing the master.

Kathy Mallory picked through the dead man's hair. Finding something she liked, she said, 'See this spot of blood on the scalp?'

Slope adjusted his glasses as he leaned over the corpse. 'Yes, and here's another one on the upper lip. So small.'

'And this drop on his shirt.' One red fingernail marked the spot. 'That's three drops total. And none of the blood is where you'd expect to find it if the shears had killed him. It's a back-strike splatter. So the wound was made with something smaller, thinner.' She leaned down to rifle her knapsack and pulled out a bag tagged by Forensics. It contained an ice pick. 'I like this for the primary weapon. I want his stomach contents. I want to know what he ate for his last meal and where he ate it. I want a screen for drugs. If he's a user, I need to know when he got his last fix. And I want—'

'Stop.' The doctor put one hand up in the manner of a traffic cop. 'First things first. A few drops of back-strike blood doesn't prove it was an ice pick. I can't even corroborate a second weapon. I've told you a hundred times, textbook scenarios don't even get close to the spectrum of trauma I see on my dissection table.'

'I didn't work this out by reading a book.' She opened the evidence bag and held it close to his face. 'Sniff that.'

No need. The odor of bleach was strong. 'Someone cleaned it.'

She turned over the evidence bag to show him the white residue of a price tag peeled from the bottom of the pick handle. 'It's brand new, a perfectly smooth surface. Heller says, even without the bleach, his luminal wouldn't pick up any blood on the metal. But *this* is the weapon. It fits with the back-strike blood.'

'You know who killed him, too?'

'An old lady.'

'Good,' said Slope, finding this only fitting since Willy Roy Boyd had murdered three women. And now he better understood police concerns about leaks to the newspapers. He envisioned the headline: Old Lady Kills Lady-Killer.

Kathy Mallory parted the hair on the dead man's scalp. 'This drop runs horizontally. The woman said they were both standing when she stabbed him.'

And blood ran down, not sideways. 'So, either the law of gravity has changed or the old woman lied.'

'No, I believed that part. He was on his feet when she stabbed him the first time. But he was down and dead when she pulled out the pick. And *that* explains the drop of blood in a horizontal streak.'

The doctor nodded. 'And then the shears were pushed into a

44

prone corpse.' He smiled. 'Congratulations. Now you can nail an old lady for mutilating a corpse, but he's just as dead either way, and hardly worth the trouble of—'

'I *want* that autopsy. I need proof that the ice pick killed him.'

'Any idea why this woman would go to the trouble of planting a second weapon?'

'Yes.'

'But you're not going to share. No, of course not. What was I thinking? So, obviously, you want evidence to dispute her claim of self-defense.'

'No, that holds up,' she said. 'Willy Roy Boyd was a one-trick pony. He was in that house last night to kill a woman.'

Though Edward Slope's brain had stripped a few gears, he was damned if he would let it show. The doctor stared at her with his best poker face, but hers was better.

Endgame.

Kathy Mallory had won a full autopsy by the chief medical examiner, for now that he had been suckered in – what were the odds that he would let anyone else touch this corpse?

Waiting for the explosion, boys?

The upper half of the wall was a wide window on the squad room, and, with the blinds open, Lieutenant Coffey's private office was a damned goldfish bowl on view for fifteen pairs of eyes. He pretended not to notice the men beyond the glass as they covertly looked his way.

The lieutenant was young for a command position, only thirty-six, but he was aging fast to fit the job. Stress had chiseled new lines into his face, giving him an expression of constant pain, and, just now, it was a fight to bite back a scream as three detectives brazenly walked up to the glass, the better to observe their boss, the poor bastard with the thinning brown hair, the tension headaches and a knotted-up gut.

The case load for Special Crimes Unit had spiraled out of control. And the new mayor, a man with the soul of a corporate raider, was planning to cut the department's allotment in manpower and funds. Every day was run at a heart-attack pace, and yet, Jack Coffey was showing no early warning signs that this was the worst possible time to jerk him around, nor had he raised his voice to Mallory and Riker, who sat unmolested on the other side of his desk. He was not even holding a gun on them, and the other detectives must find that odd.

When he glanced at the glass wall again, he saw money flashing out there in the squad room. Bastards, they were making book on this meeting.

Never let the troops see you crying like a little girl.

That was his mantra today.

Riker and Mallory were on their best behavior this morning, quietly waiting for him to finish scanning another precinct's report on a common burglary gone awry. He crumpled the cover sheet in one hand. Well, this was just *great*, this *crap*. Why would these two detectives drag this case home to an elite squad of first-grade gold shields?

'Mallory, close the blinds!'

This was a test, and he was gratified to see her do it, and so quickly, not even dragging it out to jack up his frenzy.

Big mistake, Mallory.

Now he knew that all the leverage in this room belonged to him. Better than that – with the blinds drawn and no witnesses, he could do whatever he liked with these two. He leaned forward and gave them his most benign smile to knock them off balance. The partners exchanged looks that clearly said, *Oh, shit.*

So they wanted this case really bad.

Well, tough.

But he just had to know why.

He pulled one sheet out of the pile of paperwork, the results of the fingerprint search they had requested. 'You'll be happy to know that neither one of your socialites has a criminal record. What a surprise, huh?' He also crumpled this paper into a ball and tossed it over one shoulder, then picked up a collection of forms that transferred the dead man to his own doorstep. 'And this makes it official. We've been screwed in triplicate.' He took his time crushing these sheets into another ball. He bounced it off the back wall. After spreading out the remaining paperwork, he selected two sheets from the array. 'Well, what have we got here?' Could his sarcasm be more obvious? Did he need to work on that? 'I'm looking at two witness statements, one from a little old lady, eighty years—'

'That's a typo,' said Mallory. 'Nedda Winter's only seventy.'

'And she's at least as tall as Mallory,' said Riker.

'Maybe an inch over,' she said.

'Yeah,' said Riker. 'Make that five-eleven.'

Coffey glared at his detectives, then looked down at the paperwork, saying, 'And next we have a shitpile of biblical quotations from Bitty Smyth, a forty-year-old woman of *undetermined* height.' He paused to glance at Mallory. 'Just jump right in if I get anything else wrong, okay?' His true message to her, delivered only by the tone of his voice, was *You speak – you die.*

The lieutenant turned to his senior detective, whose face was always easier to read. 'So, Riker, the catching detectives agreed with you. They figured it for a staged crime scene. Fair enough. Heller's report backs them up. But the old lady explained that in her statement. She was afraid the cops wouldn't be very understanding if she'd killed an unarmed burglar. So she put the ice pick in his hand.' Jack Coffey leaned back in his chair and clasped his hands behind his head. 'Well, I say no harm done. She gets to slide on that one. I may even send her roses for killing that butcher.' He swiveled his chair to face Mallory. 'I'm surprised that Nedda Winter isn't your new best friend. Willy Roy Boyd was your perp. You think a quick death was too good for that little freak? Would you rather wait out years of appeals before the state put him down with a needle?'

'That old woman lied about the—'

'Miss Winter gets away with everything, Mallory.' Coffey picked up the amended statement and scanned the lines for the one he wanted. 'She says her medication causes confusion.'

'Ah, bless her.' Riker flashed a smile at Mallory. 'Nedda was good, wasn't she?'

Jack Coffey was not amused. 'Maybe you guys should've brought her in here to do your talking for you. I called the old lady myself. It took me five minutes to queer the idea of an inside job. She said there was always a spare key in the planter outside the front door, and she couldn't remember setting the burglar alarm last night. So much for our perp turning off the alarm with a security code. She also solved your problem with the missing videotape. A patrol cop named Brill took it out of the security camera.' Coffey looked down at his personal notes. 'That was last week after an attempted break-in. The cop returned it to Bitty Smyth, but she never got around to reloading the camera. The ladies figure the housekeeper tossed out the videotape with the trash.'

The lieutenant picked up Mallory's report, but never bothered to read it. He preferred to make up his own more accurate summary. 'Now the catching detectives couldn't fob the case off on Robbery Homicide. And why not? Because those guys had the brains to bow out early. Then, while you two have your backs turned, the West Side dicks skate out the door and leave their mess in your lap. Now I know the two of you could've dumped this case on another squad if you'd only tried harder and talked faster. You've got thirty minutes to do the paperwork and close it out as justifiable homicide.'

Jack Coffey was shuffling all the reports and statements into a neat stack when Mallory leaned forward.

Trouble.

'There's more to it,' she said. 'West Side screwed up. Willy Roy Boyd was hired for a murder. It's all there,' she said, pointing to her own report, the one he had never read. 'It all fits.'

'Talk fast, Mallory.'

'The West Side precinct has no volume in homicides,' she said. 'They looked at the same evidence and came up clueless. If we just write this one off, then one of those women dies.'

'Not so fast,' said Coffey. No, he was not getting stuck with this lame case. 'If you guys are right about murder for hire,' and he was not conceding this, 'why wouldn't the ladies ask for police protection?' He turned to Riker for his answer.

Mallory jumped in. 'Two other people live in that house – the old lady's sister and brother. They were conveniently out of town for the attempted break-in last week, and they weren't home last night, either.'

'Even if you were onto something,' and Coffey doubted that, 'it's still not a case for Special Crimes. The department has a task force for that kind of—'

'It's not a mob hit,' said Mallory, 'and it's not gang related. Willy Roy Boyd wasn't connected that way. But he had an expensive lawyer for his bail hearing, and the bail bond cost him a fortune. He's got no assets, no job, but his wallet was full of hundred-dollar bills. He was hired to kill one of those women. If we don't work this case, no one else will.'

'And your partner collects ice-pick murders,' said Coffey. 'You left that out.'

This was no joke. His detectives had not been invited to last night's party on the Upper West Side. He knew that Riker had been tipped to the aspect of the ice pick.

Over time, word had come back to Jack Coffey, mentions of his senior detective turning up at crime scenes in every borough where an ice pick was the murder weapon. Special Crimes had only handled one such case, only one standout among the more common murders via muggings and domestic disputes. No matter how ordinary the crime, Riker had been a faithful visitor at every scene all his working life. And no one knew the reason.

'Why?' Coffey had to ask or he would have blown out his teeth trying to hold it back. If Riker would only answer him, the man could keep this damn homicide. The lieutenant's only other consideration was the possible embarrassment of having a taxpayer drop dead after the case was closed out. 'Why ice picks, Riker?'

'He doesn't have any *normal* hobbies,' said Mallory, betraying impatience with Coffey's little side trip.

The lieutenant was a second away from slapping her with a charge of insubordination when her partner spoke up.

'I collect ice-pick cases,' said Riker, 'because my father did. My grandfather collected them, too.'

'I need a little more than that,' said Coffey, and he was surprised by his own lack of sarcasm.

'Willy Roy Boyd was hired by amateurs,' said Riker, 'but maybe he was killed by a pro, somebody who had a little practice with a pick. Maybe the ladies weren't the only ones in the house last night.'

'A pro?' The lieutenant was incredulous at this escalation from a nice old lady to a professional assassin. 'A pro . . . with an *ice pick*?' He shook his head slowly from side to side. Oh, no, this was the age of miracles and wonders, long-range rifle sights equipped with infrared devices that could see in the damn dark. 'No contract hitman has used an ice pick since the forties—'

'And there's one old case still on the books, mass murder,' said Mallory. 'How would you like to wrap nine unsolved homicides this week?'

Oh, Jesus freaking Christ.

Jack Coffey could not find the words to toss these two out of his office. The partners politely waited for him to find his voice again. He did. He slammed his fist down on the desk. 'No, this is not *happening*! Riker, tell me she's not talking about Stick Man.'

Mallory answered for Riker. 'Special Crimes Unit would get all the credit, and we need good press right now. The timing is perfect.' She tacked on the reminder, 'It's budget-cutting season.'

Ordinarily, these would be the magic words, but not today. Jack Coffey, feeling slightly giddy, covered his face with both hands, worrying that tics or twitches might betray his image of a man in control of this meeting.

Mallory, of all people, should never have bought into this fantasy of a superannuated psycho from the last century. She was more jaded, better rooted in reality. Any cop could imagine the horror show of her childhood on the streets of New York, dodging kiddy pimps and pedophiles, ending every day in the exhaustion of a child's poverty, then chasing down some place where she could be safe for a few hours, where she might close her eyes to sleep. Still feral in many ways, she was suspicious of everyone she met and everything she was told. Her belief in a ghost story intrigued him more than Riker's.

A fair detective in his own right, Coffey had worked through the puzzle in the very next minute. These two were holding something back, a bombshell. There was no other explanation. 'Riker, do you have any idea how old Stick Man would be today?'

'Well, yeah.' The man's tone indicated that this might be a silly question since he was the expert on all things related to ice-pick homicides.

'All right, let me see if I understand this.' The lieutenant uncovered his tired eyes to look at Riker. 'You're planning to reopen the Winter House Massacre. Have I got that right?'

The man only shrugged to say, *Yeah, that's about right.* And his partner was busy inspecting her running shoes for smudges.

Jack Coffey shook his head. 'Riker, you've got two minutes of my time. Give me the rest or get out.'

'Okay. The old lady you talked to this morning? That was Red Winter.'

'Of course it was.' Jack Coffey wore that special smile reserved for dealing with lunatics. 'I should have guessed.' His smile never wavered, though his teeth were locked together and grinding. 'So . . .

when you asked Red Winter where she'd been for the past sixty years—'

'Fifty-eight years,' said Mallory. 'She was twelve when she disappeared. She's seventy now.'

'Shut up,' said Coffey. He only had eyes for his senior detective.

'Well, sure,' said Riker. 'We asked where she'd been, but she just yawned and went upstairs to bed. Left us to lock up the house.'

With one angry sweep of his hand, Coffey wiped his desk of papers and sent them flying to the floor. He was on the verge of the explosion his squad had been waiting on, *betting on*. And now he realized that he was still smiling – actually grinning – not a good sign, not a *healthy* sign.

Mallory bent low to pick up the scattered papers around her chair. 'We got the medical examiner to lose the ID on Willy Roy Boyd for a week.' She was already assuming that he would believe the most ludicrous story ever told within these walls. 'We have to keep a low profile,' she said, collecting the sheets and stacking them neatly on the edge of the desk, then bending down for others. 'The reporters can't get near this story.' She settled back into her chair to concentrate on aligning all the edges of every sheet. 'It might be better if the rest of the squad didn't—'

'I won't tell a soul,' said Jack Coffey. And he would not – no more than he would run naked through the streets, scattering rosebuds along the way. He continued to smile, feeling oddly calm. He just needed a little time was all, that and a bottomless bottle of Jack Daniel's. Most of all, he needed to make these two detectives disappear. So much depended on that: his sanity, his stomach lining and what was left of his hair. Though the blinds were closed, he could sense the troops massing out there, pressing up against the glass, tensing, waiting for him to crack wide open.

Any minute now.

'You got seventy-two hours,' said Coffey. 'I don't expect to see your faces for three days. Got that?'

He very much wanted to lay his head down on the desk and bang it a few times, but his detectives were still seated in their chairs, perhaps not fully comprehending that they had gotten away with this.

'Leave,' he said, '*now!*' And leave they did.

They left the door open, unfortunately, and he heard a snatch of their conversation.

Riker asked his partner, 'Where to now?'

'We're going to mess up a lawyer,' she said.

'That's my girl.'

Money was changing hands in the squad room, but the lieutenant no longer cared who had won or lost this round. He knew Mallory was going after the lawyer who had won a bail hearing, against all odds, for a cockroach who had murdered three women. The high school student, Boyd's youngest victim, had been closer to a child. Jack Coffey had been the one to break the news to her parents, to show them the morgue photograph of their daughter's face, a shot framed to expose the features least bruised and broken. The mother had touched the photo, caressing it with her fingers, then rubbing the glossy surface, as if desperately trying to break through that artificial dimension to get to her only child.

Both parents had cried.

The morale of the squad had gone down when that serial killer had walked out free on bail, spitting on the sidewalk and spitting on the law. The timing had been a gift from hell, the very hour of the schoolgirl's burial. And so the lieutenant gave no thought to blowback from Mallory's upcoming confrontation. Finally, he understood why she needed jurisdiction on the dead body of Willy Roy Boyd.

She wanted payback.

Coffey wondered if Mallory would go after the defense attorney's testicles. There were some things in life that were worth his rank and pension; neutering a lawyer was high on the list.

He picked through the cards on his Rolodex until he found the number for the parents of Boyd's last victim. He would call them first and tell them that the man who had destroyed their lives was dead – stabbed to death by an elderly woman. They might find some just irony in that.

No – they would cry.

Nedda Winter pulled back the sheer white drape of the front window for a better view of the old Rolls-Royce. Once it had been her father's car, and now it belonged to her brother. A dozen suitcases were disgorged from the car's trunk. Tall Lionel, sixty-nine on his last birthday, handled the bags with surprising ease, though he did this service grudgingly, for most or all of the luggage would belong to his sister Cleo Winter-Smyth. Bitty's description of the summer house in the Hamptons filled its closets and drawers with her mother's clothing. And Cleo's room upstairs was packed with more designer dresses like the one that she wore now.

So why this spectacle of suitcases? What was the point of two houses if one could not travel lightly from one to the other?

Without taking her eyes from the window, Nedda spoke to the small woman behind her. 'They're here, Bitty.' She glanced back at her niece, who was still holding the Bible. 'Go up to your room if you like. I'll deal with them.'

This arrangement was very agreeable to her niece, who stole up the staircase with exaggerated stealth, perhaps on the off chance that Cleo and Lionel could hear escaping footsteps through the solid walls of the house.

Nedda turned her eyes back to the sidewalk activity. Her brother stood beside the car, shaking his head. He was refusing to lug the suitcases up the stairs. Lionel put two fingers to his lips and whistled. The doorman from the neighboring condominium came running, smiling as a dog would smile if it only could. Money changed hands, and Lionel slipped behind the wheel of the Rolls and drove off to the parking garage, leaving his sister to supervise the doorman, who gathered up her bags. Cleo looked up at the parlor window, saw her elder sister standing there, then quickly looked away. This was only one small slight of many.

Nedda understood. She might never be forgiven for coming home again.

Though Cleo and Lionel had been to town only a week ago, Nedda was amazed anew each time she saw her sister and brother, these chic people so little affected by time. In her early sixties, Cleo appeared closer in age to her forty-year-old daughter. There was not a single strand of gray in the perfectly coiffed ash blonde hair, and her flesh was suspiciously smooth and firm.

Nedda let the drape fall, then sank down to the window seat. The front door opened, and the foyer was filled with the sound of dueling accents, American diva and Spanish immigrant. The doorman was making short work of the bags, stacking them inside the door, while Cleo surveyed the front room, checking for signs of sudden death. Or would she be more concerned with possible breakage?

Cleo turned to her sister with a vacuous smile; one might call it professional, the way a stewardess can smile at her passengers though she hates them and hopes they will die. 'You look wonderful. Your color's so much better.'

The yellow cast had passed off months ago in the hospice, where Nedda's siblings had expected her to pass away from natural causes.

Fooled you all. So sorry. I never meant to.

'But you're still a little pale, Nedda. You really must get some sun and fresh air. We'll have to get you out to the Hamptons one day.'

The sisters both knew that day would never come. There would be too many questions from the Long Island neighbors. It was so much easier to hide embarrassing relatives in the more anonymous city. And now, small talk exhausted, they fell into a silence – awkward for Nedda, easy for her sister.

When the doorman had lugged the last suitcase indoors, he learned to his dismay that he had not yet earned his money, not until he carried them up the stairs to a bedroom. He looked up at the winding steps – and up, and up, shaking his head in denial. Finally, the job was done, and her brother had returned from the garage on the next block. Lionel preened for a moment before a mirror, running one tanned hand through hair as white as her own.

Her brother could still be called a handsome man and surprisingly youthful in the way that a waxwork can never age. So this was what sixty-nine years looked like in the twenty-first century. Nedda rarely consulted a mirror on her own account, for she was a different creature now, and no such comparison to her former self was possible. Though she had made good use of the third-floor gymnasium, the treadmill and the weights would not give her back any of the time she had lost. She was marked by the wrinkles and stitched up scars of a difficult life.

Not so for Lionel and Cleo.

Nedda had returned to find her siblings well preserved in the amber of younger days. Every creature so preserved was dead, and still the simile held true. There was no life in their dark blue eyes, dead eyes, flies in the amber.

'Neddy' was all that Lionel said to her by way of a greeting.

She could see that it irked him to slip and call her Neddy, but he had never known her by any but that childhood name. In a cruel departure from a good-natured boy of eleven, Lionel the man reminded her of their father now. Quentin Winter had been a cold one, too. It had been said of Daddy, in his youth, that he left footprints of ice across the floor of a warm room on a summer day. She recalled Lionel as a child of five, following his father about in the month of July to see if this was true.

In part it was.

She turned to her sister, always searching Cleo's face for evidence of the child she had been. Up to the age of five, young Cleo had danced through the average day, always in motion to music that had played round the clock, a laughing child, who had no bones, who moved to the beat of drums and cornets with fluid joy. Daddy's little

Boogie Woogie Wunderkind had never been able to pronounce this mouthful, and so she had been called Jitterbug by one and all. But Nedda never forgot herself and called her sister by this old pet name. It was unsuitable now, for Cleo had become somewhat stiff on several levels.

Nedda wondered how she was remembered by her siblings. She shuddered, and this thought passed off like a chill.

Lionel walked to the center of the carpet. 'Was it here? Bitty wasn't all that clear on the phone.'

'Yes, that's where the man died.' Nedda turned from one sibling to the other, saying, 'Charles Butler was here last night. Did Bitty tell you that?'

Cleo broke into a rare wide smile. 'The *frog prince*? No, Bitty never said a word.' And now something dark had occurred to her, no doubt linked to the shrine in Bitty's room. The woman sat down, more solemn in her tone, saying, 'My God, did the police see the—'

Nedda nodded.

'And they brought Charles Butler here? They showed him—'

'The shrine in Bitty's room? Yes, he saw it.'

Lionel and Cleo turned to one another to hold one of their eerie conversations of the eyes. It was something akin to the made-up languages of small children bonding in secret alliance against the adult – herself. This time, it was easy for her to guess the content of their discussion, and, in answer to their unspoken question, she said, 'The police believe that Bitty was stalking Mr Butler.'

'Charles Butler,' said Lionel. 'Wasn't he one of the Gramercy Park Butlers?'

'Yes, dear,' said Cleo, the keeper of the social register. 'Charles is the *last* one, but there haven't been any Butlers in Gramercy Park for ages. He lives in SoHo, of all places. He owns an apartment building there.'

Trust Cleo to know the details of wealthy families who would not take her phone calls and the environs where she was not welcome.

The Winter family had fallen away from polite society long before the massacre.

'Charles Butler,' said Cleo. 'Bitty must've been *thrilled*.' And, by inflection, she conveyed the opposite meaning. 'Well, we must do something before this business gets out of hand. I'll call Bitty's father. Sheldon will know how to handle it.'

'Oh, Christ,' said Lionel, at this mention of his erstwhile brother-in-law, the attorney. 'Did the police take Bitty away?'

Both faces turned to Nedda. They were almost twins in expressing the horror of publicity.

She shook her head and stood with them in cold silence, the natural state of their every reunion, until a movement in one of the many mirrors caught her eye. Nedda turned around to see her niece slowly coming down the grand staircase, hesitating now, eyes wide and wondering if it was safe yet. Bitty had never outgrown a child's stature and a child's issues, the cowering deference to her mother and her uncle. And yet, one day, brave as any knight, this tiny woman had marched into a hellhole and plucked Nedda out of it, soul and all.

'Hello, dear. Kiss, kiss,' said Cleo in lieu of actual affection for her daughter. 'I've decided that we'll have a small dinner party tonight. I think I can arrange for the frog prince to come.'

Bitty's feet were frozen in place on the last step, and one hand drifted to her heart, as if her mother had shot her there.

'Yes, dear,' said Cleo. 'Your beloved Charles Butler. Won't that be nice?'

Bitty nodded meekly, then turned away from them and crept back up the stairs.

Lieutenant Coffey was enjoying a rare hour of calm. Two homicides had been closed out before noon, a banner day. There would have been three cases closed by now if Riker and Mallory had only cooperated. But they were both exhausted and badly in need of a rest.

They had logged more overtime than anyone else on the squad. And this was how Jack Coffey rationalized his irrational behavior of the morning, allowing them three days to work a bogus case.

Red Winter, my ass.

When he stood up to stretch his legs, he saw the wadded balls of paper he had tossed on the floor. Sooner or later, he would have to uncrumple them. He gathered them up and smoothed the pages out across his desk. Next, he picked up Mallory's report. He had the time to read it now, but his eyes could not move past the address for the crime scene. She had included the landmark credit with the formal name of the property. Miss Winter was not just another taxpayer with a common surname. She lived in Winter House.

The lieutenant stole guilty glances at the glowing computer screen only a few feet from his desk. The cold-case file would not be there, not a case dating back to the forties. Almost against his will, the chair slowly wheeled toward the computer workstation. He typed Red Winter's name into the search engine and came up with a selection of several hundred Web sites. After weeding out the sellers of books, videotapes and memorabilia, he settled upon a site for true-crime junkies.

Colorful.

Blood-red skulls marked every selection on the menu, and the Winter House Massacre was listed near the end of this alphabet of bones. When the screen changed again, he was staring at the famous nude portrait of a child with long red hair, and he could see that she had been tall for her age, all out of proportion to the surrounding furniture. Civilians and cops who knew the case had always called her Red Winter. Here, her true name was given as Nedda, the same as the woman — a *tall* woman — who had stabbed Willy Roy Boyd. Riker had guessed her height at five ten or eleven, and Mallory had placed her age at seventy. Nedda would have been a twelve-year-old girl in the year that Red Winter had disappeared.

No, no, no!

It was easier to believe that he was being set up for an elaborate pratfall. And how many bets were being made on him *this* time?

Though his blinds were not drawn and the door was not closed, no one disturbed him. His people had sensed that he was best left alone as he sat there staring at a blank space on the wall. From time to time, the men would approach the glass of the goldfish bowl to see if the position of the boss's body had changed any. And now Jack Coffey gave them a little thrill. His head moved slowly from side to side as his chair rolled back and away from the computer.

It seemed that two of his detectives had found the lost child, Red Winter, the most enduring mystery in the annals of NYPD. And he had only given them three days to expose Stick Man and break the case of the century.

THREE

Riker was telling his partner a story to distract her from a favorite sport of near-death adventures in traffic, and so the tan sedan rolled safely down Madison Avenue.

Mallory pulled up to the curb. Legal parking spaces were impossible to come by in midtown, but bus stops like this one were plentiful. She cut the engine. 'Why did they call him Stick Man?'

'The lead detective on the Winter House Massacre – *he* named the freak.' Riker stepped out onto the sidewalk. 'There're only two or three cops who'd remember why he picked that name, and they're in nursing homes.'

He paused to light a cigarette, striking three matches in the wind. Impatient, Mallory slammed her car door, and still he took his time, exhaling a cloud of smoke as he walked toward an office building at the middle of the block. 'One of the Winter kids was holding a crayon drawing when they found him. It was a stick figure, no detail. You know the way kids draw, and this little boy was only four years old. There was one small hole in the paper and some blood from the stab wound to his heart. So the lead detective – Fitzgerald was his name – he framed the kid's picture and hung it up in the squad room. At first, only the cops on the case knew how important that drawing was.'

'So Fitzgerald thought the boy drew a portrait of his killer?'

'Yeah,' said Riker, 'and, in a way, he did. There were thirty detectives assigned to the massacre. They worked it for a solid year, and they never had one lead to flesh out a suspect. You see? The kid's drawing of a stick man fit the case. It hung on that wall for years. It drove them all nuts.'

He stopped and looked up at the sky, as if he gave a damn about the weather. He was wondering how much of the story he should hold back. In Mallory's puppy days, when he was still allowed to call her Kathy, she had loved his grisly cop stories, the more blood the better – but never ghost stories. Eventually, he would have to tell her that Stick Man's killings had begun in 1860.

And then she would have to shoot him.

'My grandfather didn't work the case,' said Riker, 'but it was all he ever talked about.' And it was all that Granddad had really cared about. The old man had made a science of ice-pick wounds that spanned a full century. But Mallory did not need to know that, not yet. And now that they had reached the address of Willy Roy Boyd's attorney, the story hour was over.

The two detectives pushed through the glass doors of the rat maze, floor upon floor of lawyers' offices stacked up to the moon. Riker flashed a badge at the security guard who wanted to stop them from using the penthouse elevator. They stepped inside a carpeted box paneled with mirrors and lit by a tiny crystal chandelier. It was a style that New Yorkers would call piss elegant. The elevator doors closed and they rode upward through the tower of law firms, aiming for the most expensive one. Riker was looking forward to this meeting, and he had no plans to restrain Mallory's enthusiasm for payback.

They exited at the last stop and breezed on by a young woman at the reception desk, paying no attention to her as she called after them, asking if they had an appointment. The next woman to ask this question was a more formidable brunette, whose desk stood guard before a lawyer's door. The secretary spoke only to Mallory, or, more accurately, to Mallory's clothes, the silk T-shirt and tailored blazer, money on the hoof that blended well with the luxurious surroundings.

The brunette made it clear that Riker's suit really ought to have arrived on the delivery elevator at the rear.

Mallory's clothes leaned over the desk and said, 'We don't need an appointment.'

Did the dark-haired woman find her unsettling, possibly dangerous?

Oh, yeah.

The secretary sat very still, hands tightly folded and knuckles turning white, as the young detective reached across her desk to press the button that would admit them to the inner sanctum of Sid Henry, Esquire. Riker followed his partner through the door, glancing back at the cowed woman behind the desk.

Good job.

The door swung open on panoramic windows and brilliant light. The lawyer was reclining in a leather chair and sunning himself like a lizard in very expensive threads. The man even moved like a reptile, his head jerking upward, startled. As the attorney rose from his desk, preparing his first verbal assault, he suddenly shut his gaping mouth. Was it the sight of Mallory's lovely face? No, Riker guessed it was probably the very large gun, a .357 Smith and Wesson revolver. She had one hand on her hip, her blazer open and pulled to one side, and there was no way he could fail to see that cannon.

Sid Henry sat down – quietly.

Riker luxuriated in these passing seconds, for Mallory had not yet produced her shield, and, considering this attorney's recent client, a serial killer, the poor bastard sincerely did not know if she was crazy or a cop. Would he live or die?

It was Riker who ended the suspense, holding up his own gold shield.

Mallory pulled a manila envelope from her knapsack, tore it open, and held up the morgue photograph of a body on the dissection table – *after* the dissection, minus all the vital organs, and looking very pale. 'Recognize your former client? No? Well, it's a bad photo.

Willy Roy Boyd was the psycho who butchered three women, gutted them with a hunting knife. And you got him out on bail.' She dropped the photo on his desk. 'Remember now?'

'Blame it on NYPD.' Sid Henry grinned at her, entirely too confident that she would not hurt him. 'The case against my client wasn't exactly flawless.'

Mallory slammed her fist down on the desk with the force of a hammer. 'My case was *perfect!*'

The attorney flinched, and his eyes widened with sudden clarity, for now he understood his error: she was the lead detective on that case – and she did not respond well to criticism.

'I looked up every precedent you cited at that bail hearing,' she said. 'You had nothing. It was all smoke. You knew that judge would never admit he didn't know case law on search and seizure. You were right on the edge of perjury.'

'So,' said Sid Henry, 'this is retribution? You plan to scare me to death?' He tapped the photograph. 'This is so unnecessary.' He turned the picture over. 'The dramatics, this disgusting picture.'

Riker had predicted that the man would rally quickly. According to police lore, lawyers were as resilient as cockroaches, and one who had been decapitated could litigate for up to three days.

Mallory walked back to the door and closed it – *slowly* – smiling as she shut out all sound and sight of witnesses, and this little gesture was not lost on Sid Henry.

'So, Sid, let me guess,' said Riker. 'You're just an associate, right? Not a partner in the firm? Naw, you're too young. I'd bet even money those old geezers don't know you took a fee to bail out that butcher.'

'Maybe,' said Mallory, 'you told them it was *pro bono*. All the money you made on that hearing didn't go through the firm's billing office.' At least, she had found no record of it while raiding the firm's database. However, she *had* found a large deposit in the lawyer's personal bank account.

By Sid Henry's silence, Riker knew they had the man cold for pocketing money that belonged to his firm, and now they owned him. Oh, and best of all, there would be no charge of police harassment at the end of the day – even if Mallory left marks on him.

'You didn't ask how your client died,' said Riker, not giving the lawyer any time to wonder how the police could access the firm's billing office. 'It wasn't in the newspapers. Not on the tube, either. But you don't seem surprised.'

'I haven't seen Willy since the bail hearing.' Sid Henry picked up the photograph of his late client and forced a smile as he handed it back to Mallory. 'So he's dead. Can I assume this is your work, Detective? Rather excessive use of force.'

Mallory ignored the photo and let it hang in the air between them until the man's arm got tired and he lost the idea that he could win a staring contest with her. She pulled out the pocket watch that had once belonged to the late Louis Markowitz. 'You've got two minutes to clear yourself on a charge of murder for hire.' This little trick of time, the pressure of a ticking bomb, was another hand-me-down from her foster father. 'If you can't do that, then we get to parade you out of here in handcuffs.' She waited out the silence, her eyes cast down to the face of her watch. 'One minute, fifty-five seconds.'

Sid Henry's voice cracked. 'If you think you can—'

'We wanna know who paid for that bail hearing.' Riker snatched the photograph from the lawyer's hand. 'And don't give us any crap about attorney–client privilege. That won't cover the bastard who hired you. We know Willy couldn't afford fifteen minutes of your time. So who paid your fee?'

'One minute, fifty seconds,' said Mallory.

'You've got no right to—'

'This is a warrant.' Riker waved a folded sheet of paper. It bore no judge's signature, but it worked well as a prop. 'The charge is attempted murder. Your client tried to kill another woman last night – a *rich* woman. Now the older lawyers, the guys with their names on the door of this outfit, maybe they even know her. All these rich people know each other, don't they?' He turned to his partner. 'Curious, Mallory? We could ask them on the way out.'

She nodded, saying, 'One minute, thirty seconds.'

Riker pulled out his handcuffs, then tossed a Miranda card on the desk. 'I think we can assume you know your legal rights. I'm guessing you plan to use the right to remain silent.'

'One minute, fifteen seconds.'

Riker grinned at her. 'I think your watch is slow, kid. I say we just *do* him.'

It happened very fast. She had reached the other side of the desk before the lawyer knew she was after him. Now he was half risen from the chair and pulled forward by her hand dragging his necktie – no visible bruising that way. He was quickly bent over the desk, face pressed to the blotter, as she worked his arms behind his back.

Riker threw her the handcuffs, and, while she did the honors, he stood back and smiled, wanting always to remember this special moment – Sid Henry bending over and exposing his ass to all comers.

Evidently, the lawyer saw his own posture as a portent of things to come in lockup. 'I don't *know* who hired me!' he yelled.

No – call it a squeal.

'That's not what we wanted to hear,' said Mallory.

'I couldn't tell you if I *wanted* to!' And now, his words came out all in a rush. 'It was a cash payment – anonymous. Ask my secretary. She opened the first package. There were two installments, one before the bail hearing and one afterward.'

'And you gave the secretary a cut to keep her quiet, right?' Riker pocketed the warrant, producing instant relief in the attorney's eyes. 'Okay, I don't think we have to pursue this – *if* your story holds up.' He took one last look at the man bent over his desk, then turned to his partner. 'Can we take a picture of this before you uncuff him?'

No, he could see that Mallory was in a hurry to get on to the next interview. Well, one lawyer down and one to go. Their second target of the day was the attorney of record for the Winter family trust fund. He was also the father of Bitty Smyth.

The reception hall of the Harvard Club had the hallmark of wealth and power – wasted space on an obscene scale. The high ceiling was close to God and deceased alumni.

It was rare for Charles Butler to set foot in this place. As a child prodigy, he had not made many friends among his older classmates. Today's luncheon was at the invitation of Sheldon Smyth, scion of the oldest and most venerable law firm in New York City. Smyth had mentioned that his son, Paul, would also be dining with them. The old man harbored the delusion that Charles and Paul had been great friends at school.

Untrue.

Paul Smyth had been shoehorned into Harvard as the son of a wealthy alumnus, while Charles had been a sought-after child, the center of a bidding war among the finest schools on the Eastern Seaboard. There had been only one occasion when he and Paul had met on campus in passing. At eighteen, Charles had been on his way out, one semester away from submitting a Ph.D. dissertation, and Paul had just arrived as an incoming freshman. No thought had been given to this – schoolmate – in decades. However, last night, the birthday party photographs in Bitty Smyth's bedroom had raised old grudges dating back to the sandbox.

The main dining room, a grand oak-paneled affair, was lined with the portraits of patrons immortalized in gigantic oil paintings, their names and deeds long forgotten. However, the club's famed cheese dip was memorable.

He crossed the room behind a waiter. If not for this escort, he would never have chosen the right table, for his old enemy was so altered by time. Paul Smyth's hair had thinned, his belly had expanded, and his chin had tripled. But Charles was recognized at once, so little changed was he, with a full head of hair and only the one chin. So it

67

was a balanced universe after all. Paul stood up to shake hands with him.

In peripheral vision, Paul's father was a thatch of silver hair with thick black eyebrows. Now the older man rose from his chair to match Charles's stature of six-four. Sheldon Smyth extended one hand across the table to greet his luncheon guest. The old man's eyes were the magic mirrors that every narcissist prayed for, clear blue reflections of the egoist coda, saying to the beholder: *My God, I think you're wonderful!* Aloud he said, 'So good of you to come, such short notice and all.'

Charles was stunned, but not seduced. 'How do you do, sir?'

By Sheldon Smyth's manner and smile, the other diners might believe that they were close friends who met for lunch every day. When the three men were seated with menus in hand, the elder Smyth said, 'I understand the police got you out of bed last night. My ex-wife called this morning. You remember her of course. Cleo Winter-Smyth?'

'No,' said Charles. 'We've never met.' For that matter, he could not recall having met Paul's father either. At those gatherings where children were forcibly pitted against one another, Paul had always been accompanied by a nanny.

'But you *did* meet her once,' said Paul, 'for about six seconds when you were ten. She dropped off me and my sister at your birthday party. Bitty wasn't invited, of course, but she badgered Dad, and I had to take her.'

Sheldon Smyth cleared his throat to announce that this minor slander did not sit well with him. 'Bitty is the only child by my first marriage to Cleo.'

Charles nodded in a show of polite interest. 'I see the family resemblance.'

'Bitty's adopted,' said Paul.

This was a surprise, for the woman had features in common with her father, the shape of his large eyes, if not their color, the same chin and mouth. Paul, on the other hand, bore no—

'She's *family*,' said Sheldon Smyth, all but daring his son to say one more word. With a friendlier expression, he turned all of his attention on Charles. 'Cleo and I adopted Bitty when my cousin died in childbirth. Now tell me, why should the police bother you about a lot of photographs?'

'I believe they're required to notify me of a potential stalker.'

'But you set them straight, of course, told them she was a family connection.'

This was news to Charles, who had no surviving relatives. He politely smiled and waited for some explanation.

'Your mother's second cousin, Charles. His half brother was a Smyth. No blood relation perhaps, but there you are,' he said. '*Family.*' The old lawyer allowed this word to hang alone, punctuated with respectful silence to increase its import.

Charles was not surprised. He had long been a believer in the six degrees of separation: the theory that everyone on the planet was somehow connected to everyone else by a sequence of relationships. However, the Smyths had taken it to an elitist extreme, marrying into every major fortune in New York State.

'So you've got a *stalker*,' said Paul, not quite understanding that word as the one his father most wanted to defuse. He failed to catch the old man's eye and that look of disappointment in an idiot son. 'Just like a rock star.' Grinning, Paul punched Charles on the arm, instantly calling up the days when a child-size Paul had fired sniper shots with closed fists, jabbing and bruising on the run, then finishing off his prey by killing him with words that had an even stronger punch and power. Charles had died each time they met.

But not today.

Sheldon Smyth had finally managed to capture his son's attention. The old man narrowed his eyes in an ocular thump on the head, a warning not to punch their guest one more time. Glancing at his watch, he said, 'Paul, don't let us detain you any longer.' As he reached out for a roll and a butter knife, his face said the rest: *Go, or be impaled on the silverware.*

And now, Charles quite liked the old man.

When Paul had excused himself from the table and the waiter had departed with their menus and lunch orders, Sheldon Smyth leaned forward, voice lowered. 'So, my boy, Cleo said the house was full of police – standing room only. Why all this fuss over a burglar?'

'Well, he was a *dead* burglar. You didn't know?'

'No, my ex-wife neglected to mention a corpse. So typical of Cleo,' he said, as if dead bodies lying about the house were an everyday nuisance. 'I think she was more concerned that you might cause problems for Bitty. When I called my office this morning, I was told that the police had paid a visit. Well, naturally . . . I wondered if you'd pressed charges against my daughter.'

'No, sir, it never occurred to me.'

'Good man.'

Salads arrived during the ensuing silence. Then Charles further reassured Bitty's father, saying, 'I had a long talk with Bitty last night. I'm satisfied that she isn't the least bit dangerous.'

'Quite right. No more than a simple schoolgirl crush. I'm sure you found it quite charming.'

Charles understood this from his host's perspective. Quite comical, really. A man like himself, one with the attributes of an eagle beak and bull-frog eyes, would have so few choices; how could he fail to be flattered by the fixation of a neurotic elf?

Between one course and another, he learned that the Smyth firm had served the Winter family for more than a hundred years. The old man's eyes were always fixed upon Charles, as if he regarded his guest as the most important personage on the planet. It was an illusion from a lawyer's bag of tricks to win over juries and stalking victims alike, but Smyth had perfected it to a fine art, and Charles felt that his immunity to flattery was slipping.

Meanwhile, heads were turning at all the other tables. Mallory had arrived to work her usual effect upon a room. No one thought to stop her forward momentum across the wide floor. She was so obviously one of the power people in this gathering. What waiter would risk being trampled? There were nods of approval all around. Yes, the patrons assured one another, she was one of them, though so few of them carried guns to lunch. Hers was exposed – quite deliberately, Charles thought – as she swept the blazer to one side and reached into a rear pocket of her jeans, where she kept her gold shield.

Only now did Smyth realize that his table had become a spectacle. He looked up to see the young homicide detective standing beside his chair. She was no longer displaying the gun, but only discreetly holding out her badge.

Mallory gave Charles a curt nod. 'Hello, Dr Butler,' she said, employing a title he never used, though his credentials entitled him to do so. And with this pointed formality, she wiped away their friendship, their business partnership and the years that they had known one another. They were merely recent acquaintances – that was her message to him. And now, after forcing Sheldon Smyth to wait out this little farce, she turned her eyes on him. 'Your office told me I could find you here.'

'Really,' he said. With those two syllables, Smyth managed to convey that some minion would be parted from his head just the moment he returned to his office.

Hardly inclined to wait on an invitation, Mallory pulled up a chair at the table. As if she did not already have Smyth's complete attention, she asked, 'Can you think of any reason why someone would want your daughter dead?'

Smyth stared at her, then shook his head and kept his silence, perhaps adhering to a lawyer's code to ask no question to which he did not already have the answer. And then, of course, he could not have been more stunned if she had pistol-whipped him.

Mallory seemed to like that reaction. She liked it a lot. 'Money motives work for me. Who inherits if your daughter dies?'

The words were slow to come. 'No one,' said Smyth. 'I drew up her will myself. Her estate goes to the Legal Aid Society.'

'I know there's a family trust fund.' Mallory's tone implied that she had caught the old man in a lie.

'My daughter has no stake in that. The only beneficiaries are her mother and her uncle.'

'And Nedda Winter?'

The old man nodded.

'Tell me why your daughter doesn't benefit from the trust fund.'

It took a moment for Sheldon Smyth to adjust to the fact that he was not in control of this interview. He graced her with a radiant smile – an experiment that immediately failed. She had a natural immunity to charisma, and this seemed to irritate him. The old man made a great show of looking at his wristwatch, and he would not meet her eyes when he spoke. 'I can't discuss the trust fund with you.' He addressed the empty chair on the other side of the table. 'It's privileged information. I can tell you that Bitty doesn't *need* a draw on the trust. I provide her with a generous allowance.'

'That's not what I asked.' Mallory leaned forward and raised her voice, as if the old man might be hard of hearing. 'So, apart from you, her only source of income is her law practice?'

Charles sat up a bit straighter. 'Bitty? A *lawyer*?'

'Yes, my daughter was top of her class at Columbia.' The old man misunderstood Charles's startled expression. 'Of course, I wanted her to go to Harvard, but she preferred to stay close to home.'

Mallory called Smyth's attention back to herself. 'Where does your daughter practice law, and what's her area of expertise?'

'She used to work for my firm, but now she's on sabbatical. She's always concentrated on contract law.'

'Would that include trust-fund busting?'

'You can't mean the Winter family trust.' Smyth was incredulous. 'What would be the point if she didn't—'

'I need copies of all the documents for that trust fund,' said the detective. 'I want them today.'

72

'Got a warrant, Detective?' Smyth seemed suddenly cheered by Mallory's prolonged quiet. 'No,' he said, 'I didn't think so.'

'You're the executor,' said Mallory. 'You can give me any—'

'That trust fund has a long history. The documents – every bill and receipt and canceled check, paperwork for decades of transactions – it fills a good-size storage room.' He leaned toward her with new confidence. 'It would take a small army to copy all that paperwork, and the originals will never leave my firm.'

'Did I mention that I was trying to keep your daughter alive?'

'And were you listening when I said there was no motive for anyone to harm her?'

'It's *my* job to decide that,' said Mallory. 'You're only a lawyer. I'm the *law*.'

Sheldon Smyth inclined his head and smiled, perhaps in agreement with this distinction, but more likely in approval, a sudden change in his opinion of this young adversary. 'Detective Mallory, I can give you the basic structure of the trust. Cleo Winter-Smyth and her brother are entitled to a monthly draw.'

'And Nedda,' said Mallory, reminding him once more of this woman's existence. 'She could also be a target. So if she dies—'

'It doesn't change the amount of the draw. You should also know that the trust fund is entailed to charity. The payouts end with Lionel and Cleo's generation.'

'And Nedda,' said Mallory. 'You keep forgetting her.'

Sheldon Smyth dropped his smile and laid his napkin on the table. 'I think we're done here, Detective. Talk to my secretary if you need more information. She'll schedule an appointment.' And now, because he must sense that she did not take direction very well, he added, 'I'm afraid we're boring poor Charles with all of this.'

After Mallory had kicked him under the table, Charles was encouraged to say, 'Oh, no, sir. This is fascinating.'

'Well, Charles,' said Smyth, 'if that's the case, I suggest you have dinner with the family tonight. You've been invited by my ex-wife.

I'm sure Bitty would like to properly apologize for the unpleasantness with the police.'

'I assure you there's no need for that,' said Charles, shifting his legs beyond Mallory's long reach.

'Say yes,' said Smyth. 'I'm asking as a favor. Bitty's so easily crushed. Tell me you'll go.'

In Mallory's version of subtlety, she examined her fingernails – as if they might need sharpening.

'Of course,' said Charles.

After signing a tab for the luncheon and leaving instructions to care for his guests, Sheldon Smyth departed, and the energy level of the dining room was diminished by half.

Moments later, Riker arrived, and he proved to be another head turner, attracting attention from every quarter of the dining room. He moseyed toward the table, followed closely by a waiter, who no doubt suspected this badly dressed man of a scheme to steal the silverware. Charles stood up to greet the detective, and the waiter, somewhat relieved, melted away.

When Riker had been apprised of the fine points of Mallory's interview, he sipped his coffee and grinned at Charles. 'So Mallory promoted you to snitch. Good job. Take a nose count when you show up for dinner. There might be somebody living there that we don't know about, maybe the one who wrote this letter.' He handed over a clear plastic bag containing a sheet of paper. 'We took that from the dead man's lawyer. It came with a boxful of money.'

Charles read the scant information neatly typed. It mentioned the name of the client and an arrangement for more money if the bail hearing was successful. 'My God, I should've recognized him from his picture in the newspaper. This is the dead burglar, isn't it? Willy Roy Boyd?'

'Keep that to yourself,' said Mallory. 'Can you tell us anything helpful?'

Charles shook his head. 'Bare sentence fragments. No style or

74

turn of phrase to give the writer away. I can tell you that you're not dealing with an idiot. Does that help you?'

No, apparently not.

'Sorry.'

An afternoon of begging for warrants had come to a bad end. District Attorney John J. Buchanan had personally turned down the last request for assistance from his office. In a rare exception to protocol, he had granted an audience to mere detectives, and that alone had been enough to make Riker suspicious.

The DA had made it clear that the Smyth firm was unassailable and off-limits to the NYPD. That directive had included Bitty Smyth, a former member of that firm.

It was dark when the partners returned to SoHo, and Riker was gearing up for another unpleasant confrontation as they left the car and headed down the street to a familiar haunt. 'Well, it's an election year,' he said, as they walked along. 'Smyth must be a big contributor to the DA's war chest. Damn Buchanan.'

They stopped by the window of a brightly lit café across the street from the station house. The table on the other side of the glass was littered with guidebooks and cameras, and the chairs were filled with middle-aged ladies.

Damn tourists.

All the cops in sight had had the decency to take other tables. A gray-haired woman sat in the chair once occupied by Mallory's foster father. Unaware that she was trespassing, this tourist looked up to see the young homicide detective's face close to the window and those cold eyes like oncoming bullets. Apparently the mayor's new handout sheet for visitors had included tips that were actually helpful, like – never make eye contact with the sociopath, for now the woman quickly looked down at her menu, wishing the green-eyed apparition away.

Riker nudged his partner. 'They're ordering dessert. We can come back later.'

Carol O'Connell

No, that would have been too easy.

The woman seated in the dead man's chair looked up to the window again, and now her companions were also curious. This was Mallory's cue to clear the table – quickly and efficiently. Before his partner could casually draw back one side of her blazer to terrorize these out-of-towners with the display of her shoulder holster, Riker said, 'No, let me do it this time. Just wait here, okay?'

He entered the café and hunkered down by the ladies' table. Softly, he spoke to them about the young woman on the other side of the window glass, the one with the very disturbing eyes. Really just a kid, he said to them. He talked about her foster father, a late great cop, and how Kathy Mallory had never come to terms with the fact that she would never see him again. It was too hard to believe that Lou Markowitz would not be sitting at this very table each time she came by the café. And here Riker paused a beat to rap the table – softly.

There was always this little moment of pretend, he told the ladies, before the kid turned to the window to see that the old man's chair was empty. And then she would come in and sit down to wait for him because, bless the old bastard's soul, he was always late. And, just for a little while, Lou was still alive. He had never died in the line of duty and left his kid all alone in copland.

Just a kid, he said once more.

And he told them about Gurt, the waitress who had kept this table clear of other patrons at this same hour, until the day, not long ago, when she had retired. So now the girl had also lost another fixture in her life. Ah, Gurt, he said to them, that *saint* (a sarcastic old bat who should have retired years ago). And so, as the ladies could see – he pointed to Mallory now – the kid did not handle change very well. It . . . disturbed her.

They all turned to the window, as if waiting for Mallory to cry.

They would wait forever.

He was still talking as these women rose from their chairs, all

76

smiling with their kind faces from the heartland of America, where all the *good* people lived. They picked up their plates and glasses, silverware and napkins, and moved to a vacant table at the back of the room.

Riker faced the window, but Mallory was gone.

'What did you say to them?' She was behind his back, and he jumped. One hand went to his heart – still beating – just checking.

'I told them the truth,' he said, and that should shut her up. Mallory had difficulties with that simple concept. And the idea of human kindness would give her even more trouble.

When they were seated and waiting for their meal, Riker continued to parcel out the story of Nedda, a.k.a. Red Winter.

'You've seen the painting,' he said. 'I guess everybody has. But back in the day – remember this is the forties – a nude painting of a little girl was a shock and a half. In the other paintings the kid had clothes on, but the nude was the biggest one, nine feet tall. And Nedda was only eleven years old then. The cops raided the art gallery and took all the paintings away.'

'The artist was her father, right?'

Riker nodded. 'Her *rich* father. I guess that's why the whole thing blew over – one headline in the papers, then nothing. Some of the books about Red Winter figured her for a runaway because Daddy was a freak. And some say she killed him.'

'And everyone else in the house?' Mallory shook her head. 'A little girl on a murder spree doesn't work for me.'

That had been predictable. His partner favored money motives.

'Hey,' said Riker, 'I can only tell this story the way it was told to me. You wanna hear it or not?'

He knew that she did. Her chin lifted slightly, a vow to behave, and she was his old Kathy for a moment, just another little girl sitting around a copshop, surrounded by men with guns and human scum in handcuffs.

Riker had sometimes done midget duty in the after-school hours, making sure the tiny, semi-reformed street thief would not rob the place while her old man had been occupied with more hard-core criminals. Riker had kept Lou's foster child honest by telling her all of his handed-down family stories from the days of Legs Diamond, Lucky Luciano and Murder Incorporated – murders by the dozen in every tale.

What a deal.

Young Kathy had never gotten such bloody treats at home. Her foster mother would never have allowed it. Gentle Helen Markowitz had always held the strange notion that Kathy Mallory was a normal child, one who might have bad dreams of the bogeyman. What Helen had never understood was that little Kathy had the early makings of the bogeyman's nightmare.

'Anyway,' said Riker, 'after the raid on the art show, Quentin Winter's daughter is famous. Everybody, uptown and down, has a theory on what goes on inside Winter House. Then one day, a year later, the cops get a call from another little girl. She tells 'em she just got home from the park with her brother, Lionel. The whole house is dead – that's the way she put it – except for the baby. And the baby's crying. The little girl on the phone says her name is Cleo. She was only five years old.'

When Charles rang the bell, it was Sheldon Smyth who responded. The older man had won a footrace to the door, beating a young woman in a maid's costume, who rushed up behind him with a tray of hors d'oeuvres in hand.

'Not now,' said Smyth, flicking his fingers at her to shoo her away as if she were an insect. 'Hello, Charles.' He glanced back, satisfied to see the maid in retreat. 'Not the best caterers, I'm afraid. Short notice and all.'

Charles wondered why Smyth would tell such a lie. The truck parked outside the house belonged to the most exclusive caterer in Manhattan, one who was booked months in advance and not the sort to do impromptu dinner parties – unless of course, the fee had been doubled or tripled.

With the old lawyer's hand on his back, Charles was gently but firmly propelled into the front room, and his eyes were once again drawn to the wildly impractical staircase. The architect must have hailed from a school that regarded clients as parasites in the home, only grudgingly deferring to them by allotting space for kitchens, bathrooms and the like. And now he had exhausted every sane rationale for his sudden discomfort. In a less pragmatic part of his mind, he thought the house was hostile.

How ludicrous.

At the foot of the stairs was a fully stocked bar, and here introductions were made to Bitty's uncle. While Charles was shaking hands with Lionel Winter, he felt that his host was missing something – oh, perhaps a pulse. The man was simply not present, that or his personality was in hiding. Given the snow-white hair, the face was younger than it should be, and Charles wondered if the lack of age lines was due to the absence of an emotional life. It was pathos and comedy that creased a face with personal history.

Sheldon Smyth dismissed a young man from the caterer's staff and assumed the role of bartender. 'Let me guess your poison, Charles.' He poured a double shot of Chivas Regal into a brandy glass. 'Neat, am I right?'

'Yes, thank you.' This was indeed Charles's usual fare, but he had not ordered Chivas at lunch today. He was given further proof that Smyth had gone to a great deal of trouble over this dinner party, for now he learned that his favorite foods were on the menu. However, the elderly lawyer had not discerned that Charles's taste in music was strictly classical, though this extended to the vintage jazz that Nedda Winter had played on the radio during his last visit to this house. Tonight, he was forced to listen to elevator music, popular tunes played as boring instrumentals by an uninspired orchestra. Even the tonal quality had changed overnight. The sound surrounded him. He did not have to look at the antique radio to see that the dial was dark, that the music did not come from there.

Lionel Winter made his first attempt at conversation, going on at length about the elaborate sound system that played in every room of the house. And when Charles mentioned the jazz tunes of the previous evening, his host fell silent and only stared at him.

Sheldon Smyth filled this uncomfortable void, saying, 'The ladies should be joining us any minute now. Ah, women – never on time. Well, what's the use of a grand staircase if you can't make a stunning entrance?'

And now the ladies were coming, gliding down the stairs in long gowns. The tall woman could only be Cleo Winter-Smyth. Resplendent in a dark-blue gown the color of her eyes, she towered over her daughter.

Poor little Bitty. Her strapless dress of iridescent colors was reminiscent of a disco ball on prom night, and her gamine charm had been destroyed by a gash of lipstick, a rouge pot on each cheek, and hair lacquered into appalling spit curls. Aghast, Sheldon Smyth turned from his daughter to his ex-wife, and Charles wondered if Bitty had been transformed into a circus pony under duress. The tiny woman flinched, needing no more than her father's expression to tell her how foolish she looked.

Cleo Winter-Smyth resembled her brother, Lionel. Both were tall and fair and absent any human aspect in their eyes. The woman tilted her head to one side, and this was the only indication that she was surprised by her ex-husband's attitude. Turning away from him, she managed a floodlight white smile for their guest.

During the ensuing small talk of weather and dead burglars, Charles felt more and more ill at ease. Again, he tried to blame this on the staircase that was always in the act of running off to the top of the house. And all those tall mirrors – they picked up each gesture of a head half turned, repeating it in a herd of heads all giving alarm as animals will do when they turn to the sound or the scent of danger.

Even the small painting over the bar had a manic quality of stroke and line and color. Between one drink and the next, he learned that Bitty Smyth had grown up in this unsettling house. And so, if there was an easily startled air about her, in her eyes and in her manner, this was to be excused.

Cleo Winter-Smyth lifted her face ever so slightly as she peered into one of the mirrors lining the walls. She spoke to the reflection of another woman on the staircase behind her. 'Nedda, I didn't know you'd be joining us tonight.'

Was there something in her tone that implied the older woman was unwelcome?

Nedda Winter drifted down the stairs in a long black satin dress that called to mind a black-and-white movie from a more elegant era. A loose-woven shawl of silver threads was draped over her shoulders, and her braided white hair served as a coiled crown. She was another paradox of the house. The lines of her gown were sylvan and classical, the lady statuesque, her posture unbowed, and, despite the wrinkles and the hair gone white, the total effect was beautiful. And what quiet authority this woman had, sufficient to reduce Sheldon Smyth to a fidgeting child on best behavior. Her pale blue eyes took in the drastic alterations to her niece. If the sight was unpleasing, she never let on, but, while Bitty was looking elsewhere, Miss Winter glanced at Cleo with mild disapproval. The younger sister would not look at her.

Upon reaching the bottom step, the elder lady inclined her head and extended one veined hand to Charles. 'How nice to see you again. I'm sorry we didn't have a chance to talk last night.'

'Well,' said Sheldon Smyth, 'we'll make up for that this evening.' And with those words, the occasion of a man's violent death had been reduced to a previous social event.

Nedda placed a protective arm about Bitty's shoulders, then guided her niece into the dining room, and the rest of the party followed them to the table.

A waiter pulled out a chair to seat Cleo Winter-Smyth beside

Charles. 'I met your parents years and years ago,' she said. 'Sheldon and I were enrolling Bitty at the Marshal Frampton Institute.' Left off this long name were the words *for gifted children.* 'They seemed to dote on you.'

The woman had more grace than to mention that Marion Butler had been a bit old for motherhood. Charles's birth had been a shock to his parents, a pregnancy so late in life. His parents had died of old age before he was out of his teens. And, yes, they had doted upon him and sent him to schools that would cater to his freak's IQ. He looked down at his place setting, wondering how he could have forgotten Bitty Smyth among the limited enrollment of the Frampton Institute.

'Stop racking your brain, my boy,' said Sheldon Smyth. 'The moment my back was turned, Bitty's mother pulled her out of school. I don't think she attended for more than two days.'

The subject came up again as the first course was being served.

'It wasn't the right school for Bitty.' Cleo's tone was somewhat defensive. 'I sent her to a better one where she could make all the right connections.'

'Connections?' Smyth laughed. 'She was a five-year-old, not a socialite.'

Bitty seemed to be growing smaller, sinking down in her chair as she was talked about, but never acknowledged as a person in this room. She was so small, so easily overlooked in a family of giants. Charles imagined her life as a mouse in this house, scurrying from one bolt-hole to another. He waited for her to look his way, then smiled and said, 'It's a pity you didn't stay at Frampton. We might've gotten to know one another much earlier.'

Bitty smiled and spilled her water glass. While a waiter mopped up the table, Nedda Winter nodded her approval of Charles. The subject was closed and peace was restored for a time.

Before the last entrée had been served, the house and all its company, all save Nedda, had begun to wear on Charles. He hardly tasted his food while eating his way toward the final course. Cleo and

Lionel's smiles were flashing on and off like lightbulbs, and, by this odd behavior, he determined that the history of the house was a subject to be avoided. Every foray into this area was sharply cut off and the conversation directed elsewhere.

Odder still was the bond between brother and sister. In some respects, Lionel and Cleo brought to mind an old married couple who could finish one another's sentences or altogether do away with the spoken word. However, there was no apparent affection between them. They simply came as a set. If you got one, you got the other.

Charles picked up the challenge of cleaving the pair. 'Lionel, what sort of work do you do?'

'Work?'

Cleo translated for her brother. 'Investments, dear, the stocks and bonds.'

'So you work on Wall Street,' said Charles in an attempt to be helpful. Oh, wait. There was that pesky word again. *Work?* Us?

'No, we manage our own investments,' said Lionel. 'But it *is* time consuming.'

Somewhere between the chocolate mousse and post-prandial brandy, the conversation had turned to the subject of fortunetellers. Where this topic had come from, Charles could not say, but he suspected that Bitty had raised it in a small voice and wafted it across the table to her mother, a willing receptacle.

'I've had a few tarot card readings,' said Cleo, 'and it was worth years of therapy. But there's nothing mystical about it. The fortune-teller reads the person, not the cards. Some readers are remarkably intuitive.'

And Charles took this to mean that a fortuneteller had once flattered her. No, that was unkind and in conflict with his heightened sense of empathy. He suspected a wound at the core of this woman, some serious misadventure of the psyche. It was a certainty that she shared this affliction with her brother, hence the odd bond between them. Something had happened to them, some great trauma.

Bitty gulped down her brandy and reached for the decanter, saying, 'Aunt Nedda can read tarot cards.' Out of the entire company, Nedda Winter was the most surprised by this news. Bitty quietly slipped away from the table and left the dining room door ajar as she made her way across the front room, wobbly but stumbling only once.

Upon finally noticing her daughter's absence, Cleo shrugged her apologies to Charles. 'I'm sure she'll come back.'

'It might be better if she didn't,' said Lionel. 'She's had way too much to drink.' He turned to Charles, saying, 'My niece isn't accustomed to alcohol. The religious life, I suppose. Her current church—'

'*Religious?*' Sheldon Smyth pronounced this word as if he had never heard it before. 'Bitty? She's never even been to Sunday school.'

'It's a phase she's been going through,' said his ex-wife, 'for the past *three years*.' There was a clear comment here on Sheldon Smyth's apparent lack of interest in his own child.

Lionel turned to his erstwhile brother-in-law. 'So Bitty never told you when she joined the Catholics.' There was nothing in his voice to say that Sheldon's ignorance surprised him. 'Well, that's old news.'

In an aside to Charles, Cleo said, 'Bitty's a Protestant now – Bloody Heart of the Redeemer, I think. Something like that. It's a sect – no, actually, more like a cult. Lots of traveling on holy missions to recruit heathens.'

'I'm sure,' said Lionel, 'Bitty finds it a damn shame that the Protestants have no nunneries.'

'It's a shame they have no confessionals,' said Bitty, reappearing from behind her uncle's chair, weaving slightly and producing an awkward silence all around the table. 'Imagine a little room where you can take your soul to get it cleaned.'

This comment was met with dead quiet. Charles affected the distance of outsider status. Eyes cast down, his spoon served only to move the dessert about on his plate.

'You've had quite enough to drink.' Cleo was firm and apparently still had the power to forbid her forty-year-old child, for now she moved the brandy snifter far from her daughter's place setting.

Ignoring her mother, Bitty passed by her own chair and moved toward Nedda in a slow, somewhat unsteady march. She held a boxed deck of cards in her hands. The cardboard was worn with ages of handling and bore a tarot illustration of the hanged man. She set it down on the table before her aunt, as though bestowing a precious artifact. 'Maybe you could read the tarot cards for Charles.'

Nedda Winter stared at the deck with a trace of alarm. This might as well be a dead animal that her niece had laid on the dinner table. She was slow to recover her composure, and then she slipped the deck into her lap beneath the cover of the tablecloth. 'Not tonight, dear. I'm rather tired.'

'What you need is a good stiff drink.' Sheldon Smyth rose to gallantly pull out her chair, then led her away from the table, and the rest of the party followed them to gather around the bar in the front room. While the lawyer poured out their drinks, Charles renewed his fascination with the staircase.

'You feel it, too,' said Bitty, nodding. 'It's haunted.'

He noticed a sudden dismay about her and turned to see what she was staring at – another damned mirror. It was impossible not to encounter one's self at every turn. Bitty had caught her reflection alongside his own. How he dwarfed her in size. They resembled a sideshow team of giant and midget. She turned her eyes this way and that, finding the same tableau in every direction.

They both looked up to escape the mirrors, and now they shared a view of the winding banister encircling a skylight dome at the top of the house. In another era of horse-drawn carriages and clearer skies, there might have been stars up there.

'Lots of history in this house,' he said.

'You mean all the murders,' said Bitty.

Cleo's smile clicked on slightly out of sync and all for Charles.

'I'm sure you know the story of Winter House. Everyone does.' Glancing back at her daughter, she said. 'It's a *tired* old story, dear.'

Every pair of eyes was fixed on Charles, reading the stunned surprise on his face. He was recalling a bit of history that appeared in newspapers every ten years or so, the regurgitation of a mass murder for the reading pleasure of the public on a Sunday afternoon.

Oh, bloody hell.

Riker and Mallory should have told him, warned him.

Forgetting his manners, he looked over Bitty's head to gape at the surviving Winter children all grown up.

'There was another murder that wasn't famous.' Bitty addressed Charles's shoes. 'You're standing on the place where Edwina Winter died. She was Aunt Nedda's mother.'

He backed up a few steps. 'She fell?' He looked straight up. The body could not have landed in that spot, not after falling down the stairs. The woman must have gone over the—

'Nedda is our half sister,' said Cleo, as if this might be what puzzled her guest. 'Different mothers. And *her* mother drank quite a bit. Well, there you have it, the oldest family scandal. Edwina Winter was drunk when she went over the banister.'

'My father and his brother, James, saw her fall,' said Lionel, directing his gaze upward to a large picture hanging on the second-floor landing. 'That's their portrait.'

Charles looked up at the oil painting of two adolescents. Even at this distance, he would call it a very bad piece of work, almost a cartoon.

'Their account wasn't quite accurate,' said Bitty.

'Daddy and Uncle James gave the *only* account,' said Cleo. 'How can it—'

'Quentin and his first wife hated each other.' Bitty sipped sherry, stocking up on a little bravery from a glass. 'I found the divorce papers filed just before Edwina died. They were charging each other with infidelity.'

'That's enough, Bitty,' said her mother. 'Have some consideration for your aunt.'

'No, don't stop because of me,' said Nedda. 'I never knew my mother. I was a baby when she died.' She gave her niece an encouraging smile, apparently approving of this uncharacteristic demeanor.

'All the money belonged to Edwina Winter.' Bitty was running out of false courage. She went to the bar and poured herself some more. 'The staircase is full of ghosts. It's a nervous kind of haunting. Can't you feel it?'

'I know what she means,' said Sheldon Smyth. 'There's always been something queer about this house. Always felt it, just as she says. And that damned staircase. It's just plain wrong.'

'It's the pride of the house,' said Cleo. 'It was featured in *Architectural Digest*. The writer called it the absolute triumph of form over function. His very words.'

Sheldon Smyth wore a condescending smile. His ex-wife had missed the insult in that quotation, and she was doomed to repeat it to anyone who would listen to this joke told by herself at her own expense. Politeness prevented Charles from enlightening her, informing her that life was not lived on the stairs, but in the rooms where people might take creature comforts, procreate and dream. But not in this house. Here everything revolved around the tension of the staircase; the inertia of lines rushing upward appeared to be all that kept it from falling down.

Taking Charles by the arm, Bitty smiled with newfound boldness. 'You decide.'

Helplessly bound by good manners, he climbed the stairs with her until they gained the second floor. The rest of the party was also being pulled along, straggling upward without wills of their own. The dynamic of the dinner party had changed. Oddly enough, Bitty was running the show. She paused and, with the air of a tour guide, pointed to the place along the stairs where Quentin Winter had died in the famous massacre. Charles glanced back to see Nedda, last in line, giving wide berth to this area, as if she must round the dead body of her father before she could continue upward.

The staircase was not haunted – Nedda was.

'Edwina Winter died almost twelve years before the massacre.' Bitty stood beneath the painting of the Winter brothers and instructed Charles to remain by the railing. 'That's where she was standing when she – *fell*. Now remember, all the Winters were tall, and they married tall people, like you. Think you could fall by accident?'

He stood with his back to the railing, which was higher than one might expect, yet another design flaw, and he tried to imagine a scenario where he might go over the side; perhaps if the floor were slippery or he were to stumble. No, that would not work. His center of gravity would still be below the rail.

'Tricky, isn't it?' Bitty rested one hand on the smooth, round wood. 'Now if it had broken, that would explain everything, but this is the original – perfectly sound. Give up?' Without waiting for a reply, she turned her back on him to open a door into the blackness of a bedroom. She pointed to the spot where he was standing. As if commanding a very large dog, she said, 'Wait there.'

The tiny woman was swallowed up in the shadows. Seconds later, she was rushing back into the light, running toward him, hands extended and palms flattened back, as if to push him. And she was fast. There was no time to grip the rail, nor even to raise his arms. Bitty stopped – dead stop – when her hands were a bare inch from his chest. She turned her smiling face up to his. 'That's the only way it could have happened. Quentin Winter murdered his first wife.'

'That's enough,' said Cleo, 'I won't have you saying these things about my father.'

'Why not?' said her ex-husband. 'Neither one of the Winter boys was a saint, not according to *my* father. It's as good a theory as any.'

'And now – the other ghosts.' Bitty was gleefully potted as she descended the stairs to a midpoint between the high ceiling and the parlor floor. She turned to look back at Cleo. 'This was where *your* mother died.' Bitty turned her eyes to Charles. 'Alice was her name. The second Mrs Winter was my grandfather's favorite model. He was an artist, you know.'

All eyes followed the dramatic point of Bitty's finger. 'There was another body in the—'

'Stop! You weren't there!' Cleo yelled at her daughter. 'You weren't even born yet! You don't know *anything*!'

Nedda Winter was not taking this well, either. She gripped the rail with a sudden need of support.

Had both these sisters witnessed the massacre of their family? Charles's sketchy knowledge of this old story held no such detail.

Bitty was prattling on about the other deaths and where the bodies fell as she led the party down the staircase. 'And then there was the baby,' she said, almost as an afterthought. 'A newborn. Sally was her name. She survived the massacre. What happened to her after that, Mother?'

Nedda paused on the last step and stared at Cleo, waiting on the answer to that question. Clearly, she had no knowledge of her baby sister's whereabouts. How curious. Charles wondered if another of the Winter children had been . . . lost.

'Sally Winter.' Sheldon Smyth was the first to reach the bar. 'I haven't heard that name in years.' He smiled at Charles. 'Everyone called her Baby Sally. I was just a boy, away at school when I heard the news. She ran off. Isn't that right, Lionel? Isn't that what the nanny told the police?'

'The nurse,' said Cleo, 'Sally had a nurse.'

'Quite right,' said Sheldon. 'As I recall, your uncle James fired that woman for stealing.' He spoke to Charles, for the outsider would need a running translation. 'James Winter was their guardian after the rest of the family was murdered. Yes, I remember him confronting the nurse about stealing.'

'You're confused, old man,' said Lionel. 'It was Uncle James who was stealing.'

'Yes, of course,' said Sheldon Smyth. 'That's why he left town so suddenly. If I remember correctly, that was the year you turned twenty-one.'

Lionel turned his back on the man, then poured a double shot of whiskey from the bar and downed it quickly.

Nedda's face had gone bloodless. She drifted back to the stairs, passing all of them by, and without a good night to anyone. In dead silence, they all watched her climb and climb, then disappear behind a door on the floor above. Bitty, the living portrait of contrition and regret, trailed after her aunt.

Sheldon Smyth was quick to retrieve a briefcase from the floor of a closet, and now he made his retreat, backing up to the door, pleading an early appointment and urging his guest to stay on for a nightcap. The caterers were gone, and so were Cleo and Lionel. Charles opened the door to the dining room, hoping to find them there, to say good night and beat a hasty retreat.

Not there. Where then?

They had not gone upstairs. After searching the kitchen and the sewing room, he returned to the front of the house to find Cleo and Lionel standing by the entrance to the foyer. With only a nod to their guest, they turned around and left. Charles heard the front door close behind them. Well, this was a bit backward, the hosts leaving the house in advance of the guest.

'A most unconventional dinner party,' said Nedda Winter.

He turned to see her standing behind the bar, uncorking a bottle of wine.

'My family doesn't entertain much anymore.' She smiled, quite her old self again, such a charming smile. She tapped a button on a control panel next to the bar, and the sound system died off to blessed silence. 'Ah, that's better. I'd like to thank you for not asking me where I've been for all these years.'

'To be honest, I wasn't sure that you were Red Winter. I don't know the story as well as I thought.'

'Do you like jazz, Mr Butler?'

Old-fashioned record albums had appeared on the bar, stacked up beside two wineglasses. Charles examined them one by one. Any audiophile could date them back to the middle of the last century. 'This is a wonderful collection.'

'Unfortunately, they're all warped and scratched. And all the records that my sister stacked up for the party are not my idea of music.'

'Mine either.' He pulled a record from the album cover. It was made of hard plastic that predated vinyl, cassettes and magnetically encoded discs. And it was ruined. What a great pity.

Nedda turned away from him to study the control panel for the sound system. 'I was hoping you could show me how to play the radio on this thing. It has a beautiful sound quality, and I know a station that only plays jazz from the thirties and forties. I tried to tune it in once, but that made Cleo cry. She said I changed the programming for all her favorite stations. She doesn't know how to work it, either.'

'And neither do I.' For a birthday present, Mallory had rewired his apartment with a similar sound system, and, yes, the sound quality was incredibly beautiful, but the control panel she had installed was equally daunting. 'I have one at home, but it's a different model and the buttons are color coded.' Mallory had programmed his stations and painted the selection buttons with red nail polish.

He strolled over to the antique radio that she had played last night. 'Well, we know this works.'

The front windows were open. The curtains blew inward, Duke Ellington and his band flowed out into the street.

Charles Butler was in Luddite heaven. He ended the evening painlessly, sitting outside on the stone steps. The warm wind of Indian summer ruffled his hair to the tune of rippling piano keys. They were finishing off the last bottle in a prolonged goodbye.

'I haven't gotten soused on wine since I was twelve years old,' said Nedda Winter.

'I gather your upbringing was rather liberal.'

'You have no idea.' She looked up at the face of her house and smiled. 'It was a party that went on for years. My parents were jazz babies, and they were never bothered by nice people from good families. Our guests were miles more interesting.' She ticked off an impressive list of actors, writers, gangsters and gamblers who had passed out at the dining room table. 'But I liked the chorus girls best. They gave me a taste for cold beer and taught me to curse.' She produced a pack of cigarettes from the folds of her shawl. 'And they taught me how to blow smoke rings.' She blew one now and it hung in the still night air. 'You don't like my house much, do you?'

'I suppose it makes me nervous.'

'Yes, I noticed that. But it didn't bother you the other night, did it? Not with all those policemen, all that activity and this music on the radio.'

'Well, no.'

'Oh,' said Nedda – *big* smile, 'how the house loves a good party. I'm afraid we put on a rather poor show tonight. Not nearly enough people – and that dreary music.' She caressed the wrought-iron railing. 'Poor house. It was made for a wilder nightlife.'

Though he would not describe the crime scene as a wild party, he took her point. 'So, tonight, I'm seeing the house out of context. The interior – that was actually *designed* for large gatherings, wasn't it?'

She nodded and refreshed his glass with more wine. 'My father's work. He gutted the front room years before I was born. The staircase was the main event. It works best with a hundred people lounging on the steps, slugging back whiskey and tapping their feet to very loud music. Late in the evening, the music was live. Musicians came by from every club in town. Jam sessions till sunup. Piano men and men with horns, women with voices that could belt out a song to bring the roof down. Everyone in motion, dancing, even when they were sitting down. Now the mirrors – Daddy hung them up to create a bigger crowd than the house could hold. He even slanted the walls to give the mirrors more scope.'

'That's why you can never avoid the multiple reflections?'

She nodded. 'You could never escape my father's illusion. All that energy. The people and the music fed the house.' Her hand rubbed the stone step she sat upon. 'Poor house. Now it's starving – dying for the next big party.'

As Charles lit the last of her cigarettes, he glanced at his watch, startled to realize that another hour had passed. He liked this woman tremendously. However, he knew she must be tired. With some regret, he rose to take his leave, to see her safely behind the door, and to lose the pleasure of her company.

Lionel Winter loved one thing in all the world, the 1939 Rolls-Royce – the Wraith. In the last two years of production before the war, only 491 had ever existed. The Wraith had been his father's car, and it was in near-perfect running condition. The ride was smooth and utterly quiet. He paid lavish tips to the garage attendant for a little magic from an aerosol can that always made the leather smell like new – like 1939, the year when he had sat upon his father's lap and steered the Wraith down city streets. Whenever he drove this car, he lived in that year.

Tonight, however, it was difficult to escape the twenty-first century, and all his thoughts were centered upon his niece. What was she playing at? Since Bitty had abandoned the practice of law at her father's firm, she had become more and more peculiar, or so it seemed on those days when she appeared in his line of vision. Most of the time, he hardly noticed her. He could not entirely blame the wine for the night's disaster. How long had she been harboring these suspicions, and how much could she really know?

Flying down the Henry Hudson Parkway, boats on the water, the town alight – electric – New York at night. How he loved to drive, always shuttling between the summer house and town. That was his whole life, going nowhere with great speed and always alone.

His solitary thoughts turned to Nedda. Why was she still alive? At the hospice, an ancient doctor had virtually promised him that his older sister would be dead before the month was out, that no tests were necessary to tell him that there was no hope of a cure. All the signs of end-stage cancer had been there, her skin a ghastly yellow, her belly bloated, and the rest of her body wasted. And yet, months later, Nedda had come home to Winter House, and there she resided – in splendid good health.

Doctors were so untrustworthy. Hardly science, was it?

Obviously, his older sister had been woefully misdiagnosed. So she lived – in his house – and every day Nedda summoned up the gall to look him in the eye. Every smile in his direction was a mockery. And now she was using Bitty, turning his niece against her own family. Lionel's fingers tightened around the steering wheel, and the car accelerated down the parkway. He sped past the taillights of slower cars, the electric yellow windows of tall buildings and bright reflections on the river, going faster and faster.

Why did you come back, Nedda?

Uncle James had promised them, over and over, that their sister would never return to Winter House.

He turned toward the passenger seat to look at his sister in her own neighboring galaxy on the other side of the car. Her face was bathed in dim light from the dashboard.

'Cleo? You don't remember very much, do you? When we came home from the park that day . . . and found them all dead.'

'No.' She shivered slightly, as if awakening and shaking off dreams. 'No, I don't.'

That was not surprising. His sister had been only five years old when the two of them had come home to find their parents' bodies sprawled on the stairs. And the dead housekeeper – what was her name?

94

No matter. He could not remember the nanny's name either. Oh, but the others, his brothers and sisters. He saw them now, white and still.

His parents were his most vivid memory. What a picture for the family album: little Cleo clinging to their dead mother, the corpse warm to the touch, and by that warmth, still giving comfort to one of her children – but not to Lionel. While standing on the stairs, only inches from his father's body, he had been a zillion miles distant from that scene, wishing himself to the moon and listening in on the world from a great distance.

Listening to a memory now – truly a long way off – he could still hear Cleo's sad little conversation with the police on the telephone, numbering and naming the dead, then ending by asking them so innocently, 'Are you coming?'

Lionel looked at his mask of a face in the rearview mirror, then glanced at his sister's mask before turning back to stare at the windshield.

Alone again.

FOUR

Charles Butler's suite of offices was equipped with an ultramodern kitchen, and Mallory was always upgrading the technology. Most of the appliances had secret lives of their own and functions that he could only guess at, but the one that he resented most was the high-tech coffee-maker. As a confirmed Luddite, he preferred his brew untouched by computer chips.

This morning he ground his own beans, as usual, percolated the coffee over an old-fashioned gas flame, then carried the cup and saucer across the hall to a door that bore the gold letters of Butler and Company on frosted glass. Once it had said Mallory and Butler, but again, the police department had frowned upon this flagrant breach of policy against using investigative skills in the private sector. The absence of her name on the door was at least an attempt at discretion.

Charles took a deep breath while fitting his key in the lock. He would only have six seconds to disable the burglar alarm, all the time that Mallory's programming would allow him, and he was not likely to forget that – ever. The deafening siren had once jangled his brain and entirely cured his absentmindedness.

But the door was not locked.

Well, this was not a promising start to any day, not in New York City. Only two other people had keys: his cleaning woman, Mrs Ortega, never came this early, and his business partner never came this late. He glanced at his wristwatch. Right about now, Mallory would be entering the SoHo police station, her only legally sanctioned workplace.

He pushed open the door and found that the reception area was in good order, and nothing appeared to be missing. The antique furniture in this room was costly, but burglars would probably prefer more portable items – like Mallory's wildly expensive electronics.

He walked down a narrow hallway to the back rooms, moving at the leisurely pace of a man who is heavily insured. Mallory's private office was dimly lit by the glow of a computer projection on a large pull-down screen. He stared at the wall-size portrait of a redheaded child standing nine feet tall. A smaller scale of this same picture appeared on three computer monitors, but for some reason, the detective felt the need to see this little girl blown up. So absorbed was Mallory that she had not noticed him yet.

Charles watched one painted image blend into another. In this new portrait, the red-haired girl wore the uniform of a private school, and she posed with her legs draped over the upholstered arms of a chair. Just a trace of white underpants was showing. Computer clicks and whirs announced the next painting, and this one was memorable. This was the jewel of the Quentin Winter collection, the only major work of art by an otherwise minor painter. This was the artist's child, and she was naked. There was only a gentle swelling where breasts would be one day. More paintings clicked by in quick succession, and he felt like a voyeur watching Nedda Winter go through all the stages of her prepubescent life, nine feet tall on Mallory's wall, a young giant.

'Do you see what I see?' asked Mallory, without turning around.

So much for being able to walk up behind her unnoticed. After the next click, Mallory was once again bathed in the light of the famous Red Winter painting. He well understood her question. 'Well, the artist wouldn't be the first to paint his own child *au naturel*.'

'That bastard singled her out,' said Mallory. 'Nedda was one of nine kids. He painted a lot of nude women, but she was the only child.'

'You believe he molested his daughter based on nothing more than a painting?'

'I'm ninety percent sure.'

Charles did not care for the sound of that. He would prefer not to go to certain corners of Mallory's early life, undoubtedly the source of her expertise. Turning to face the projection on the wall, he recalled a wallet photo that his old friend Louis Markowitz had carried, a small portrait of his foster child. At the age of the young girl on the wall, Kathy Mallory had possessed those same wary eyes. Her early days on the streets had been hard and hardening. Nedda Winter, however, had been a child of wealth and luxury. Not at all the same case, and this might argue for a troubled home life in Winter House.

And molestation?

His mind now poisoned, he had to wonder, against his will, if the title word *red* denoted the color of young Nedda's hair or her rape.

Mallory switched on the overhead fluorescent tubes, and the room became entirely too bright. Light bounced off glass monitors, gleaming metal furnishings and electronic components. The carpet was an institutional gray, no doubt selected to disguise the wood floors as cement. She crossed the room, heading toward the steel blinds that hid the graceful lines of arched windows. Her computers were dead for the moment. When they were powered up, they hummed in communication with one another, and she with them. When the machines were alive, the psychological temperature of her private office was always ten degrees below a normal person's comfort zone.

The viewing screen was raised with the press of a remote-control button and sent rolling back up into its metal cylinder near the ceiling molding. A cork bulletin board that spanned the entire wall was now exposed with all its papers pinned up at perfect right angles, and each sheet was equidistant from the next. Mallory's pushpin style had machine precision.

If her lovely face was incongruous in these environs, what lay beneath was not. And what truly moved him, what touched him most, was that she could have no idea that this room exposed her personal quirks, her own clicks and whirs, all the most chilling departures from her fellow creatures. This office was Mallory naked for all to see – so vulnerable.

And what did she see when she looked at him? Was it something sad and pathetic? Or was he comical in her eyes?

They could never tell one another the truth. They were friends.

'All right,' said Mallory. 'Let's say Quentin Winter molested his daughter. Could you make a case for the girl as a spree killer?'

'What? Nedda? I was under the impression that an outsider killed all those people.'

'An ice pick killed them,' she said. 'And that dead burglar the other night? He wasn't killed with the shears. It was a pick to the heart, same as all the victims in the massacre.'

'I see the problem.' He sat down at the edge of Mallory's desk. 'Back in the forties, did anyone suspect the child?'

'No, but *I* might.'

Ah, but then Mallory suspected *everyone* of *something*.

'So I gather,' said Charles, 'that the father had multiple stab wounds?'

'No. It was a single strike to the heart, all nine victims.'

Here he might point out that this indicated no rage, zero animosity, but Mallory had not asked him to point out flaws in her logic. And now he had to wonder if she was putting herself in Nedda Winter's place. Perhaps this was the way Mallory would have done it – as a child – in cold blood, efficient and quick.

'Revenge,' he said, mulling over this idea. 'So she kills her father for molestation, and then she does in the witnesses – all those people? Nedda was what, twelve years old?'

'Very tall for twelve.' Mallory powered up the computer to display the *Red Winter* painting, and there was the evidence in the child's proportions relative to her surroundings. 'And after the massacre, this girl didn't wait around for the cops.'

'I thought the newspapers ran with the theory of a psychotic killer and a kidnapping.'

'So did the cops,' said Mallory. 'What of it? It's my case now. This killer was cold and precise. You can't see it, can you? A very cold little girl working her way through the house, stabbing all those people.'

He could, but it was a smaller version of Mallory, and he would be a long time getting that picture out of his head.

She blanked the screen. 'The only other option is a professional hitman with a money motive. Nothing personal, just a neat quick job. But there's a hole in that theory.'

'All right, I see the stumbling block.' And this time he found no fault in her logic. 'If the children are the only ones who profit from the trust fund, then who paid for the—'

'No, that's not it. I could work around that.'

'All right.' A moment to regroup, thank you. 'Professional killers don't usually kidnap children.'

'They never do.' She inclined her head, prompting him to continue.

'And it's probably quite alarming to have one turn up in a house full of people.' So far so good, no stumbles yet. 'Whereas, a member of the family could move through the house at leisure, taking victims by surprise without alerting the entire household.'

She nodded to say, *Now you've got it.*

'Well, not to be argumentative.' He held up his hands, even realizing that this was a defensive posture that said, *Don't shoot me, all right? It's only conjecture.* 'Here's another scenario. What if it *was* a professional assassin? And what if Nedda saw him in time to make a run for it?' Charles knew he was making a mistake in offering his own theory, but he could not stop himself. 'The killer would have to chase her down, wouldn't he? Suppose he lost her outside, maybe in the park across the street? Then you'd have a little girl who thought she couldn't go home again. Home was where the monster would be waiting for her. So the theory of a runaway child could—'

'It works for me.' Riker stood in the open doorway, wearing a suit and tie of a different color; otherwise, it would not have been apparent that he had changed his clothes from yesterday. 'Yeah. A runaway. Good work, Charles.' The man smiled, and this was tantamount to squaring off against Mallory when he faced her and said, 'I don't think Nedda Winter killed all those people.'

Mallory's arms folded across her breast in a warning sign that she was not happy with this division in the ranks.

Riker shrugged and lit a cigarette to say, *Well, that's just tough.*

And now she turned on innocent Charles, who had only offered the most—

'So,' she said. 'I'm guessing Nedda didn't volunteer any details about where she'd been for the past fifty-eight years.'

'No,' said Charles. 'Sorry. I never thought to ask.'

'Did you get us anything,' asked Riker, 'anything at all?'

'Maybe,' he said. 'Breakfast, anyone?'

Long ago, Bitty's room had belonged to Robert the Reader, eight years old with thick lenses in his spectacles that made his blue eyes larger, more tender. Each time Nedda Winter entered this bedroom, she saw her brother sprawled on the window seat, a book held by small dead hands, a tiny hole in his pajamas and a bit of blood from his young heart.

Nedda sat down at the edge of the bed and lifted a glass to Bitty's lips. 'Just drink it, dear. You don't want to know what's in it.'

Her niece obediently swallowed a mixture of raw egg, milk and steak sauce.

'My father favored that hangover remedy,' said Nedda.

'Was he a drunk?'

'Well, yes, dear, but, in those days, who wasn't?' She took the emptied glass and set it on the bedside table. 'And he only drank after three o'clock. He had rules.'

'Was my grandfather a violent man?'

Ah, back to the theory of Edwina Winter's murder. 'No. The only thing that aroused any passion in him was a fight with my stepmother. Sometimes Lionel got a light swat on his backside. He was always getting in between his parents, trying to protect his mother. Not that she needed any help. She always had something heavy in her hand whenever she went after my father.'

'I can't imagine Uncle Lionel as a boy.'

'I think you would've liked him then. He was the only one of the children who ever stood up to my father. He was a brave one. I loved him for that.'

'Did you love your father?'

'Yes, but Lionel loved him more. Sometimes I think he took those hits just to get Daddy's attention.'

Bitty pushed her covers aside, then, after a grimace of pain, thought better of moving so rashly. She lay back on her pillow. 'What about the others? Do you remember Sally?'

'Of course. She was the baby of the family, a newborn. She cried a lot. That's why the nursery was at the top of the house. And she wasn't well. I remember a steady stream of doctors marching up the staircase to examine her.'

'What was my mother like?'

'She was only five when I – left. A very loving child. Big sunny smile. Poor little Cleo. She must've thought that I'd abandoned her. And I suppose I did.'

'Aunt Nedda, I'm so sorry about last night. That business about your mother—' She turned her face into the pillow.

'It's all right, Bitty. I told you, I never knew my own mother. Your murder theory didn't upset me at all. I know my father didn't kill her. His second wife, Alice, was a copy of Edwina. What does that tell you?'

'He loved her?'

'Madly. Once, before I was born, they were separated for a week. They wrote to each other every day. Their love letters are in her trunk up in the attic. You should read them. I know all the lines by heart.'

A small voice screamed, 'What?' It was Rags. The lame cockatiel had left its cage and now worked its way up the bedspread, climbing toward its mistress by beak and claw.

'Poor thing,' said Nedda. 'What happened to him? Why can't he fly?'

'His wing was crushed by the window sash. It just fell on him. No, it *slammed* on him. I saw it happen. Mother said the house doesn't like birds.'

'No, it doesn't,' said Nedda. 'Every year after the first frost, we'd find a dead bird outside on one of the window ledges. The house doesn't like flies, either.' She stared at the dead dry insect on Bitty's sill. 'That's what old Mrs Tully used to say. She was the housekeeper when I was a little girl. Tully always said, "You might see a dead fly every now and then, but you'll never hear a live one buzz – at least, not for long."'

'Was she *insane*?' Bitty's hand flew up to cover her mouth, as if she had just committed a social faux pas, calling attention to an infirmity in front of a cripple. And now, realizing her blunder, she seemed on the verge of tears.

Nedda gave her niece a smile of reassurance, then dipped one hand into the pocket of her robe. 'There's something else we have to talk about.' She withdrew a small worn box and held it up for Bitty to see. 'Remember this? Last night at dinner?' The box was heavily lacquered cardboard, not machine made, but one of a kind, hand-crafted and painted with the tarot image of the hanged man.

A *memento mori* from days in hell.

Nedda opened the box and pulled out the deck. The card of destruction, an image of a burning tower, was on the top. 'Tell me where you found my tarot cards.'

The bookcases that lined Charles Butler's library were fifteen feet tall, necessitating a ladder slanting from the top-shelf railing to the floor.

High in the air, he rolled along on its wheels as he searched for the volume that Mallory wanted. 'A friend of my father's gave it to me. He said my New York History section would be incomplete without it.'

Though he had never considered reading the book, it had been stored on the upper shelf with similar volumes. After perusing the first page, he had found the writing inferior, but it would have been bad manners and literary heresy to toss the book in the trash. Now where was it?

Well, this was embarrassing.

The book was not where it ought to be. A few years might have passed since he had placed it here, but how could it be lost? After generations of librarians had inculcated him with rules, he was virtually incapable of losing a book by placing it on a shelf out of order. Each volume's spine was tagged with the Library of Congress number to ensure against such losses. But now he noticed that *none* of the books on the top shelf were in their proper places.

No, this could not happen, not to him.

He glanced down at Mallory. She was staring at his recently delivered club chairs, six of them arranged in a circle. In their midst one might expect to find – oh, say, a priceless piece of furniture with a provenance dating back to 1846 and great historical significance. However, inside the wide circle of chairs there was nothing but his memory of a page from an antique catalogue.

She lifted her face to his. 'Charles, you've been robbed.'

'No, I gave away my card table after I bought another one. It would've been delivered this morning . . . if not for a warehouse fire last night.'

He turned back to his problem of the lost book and discovered that the top shelf was free of dust. All was clear to him now. Apparently, his cleaning woman had actually dusted up here, fifteen feet in the air, then rearranged all the books by height so the line of the topmost shelf would not appear so uneven. Mrs Ortega's mania for neatness was second only to Mallory's. Rather than undo all of the woman's hard work, he politely memorized the new order of his books.

Mallory called up to him from the foot of the ladder. 'So you thought a new table might improve your poker game?'

'No.' Well – yes. Charles was not as crippled by magical thinking as some people, but historical memorabilia could be psychologically empowering. And in the game of poker—

'You know,' she said, 'you'd have to cheat to beat those bastards.'

He sighed.

She was right. Psychology would not save him. He had the wrong sort of face for the game, expressions that gave up every thought and emotion. Worse, he had inherited his mother's deep red blush that made a lie or a bluff nearly impossible to pull off. Regrettably, he had been genetically programmed to be an honest man and a poor poker player.

The bastards, as Mallory affectionately called them, were the charter members of a very old floating poker game. Upon the death of her foster father, Louis Markowitz, Charles had inherited a seat in the game and three new friends. Next week, the poker game would have been in his apartment, played at an antique table once graced by a famous politician and worldclass card player. 'The table wasn't exactly new. President Ulysses S. Grant once sat in on a game at—'

Oh, what the hell. That bit of history was burned to a crisp.

He knew that Mallory took a dim view of the weekly poker game. It was entirely too friendly for her tastes, only penny-ante stakes, or, as she would say, chump change. She also objected to wild cards that changed with the phases of the moon or the dates for recycled trash pickups. Once, she had complained that the game was a close cousin to an old lady's Bingo night at church.

'This week,' said Charles, 'the game's at Robin's house. If you want to come, I'm sure they'll all be happy to play by your rules.'

Apparently, fleecing her father's old friends in a fast game of cutthroat, rob-and-run poker was hardly tempting. *Fat chance*, said her eyes. However, she did run one hand over the new chairs, approving the grade of leather.

He rolled the ladder down to the end of the wall, and his eyes locked onto the title he had been searching for. 'Found it. It's roughly a thousand pages.'

This news seemed to pain her. 'Can you give me the gist of it?'

'I never read it.' He looked down at his copy of *The Winter House Massacre*. 'Not my sort of thing.'

'It's that bad?'

'Well, the information should be sound enough. The author's an accredited historian. Now I wish I *had* read it. Would've saved me some embarrassment last night.' He climbed down the ladder to stand beside Mallory. 'You might've warned me that Nedda was Red Winter.'

'Honest surprise worked better.' She stared at the dust jacket and its single drop of illustrated blood.

'But I *knew* the story of Winter House.' What New Yorker, born and bred, did not? 'Where does the advantage of surprise come in?'

Mallory patiently waited him out, and now he must admit that he had not even recognized the address while visiting the crime scene. And, like most people who believe they know all the details of historical events, he had not understood the significance of an ice pick in Winter House of all houses.

'Last night,' she said, 'it would've been suspicious if you knew who Nedda was.'

'She's right,' said a voice behind him.

Charles turned to see Riker walking across the library, a cup of coffee in hand and probably wondering when the rest of his breakfast would be ready. The detective lacked the patience for homemade croissants.

'Don't feel bad,' said Riker. 'After fifty-eight years, only a cop would've made the connection to Nedda Winter – and not just any cop. It even took me a while, and I was raised on that story. The only name most people knew her by was Red Winter.'

Mrs Ortega's vacuum cleaner preceded her into the library, and all conversation stopped. The wiry little woman with dark Spanish eyes and a Brooklyn accent said, 'Pick up your damn feet,' as she moved the sucking nozzle perilously close to Riker's scruffy shoes. She switched the machine off just long enough to curl her lip while passing judgment on his suit. After pulling a wad of paper slips from her apron, she stuffed them into the man's breast pocket. 'Those are dry-cleaning coupons. You know what you have to do.' And now the vacuum powered up to move back and forth across the rug.

Charles handed the book to Riker and raised his voice to be heard over the noise. 'Here, a gift. Might be rather dry reading. This author is known for that.'

'I read it,' said Riker.

'You what?' The vacuum cleaner switched off, and Mrs Ortega observed a moment of silent disbelief. Previously, this detective had only admitted to reading the sports pages. And never mind the book's cover art. Lurid drop of painted blood aside, this was a thick book. She steered the vacuum cleaner out of the room with mutterings of damn miracles.

As an apology for literacy, Riker shrugged and said, 'I *had* to read it. The massacre was my bedtime story when I was a kid.' He hefted the book in one hand. 'But this wouldn't have helped you last night. The guy who wrote it never mentioned Nedda's real name. He only calls her Red Winter. So much for historians, huh?' He opened the volume to the title page. '*My* copy's autographed.'

When they were all seated around the table in Charles's kitchen, the batch of oven-warm croissants quickly disappeared. The detectives had not paused to savor the buttery flakes; they had inhaled them with their coffee, then made short work of the crepes. Now and then, one of them would stop feeding to extract information from him, rather than relying on his recollection of events. Perhaps he was inclined to be too wordy, possibly trying their short—

'At the time of the murders,' said Mallory, keeper of the body count, 'there were nine children and four adults living in Winter House.'

'And four children survived the massacre.' Charles used a napkin to mark the book page that would allow him to recite their names in birth order.

'But there're only three left,' said Mallory. 'You didn't buy the story of Sally Winter as a runaway?'

'I didn't say that. I said it didn't quite ring true in all the details. Lionel had an odd reaction that I couldn't put down to – Oh, how should I put this?'

'Put it briefly,' said Riker. 'If you weren't such a good cook, Mallory would've shot you twenty minutes ago.'

She nodded, as if in agreement, while reading the marked passage on the youngest Winter child. 'This author follows Cleo and Lionel from grammar school through the college years. He's got dates of enrollments and graduations. But all he's got on Sally is her date of birth.' She looked up at Charles. 'Could be another homicide. Did you question them about it?'

'Well . . . no. After Bitty's little exhibition on the staircase, the rest of them were sliding into shock. It would have been rude to ask if they'd murdered Baby Sally.'

By the rapid clicking of Mallory's pen, he deduced that a simple *no* would have sufficed.

'Good for Bitty,' said Riker, who was apparently allowed to make extraneous remarks between forkfuls of strawberry crepes. 'I never thought she had it in her.'

'She had to get drunk to do it,' said Charles. 'She's a passive-aggressive personality. It was wildly out of character to—'

'*How* aggressive?' Mallory leaned forward, liking this detail.

'Oh, not in the physical sense. She'll take a sniper shot from the woods, but it's strictly verbal. I think Nedda was being truthful when she confessed to killing that burglar the other night. Bitty simply could not have done that.'

'I never thought she did,' said Mallory, and her tone was a rather pointed reminder that she had said as much the other night and disliked repeating herself. 'Bitty's a mouse.'

Riker was more charitable. 'But last night she nailed her whole family.'

'I'm guessing that was a tactic to get attention,' said Charles. 'Bitty's emotional maturity is a bit stunted.'

'What gave her away?' asked Riker. 'Was it the prom dress or the teddy bears in her room?'

Charles ducked this sarcasm by filling his mouth with food. Last night, the significance of Bitty's outlandish makeup and dinner dress had nearly escaped him. At first, he had believed that her mother must have engineered that fashion travesty. Later, he had realized his error. Cleo Winter-Smyth would never have taken that much interest in her daughter. The mother had simply neglected to save her child from ridicule. The absence of parental bonding would explain a great deal. And now he quietly cleaned his plate, having learned not to volunteer any more elaborate explanations.

Riker wore a satisfied smile as he laid his napkin to one side. 'So it's a dysfunctional family.'

'A bit more bizarre than that,' said Charles, filling Riker's coffee cup and instantly forgetting all his lessons in brevity. 'There's no real family dynamic. They're like islands, all of them. I had the distinct feeling that Sheldon Smyth was only going through the motions of playing a father to Bitty. Same thing with Cleo and Lionel. Correct responses without any matching nuances in tone or expression.'

'I got it,' said Riker. 'Like a pack of aliens imitating a human family?'

'Exactly. It suggests—'

'You haven't mentioned Nedda yet.' Mallory tapped her pen on the table. 'How did she fit in?'

'She didn't. I'd say she was more of a watcher on the sidelines. Though I did see genuine affection for Bitty. And there was a bit of tension with her sister and brother. Nedda never exhibited any aberrant behavior – if that's what you're asking.'

'But she's been away for a long time,' said Riker. 'We think she's been institutionalized.'

'Well, I could be wrong,' said Charles, 'but in a case like that, you'd expect to see more signs of—'

'I'm *positive*,' said Mallory, 'and I know it wasn't prison. We ran her prints. No criminal record.'

Charles pushed back from the table. 'So you think she's been in an asylum all these years? Well then – that dinner party should've made her feel quite at home. But she was the normal one at the table. And quite charming.'

He could see that Riker was also rejecting Mallory's idea of Nedda as a certified lunatic with a bloody past. This detective was Charles's only ally in the theory of an innocent runaway child. The man seemed very much on Nedda's side, wanting to believe in her.

However, when the subject turned to an old deck of tarot cards produced at the dinner table last night, a deck belonging to Nedda Winter, the light in Riker's eyes simply died.

A light breakfast had revitalized Bitty Smyth, and now she climbed toward the top of the house, almost cheerful as she led the expedition to the attic.

Following close behind her niece, Nedda Winter pressed close to the banister to avoid treading upon the corpses of her stepmother and her father. On the third floor, they passed the door to Henry's room, where the budding artist, four years of age, lay dead among his sticks of chalk and pencils and drawing papers. Her little brother

Wendell, only seven when he died, lay on the floor of the next room.

Upward they climbed, passing a hall closet where her nine-year-old sister, Erica, huddled in terror and absolute darkness, listening for the footsteps of a monster and hoping that death would pass her by. Nedda trod quietly past this door and fancied that she could hear the beat of a child's wild heart.

I'm so sorry.

The staircase narrowed as they approached the last landing below the attic. Here she skirted a small corpse on the stairs. Mary had escaped the nursery in a two-year-old's version of mad flight, and she had died in a toddle down the steps.

The dead were invisible to Bitty, who resided solidly in the present. Nedda lived much of her life in the past, where the nanny on the hallway carpet was more recently deceased, the flesh still warm, and the bit of blood on her breast had not yet dried. Nedda looked down at the face of this teenager, Gwen Rawly, who had previously believed that she was immortal. The girl's lips were parted, as if to ask *Why?* Beyond the young nanny's body was the door of the nursery.

It was closed in the current century.

Bitty and Nedda paused beneath the great glass dome that crowned the fourth floor and divided the two attics. Here the stairs were split like a forked tongue. The steps curving to their right led to the north attic used for storage. Bitty climbed toward the south attic, a repository for personal effects of the dead. This was a family custom begun in the eighteen hundreds.

Following her niece, Nedda entered the narrow room of slanting rafters and the old familiar smells of rotting history and dust. It was illuminated by a row of small gabled windows, and appeared to be unchanged. Early memories were clear pictures in her mind, all that she had had to feed upon for so many years.

She looked at the trunks stacked in rows and representing generations of her forebears. The contents were the odds and ends of life on earth. Her eyes gravitated to her mother's trunk. As a child, she had spent many hours counting up the dresses, lace handkerchiefs, hairpins and such, souvenirs of a woman who had loved her, a woman who had died when Nedda was too young to memorize her living face. This morning, she passed it by, following her niece between the rows of the murdered Winters, adults and children.

'You know what this place reminds me of?' Bitty reached up to pull on strings that switched on the overhead bulbs as she walked the length of the attic. 'Early Christian catacombs, corpses stacked up like cordwood. Of course, there are no actual bodies.'

All the brass plates on this row of trunks had been polished by a finger through the dust, the better to make out the letters etched in old-fashioned script. Nedda knelt on the floor to read the names.

Bitty squatted down beside her. 'I couldn't find a trunk for Baby Sally. It's not in the north attic or the basement.' She looked up at her aunt. 'Sally had a trunk of her own, didn't she?'

'Yes, dear, we all did. I remember Sally's trunk was at the foot of her crib.'

There had been no family conversation on this subject, no catching up on one more death in the family. She had asked no questions of Lionel and Cleo, not wanting to open the door to any more sorrows. And she had thought it unnecessary. An early demise had been foretold for the baby on the day she was born. Her heart ailment had been some grave defect in the bloodline of Quentin Winter's second wife, Alice.

'You might find this interesting.' Bitty reached behind the row of trunks and pulled out a canvas sack, yellowed and cracked with age. 'Have a look.'

Nedda opened the drawstring and emptied the contents onto the floor. Among the clothing was a little girl's sailor suit of rotted fabric. The years had been unkind to these artifacts stored outside of the cedar-lined trunks. The next item retrieved from the pile was a christening gown, and it fell apart in her hands. All that held together was the little bit of material embroidered with Sally's initials. Nedda's hand passed over small moldy stuffed toys and books of nursery rhymes. She tenderly picked through the rest of the clothing in the varying sizes of a growing child who had lived for three or four years following the massacre.

Bitty folded the child's clothing and placed it in the sack. 'My father said Sally ran away the year that Lionel turned twenty-one. So she would've been ten years old. But where's her trunk? Can you imagine a ten-year-old girl dragging her trunk with her when she ran away from home?'

'No,' said Nedda, 'I can't.'

Sally had never run anywhere. A legion of heart specialists had all predicted a very short life of invalidism. Did Bitty know this? Nedda could not ask, and there were other questions that would never be answered. Had Sheldon Smyth lied about Sally running away from home, or had someone, Cleo or Lionel, lied to him? Nedda had lost the heart to go on with this disturbance of the dead. 'Where is my trunk?'

Bitty stood up and walked to the end of the row of murdered children. One trunk had been segregated from all the rest and pushed to the wall. 'This one. You were never legally declared dead, but I guess they gave up on you after a while.' She opened the lid. 'But this isn't where I found your tarot cards.'

Nedda joined her niece by the wall and read her own name on a brass plate. In the context of this attic, it was like viewing her gravestone. She followed Bitty to the far corner of the attic, the resting place of an old standing trunk larger than all the others and plastered with travel stickers. What was this old piece of luggage doing in the attic of dead Winters?

Bitty opened it like a closet. 'I found Uncle James's passport in here, and that's odd because he has a regular trunk like the others. It's stored in the north attic.'

'This is a steamer trunk,' said Nedda. 'Your grandparents used it for ocean voyages.' She examined the drawers that lined one side. In the last one, she found a jumble of bright colors, cheap, gaudy clothing that stirred a memory.

'I found a long red hair,' said Bitty. 'It was snagged in the tarot card box.' She turned to look at the bottom drawer her aunt had opened. 'That's where I found the cards. And there were short red clippings in all of those clothes, so I wondered if your hair—'

'Yes, it was cut off . . . very short.' Short as a boy's. Nedda recalled her waist-long hair falling to the floor. The snip of the scissors – it seemed like only this morning. She had been sitting on a wooden chair in a small shabby room with tattered pulled-down shades while this mutilation covered the floor. The red strands had come alive, curling and writhing in the wake of a large cockroach moving through the pile of clippings. And Nedda had cried all the while, listening to the steady beat of rain against the window – the snip of scissors.

Bitty pulled a dress from the lower drawer. 'Now this is the same size as the ones in your trunk, but otherwise nothing like them.'

Indeed, this was rather poor fare for the child of a wealthy family. Nedda well understood her niece's curiosity. Unable to get any reliable information from her family, Bitty had produced the tarot cards at the dinner table, hoping for answers via surprise attack. And now this – gentle ambush.

'I had a theory about Sally,' said Bitty, 'I thought maybe years after the massacre – you came back for her.'

Intrepid Bitty.

The detectives talked as they walked through Greenwich Village, breaking off their conversation whenever they were assailed by tourists with a wild, lost look about them. Grid logic was abandoned here, where West Fourth Street ran amok to bisect West Tenth Street. Two gray-haired people stood at this crossroad, unable to move on, gaping at the improbable street sign and willing it to make sense.

'I can't believe we're doing this.' Annoyed, Mallory waved off this elderly couple, souring the message on their I-Love-New-York tote bags.

'It's not much farther.' Riker flicked his cigarette into a gutter. 'And it's worth the trip. This is the only place in town where you can find a tarot card reader and an ice-pick murder in one conveniently located square block. It's the neighborhood where Stick Man screwed up royally – a killing close to home.'

Mallory opened her borrowed copy of *The Winter House Massacre* and removed the brochure she had used for a bookmark. It had been written by the same author, and now she reiterated the title with sarcasm. 'A guided tour of murder in Greenwich Village?'

'The guy never made much money publishing the book. Bad writer if you ask me. So he makes a living with this walking tour.'

'If you've already taken the tour, why do we have to waste—'

'And there he is now.' Riker nodded toward a small cluster of people on the sidewalk and their tour guide, a middle-aged, chinless, hairless man, who was barely five feet tall.

Martin Pinwitty was addressing his less than rapt audience of out-of-towners. Only tourists would politely listen to his monotonous drone while their eyes glazed over with fatigue. Any New York crowd would have left footprints on the author's face by now. The man actually managed to bore them with the story of a mob-financed killing machine and details of murders by gun and baseball bat and, Riker's personal favorite, the ice pick. The group's interest was suddenly revived when Pinwitty told them that they were standing on the very site of an ice-pick murder. They all looked down at their feet, perhaps expecting to find bloodstains more than half a century later.

'They always do that,' said Riker, hanging back with Mallory at the edge of the tour group.

'How many times did you take this tour?' Something in her tone of voice implied that she had lost all respect for him.

'I check in once a year. This guy's still doing research, and his spiel is always changing.'

Martin Pinwitty and his tour group walked a few paces down the sidewalk, and the lecture continued. 'The victim was a reporter who covered the hearings on Murder Incorporated in the early forties. Now that investigation was over years before this murder took place. I believe the reporter had uncovered some new evidence on a professional assassin.'

Mallory glanced at Riker, who nodded, saying, 'I think he got this part right.'

And the author droned on, saying, 'The police made a very thorough search of this area. They spent days questioning all the residents on this block. And then it was the fortuneteller's turn.' He pointed to a narrow building across the street. 'The woman's storefront was right there.'

The tour group turned in unison to stare at a bodega with neon signs for beer and smokes. A drunk stood before its front window vomiting on his shoes. Yet this view held special charms for the sidewalk audience.

'The police took great interest in the fortuneteller,' said Pinwitty. 'She was the only one they brought in for questioning at the police station. And there she died. According to the obituary, it was a cerebral hemorrhage.'

'That's wrong,' said Riker, speaking low so as not to interfere with the dry static of the ongoing monologue. 'It was way more interesting than that.'

'So what's the real story?'

'This is secondhand. I was only a kid when I heard it, and this was more than twenty years after it happened. The detectives left the fortuneteller sitting on a bench for maybe five minutes while they freed up an interview room. When they came back for the old lady, the cop on guard duty was bending over her dead body. The uniform tells the detectives she was sitting up one minute, dead the next, and there was nobody near her when she keeled over. Well, they're hunting for an ice-pick killer, right? And thanks to a slew of exhumed corpses in the early forties, they're hip to the ice pick in the eardrum. It simulates a stroke. Well, sure enough, they shine a light in the woman's ear and find blood from the pick. Now they interrogate the shit out of that cop.'

'The cop was dirty?'

'That's what the detectives figured. Maybe the uniform took a few bucks to look the other way. Or maybe he did in the old lady himself. But no. According to the other witnesses, the cop just wasn't paying attention when somebody stopped to talk with his prisoner. The old lady's visitor was only there long enough to say hello and goodbye. A few seconds later, the old woman slumps forward. The cop jostles her shoulder and asks if she's okay. That's when she falls to the floor, stone dead. The killer walked right into a police station and killed this woman right under their noses. A real pro.'

'And the detectives covered it up.'

'You bet they did. This happened maybe ten or twelve days after the Winter House massacre. The newspapers would've crucified the whole department. So an ice-pick murder was passed off as a stroke and buried on the obituary page. Oh yeah,' he said as an afterthought, 'and that old lady was no crystal-ball gypsy. She only read tarot cards.'

'And she had a solid connection to the hitman.'

Riker nodded in Pinwitty's direction. 'He's getting to that part now.'

The author pointed upward to a window on the second floor. 'After the fortuneteller was taken away, that very night, in fact, that apartment was searched by detectives. On previous calls, the tenant had never been at home. That night they didn't even bother to knock. Sadly, the tenant was gone and so were his things. No one was able to give the police a name or description. In fact, no one in the neighborhood could recall ever having seen the mysterious tenant even once, though he'd held the lease for years.'

Mallory nudged Riker. 'So the fortuneteller's storefront was a drop site for money, and the old lady brokered the hitman's murders?'

'Yeah. Two different fortunetellers used the same location. They were both murdered, but Pinwitty doesn't know that.' Riker looked on as the author lost his audience. One by one, the escapees peeled off from the tour group. 'But he did get a few things right.' He looked up to the second-floor window. 'When the detectives broke down the door, that apartment was clean, and I mean spotless. No prints anywhere. Ballsy, huh? Cops breathing down his neck, and he takes the time to wipe down the walls and the furniture.'

'And now we've got Nedda Winter with tarot cards at the dinner party,' said Mallory. 'You think Stick Man would kidnap a twelve-year-old girl to replace his old fortuneteller?'

'It's a stretch. Remember, the girl disappeared from Winter House twelve days before the fortuneteller died.'

'If Stick Man thought the cops were closing in on his drop point, maybe he planned to break in the girl as his next tarot card reader – before he killed the old woman. Nedda was tall for twelve. She could've passed for a teenager.'

'Could be.' In fact, Riker had already thought of this. But why would a hitman believe that a little girl might go along with that idea?

The spooky brat beside him read his mind. 'Maybe,' she said, 'Nedda wasn't all that broken up about the murders. Maybe she knew what was going to happen to her family before Stick Man showed up at the door.'

Riker gave this idea half a nod. 'It's possible.' There were too many possibilities and they might all be wrong.

Mallory turned back to the author and his few remaining tourists. He had moved on down the street to the scene of another crime. She listened to the fading banter for another moment. 'You said his research is an ongoing thing?'

* * *

At the bottom of the stairs, Lionel was waiting for them. Bitty shrank back, thinking of something better to do on the upper floor, and she retreated.

Sensible.

After last night, Bitty would not want a confrontation with her uncle.

Nedda accepted a cup of coffee from her brother's hand. She was so absurdly grateful for this small gesture and hoping for something more, but he looked at her with such wariness. And hate? It was difficult to read Lionel's thoughts anymore. As a child he had never been cold to her. There had been a bond between them once, the two eldest children against the confusing and sometimes violent world of their parents' making.

When brother and sister were seated in the dining room, Nedda turned her gaze to the glass-paned doors that opened onto the back garden. It looked so mournful now, pruned back to a few shrubs and a single tree. Once, there had been a swing attached to the lowest bough. Her brother had preferred the higher climbs, the branches closer to the sky. He had been a beautiful, nimble boy with a sunbrowned face and perpetually skinned knees.

'And now,' said Lionel, 'you're wondering about Baby Sally.'

Nedda shook her head. No, she had been hunting out of doors for some old memory to share with him, a common ground. She wanted only a bit of conversation and his company – nothing more.

'Cleo and I were away at school when Sally . . . when she left. I've given a lot of thought to that day. It was nothing that we did. We were—'

'Old history.' Nedda dismissed the rest of his words with a wave. And now she wanted so much to reach across the table, to take his hand in hers and tell him how good it was to be home. However, in this moment, she was more the coward than Bitty. She anticipated

Lionel shrinking away from her touch, withdrawing his hand and turning to ice.

Her own hands remained folded in her lap.

Martin Pinwitty was beside himself with happiness. Two genuine homicide detectives were visitors in his humble home – underscore the word *humble*. There was only one room, unless one counted the closet that housed a toilet, and Mallory did not. The bathtub, concealed by a broad wooden board, did double duty as a table, and the hide-a-bed sofa had been hastily folded away, one more sign of an impoverished make-do life.

Mallory could guess how much of this man's meager income was daily sacrificed for stamps. Correspondence was piled on every surface that was not cluttered with page-marked books. The postmarks on his mail were wide-ranging, and a few envelopes had the return addresses of police departments in other states.

On the way to his apartment, Pinwitty had insisted on stopping at a bodega so that he might treat them to doughnuts on this special occasion, believing, as all civilians did, that this was a staple of every cop's diet. And now both detectives, stuffed with Charles Butler's croissants and crepes, ate their sugar doughnuts, while feigning gratitude and swilling tea that was unspeakably bad.

Riker shoveled more sugar into his cup. 'So the reporter who died in the Village – that was the last ice-pick job?'

'For a professional assassin? Yes, I believe it was,' said the author. 'I have sources everywhere. If there's an old unsolved murder with an ice pick, I hear about it. The pick was going out of vogue years before that man was murdered.'

After scanning one of Pinwitty's files, a lengthy list of muggings and murders, Mallory set it aside, agreeing with Riker that this was an amateur investigation. 'What about the freak who killed the Winter family? You think he retired after the massacre?'

'Oh, definitely,' said Pinwitty. 'That or he died. You know, once,

I actually thought Red Winter had killed him. A man was stabbed with an ice pick in the state of Maine.' He stood up and walked to a bookshelf crammed with texts, papers and manila envelopes. 'I have a separate file for that one. Nothing ever came of it.' He pulled out a folder and smiled. 'I even went up to Maine for a few days to check it out.'

This piqued Mallory's interest, for that little junket would've represented a lot of money for this impoverished little man.

Pinwitty settled into a chair and opened the folder on his lap. 'I'll tell you what made this incident so interesting. The victim of the stabbing was a man named Humboldt.'

Riker's teacup was suspended in midair, all attention suddenly riveted to the author, and Mallory had to wonder what that was about.

Pinwitty continued. 'Humboldt once shared a cell with a murder suspect in New Orleans. The cellmate was charged with the ice-pick murder of a politician.'

Riker's cup clattered back to its saucer.

'Now this suspect—' The author paused to bring the page a bit closer to his nearsighted eyes. 'Oh, I don't have a name for this one, but I know it began with an *H*. Well, no matter. Turned out the man was innocent. There'd been another murder while he was in custody. However, it occurred to me that Red Winter didn't know that, and she might have mistaken Humboldt for the suspected ice-pick killer. Maybe she heard a confused report of the New Orleans murder. You see, the first time I heard this story – more like a rumor, actually – Humboldt was killed by a girl with red hair. I postulated that Red Winter might've hunted down the wrong man and killed the cellmate by mistake, believing that Humboldt was the one who murdered her parents.'

Mallory smiled. Ah, the penalties of bad scholarship – death. 'And this happened when?'

'Two years after the massacre. I was originally led to believe that it happened much later than that. In any case, it wasn't Red Winter who killed Humboldt. She would've been a fourteen-year-old child at that time. When I went up to Maine, I discovered that he was killed by a full-grown local woman.'

At the time of this ice-pick homicide, Red Winter would have been tall enough to pass for someone older. Mallory glanced at Riker, who nodded to say that this was also his thought.

Unmindful of their silent conversation, Pinwitty continued his thought, saying, 'The stabbing wasn't premeditated either. So that was another indication that my theory wouldn't work. The police put it down to self-defense. It seems that the man broke into this woman's bedroom and attacked her. However, I should mention that I got this information many years after the fact. Originally, I only had one source for the story, a very old man who later died in a nursing home. There was no police report on file.'

Mallory and Riker were both paying edge-of-the-chair attention.

'Oh, I know what you're thinking,' said the author. 'I also thought it was odd. But this was a small town, more like a truck stop. And I couldn't interview the residents because there weren't any. A new highway project wiped out all the houses and public buildings. The records of births, deaths and taxes were relocated, but police records simply didn't exist. You see, the town had a police force of one. That was Chief Walter McReedy. I thought he might have taken the records with him when he retired. So I hunted down his daughter, Susan. She was rather young at the time of this incident. Barely remembers it. Now the woman who stabbed Humboldt was a redhead, and Chief McReedy's daughter agreed with that much, but after she had a minute or two to think it over, she couldn't swear that red was the woman's natural hair color. In fact, a minute later, she thought otherwise. She did recall that the woman was a local, but couldn't remember her name. Susan McReedy thought the redhead might've been middle-aged, but then everyone seems old to a child of seven. At any rate, it was a wasted trip for me.'

Mallory held up her copy of *The Winter House Massacre*. 'So there's nothing in your book about Humboldt?'

'Well, no. What would be the point? He was only the cellmate of a man wrongly accused of an ice-pick murder. That doesn't confer even a peripheral significance.'

But the author had failed to see the significance of Humboldt's death by ice pick; he had tripped over this large messy fact and not seen it. Mallory was undecided: either Martin Pinwitty was more inclined to believe in coincidence than the average cop – or he had not told them everything. There was something *not right* about this little man. And she could say the same for her own partner.

After warding off more stale doughnuts and bad tea, the detectives escaped from the author's apartment with the borrowed file on the incident in Maine. Riker paused on the stoop outside the building, as if unable to go on.

'Nedda killed Stick Man,' said Mallory.

He hanged himself with a slow nod. Riker was definitely holding out on her, just as the daughter of the cop from Maine had held out on Martin Pinwitty.

On the drive back to SoHo, she waited for her partner to save himself, to explain how he had recognized Humboldt's name, a name he had never read in any book.

And he said nothing.

Cleo appeared in the dining room with a coffee cup in hand, nodding in Nedda's general direction as she sat down on Lionel's side of the dining room table. The line of demarcation was always drawn this way – two united against one.

'Did you sleep well, Nedda?'

Her sister's tone of voice might better fit the question *Why aren't you dead yet?* After all, Nedda had unwittingly reneged on the prognosis, the virtual promise, of an early demise.

Cleo's eyes narrowed. 'Bitty's not joining us this morning?'

'She had an early breakfast,' said Nedda.

'She's hiding, isn't she?' Not waiting for a response, Cleo rose from her chair and quit the room, followed by Lionel.

Nedda was left alone and lonely. The fantasy of her homecoming was in ashes. She pulled the tarot deck from her pocket and bowed her head as she spread the cards on the table, looking there for hope and finding the burning tower in every arrangement of painted images. An old woman had given this deck to a very young Nedda, tapping the box illustration of the hanged man and saying, '*Memento mori*, a reminder of your mortality.' It had been a warning then, but the child had failed to recognize it as such.

Charles Butler politely ended his long-distance telephone call to Susan McReedy in the state of Maine, then replaced the receiver in its antique cradle and shrugged his apologies to the two homicide detectives seated on the other side of his desk. 'Sorry. Miss McReedy wasn't very helpful.'

'What do you think?' asked Riker. 'Is the lady holding out?'

'Oh, definitely,' said Charles. 'The fact that she was suspicious and guarded would indicate as much. And she had a few questions of her own. Where did I meet the redheaded woman? What name did she go by now? And how did I know the dead man was called Humboldt? She wasn't very happy when I didn't give her any answers.'

'You're a shrink,' said Riker. 'Can't you give us more than that?'

'Based on a telephone conversation?' Charles sighed. He hated the word *shrink*, and it would not apply to him. Although he had the proper credentials and a special interest in abnormal bents of mind, he had never had a private practice and never treated a single patient.

Mallory leaned forward. 'McReedy lied to Pinwitty, didn't she?'

It was a mistake to encourage her idea that he was a human lie detector. Her belief was founded on the fact that he could always tell when *she* was lying. However, this time she was correct. Ten years ago, Miss McReedy had lied in her interview with the author. The proof was all here in the folder that lay open on his desk. Pinwitty had been a word-for-word recorder of conversations.

'Well, if we begin by assuming this woman wanted to mislead Pinwitty—'

'She did,' said Mallory.

'Fine. Then the redhead who killed Humboldt was young, not middle-aged. I'd say the mystery woman's hair was naturally red, not dyed. Otherwise Susan McReedy wouldn't have made a point of mentioning that small detail – while pretending to forget the woman's name or what had become of her. Rather difficult to misplace a local murderess in a small town described as a truck stop. And her defensive posturing on the phone might suggest a protective relationship with the missing redhead.' He shrugged to say that was all he had. 'So you'll be going up to Maine to interview her?'

'No,' said Mallory. 'She'll call you back. And when she does, you'll get more out of her than we would.'

'And you know this *how?*'

'She didn't brush you off,' said Riker. 'She asked a lot of questions. That means you've got something she wants.'

'And she's wanted it for a long time,' said Mallory.

'Good logic.' Charles turned to the window, looking up to a blue October sky and wondering where his own logic had flown. How could he have been so far off the mark in his initial assessment of Nedda Winter? 'I nearly forgot. I gave Miss McReedy a date for the stabbing. I was off by two days, and she corrected me. I think that was a slip on her part. What's her profession? A teacher, something like that?'

'A librarian,' said Mallory. 'Retired.'

'Close enough. So Nedda Winter was a fourteen-year-old child when Humboldt was stabbed to death. You really believe that she—'

'Yeah,' said Riker. 'Everything fits. Ice picks seem to be her lifelong weapon of choice.'

Mallory leaned far back in her chair, and Charles was immediately on guard. If she were a cat, her tail would be switching like mad.

'You *like* Nedda Winter, don't you.' This was not a question. She was making an accusation, for Miss Winter was now solidly in the enemy camp. Mallory also turned a cold eye on Riker, no doubt suspecting him of the same treason.

'I do like her,' said Charles. 'Can't say I thought much of the rest of Nedda's relatives.' Though Bitty certainly deserved his pity.

'You know it's a dysfunctional family,' said Riker, 'when the one you like the best is a mass murderer.'

FIVE

Nedda's body remained at rest. There was no anxious wringing of hands, nor was there any furtive sign of panic though she was alone.

The new housekeeper, the latest in a parade of transient hires, was out grocery shopping, and Bitty was off on some errand. Nedda had no idea where her brother and sister had gone. Lionel and Cleo had simply walked out the door without a word to her. And why not? She was dead to them. One did not consult with the dead about the day's plans. The sadness of this slight never showed in her eyes. She continued to behave as if she were constantly being observed from all quarters of every room and would not betray any emotion that might be noted or charted.

Poor Bitty.

Her niece must have had great hopes for the first family reunion. Nedda recalled the startled faces of Cleo and Lionel on the day they had visited the hospice. What a grand surprise that had been. Bitty had dramatically thrown open the door to the private room and exposed their long-lost sister, whom they had always believed to be – *hoped* to be – dead. True horror had set in after their barrage of questions which only a true sister could have answered. Finally, Cleo and Lionel had been convinced that Nedda was no grifter, no fraudulent heiress, and they had asked, almost in unison, 'Why did you come back?'

Nedda's joyful face had frozen into a fool's grin, and she had been trapped in that expression until her brother and sister had quit the room. How mad she must have seemed to Bitty in that next moment. Anguished crying – foolish smiling.

Mallory turned her small tan sedan eastward into the center lane of Houston at the optimum time for the greatest flow of commuter traffic. Riker sat beside her unaware that anything was amiss in their relationship.

She braked to a full stop and killed the engine. Vehicles in flanking lanes whizzed by, the drivers craning their necks at the odd sight of her stationary car in the middle of rush hour when all New York motorists went insane en masse. The yellow cab behind her screeched to a halt, and a long line of cars behind that one were also unable to change lanes. Mallory only stared at the windshield, as if checking it for spots and bugs, unruffled by the song of the city – drivers honking, putting great feeling into their horns, leaning on them for maximum noise, and the rising lyrics of shouted obscenities. In peripheral vision, she watched Riker's head swivel in her direction, silently asking, *What are you doing?*

'You're holding out on me.' She never raised her voice to be heard over the hell choir of honking and screaming, and this forced Riker to lean toward her, straining to hear every word.

Good.

She had his attention now. 'When Pinwitty mentioned Humboldt's name, I know you recognized it, but you didn't get it from a book or a—'

'Oh, sure,' said Riker. 'I know all of Stick Man's names.'

Bastard!

While she waited for him to elaborate on this little throwaway bombshell of his, the trapped cars were stacked up all the way back to a grid-locked intersection. The horns had doubled their number and volume, and now a new note was added to the mix. She could hear the angry, tinny slams of compact cars and the heavy-metal sound of trucks as drivers left their vehicles, intent on laying some blame and taking some satisfaction out of her hide.

Yeah, right.

But one glance at Riker told her that he was a believer in road rage. A traffic jam like this one could make killers out of the best-tempered nuns.

'So tell me something.' Mallory's words were slow and dead calm, as if she had all damn day for this conversation. 'When were you planning to share all these names?'

An old man stood on the cement strip that divided the traffic bound east and west. The elderly pedestrian had no stake in this event, yet he was as outraged as any of the drivers gathering around her car. He shook his fist and mouthed toothless angry words that were lost in the fray. Other men were massing near the windows on all sides. Riker held up his badge, as if that would fix everything.

Mallory slowly turned her head to glare at him, to warn him. He had better start talking and fast. The people surrounding this car were murderously angry, and this was definitely not the time for one of his long-winded stories.

And so Riker told her a story.

Charles Butler sat at his desk, reviewing paperwork on the latest client of Butler and Company. This one was the most brilliant to date – and the most troubled. The teenager had dropped out of college, descended into profound depression, and continued his fall by dropping off the planet. Mallory had found a lead with an illegal perusal-for-profit of police reports on missing persons. She had then tracked the boy down to a hole in the swamp at the edge of the world (her euphemism for a motel in New Jersey).

During the employment evaluation, all the right answers had been provided for every question on the personality profile, and that had been a clue to a problem; no one was so well balanced. However, the first warning had been the boy's rolled down sleeves on an unseasonably warm day. Mallory had suspected drugs. Charles had believed the sleeves would hide the scars of an attempted suicide.

He looked up from his reading and noticed his copy of *The Winter House Massacre* lying on the end table by the couch. So Mallory had decided not to read it after all. Wise. What a deadly bore was history in the hands of a bad writer. He turned back to the matter at hand, reading his business partner's most recent research on their young job candidate.

She had turned up a history of no less than six therapists, thus explaining how the youngster had sailed through all the psychological examinations – practice. Charles read the headings for each of Mallory's documents; all of them had been raided from hospital computers in the tristate area. She could not have gotten them by any other means. Even at one remove from theft, it would be unethical to read this material. And what would Mallory's foster father have said of this – theft of confidential patient files?

That's my kid.

And Louis would have said that with great pride.

Thoughts of this dead man linked up with the image of Nedda Winter skirting her ghosts on the staircase the night of the dinner party. He had never mentioned that to Mallory as an indication of a mind gone awry. If that held true, then he must count himself as a loon and a half.

The brown armchair beside the couch was the most comfortable seat in this office, and yet he never sat there. It was Louis's chair even now. That good old man had sat in this room on many a night when sleep was impossible because his wife was dead. In a way, all of Louis's stories of life with the incomparable Helen Markowitz had been ghost stories. Had she not come alive in this room? After a time, Charles had also come to grieve for Helen, though he had never met her. And he still grieved sorely for Louis. He missed that great soul every day.

And Charles could see his old friend, clear as day, seated beside him now, gathering up hound-dog jowls in a dazzling smile. And was there just a touch of pity in the old man's crinkled brown eyes? Oh, yes. Only Louis could fully appreciate Charles's predicament with Mallory's purloined documents. As the former commander of Special Crimes Unit, Inspector Markowitz had made such good use of his foster child's skill with computer lock picks.

Charles looked down at the raided information, poisonous fruit from Mallory's hand. Well, it was definitely in a good cause – life and death – if his suspicions about their client proved true. He read every line of the stolen data and discovered that each of the boy's psychiatric examinations had followed police custody for a suicide attempt on Halloween. And what were the odds that he might forgo his yearly wrist-slashing?

Well, job placement was out of the question, but now he could make the proper referral for long-term therapy. Mallory may have saved the boy's life with this information, stolen or not. Charles looked up at the armchair – Louis's chair. His old friend, the dead man, shrugged, then splayed one hand to say, *This is how it begins – the seduction.*

Charles found himself nodding in agreement with a man who was not there. Yes, he had actually rationalized a breach of ethics, an unnecessary violation. In truth, Mallory's theft had only supported his own suspicions. He was actually quite good at his craft, though he applied his skill to analyzing a potential client's gifts and suitability for employment.

Retiring to the couch, he stretched out to finish his reading in comfort. He was surprised to turn a page and find Mallory's job proposal for placing the boy in a remote scientific community. There, he would not be a solitary freak, but one of many such freaks, and he would cease his ritual attempts to kill himself every Halloween; this had been Mallory's argument for selling an unbalanced job candidate.

Oh, *of course*. Never mind the fee. And here he countered with her own trademark line, 'Yeah, right.'

131

Mallory, the *humanitarian*, had also secured the client on the profit side of this transaction. The New Mexico think tank was funded with a truly obscene amount of grant money. Best of all – and this was her final salvo – the personnel director had not balked at the disclosure of the boy's suicidal ideation, and the project would provide long-term therapy.

Thus far, this was the only argument for job placement.

All that remained was the detail of signing off on Mallory's paperwork. He slowed his reading to a normal person's pace, for his partner sometimes deviated from the standard boilerplate contract, and he had learned to go slowly and scrutinize every line before signing anything. True to form, she had named a staggering fee that he would never have had the gall to charge, and her conditions straddled a borderland between ethics and all that the traffic would bear. She had added a penalty clause, doubling their fee if the New Mexico project failed to keep the boy alive through Halloween.

Charles stared at the ceiling, averting his eyes from the laughing dead man.

Reading that final contract clause in the best possible light, Mallory was not actually planning to profit on a death. No, she only wanted to ensure the boy's ongoing survival. He turned to face his memory of the late Louis Markowitz, who knew her best.

The old man lifted one eyebrow to say, *But you're not really sure, are you, Charles?*

On a normal day, he would be madly rewriting the terms of Mallory's contract, but now he simply bowed to the absurd and signed his name on the dotted line.

Done with the business of the day, he turned his attention to the telephone on the other side of the room, willing it to ring. He was looking forward to another conversation with Susan McReedy, the lady from Maine. Mallory had insisted that the woman would call again. The detective's contracts were a bit dicey, but her instincts were superb. Yes, Ms McReedy would definitely call back. He could see the woman clearly now, sitting by her own telephone, her hair gone to gray and her life as well, facing the tedium of her retirement years. This very moment, all of Ms McReedy's thoughts would be consumed by old acquaintance with a memorable ice-pick-wielding redhead.

He reached out to the near table and picked up his history book. As he turned the pages, he marveled anew that Riker could have ingested this dry text without the skill of speed reading and the mercy of a quick end. While scanning the pages, Charles revisited Mallory's theory on a twelve-year-old girl's involvement in the Winter House Massacre.

In a bibliophile's act of heresy, he threw the book across the room. Next, he abandoned logic, replacing it with faith and feeling. He liked Nedda Winter. Between dinner at eight and the last bottle of wine in the early hours of a morning, he had come to think of her as a friend.

Head bowed over her plate, Nedda Winter finished supper in the kitchen, then disregarded the automatic dishwasher to clean her plate in the sink. She planned to retire early and spare her siblings one more encounter, though she craved their company, any company at all, rather than to be alone, that state where memory consumed her.

One benign recollection was of Mrs Tully, wide as she was tall, the cook and housekeeper who had died in the massacre. This kitchen had been that old woman's domain, and October had been Tully's favorite time of the year. For weeks in advance of Halloween, she had always been allowed free rein to terrify her employer's offspring. That last time, when five of the Winter children had only a few more days to live, they had all gathered in the kitchen, all except Baby Sally. The youngsters, rocking on the balls of their feet, had wafted back and forth between terror and delight. And then the long-awaited moment came when the housekeeper threw open the cellar door to absolute darkness and led them all down the stairs.

Five-year-old Cleo had alternately laughed and squealed in anticipation before Tully had even begun her scary work. Erica, who had turned nine that year, was much more ladylike, practicing to be blasé and determined that the old woman would not make her scream. And the rest of them could hardly wait to be scared witless.

'I never use mousetraps,' the old woman said, as she led the parade of children into the dank basement by the light of a single candle. She held the flame below her face to make it seem evil when she grinned at them. 'No, traps won't do. Might catch a child or two by mistake and break your little fingers and toes. But no fear. The house likes you – all of you. But the house hates vermin. Kills 'em dead, it does.' Tully had bent low to hold her candle over the small moldering body of a field mouse underneath a fallen box. Another mouse was found crushed by a wrench that had dropped from a shelf of tools. 'Looks accidental, don't it? But look around you, my little dears. Did you ever see so many accidents in one place?' And then she had laughed, high-throated, wicked, shining candlelight into corners, illuminating other tiny corpses caught and crushed in the circumstances of apparent mishaps.

So *many* of them.

Erica screamed.

Nedda glanced at the clock on the kitchen wall. She should go upstairs now. Lionel and Cleo might come home at any moment.

After passing through the dining room, she walked toward the stairs at an odd angle so that she might avoid the prone and lifeless Mrs Tully in her plain gray dress. Nedda began her ascent by hugging the rail and keeping to a narrow path so as not to tread on any part of her father's body. She paused, as she always did. Farther up the staircase was her stepmother's corpse. A small spot of blood marred the breast of a blue silk dressing gown, and the eyes were rolled upward, as if mortified to be seen in this unflattering sprawl of limbs.

Nedda lifted one foot, for she had just stepped on her father's dead white hand.

Sorry, so sorry.

She looked down at his upturned face, his startled eyes, so surprised to be dying.

Behind her, she heard the familiar voice of Uncle James calling out to her from across the room and more than half a century, asking in a plaintive tone, 'My God, Nedda, what have you done?'

Mallory climbed the stairs behind her partner. His new apartment was located on the floor above a saloon – Riker's big dream.

'My grandfather was never on the case,' he said, 'but the old man worked it on the side – worked it all his life. He visited every crime scene where an ice pick was used as weapon.' After opening the door and flicking on the light, he waved her inside.

Mallory remained standing while her partner flopped down on the couch, raising a cloud of dust from the cushion. Every littered surface was filmed with gray, though he had only occupied this place for a few weeks. Where was he getting his dust supply?

'So your grandfather covered domestic disputes and bar fights?'

'Everything,' said Riker. 'Have a seat.'

'What for?'

Misunderstanding her, he stood up and, with no offense taken, swept the leather seat of an armchair to send his unopened mail and smaller, unidentified flying objects to the floor. 'There you go.'

She sat down, careful not to touch the padded arms, for she could not identify what he had spilled there. Next, she flirted with the idea that he had brought some of his trash from the last apartment, perhaps regarding this formidable collection of crushed beer cans as a homey touch. 'Why would your grandfather cover the nickel-and-dime scenes? It's not like he expected them to tie back to Stick Man.'

'My father thought that was strange, too.' In Mallory's honor, Riker walked about the room, bending low to pick up dirty socks and stuff them behind the couch pillows. 'When Granddad retired, he lost access to crime scenes, so Dad collected all the details for him.'

'And now *you* do it.' And when would they ever get to the reason why? She tapped one foot as Riker opened the refrigerator and pulled out two cold beers. Accepting one from his hand, she asked him again. 'Why, Riker? What can you learn from garden-variety stabbings?'

'Every way you can stab another human with an ice pick.' This time he eased himself down on the couch, cutting the dust fly by half. 'The lead detective ruled out a pro in favor of a psycho, but not my grandfather. Gran developed a signature for Stick Man. Now this is something you won't see in a rage killing. The pick was *pushed* into the body, perfectly level to pass through the rib cage. No false strikes, no bone chips ever. Just perfect. The picks were honed, narrow and needle sharp. Easier to pass through clothes and muscle. Then Stick Man made a little jog to the right and shredded the heart. That enlarged the entry wound. He eased the pick out. No blood fly that way. And he wiped the bloody end on the victim's clothing. He could've slaughtered a battalion without getting a drop on his clothes. After Granddad retired, my father used his clout to pull hundreds of old autopsy reports, and they found matches. There was no other stab wound quite like Stick Man's. He used that same MO for almost a hundred years. The cops caught him twice – and twice he died.'

A ghost story.

Mallory's hands balled into fists. She *hated* ghost stories.

Nedda backed away from the staircase, then stopped – dead stop.

What was that?

The million fine hairs of her body were on the rise as she sorted out the noises of the house. A light slap on glass came from the garden, where a leafy branch licked the panes of the doors. Elsewhere, a clock was ticking. She turned around, looking across the front room to the foyer and the burglar alarm. There was no glowing light to assure her that the alarm was working. She rationalized this away. The new housekeeper had not set the alarm before going out, and that was common enough. They never stayed very long, and few of them had found the time or inclination to memorize the daily change of the code that disabled the alarm upon reentering the house.

Was the door even locked?

Another noise, a knock, then a thud, was followed by the sound of breaking glass.

Nedda drifted across the room and down the hall toward the kitchen, the source of her fear. She could not stop herself, though her legs threatened to buckle and fail. She was like one of those elderly women on the hospital ward, driven by a compulsion she could not name, her limbs moving of their own accord.

On the kitchen threshold now, eyes on the cellar door, fascinated and afraid, she was moving toward it. One hand trembled on the knob, and she opened the door to absolute silence, that moment between one footstep and the next, the still vacuum of holding one's breath. And now she heard another noise. By the dim light filtering downstairs from the kitchen, she saw a mousetrap at the edge of the first step. She wanted so much to believe that it was a rodent down there, a big one with enough weight to make the sound of crunching glass underfoot. But she was not so gifted at delusional thinking.

Nedda backed away from the door, keeping her eyes trained upon it as she reached out for the nearest drawer. This was where Bitty had found the old wooden ice pick the other night, the one used to satisfy the curiosity of Detective Riker. And now that pick was in Nedda's hand.

She backed out of the kitchen, never taking her eyes off the door until she turned and ran light-footed down the hall, heading for the staircase. Bitty's room on the floor above had a good strong bolt on the door.

Nedda gripped the banister, and stood there very still, one foot upon the stair. She shook her head. She could not hide; she could not take the chance. What if this intruder surprised the next innocent to come through the front door?

Well, she would call the police.

And say what?

I hear noises in my house? My burglar alarm isn't working?

The night of the break-in, she could not remember having the luxury of time to question what she should do next. Nedda looked down at the ice pick in her hand.

She could do it again.

Riker stood on a chair to reach the box at the back of his closet. He hoisted it down and dropped it on the floor at Mallory's feet. 'I was just a kid then. Every night after dinner, they'd spread all this stuff on the kitchen table. Mom called our kitchen the murder room.' He lifted the box and carried it to his own kitchen table. 'The earliest cases date back to the eighteen-hundreds, but they all used Stick Man's signature. They ended in the forties, the year of the massacre.'

Somewhat mollified by Riker's hasty disavowal of a ghost story, Mallory asked, 'How many generations of hitmen?'

'Three.' He sat down at the table and opened the box. 'The first one was a crazy little bastard in Hell's Kitchen. He worked for the Irish gangs. Started when he was only thirteen. Back in those days, they called him Pick. What really spooked the locals was the daylight killing. He'd walk up to a guy on the street at high noon and just do him on the spot.'

'Too crazy to worry about witnesses.'

'Right. And who wants to make an enemy of the neighborhood nutcase? So everybody knew who he was, even the local beat cop, and nobody talked.'

Riker pulled out a handful of yellowed papers and photographs, diagrams and scraps of paper with notes in faded ink. He tapped a picture cut from an ancient newspaper and preserved in laminate. 'This is his mother. Smart lady. She was the broker for all his jobs. And – surprise – she read tarot cards. That was her front for the murder contracts, and she never did one day in prison. Well, her son was nuts, and I mean a real standout kind of crazy. But the mother paid off the cops when they started asking questions. Then one day, there's a new commission to investigate police corruption, so the cops run out and pick up her son just for show. That closes a few dozen homicides in an afternoon, and the department really shines in the morning paper.' He grinned at Mallory. 'Don't you love this town?'

'That's when Pick died?'

'The first time? No, not yet. After the arrest, he was committed to an asylum. And that's where he hooks up with his replacement – an orderly named Jay Holly.'

Riker had covered every inch of the table, laying out his files in stacks of a dozen folders, each one another death. 'You won't find this stuff in police reports or history books. Pinwitty's research was pathetic next to Granddad's.' He found a mug shot from the New Orleans Police Department and handed it to Mallory. 'That's Jay Holly. He did a deal with the fortuneteller.'

'Wait – she put out a contract on her—'

'Her own son? Yeah. Her crazy son was too dangerous to keep alive. It was just a matter of time before his mother was tied to the murders.' Riker shuffled through more papers, producing a list of assets: expensive homes and purchases beyond a fortuneteller's means. 'But the old lady didn't wanna give up a good income. So she hired Jay Holly to kill her son in the asylum. Pick was smothered with a pillow.' He pushed an old copy of the death certificate across the table.

Mallory glanced at the date, then picked up a column cut from a yellowed newspaper. 'And five days after that, there's another ice-pick murder. All right, I get it. She pays Jay Holly to make her dead son look like an innocent man. Now the old lady's in the clear, too.'

'Yeah.' Riker placed another file in front of her, another death. 'And then—'

'The next day, she's back in business,' said Mallory, 'as the new hitman's broker. But the cops don't bother her anymore.'

'My grandfather would've loved you, kid. Yeah, that's the way he figured it. Jay and the old lady did real well, until she died – of a stroke. More likely it was murder. There was no autopsy. Granddad figured that must've been the first instance of the pick in the eardrum. Another fortuneteller took over the same storefront, and this one was young and good-looking. Then Jay Holly got caught in New Orleans. That's where he hooked up with our guy in a holding cell.'

'Humboldt.'

'Yeah, but that wasn't his real name.' He handed her another sheet. 'These are Humboldt's aliases. He did time all over the South for fleecing women out of their savings. A real charmer. The last lady withdrew the charges. So Humboldt was about to get out of jail around the time Jay Holly was taken into custody.'

'They share a cell – they do a deal.'

'Yeah. So now Humboldt knows the style. The day he gets out of jail, there's another ice-pick murder, same MO, and the cops release Jay Holly. Then Holly dies, but it's not an ice-pick kill. Humboldt's smarter than that. Jay Holly was found dead on a barroom floor. He'd been poisoned, and the cops had no leads on the man he was drinking with that night.'

'Humboldt goes back to New York and uses the same fortuneteller for his broker.'

'Right. And he keeps this one alive for a long time. She was an old woman before he murdered her in the police station.'

'Twelve days after the murders at Winter House.' Mallory drummed her fingernails on the table. 'And your father keeps working on this?'

'No, he stopped the night my grandfather died.'

'You think he could help us?'

'No, I could never ask Dad to do that. It's a long story.'

Mallory's face was a study in grim resignation.

* * *

There was no need to touch the light switch for the cellar. From the top of the stairs, Nedda could see shards of broken glass clinging to the socket of the hanging bulb. The last time she had visited the cellar, it was to help one of the housekeepers replace a blown-out kitchen fuse, and then her own head had cleared that bulb by only a few inches. So the intruder must be a tall one, over six feet.

The new housekeeper was also tall, but Nedda had no illusions about finding the woman down there on some innocent errand. However, this might explain why an intruder had dared to come in by the front door. He must have been watching the house. He would have seen them all leave and go their separate ways, perhaps mistaking the housekeeper for herself. And then, he must have heard approaching footsteps and fled for the cover of the basement.

Nedda raised the pick high. And, because she was afraid, she gathered dead brothers and sisters around her. Mrs Tully, an animated corpse of formidable girth, led the procession down the cellar stairs.

Just like old times.

The kitchen light petered out beyond the bottom step. There would be a flashlight on top of the fuse box to her left. But now she saw the bright rectangle of an open door on the other side of the basement. Whoever had broken into the house was long gone. Beyond the threshold, ten steps led up to the backyard and escape. A breeze called Nedda's attention to a high window. Its heavy wood frame was propped open with a stick. This was how the intruder must have gained entrance. As she drew close to the window, dead brothers and sisters walked with her, lending comfort. All of them looked up to see a field mouse at the window, testing the cellar air, nose high, whiskers twitchy. Its small pink hands were almost human as it gripped the wooden sill. The tiny creature was half in, half out. And, though the wind had ceased and there was no visible agency to move the propping stick, the stick did fall. The slamming wood frame broke the back of the mouse. Its mouth opened wide and, in surprise, it died.

Mrs Tully laughed.

Nedda, in concert with the children, moved back from the window. By the good light of the open door, this small audience of the dead and the living could see wet drops of blood on the steps leading up to the backyard.

What had the house done to the intruder?

'My father doesn't even know I have this stuff,' said Riker.

'You *stole* it from him?'

Riker shook his head. 'I came by it the night Gran died. That old man literally worked this case right up to the end. He had coroners' reports from six states, patching time lines and murder contracts together, but nothing after the date of the Winter House Massacre. So, it's twenty years later, and the trail is as cold as it ever gets. That's when Gran figures Stick Man must've died back in the forties, the year of the massacre.'

'Well, he was only off by two years,' said Mallory, examining her nails, 'if Nedda killed Stick Man in Maine.'

'Yeah. Too bad the Maine police weren't on Gran's radar. He might've closed out the case.' Riker knew she was wondering when this family saga would finally end. He was always trying to connect with her on some human level, forgetting who and what he was dealing with.

'Your dad,' she said, prompting him for an explanation of why this door was closed to them.

'Okay,' he said. 'Now remember, Gran and my dad worked this case together for years – from the day my grandfather retired until he died. Well, Granddad was always pumped. Dead or alive, he wanted to bring Red Winter home. All those nights at the kitchen table, looking at clues and kicking around ideas – that was the only time my father's old man ever talked to him.'

And this family custom of stone silence had carried into Riker's generation.

'The only time Dad was really happy was when he was filling the kitchen with cigar smoke, emptying a whiskey bottle with my grandfather and talking shop. So it was hard to understand what Dad did when his old man died. That was the night my father brought home a twenty-two-year-old autopsy report on the second fortune-teller, the one who died after the Winter House Massacre. After Granddad read it, he got all excited. He couldn't get the words out. He stood up, hugged my dad – for maybe the first time ever – then fell across the kitchen table dead.

'Later that night, my mom was out on the porch, waiting for a hearse from the mortuary. And Dad was in the kitchen with his father's corpse. I can still see him on the floor, crawling around on hands and knees, picking up all the papers that scattered when Gran had his heart attack. After my father had the whole file all bundled together, he dropped it into the garbage can and never talked about the case again.'

The files young Riker had rescued from the trash still bore faint stains of what the family had dined on that night.

'As much as your dad couldn't stand the sight of that file,' said Mallory, 'that's how much he loved your grandfather. It was just too much pain. That's why he tossed it in the garbage can.'

Riker nodded. He had come to understand that over the passing years, but Mallory the Machine should not have been able to work it out – and so quickly. 'But that's not the reason I can't ask for Dad's help with this case.'

'I know.' Mallory pushed her empty beer bottle to one side. 'It's because now you understand why your grandfather was so excited he couldn't talk. For those twelve days between the massacre at Winter House and the fortuneteller's murder in the police station – Nedda was learning to read tarot cards.'

᛫ That was the pattern: a new fortuneteller to replace the old one. What other reason could a hitman have for stealing a child? And what a tall child; one who could pass for a woman, but so much easier to

143

control – an heiress who could one day reappear to claim a fortune.

This last piece dropped into place so neatly, he could almost hear an audible click in the gears of Mallory's mind.

Riker stared at her for what seemed like a very long time, perhaps no more than a minute, but how those seconds crawled along. She could still surprise him, and sometimes this caused him pain. He had watched her grow up, but he could never really know her. And, fool that he was, he was always tripping over himself each time he underestimated her – and yet he never learned.

He nodded now. She had gotten it right.

When his grandfather had felt the onset of a massive coronary, when joy had overpowered fear and pain, that must have been the moment when the old man realized that the stolen child could still be alive. Riker looked down at the sprawl of papers on his own kitchen table – the family tradition of fathers and sons.

'My father was a great cop. None better. That murdered fortune-teller was the key. If he'd gone on working this case, Dad would've followed through on Humboldt. He would've run him down to the ice-pick stabbing in Maine and a red-haired girl.'

Mallory nodded. 'He would've brought Red Winter home forty years ago.'

'I can never tell him that.'

'We have to stop meeting this way. People will talk.'

'Yes, ma'am.' Officer Brill gallantly strained to smile at this line, which had been an old one before Nedda was born. After opening the cellar door, he clicked on his flashlight, and she followed him down the stairs. The yellow beam roved over the broken glass on the floor. He had found one piece that he liked and put it into a plastic bag.

'Is that blood on the glass?'

'Yes, ma'am, it is. Did you cut yourself?'

'Not my hands.' She examined the backs of them. 'And I had shoes on my feet.'

'You didn't stab anybody, did you, ma'am?'

'No, I'm off that now.'

Officer Brill's polite smile widened into a genuine grin. 'Good to know.' He looked up as he redirected the beam of his flashlight to the broken bulb overhead. There was more blood on one of the shards that still clung to the socket. 'So, we'll be looking for a tall man wearing a bandage on his head. That's more of a description than we usually get.'

Back upstairs again, the patrolman accepted her offer of tea, but insisted on preparing it himself. He seemed at home in a kitchen. She guessed that he had a grandmother her age, and, during the course of their conversation, this proved true. The young man lived in the Bronx with a large extended family that included both of his grandparents. He spoke of them warmly as he pulled out a chair for Nedda and seated her at the table.

When the kettle released its steam in a shrill whistle, he was quick to kill the flame of the burner. As he poured hot water over the tea bags in their cups, he noticed the tarot deck on the kitchen table, and he smiled. 'My grandmother spends ten dollars every Monday to have her fortune told.'

'Well, that's cheap. She must know an honest fortuneteller.'

By the expression on the young man's face, Nedda could tell that he considered this an oxymoron. How could a fortuneteller ever be honest?

'An old woman taught me to read tarot cards.' Nedda unboxed the deck. 'These belonged to her.' She selected the card that most resembled the young policeman. 'This is your significator, the Knight of Swords. It's what you are. Now think about the problem that troubles you most.' She shuffled the cards. 'I'm guessing that's me.' After cutting the cards three times, she laid them out in three piles. 'Put the deck back together and hand it to me.'

He did as she asked, and she knew it was only to humor an old woman, for he was a child of the new century, a firm believer in scientific explanations for everything.

145

She lifted one card from the top and laid it down upon the knight. 'This covers you.' And with the next card laid lengthwise, she said, 'This crosses you for good or ill.' In quick succession, she placed four cards at compass points all around the first three, then dealt four more cards in a row to one side.

'And now you're going to tell me my future.'

'No, that's for the fool,' said Nedda, 'the kind of person who seeks patterns that aren't there – the sort who sees the Virgin Mary in a grocer's deformed potato, then pays a ten-dollar admission fee to worship it. Given a fool's nature, he deserves what he gets – a lighter wallet and nothing more.'

She covered the policeman's hand with hers. 'You're not like that. You wouldn't want to see the future, not even if you believed it was possible.' No, this boy would never bow to the idea of a destiny writ in stone. 'You already see a *possible* future – the one you can forge for yourself.'

Nedda pointed to the west card. 'This is where that future begins, in your past. You became a policeman, not for the good pension plan, but because you wanted to help people. That's your nature.' She pointed to the south card. 'This is the foundation of the matter. You're exactly where you should be in the world. You like what you are, and that's rare.' Her hand drifted toward the north card. 'You strive to create order out of chaos.' Her finger landed on the east card, the immediate future. 'And you will do this every day in small ways and big ones. But you already know that. You've made it your mission.' She studied the remaining cards. 'Now, if I'm right and your worry of the moment is me . . . I can tell you that you'll see me again.'

But would she be dead or alive?

'That was an easy one,' she said. 'I spend a great deal of my day at the windows. I've seen you drive by from time to time, probably more often than you should. You always slow down when you pass my house. I suspect that you keep an eye on me.'

A good guess. She had taken him by surprise.

Her hand drifted up to the last card dealt, the culmination of all that had gone before. 'In this matter where our paths have crossed, we will each reap what we deserve. But then, that's true for everyone. Hardly magic or psychic phenomena.' She swept all the cards together. 'Just a tool to keep you focused on the road ahead.'

He must have intuited that this card play was a ruse to keep his company a while longer, for he leaned toward her, saying, 'Shock is a funny thing.' He cleared their cups from the table and set them in the sink. 'Sometimes it makes people weak in the legs. Sometimes they're afraid to be alone. If you hear any noises, or if you just feel jumpy, you can call and ask for me. I'll be on duty for another six hours.'

The cleaning lady entered into a street fight of sorts, or so she would tell it later on, as she wrestled over a wire cart filled with her supplies. The young policeman insisted on carrying it up the stairs for her, and by brute strength he won.

'I don't tip cops!' yelled Mrs Ortega in Brooklynese.

'Suits me fine,' the young officer countered with his Bronx accent. 'Chump change ruins the line of my uniform.' And now that he had settled her cart by the front door to the mansion, he tipped his hat and left her standing there agape and with no comeback line.

No need to ring the bell. The door was opened wide by a woman as tall as Detective Mallory, but much older. The hair was white, her eyes pale blue, and what a curious smile. 'You're from the temp agency?'

'Lucky guess, lady. Here, you gotta sign this.' The smaller woman handed her a work order tapped out on Mallory's computer and guaranteed to pass for the genuine article. 'The name's Ortega,' she said. 'You can call me *Mrs* Ortega.' And by the signature, she knew this was Nedda Winter.

And now the cleaning lady had to fend off more good manners, offers of tea and conversation, for God's sake. But she was firm. 'I only got a few hours.' Mrs Ortega powered up her vacuum cleaner and kept her mouth closed until, an hour later, she opened the door to the closet in the foyer. 'What the hell?'

The shelves were narrow for a linen closet, and they were lined with women's hats.

'It's a hat closet,' said Miss Winter.

'There's no such thing,' said Mrs Ortega. 'You know how many years I been cleaning houses like yours? Hell, even fancier than this one, and there's no such a thing as a damn hat closet. This is a *linen* closet, and you never find a linen closet in a damn foyer. But that's not what I was talking about.' She leaned down and picked up one hat that had fallen from a lower shelf, then pointed to a hole in the wall. 'What's that?'

'A mouse hole, I suppose. Would you like a cold beer?'

Two blocks west of Winter House and two hours later, Mrs Ortega was sitting in the front seat of Mallory's car. 'So I says to Miss Winter, you got real classy rodents here – that's a nice round hole. Between you and me, Mallory? I'd say that mouse used a drill with a four-inch bit. And it was a damn tall mouse. That hole was two feet off the ground.'

Mallory nodded, hardly listening.

'The back of the closet was cheap plasterboard,' said the cleaning lady, attempting to liven up her story. 'Now that's odd because the sides are cedar. It don't make sense. You see the problem?' No, she guessed that Mallory had lost interest in the closets of the rich, and Mrs Ortega was still unclear about what service she had done to warrant a hundred-dollar bill on top of her regular cleaning fee. And so she felt obliged to elaborate, drawing on her vast reading in true-crime paperbacks. 'You know that house has a history, right?'

Mallory's face had no expression that the cleaning lady could read. Mrs Ortega offered a hint. 'The Winter House Massacre? Ring any bells?'

'That's way before Mallory's time,' said Riker. 'Mine, too.' He had returned from his deli run. After settling into the backseat, he handed Mrs Ortega her requested bagel and coffee. 'Now here's our problem.' He held out a sheet of paper with the letterhead of Crime Scene Unit. 'A rookie investigator has a note here. Suspicious hole in shallow closet.'

'Crime scene, huh? Another murder. Do you know how many—'

'Don't get excited,' said Riker. 'It was a robbery.'

'Oh, sure,' said Mrs Ortega. 'You two turned out for a robbery.'

'That's right,' said Mallory, pressing another large bill into the woman's hand. 'Is there a problem here?'

'Absolutely not.' Mrs Ortega pocketed the bill. 'So this rookie – did he mention the seam around the closet hole?' Well, that got their attention. 'The backing on that closet is old and rotted. But the hole and the seam? Not so old. Somebody cut out a section and then put it back in place. There's a ridge of glue around the seam for the patch. And there's dust on that ridge.'

'Well, that tears it,' said Riker. 'Whatever got walled up in the closet, it's long gone now.'

'Tell me about Nedda Winter,' said Mallory.

'Real jumpy. Followed me everywhere, and it wasn't like she thought I was gonna rob her blind. She just wanted the company. Didn't wanna be alone. That was my take. I cleaned her room. Hardly needed it. Very neat. No personal items. There's a metal suitcase stashed under the bed. I thought that was her house, but she acts like a real polite guest who isn't sure how long she wants to stay. So then the little one comes home.'

'Bitty Smyth.'

'Right. Soon as I saw her, I knew which room was hers. Never had to ask. It had to be the one with all the stuffed toys on the bed. Like a kid's room. Now that's because she's so small. I bet people still pat her on the head. She'll have teddy bears on the bed when she's ninety years old. Well, as soon as she showed up, I left.'

'Good job.' Mallory nodded to the police cruiser behind her car. 'That officer will drive you anywhere you want to go.'

Mrs Ortega looked back over her shoulder to the rear window and its view of a policeman in uniform, the same cop who had wrestled her for the cleaning cart. 'Good. A rematch.' As she closed the door of the car, she leaned down to the open passenger window. 'Just one more thing, you guys. Instead of asking yourselves *what* was walled up in that closet, you might be wondering *who*. It was a damned big patch.'

No intruder could hide in the dark of an old house. Every creak of a timber and each footfall on the stair was kettledrum and timpani; moments of silence were suspect and fraught with tension – waiting, waiting.

Nedda rose from her bed and walked to the window. Evidently, Officer Brill had not been impressed by the most recent break-in. There were no police cars parked out front. She held the opera glasses borrowed from her mother's old trunk in the attic. Raising the lenses to her eyes, she looked out over the park, bringing leaves into sharp focus and searching for a sign of movement among the branches.

Her brother and sister had not returned. They had been absent for yet another break-in, and she wondered what the police would make of that coincidence.

Cleo and Lionel spent so much of their time at the summer house, and Nedda blamed herself for making the town house unbearable. Bitty had offered another theory: they simply liked to drive; it was nothing for them to make the round trip in a day, only spending a few hours in one place or the other. Her niece believed that they used the summer house as an excuse, needing some destination for their drives, else they would drive in circles. The pair had longtime acquaintances, but no real friends to visit in the Hamptons.

But they had each other. And what of Bitty? She had no one but a lame cockatiel.

Nedda refocused the opera glasses and strained to see a man in the mesh of leaves. No, there was no one there, but she imagined him behind each tree. The wind was rising, and the branches lost more of their cover with every gust.

Waiting, waiting, anticipating.

She closed the drape and lit the lamp. Next, she sat down at the writing desk and picked up her pen. Nedda meant to explain her actions to her family, or that was her intention, but she could think of no way to begin her letter. Instead, she wrote the same line, over and over, filling both sides of a paper, then reaching for another sheet. If things should go wrong tonight, this might be the most eloquent explanation she could leave behind. Or was it a confession of sorts? Pages covered with her handwriting drifted to the floor as the hour grew late. Over and over again, she wrote the same line: *Crazy people make sane people crazy.*

Rising from the desk, she switched off the lamp and returned to the window. There were no pedestrians in sight, and the traffic was light to nonexistent. She focused the opera glasses. There, a face moving behind the trees near the stone wall, that low barrier between the sidewalk and the park. Nedda looked back at the clock on her bedside table. Officer Brill would have gone off duty hours ago. What would she say if she called the police station?

I see a pale face in the woods?

No, they would not send anyone to search Central Park for suspicious persons, not on her account. They would write her off as a crazy old woman, and perhaps this was true. She watched the wood across the way and saw him more clearly now, but just the back of him moving deeper into the foliage.

Nedda disrobed to stand naked before her closet, moving hangers, hunting for something night black. When she was dressed, she reached beneath her pillow to grab up the wooden handle of the ice pick. With great stealth she slipped down the hall to the stairs, finding her way in the dark, descending slowly, minding the steps that made noise. The alarm light was on in the foyer. She tapped in the number code to disarm it, then found the switch to turn off the light above the outside stairs.

Charles Butler returned home from a charity auction, his wallet lightened by a donation, but no purchases had been made aside from cocktails at the bar. None of the antique furniture had remotely resembled the gaming table of his dreams. And now he had less than a week to replace the one that had been destroyed. Before he could insert the key into the lock for his apartment, he saw the lighted glass of the door to Butler and Company.

Mallory? She liked the late hours.

He entered the reception area and saw a light at the end of the hallway, but it was his own office and not hers. Charles found his cleaning woman fast asleep and slumped over a book in her lap. Now that was odd. Oh, wait – not odd at all. She had been reading the book on Winter House, and that would put anyone to sleep.

He put one hand on her shoulder. 'Mrs Ortega?' When her eyes opened, he said, 'I've never known you to work so late.' He glanced at his watch. 'It's after midnight.'

This took some convincing. She had to look first at his watch then her own. 'I'll be damned. I couldn't clean your office this afternoon,' she said. 'I had to do an errand for Mallory. I didn't think you'd mind if—'

'Oh, but I *don't* mind. So what sort of errand did you do for Mallory?'

'I can't tell you.'

'Ah, sworn to secrecy. I understand.' He walked to the credenza behind his desk and returned to join her on the couch, holding a bottle of sherry and two glasses. 'However, it wouldn't count if I guessed, would it?'

Undecided, she accepted a glass and allowed him to fill it – several times in quick succession.

He pointed to the book in her lap. 'I'm guessing it's something to do with Winter House.'

'Maybe,' she said, and then she smiled. 'Are you a betting man?'

'You know I am.' Indeed, he never tired of losing at poker. 'What's the wager?'

She held up the thick volume. 'I know what happened to Red Winter.'

'Fascinating.' Charles dipped the decanter to refresh her glass. 'Twenty dollars and a limo ride home to Brooklyn?'

'It's a bet. I say Red Winter was never lost. That kid never even left her own house. The body was walled up in the foyer closet. That's *my* theory.'

'Really.' He filled her glass again. Mrs Ortega had a high tolerance for alcohol, and it might take a while to get the entire story.

Nedda stood on the sidewalk in a long black leather jacket and slacks. She felt cold – exposed. A single car rolled by, and she turned away from the headlights, hiding the ice pick in her side pocket. She ran full out to cross the boulevard. When had she last run for her life or any other reason? It made her young again. The wind hit her face and picked at the loose weave of her braid. She approached the low stone wall as a twelve-year-old girl and easily scaled it, her feet hitting the broken branches and cracking dead leaves on the other side. And now she played the child's game of statue, quieting her heart the better to hear a stranger's footfall.

She was terrified, exhilarated – *alive*.

This was a better plan than waiting for him to come for her. They were old friends now, she and Death. It got easier each time they met. And this time, she had selected the meeting place. Her head snapped right with a sound of a dry stick broken underfoot, and she walked that way, pushing branches to one side, going deeper and deeper into the wood and losing the light of the path lamps.

'Red Winter,' said a man's voice just behind her back.

Her hand closed around the ice pick in her pocket. She turned around to face him, but there was no one there.

153

'My God, it's really you.' A tall figure stepped out of the foliage. Only a shadow and only his voice discerned his sex. 'Red Winter. You don't remember me, do you?' He clicked on a flashlight and shined it on his own face, making it ghoulish with sharp shadows riding the planes of his cheeks and the deep eye sockets. Yes, he was a tall one, and, just as Officer Brill had predicted, he wore a bandage high on his scalp where the lightbulb's broken glass had scratched him.

'We met when you were very sick,' he said, in a surprisingly normal voice, hardly threatening. 'You made a nice recovery, didn't you?'

She had not expected this – a civilized conversation replete with polite inquiries on the state of her health. Had they met in a hospital? There had been so many of them over the years. And then there had been the nursing homes and finally the hospice. Her grip on the ice pick remained very tight.

'No,' he said, lowering the flashlight. 'You wouldn't remember, would you? You were really out of it then.'

And now she must pin that down to one of three places. They might have met in the last hospital where her health had severely declined, or the nursing home where her life would have ended if not for Bitty. Or was it the hospice?

The man was coming closer, his white hands dangling from the arms of a loose flannel jacket that might conceal any number of weapons.

'Were you a patient, too?' she asked, as if this might be a normal chat with some acquaintance who had slipped her memory.

'Me? In a nursing home?' He actually smiled. 'Not likely.'

No, he was only thirty years old at the outside. So he had met her in the Maine nursing home.

He placed his flashlight in the crook of his arm, shining its light on the trees behind him, and freeing both hands to open the buttons of his jacket. Did he have a gun? An ice-pick could not beat a bullet.

He was one step closer, his right hand still concealed.

His backward-shining beam spotlighted another figure in the wood, a lovely face with the luminous skin of a haunt.

Mallory.

The young detective was only a few yards away. Holding a very large gun in one hand, she crept closer with no clumsy breaks of twigs underfoot, but padding like a cat, taking her own time in Nedda's elongated sense of seconds expanding in slow motion.

The man was pulling his hand from the folds of his jacket. What was that dark object in his hand?

Mallory was smiling as her gun hand was rising. The young policewoman was enjoying this moment, and a moment was all it was before Nedda heard the connection of heavy metal on bone. The man made less noise when he dropped to the ground.

A uniformed policeman stepped out of the woods in the company of Detective Riker, who hailed her with a broad smile and, 'Hey, Nedda. How's it going?'

Mallory waved one hand toward the younger of the two men. 'You remember Officer Brill.'

'Yes, of course,' said Nedda. 'He comes to all of our crime scenes.' She smiled at the patrolman. 'How nice to see you again.'

'Evening, ma'am.' Officer Brill tipped his cap, then turned to the chore of helping Riker pick up the fallen man. They carried the unconscious body up the path that would lead them back to the stone wall. A police car was waiting for them, its red lights spinning through breaks in the trees.

Nedda was left alone with Mallory, who was slow to holster her gun.

'What brings you out so late, Miss Winter?' The young detective circled around Nedda, then dropped her voice to a whisper behind the older woman's back. 'Hunting?' Louder, Mallory said, 'Not enough action back at your house?'

All Nedda saw was the flash of one white hand before she felt a light tug on her jacket. The movement was so quick, there was hardly time to be startled before she realized that the detective had just robbed her pocket of the ice pick.

'Brill was so worried about you,' said Mallory. 'And he even knows how good you are at taking down violent criminals.' She glanced back over one shoulder, perhaps wanting the assurance they were alone – without witnesses. 'Incidentally, that man had a gun, but it was still holstered behind his back.' The detective held up a small camera. 'This is what he had in his hand. So it's lucky I interrupted you before you killed *another* unarmed citizen.'

Lucky indeed. Nedda jammed both hands into her pockets, not wanting this young woman to see her tremble so.

The detective was looking down at the ice pick resting on the flat of one palm, then the camera in her other hand. She seemed to be weighing one thing against another. 'I don't know who to charge tonight. It's a real crap-shoot.'

'If you don't mind a suggestion?'

'Go for it.'

Nedda looked to the shadows where the police and their prisoner had disappeared. 'It might be better if you charge *him* – since you cracked his skull.'

'Good point.' Mallory held up the camera. 'You run pretty fast, Miss Winter. Yes, we were watching you from the woods. Nice sprint.' She held up the camera. 'Three more shots left on the roll.' She pointed through the trees toward a path that was well lit. 'I want you to run that way – fast as you can.'

When Nedda hesitated, Mallory said, 'Do it. Now!'

And Nedda ran. She stumbled the first time she heard the click behind her. She had been shot with the camera. She looked back over one shoulder to the startling sight of Mallory running behind her and shooting her again.

'That's good! Now stop!'

Nedda halted on command – like a pet – and turned around to see the detective removing a roll of film from the camera.

'If anyone should ask,' said Mallory, 'my prisoner took those last three pictures.'

'You're asking me to falsify—'

'You've got a problem with *that*? Would you rather visit the local station house and explain what you were doing in the woods with a concealed weapon?' Mallory rested one hand on her hip. It was a gesture of total disbelief. 'I see you at the window every night. Always looking out at the park. You're holding out on me. That man – you were waiting for him to show up. Am I right?' Mallory held up the ice pick. 'You want to talk about this now? No? Then meet me downtown in six hours.'

'What do you want me to do? Make a statement or—'

'You didn't get my message? You agreed to take a polygraph exam, Miss Winter. I set it up for this morning. Were you planning to back out?'

'No, I'll be there.'

The detectives rode in the back of the patrol car with their unconscious prisoner propped up between them. Mallory was going through the man's wallet.

'This is trouble,' she said, holding up a private investigator's license issued in the state of Maine.

'So now we know he's got a permit for the gun,' said Riker. 'Damn. Too bad you didn't shoot him, kid. Fat chance we can keep Nedda out of the papers now.' He rolled back one of the prisoner's eyelids and waved his hand back and forth between the man's eyes and the car's dome light. 'The pupils don't react. I think you might've caught a lucky break. He's not gonna wake up anytime soon. Maybe never.'

'*Okay*, you *win*!' Annoyed, Mallory leaned toward the driver. 'Cancel the SoHo station. Aim this car at the nearest hospital.'

The prisoner transport swerved off Seventh Avenue and rolled into the emergency entrance for Saint Vincent's Hospital in Greenwich Village.

Riker, sarcastic alarmist, gave her no credit for knowing how to pull her shots. She had not hit the man all that hard, and he would certainly live. Also, and this was a bonus, a prolonged awakening worked in her favor. She could have the photographs developed before the man regained consciousness.

Nedda parted company with Officer Brill on the stairs outside her front door. She entered the house by herself despite his kind offer to come inside with her. After crossing the room in the dark, aided by memory alone, her hand closed on the banister, and she made the long climb to the second-floor landing with time enough for deep regret to settle in.

Why had she ever gone into the park?

The man with the camera was most likely a reporter, and now irreparable damage had been done. Cleo and Lionel would have to bear the consequence of her little walk in the woods tonight. Very soon, perhaps in the early morning hours, they would be accosted by microphones shoved in their faces, cameras and questions to fend off.

Gone was every hope for reconciliation.

She entered her room and switched on the bedside lamp, then examined the disarray of her clothing. Her leather jacket was scored with the scratches of tree branches, her slacks were ripped open in places, and dirt caked both her shoes. She turned to the only mirror in the room.

What a fright.

Strands of hair had escaped the braid in wild profusion. A branch had sliced into her neck and broken the skin. She touched the wound and her hand came away with drops of blood on it. She removed her jacket, then jumped when the ice pick fell to the floor. Mallory must have covertly slipped it back into her pocket, but why would an officer of the law do such a thing?

Behind her, there was a sudden intake of breath. Realizing that she was no longer alone in this room, she whirled around to see her small niece standing in the open doorway, all eyes and staring at the weapon on the floor – the blood on Nedda's fingers.

'Oh, God,' said Bitty, 'what have you done?'

The elder woman started at these words – echoes – of Uncle James, her first accuser. Bitty was back-stepping into the hall, and Nedda bowed her head, so sorry, so utterly destroyed.

SIX

Riker's back was broken after five hours of bad dreams on a lumpy couch in the hospital lounge.

A voice close to his ear said, 'I know you're awake.'

Mallory sounded so damned alert, but she was young; she could string three days together with catnaps and never miss the sleep. Well, he might be awake, but she could not force him to open his eyes.

'I talked to the state cops in Maine,' she said. 'They went out to Susan McReedy's place.'

Riker rolled over and away from her, burrowing into the upholstery.

Mallory's voice was louder, more testy. 'McReedy's *gone*. The neighbors said she left town doing eighty miles an hour. She's on the run. I ran her credit cards. No charges. She's paying cash for her gas.'

Riker mumbled, 'Some people still use cash, Mallory.' Morning light was breaking through the slits of his sore eyes. 'Maybe the lady just needed a vacation.' Life in the boondocks of Maine might be more exciting and stressful than he had previously supposed. He rolled on his back, eyes all the way open now, and decided that – naw – Susan McReedy was on the run. 'Damn. So that private dick upstairs is all we got left.'

He was talking to the ceiling. His partner was crossing the lobby, forcing him to rise and lope after her.

* * *

Nedda faltered on the stairs as she made her way up to the south attic, where the trunks of the dead were kept – all but Baby Sally's. The light from the gabled windows was waning. The morning was turning dark and promising rain. She wandered the rows of stored effects until she found her mother's trunk and opened it. The lid was heavier today.

So tired.

Nedda dropped the opera glasses inside and closed the trunk softly, reverently. She moved on to the neat row of murdered parents and children. One by one, she dragged their trunks to an open space. The sky was rumbling over her head as she arranged them in a circle, and lightning flashed in every window when she sat down, tailor fashion, surrounded by all that remained of her dead.

This was the family.

Following a crack of thunder, rain streaked the glass panes. As Nedda cried, so did the house.

Nestled in her lap was the canvas sack of Baby Sally's rotted clothes. This child was never far from her thoughts, though she could only see her youngest sister as a newborn with hair of soft down – fingers and toes impossibly small. Nedda called up a memory of solemn children gathered in the kitchen. Old Tully the housekeeper had taken it upon herself to explain this impending death of their baby sister, and she had done it badly, telling them that they were all dying from the moment they were born. 'That's what life's about,' said Tully.

Not good enough.

The children, not one philosopher in the pack of them, had demanded a more concrete explanation. Obligingly, the housekeeper had gone out into the yard, captured a slug and returned with it, laying the slimy creature on the kitchen table. 'This is death,' she had said, holding up a heavy mallet used for tenderizing meat. The old woman had brought her weapon down upon the slug and smashed it

161

into a smear on the tabletop. 'There,' said Tully, 'it's gone to live with Jesus.'

Nedda held up a little dress that a four-year-old might wear.

Sally, my Sally.

A child-size wraith in a white nightgown hovered by the attic stairs. Only Bitty.

Nedda swiped her wet face with the back of one hand, then turned to her niece and braced herself for some new accusation. Bitty was lit by a flash of lightning. Her eyes rolled up toward the rafters, and she stiffened slightly, waiting for the thunderclap.

It never came.

'I'm sorry, Aunt Nedda – about last night. I got a call from Officer Brill this morning. He wanted to know if you were all right. He told me what happened in the park. After everything you'd been through, I made you feel like a criminal.'

'Don't give it any thought, dear. It was perfectly understandable.'

Bitty pulled a piece of paper from the pocket of her robe. 'You had an earlier call last night after supper. I didn't want to disturb you. I thought you might be sleeping.' She held out the piece of paper as she walked toward her aunt. 'It's a message from that detective,' said Bitty, 'the tall blonde one.'

BANG!

The thunder cracked overhead. Bitty jumped and her hands flew up like wings. The note wafted to the floor.

Nedda reached out to retrieve the fallen paper, already knowing its contents before she unfolded it. This was Detective Mallory's demand to appear at the police station this morning. She looked up to see that Bitty had recovered nicely from the inclement weather.

'Aunt Nedda?' Lightning returned to light up her face, her worried eyes. 'I've never practiced criminal law, but I know it's always a bad idea to take a polygraph. I don't think you should do it.'

'Don't worry, dear. I can deal with this.'

BANG!

* * *

When the patient regained consciousness, Mallory was the first thing he saw, and Riker felt sorry for Joshua Addison, a private investigator licensed in the state of Maine.

Mallory leaned over the hospital bed, both hands curling round the metal rail. Such long red fingernails. And Riker saw that old look on her face – hungry – as if she had not been fed for days and days.

Startled, the patient appeared to be playing dead with his eyes wide open. Riker watched the man's chest, fascinated and wondering how much longer Addison could hold his breath. The private investigator's survival instinct was slow to kick in, and when he finally sucked in air and tried to raise his arms in a protective reflex, he discovered that his right hand was manacled to the side rail. 'What the hell is this? What happened?'

'The way I remember it,' said Riker, 'you were making a move on a woman in the park – when you tripped and fell. Now you're going down on a pervert charge.'

'That's ridiculous,' said Addison. 'You can't—'

'You need a lawyer,' said Riker, thinking it best to bring up the subject first. The moment their suspect asked for counsel, the interview must end. 'Yeah, and make it a damn good lawyer. A pervert charge is—'

'What? You're crazy!'

'Addison, you were stalking an old woman. And maybe we should add an assault charge.' Mallory reached out to touch the bandage on the patient's forehead. Her long nails were dangerously close to the man's eyes and he flinched as she peeled the bandage back to expose a jagged cut. Though there was no doubt that the wound had come from the broken lightbulb in the basement of Winter House, Mallory said, 'We need a picture of this scratch. Looks like the old lady tried to fight him off.'

On cue, Riker pulled a disposable camera from his coat pocket and snapped a close-up photograph with a burst of light in Addison's eyes.

'You're both nuts!' Half blinded by the flash, the private investigator squinted at his accusers. 'I never *touched* that woman.'

Mallory laid three photographs on the bedsheet. Riker knew that these pictures had been taken by his partner, though she had given him the gift of deniability by lying to him. Unlike all the other shots from Addison's roll of film, these three had Mallory's center fixation. Nedda Winter's head was in the precise center of each frame, as if she had been shot through a gun sight. In the first one, the camera was facing the startled woman. In the next one, she was running away. The third shot, a personal favorite, had Nedda, still on the run, looking back over one shoulder – a documented chase.

'We have a lock on this case,' said Mallory. 'These shots came from *your* camera.' She laid the private investigator's license on his pillow. 'And you can kiss this goodbye. We've got you cold for breaking into that woman's house.' She pulled out an evidence bag with Officer Brill's signature. It contained fragments of glass. 'This came from a broken lightbulb in her basement. It's your blood type, O negative.'

'Ordering a DNA test would be overkill.' Riker smiled. 'Real jail time, pal.'

'An old woman like that,' said Mallory – as if she had ever been sentimental about old ladies. 'You *freak*.'

'I was working a case.'

'We don't think so,' said Riker, more affably. 'We like the pervert charge.'

'I was working for a client, and I can prove it,' said Joshua Addison.

Riker was loving this. Normally it was like pulling teeth to get a client name from a private investigator. 'Who've you got lined up? Your mother?' He looked up at his partner. 'Let's book him. I'm tired. I wanna go home.'

'That old woman,' said Addison, 'I think she's Red Winter.'

Riker feigned mild surprise. 'You're planning an insanity defense?'

He turned to Mallory in the guise of a translator. 'Red Winter was a little girl, a kidnap victim. She disappeared maybe thirty years before you were even born.' He looked down at the man on the bed. 'And, last I heard, she's *still* lost.'

'No,' said Addison. 'Her house is across the street from the park. She's back.'

'You're kidding,' said Mallory. 'That's your story? You were waiting for her to come home?'

'You know,' said Riker, leaning on the bedrail as he opined, 'this job is definitely losing its edge. The perverts get dumber every year.'

'I was hired by Bitty Smyth,' said Addison. 'At the time, I didn't know she was Red Winter's niece. I had to do some checking. But now I—'

'Yeah, right,' said Mallory. 'The niece hired you to stalk her aunt.'

'No, she hired me to *find* her aunt.'

'This is too confusing,' said Riker. 'The lady wasn't lost in the park. She just went out for a walk.'

'*Listen* to me!' Frustrated, Addison raised himself up on one arm. 'She was lost for fifty-eight freaking years!' He searched one detective's face and then the other's, only finding signs of disbelief. 'She's Red Winter. And I wasn't planning to hurt her last night. I just wanted a photograph, some proof that it was the same woman I found in the nursing home. It was the Bangor Rest Home in Maine. She looks so different now. Six months ago, she was all bloated and yellow. But her eyes – those eyes.'

Riker pulled a small notebook from his coat, then fished the rest of his pockets until he found his pen. 'So let me get this straight. You wanted to pass this woman off as Red Winter, and you needed a picture.' He jotted down a few words. 'A photograph you could sell to the tabloids?' Riker looked up from his notebook. 'You're telling us you're a con artist?' He shrugged. 'Okay with me, pal. We'll add that to the charges.'

Riker and Mallory moved away from the bedside, as if they could not leave this man fast enough.

'Hey, wait a minute,' said Addison. 'Wait!'

They did not.

Bitty Smyth hung up the receiver on the kitchen wall phone, then faced her aunt with a smile. 'The arrangements are done. I talked to Detective Mallory's superior, a very nice man – Lieutenant Coffey. It took a bit of negotiating, but I got everything I asked for.'

'How handy to have a lawyer around the house.' Nedda spooned scrambled eggs from a pan onto oven-heated plates. Behind her on the stove, bacon sizzled and hot water bubbled in the kettle. 'You should go back to your father's firm.' And perhaps that would assuage her guilt over Bitty's long sabbatical, all that time lost to the search for a long-lost child.

Her niece shrugged off this suggestion. 'I lined up an independent polygraph examiner. Lieutenant Coffey said I wouldn't be allowed to stay in the room during the examination, but I think I can get him to change his mind.' Bitty sat down at the table and took up her fork, waving it in the air as a baton. 'Good timing is very important in every negotiation. We'll make a stand right before they—'

'No, Bitty. It's better if I do this alone.' Nedda picked up the teakettle before the whistle could startle her niece, then poured boiling water over the tea bags in their cups. 'And then, this afternoon we might visit some real estate brokers.' She sat down at the table and picked up a newspaper opened to listings for co-ops and condominiums. Several advertisements had been circled in blue ink. 'I'm going to find a place of my own in some other part of town. I think Cleo and Lionel would like that.'

'But this is *your* house. No, Aunt Nedda. It's all my fault. I'm the one who upset you. First that scene at the dinner party – and then last night. I'm so sorry. You can't leave. You *love* this house.'

Yes, she did. But the house did not love anyone – not anymore.

The house was sad and crazy and sick to death of love.

'It has nothing to do with you, Bitty.' Nedda reached out to cover her niece's small hand with her own. 'You can come with me if you like. Call it a stepping stone to a place of your own. You can't live with your mother forever, can you?'

The expression on Bitty's face was one of instant sorrow, and Nedda realized that she had trod upon one of her niece's many closet secrets. Though others seemed to underestimate this little woman's complexity, Nedda never did. Sometimes even a simple conversation was like navigating a labyrinth with wrong turns aplenty. She had learned to avoid every path of discourse that led to pain, and now she folded the newspaper into her lap and out of Bitty's sight.

The detectives had finished a leisurely breakfast in the hospital cafeteria, and now they were tying up a critical loose end: how to explain away Mallory's behavior last night, the pistol whipping in Central Park.

They stood in the dark of a small room in company with a hospital physician, who flicked on a light to illuminate Joshua Addison's X-rays. The doctor pointed to a fault line, saying, 'Definitely a concussion. That's why he can't tell you what happened right before he lost consciousness. Judging by the wound, it looks to me like somebody hit him very hard with a——'

'A rock?' asked Mallory, raising a plastic bag with said rock neatly pocked with red. 'Like this one? We found it underneath his head.' She smiled so hopefully, as if she cared about this man's opinion. 'Or do you think he might've fallen and hit his head on the rock?'

'Yes, that would do it,' said the doctor, who was young, who had no experience in forensics – who had never met Mallory before. 'Yes, an accident.'

Riker had to wonder how she made her prop so realistic. He stared at the red fluid that spotted this rock taken from a construction site across the street. It *looked* like real blood. He could well imagine her smashing it down on the nearest living creature that came to hand – so many small dogs in this neighborhood – but he hoped it was catsup from the hospital canteen.

Mallory glanced at the clock on the wall, a signal that they had killed enough time. They rode the elevator up to Joshua Addison's floor for a final word with the private investigator. When they entered the room, the man in the bed had a worried look about him.

'Your story doesn't check out,' said Riker. 'We called that nursing home in Maine. According to their records, this woman's the wrong age.'

This was actually true. The sketchy records had overestimated Nedda Winter's age by eight years.

'And one more thing,' said Mallory. 'Your name is on the nursing home's discharge papers. They've got you listed as her next of kin. And they've never heard of Bitty Smyth.'

'Yeah,' said Riker, 'explain that one. Are you trying to con the Winter family out of some money?'

'Hell, no. The niece asked me to make the arrangements to move her aunt to a hospice in New York State. She wanted it done quietly.'

Mallory shook the bedrail to get the man's attention. 'Did the niece try to cut you out of the deal? Is that why you were stalking that old woman in the park?'

Addison could barely get out the word 'No'.

'We're just going by your own statement, pal,' said Riker. 'It looks like a scam to us.'

'Then it's the niece, Bitty Smyth. It's her scam. All I did was find—'

'Oh, yeah, I forgot,' said Riker. 'You did what thirty thousand cops couldn't do. *You* found Red Winter.'

'Just one snag,' said Mallory. 'It's not her.'

Riker tossed a yellow pad on the bed. 'Make out a complete statement. If we don't find any more lies, we'll sit on the paperwork for a few days. But if we find out that you passed this woman off as a member of the Winter family, then all the charges are solid, including fraud. And, pal, we read the newspapers – all of 'em.'

And that should neatly kill any idea of selling Nedda Winter to the tabloids. To further the impression that the detectives were bored with the improbable story of Red Winter's return, Riker stretched out on the bed beside Addison's. Before the private investigator had filled out half the sheet, Riker was snoring convincingly and sleeping soundly.

Half an hour passed before Mallory woke her partner, handing over the yellow sheets, one by one, as fast as she could read them. The handwritten lines of the statement were filled with every detail of the search for an old woman in the state of Maine. Joshua Addison had done hundreds of interviews looking for someone who would fit Bitty Smyth's specific list of characteristics. For two years, the man had covered the entire state of Maine.

Well, now they knew that Bitty had not been leaving town on religious missions. She had been visiting nursing homes up north. But how had the woman known that her aunt was hiding out in the state of Maine?

Mallory carried a clipboard into the interview room and walked to one end of the long table. She was ignoring the surprised polygraph examiner as she made a show of consulting her watch and writing down the time.

Nedda Winter was wired into the machine by rubber tubing around her chest and abdomen to measure her breathing, a padded cardio cuff on her arm to keep track of her blood pressure, and metal fingertips to catch her in the act of sweating.

The polygraph examiner cleared his throat – twice – but failed to get Mallory's attention. 'Excuse me, Detective,' he said, hardly disguising his annoyance, 'I work *alone*. If you have any questions, I suggest you write them down. Then I can ask them during the—'

'I'm not here to question Miss Winter,' said Mallory. 'I'm here to evaluate *you*.' She glanced at the civilian's polygraph equipment with a moue of distaste. 'How far out of date is that machine of yours?'

The examiner only stared at her, casting about for some comeback.

'Obviously,' said Mallory, making a note on her clipboard, 'you don't know how old your equipment is. I'm guessing at least ten years.' She leaned down toward Nedda, showing the woman no more regard than furniture when she examined the padded arm cuff. The detective made another note on her clipboard, speaking the words aloud as her pen moved across the paper, 'Still using cardio cuffs for blood-pressure readings.' She turned back to the examiner. 'We gave you a chair with stress plates. Why aren't you hooked in?' She tapped her pencil on the notebook, waiting on an answer, then examined the back of his machine where the wires connected. 'Never mind.' She made more notes, saying as she wrote, 'Out-moded machine. No connections for stress plates.'

She removed her blazer and draped it over a chair, a clear signal that she planned to stay awhile. And now her gun was exposed in the shoulder holster, breaking all the rules of interviews and civilian etiquette. All the power and authority was weighted to her side of the room. She leaned against the back wall, just visible to the examiner's peripheral vision and in full view of Nedda Winter. 'You can start now.'

If any arguments had occurred to the examiner, he swallowed them. Reaching into his briefcase, he pulled out a deck of playing cards. Mallory rolled her eyes. And Nedda Winter smiled, vaguely amused by the show.

On the dark side of the mirror in a small theater of chairs tiered in rows, two men sat up front near the one-way glass. They were observing Mallory's humiliation of the independent polygraph examiner.

Charles turned to Riker. 'What was all that about?'

'Mallory wants him out of the way so she can do the exam herself.

Poor little guy. He's toast.' Riker reached over to a panel on the wall and turned off the volume. 'Fun's over. I've seen this next part a hundred times. Most of these idiots went to the same school for the ten-week course.'

The polygraph examiner leaned toward Nedda Winter and appeared to be speaking in a friendly fashion. In the absence of sound, Riker translated. 'Right now he's telling Nedda that he wants to put her at ease. That's a lie. His whole job is to jack up her anxiety. If he can't do that – if she's not afraid of his machine – he won't get any responses worth measuring.'

'If Mallory keeps smirking at everything he says, it's hardly—'

'He won't last another five minutes. Now he's telling Nedda what all the tools do, what they measure. She doesn't seem too impressed. That's because she's taking all her cues from Mallory.'

The examiner laid four playing cards facedown on the table. Nedda selected one, lifting up a corner to see which card it was. The machine was turned on, and the man stared at the rolling paper as he spoke again, watching wavy lines and hard-edged spikes, jotting down small notes on the paper as it rolled by at the rate of six inches a minute.

'This is the getting-to-know-you stage,' said Riker. 'He told her to give him a negative response every time he tries to guess her card – even if he guesses right. He's telling her he needs to gauge her physical responses when he guesses the right card and she lies to him. That's bull. If he didn't know which response was a lie, the polygraph wouldn't help.'

'So he memorized the order of the cards,' said Charles. 'He already knows which one she picked. Well then, what's the point of this exercise? If she's following his instructions, then there's no attempt at deception.'

'It's a lot like voodoo. Nedda has to believe in the polygraph. When he guesses her card, that's supposed to convince her that the machine can read her mind. But see? She's not buying it. This test is only as good as the examiner, and Mallory made him look like a moron.'

'So it's true what they say,' said Charles, and by *they* he meant the Supreme Court of the United States. 'A polygraph has the same chance of detecting a lie as the flip of a coin.'

'Right, but that's not why we use it. When a cop does this test, it's a full-blown interrogation without a lawyer. Sweet, huh?'

'But this examiner isn't—'

'No, he's an independent. That was the deal we did with Bitty Smyth. We picked the time and place – she picked the examiner. This guy's only experience is interviewing applicants for low-level jobs.' Riker leaned back and closed his eyes, saying, 'Let me know when Mallory takes over. I'll turn on the volume again.'

While Riker slept, Charles watched the tableau in front of him. The lame card trick was set aside, and they were moving on to other questions. After each response, the examiner made notations on the rolling paper. Mallory was drumming her nails on the clipboard, regarding the man as a bug. Nedda always glanced at the detective before answering a question. And now Charles intuited Mallory's stance as a prelude to a lunge. He nudged Riker to wake him. 'She's almost ready.'

Riker's eyes opened. 'Good. Time to rock 'n' roll.' He turned on the volume.

The examiner asked his next question. 'Did you ever kill anyone?'

'You know I did,' said Nedda Winter. 'I already signed a statement to that effect.'

'Once again, if you could confine your responses to *yes* or *no*.'

'Yes,' said Nedda.

Mallory stood behind the examiner, watching over his shoulder as the paper scrolled across the top of his machine. 'You're botching it.' She ripped the paper out. The man half rose in protest. She glared at him. 'Sit down.'

And he did.

The detective made her own notations, matching up the responses with respiration and heartbeats, then tapped the different spikes on the chart each time she said, 'Inconclusive, inconclusive, inconclusive.' She turned on the examiner. 'You don't know what you're doing.'

Riker turned the volume off again. 'That might be the last true thing you hear from that room.' He looked back to the glass as Mallory slapped the top of the polygraph machine. 'She's telling him his equipment is crap.'

'I think I guessed that,' said Charles.

The examiner's mouth had stopped flapping. He could only gawk at the detective in disbelief.

'Fortunately,' said Riker, 'she just happens to have a brand-new, state-of-the-art polygraph parked right outside the door. Our machine doesn't work any better, but it has more bells and whistles. So Mallory won the pissing contest. The guy's out of the game, and he knows it. There's no way to make a recovery now that Nedda thinks he's a clown. But don't feel sorry for him, Charles. He's young. He can still find honest work.'

Mallory carried a heavy suitcase into the room and placed it on the table. She undid the snaps and opened it with a sideways glance at the civilian examiner, saying, 'Now *this* is a lie detector.' She held up a large clip of plastic and metal trailing a wire. 'And this is a transducer.' She attached it to Nedda's thumb, treating the woman as an inanimate part of her show-and-tell exhibit. 'This is what we use for cardio readings in the twenty-first century.' The detective proceeded to strip Nedda of all the paraphernalia that belonged to the independent examiner, then neatly packed it away in the man's suitcase.

She spoke to Nedda for the first time. 'We can put this off for another day or get it over with now. Up to you.'

'I'm ready.'

When Mallory turned around again to face the examiner, she feigned surprise to see him. 'Still here?'

The man slunk out of the room, lacking the energy to entirely close the door behind him. Mallory slammed it shut. Her voice was icy when she turned to the woman seated in the chair and said, *commanded*, 'Take off your shoes.'

Charles turned to Riker. 'Her *shoes?*'

'Yeah.' The detective shrugged as he slouched lower in his chair. 'Some perps use countermeasures like a tack in the shoe. It jacks up the response to a control question. Any question that raises a real sweat looks kind of pale by comparison.'

'So the response to a small anxiety disguises the larger one.'

'Now you got it.' The detective was watching the other room as Nedda, following another order, dragged her chair across the floor. Barefoot and wired to the machine, she sat down with her back to the wall. 'That chair is set up with a stress plate to catch muscle tension. That's another trick the perps use to beat the box.'

'But I'm guessing that you're not actually worried about Nedda using countermeasures.'

'No.'

'In fact, Mallory's not even certified for this sort of thing, is she?'

'Charles, it doesn't matter. No polygraph exam is admissible in court. But now we get to ask questions that no lawyer would ever let her answer.'

'I can't believe that Bitty Smyth would allow her to take this exam.'

'Bitty's a contract attorney. Never handled a criminal case.'

Charles watched Mallory fasten restraints to the older woman's legs. 'I think I can guess what that's for. She's pinned now, helpless.' He turned to Riker in the dark. 'You know this isn't right.'

'I know, but it's what we do.'

* * *

Nedda Winter stared at the wires that made her seem part machine. 'Bitty arranged for the independent examiner. Maybe I should talk to her before—'

'Good idea.' Mallory stood before her suspect. 'But I need answers today. Your niece is downstairs. If you don't feel up to this, I can strap her in instead. I'm sure she'll be happy to take your place if this is too stressful.'

Yeah, right.

No lawyer ever born would consent to a polygraph examination, but Nedda was nodding her head, wanting to spare Bitty Smyth any – unpleasantness. Barefoot and pinned by rubber tubes and wires, restraints on both her arms and legs, the old woman would not be able to imagine her timid niece in that chair.

Mallory sat down at the table before the equipment. She gave a cursory glance at the sheet of paper she had torn from the civilian's machine. 'You've got too many mixed responses here. We have to start over. If you like, we can wait a few hours while we find an independent who knows what he's doing. Or would you rather get this over with?'

'I said I'd take the test, but I don't—'

'Fine.' Mallory reached into the back pocket of her jeans and pulled out the deck of cards she had stolen from the civilian examiner. 'Let's try another trick. That fool only used four cards.' She shuffled the deck as she spoke. 'Let's try it with fifty-two possibilities. Pull out a card, any card.' Fanning the cards, Mallory held them just far enough away to make the older woman strain to reach one. Nedda had no sooner taken her selection from the deck, when Mallory said, 'Seven of hearts.'

Nedda nodded, surprised.

'I palmed the only cards you could reach, and I memorized their order.'

Riker leaned far forward in his chair, caught between surprise and confusion.

175

'You heard right,' said Charles. 'She just told the truth.' And he understood why. Nedda must believe in Mallory. Hang the damned machine.

'The examiner your niece picked out was a useless cheat,' said Mallory, setting the deck on the table. 'Bad card tricks are a hack's game. He wanted you to believe that he could read your mind. Now me? I don't care *what* you believe.' She pointed to the waving lines at the top of the machine. 'If you hold your breath, I'll know.' One long red fingernail moved down through the other lines. 'If your heart beats a little faster, I'll know. When you break a sweat, I'll see it on the machine before it shows up on your face.' She held up the sheet she had torn from the examiner's machine. 'His last question was inconclusive, so we'll try it again.' She wadded the paper into a ball and threw it across the room. Nedda Winter flinched, perhaps believing that it was aimed at her.

A good start.

Turning on the machine, Mallory said, 'Now, let's go for a ride.' She picked up her pencil and watched the scrolling lines, asking, 'Did you ever kill anyone? *Yes* or *no*.'

'Yes.'

Mallory consulted the spikes on the scrolling paper, making notes here and there. 'You were very calm the night we came to your house, but now your heart is beating way too fast. Is the burglar the only man you ever killed?'

Nedda's voice was not much above a whisper, asking, 'What does this have to do with the—'

'*Yes*, or *no*. If I knew your total body count, would I be impressed?'

Charles sank low in his chair. 'I think I prefer the dark old days of thumbscrews and the rack. Does Mallory understand that she's reading signs of stress – not guilt? Just being in the same room with her is enough to—'

'She knows,' said Riker. 'With a little preparation, a brain-dead Girl Scout can beat the box. But you can tell the truth and still fail the exam.'

'So it's totally useless. Why would—'

'Nedda's our only lead. We sent the Maine cops to Susan McReedy's house to ask a few questions and check out her story. Seems the lady disappeared. Nedda's all we got left.' This was not entirely true. The last resort would be Bitty Smyth, who would lawyer up immediately. And then they would lose their leverage over the woman on the other side of the glass.

'I know you like Nedda Winter,' said Charles. 'Why can't you do the interrogation instead of Mallory?'

'No,' said Riker, 'I could never do what she's gonna do.'

Mallory turned off the machine. 'This looks bad for you. I can't help you if you hold out on me. So we have to clarify your response. Right now, all I know for sure is that the burglar wasn't your first kill.'

The detective leaned far back in her chair. No need to consult the machine – Nedda Winter's face said it all. The woman had just been assaulted with no bruising, no blood loss. All the pain was in her eyes, the mouth half open, hands clenching.

'So let's clear up that previous death. Suppose you had an accident, ran somebody down in a car. That would explain the readings I see on this machine. Give me the circumstances, and then I can eliminate the last question.'

Nedda was flailing, arms raising, wires dangling from her body parts. She looked at her right hand, mechanized now, and she was horrified.

'All right.' Mallory turned the machine on. 'Let's take an easy question, a throwaway. The other night at the dinner party, I understand your niece gave you an old pack of tarot cards. She said they were yours. Was that true?'

'You've been talking to Charles Butler.' Nedda turned to the mirror. 'Is he there now? Bitty said she'd picked him for the neutral observer.'

Charles turned to Riker. 'When were you going to tell me that?'

'Never. No reason to. If Bitty hadn't made you a condition of the test, Mallory would've asked you to come. The key word here is *neutral*. You're Switzerland, Charles.'

'The hell I am.'

'Next question,' said Mallory, 'another easy one. Have you been reading tarot cards for a long time?'

'Yes. Wait.' Nedda Winter erased her answer, wiping the air with both hands. 'I mean . . . no. That was so long ago. I was a child the last time I saw that deck.'

'A child? Was this before the massacre?'

Nedda looked up in dumb surprise. Her mouth opened to speak, but she had no words.

'Did you get your tarot deck before the Winter House Massacre? *Yes*, or *no*.' Mallory drummed her nails on the table. 'What's the problem, Miss Winter? Too many murders? I'm talking about *one* massacre, your father, your stepmother, five small children, the nanny and the housekeeper – *nine* people. Did you get that tarot deck before they—'

'No!' Nedda lowered her voice to a whisper. 'No.'

Mallory switched off the machine. 'All right. You didn't hold out on that one, but now I've got another problem.' She waited a beat, then asked, 'Why did you come home again?'

The woman looked down at her hands, her head slowly moving from side to side.

The machine was switched on again. 'Are you telling me it wasn't your idea?' She glanced at the readings, though she had no need of them since she already knew the answer. 'That's it, isn't it? Someone else brought you home. Was it Lionel Winter?' Mallory made a note below a spiking line. 'No, not him. Was it Cleo Winter-Smyth? No. I'm getting odd responses here, Nedda. Your brother and sister – they didn't welcome you back, did they?' The spikes on the scrolling paper were climbing. 'Not a very warm reception?'

Nedda shook her head. No, it was not.

And now Mallory leaned far forward. 'Was it your niece? Did Bitty Smyth bring you home?' The detective's head dropped closer to the machine as she made the next notation. 'Yes, it *was* Bitty.' Mallory looked up. 'And where did she find you?'

'In a hospice. No, wait. I'm sorry. The nursing home – I think. I wasn't very clearheaded then. I was moved into a nursing home after a diagnosis of end-stage cancer. The hospice was the last place. I was taken there to die.'

'But you weren't dying, and you knew it – even if your doctors didn't. Nobody comes back from the end stage. So, before the nursing home, you were in a hospital?'

Nedda nodded her head.

'But not a regular hospital, not a place where they would've cut you open to look for a malignancy. No expensive tests. Maybe a state asylum with a clinic? Nothing else fits, Nedda. A real hospital would've gone looking for that cancer. Did you *want* to die? Was that it? An asylum is junkie heaven – all those drugs. Did you steal medication from other patients? Is that why you had yellow skin and odd results in your blood work?'

Nedda nodded.

'How did Bitty Smyth know where to find you?'

Nedda looked up, genuinely curious, as if she had never considered this problem before. 'A private investigator, I think.'

'No,' said Mallory. 'That doesn't work for me. It's a country of three hundred million people, six million square miles.' The detective unfolded a dust jacket from one of the pulp books written about the murders at Winter House. It was illustrated with the *Red Winter* painting. 'Do you see any resemblance between you and this little girl? No, even old family photographs wouldn't have helped to find you. Don't you wonder what Bitty's hiding? Why would your niece zero in on the state of Maine? She was working with insider information, knowledge she could only get from her family. You know what this means? Your sister and your brother always knew where you were.'

Nedda moved her head from side to side.

'And they let you rot,' said Mallory. 'Do they hate you that much? They never wanted you back. Why? Do they believe that you slaughtered their family – parents, sisters, brothers? Do they want you dead?'

The old woman's head tilted at an odd angle and her eyes were suddenly vacant, as if the detective had just turned her off with the same switch used to shut down the machine.

'Tell you what,' said Mallory, rising from the table, 'you think about it for a while.' She ripped her long tract of paper free of the polygraph. 'I have to review my readings. Maybe you'll feel better when I get back.'

Riker was quick to disillusion Charles of the idea that Mallory was showing the woman any kindness. 'Welcome to hell.'

'You have to stop this. She's poisoning that poor woman against her whole family.'

'Can't. It's a big mistake to get between Mallory and a case. And we're so close, Charles.'

'Close to what?'

'The only good result from a polygraph exam is a confession.'

'Confession to a mass murder? I'll never believe that.'

Mallory stood in the doorway. 'Maybe the killer was breaking in an apprentice. Does that make it a little easier to believe?'

'A twelve-year-old girl?' Charles shook his head. 'I don't think so.'

'New York has a criminal class of children,' said Riker. 'Adults use them for robberies 'cause the kids are too young to do time. They make the perfect little perps, and sometimes they carry lethal weapons.'

'And sometimes they kill people,' said Mallory. 'Now take that dead man on Nedda's rug the other night.' The detective was watching the glass window on the other room. 'She killed that man in the dark. No hesitation marks. She just did him without even thinking about it. I say she's had some practice.'

'She was protecting herself and Bitty.'

'And then,' said Riker, 'there's history – the one you won't find in Pinwitty's book. There were three generations of hitmen with the same signature as the Winter House Massacre – so they had apprentices.'

'And,' said Mallory, 'the apprentices killed the masters. The ice-pick murders stopped when Nedda was a little girl, when she killed Humboldt.'

Charles's attention was riveted to Nedda, and she was looking his way by chance. Was she searching the mirror side, seeking him in the looking glass, wanting an ally, needing a friend? 'You can't go on with this. I know what you're doing. You're cutting this woman's legs out from under her. After you strip her of family support, the only one she'll be able to turn to is you.'

'She's safer with me than her relatives,' said Mallory. 'The one crime nobody expects me to care about is the death of Willy Roy Boyd. He was a piece of scum, but he was *my* piece of scum, and that's the case I'm working here. Somebody hired him to kill a woman that night – probably Nedda. She's key to everything. So I torture her a little and she lives . . . or I can let her go and watch her die. Pick one.'

'Find another way,' said Charles. 'This has to stop right now. You can see how fragile she is.' And badly wounded. Indeed, Nedda had just been flayed to the bone of psyche.

Mallory returned to the interview room, but not to end the

interrogation. She started up the machine again, and Nedda lifted her head, slowly, sadly, to face her interrogator.

'Let's get back to the man you stabbed the other night.' Mallory turned the machine on again. 'Do you think your relatives hired that man to kill you?'

'No, of course not.'

'You don't think they're capable of murder?'

Nedda shook her head.

'Somebody hired him to kill you. Think about it, Nedda. Your brother and sister are always out of town when something happens. How many people knew you were back? And what happened to your baby sister? We can't find any school records for Sally Winter. You think she lived long enough to go to school?' Mallory looked down at the machine. 'Your heart is racing, Nedda.'

'Stop it!'

'Maybe they committed the perfect murder. That little girl was—'

'Detective Mallory, *please* stop.'

'Now, the attempt on *your* life – that was a total screwup. But what about your baby sister? What do you suppose they did with her body? Don't you care? We can't find any trace of her dead or alive.'

Nedda's hands rose to her head, warding off the words, her head making small jerking movements, hands rising like white fluttered wings, playing bird to Mallory's cat.

The detective pushed her chair back from the table. Her work was done. She could roughly predict the moment when Charles Butler would come barreling through the door. Oh, and here he was now. Such a gentleman, and so angry.

Mallory joined Riker in the observation room. They watched the ongoing show from the dark side of the glass. Charles removed all the mechanical devices that had bound Nedda Winter to the chair and the machine.

'She'll talk to Charles.'

'Yeah,' said Riker, 'but I'm not sure there's anything left for her to tell.'

Her partner had been against this idea of replacing the niece with a brand-new confidant for the old woman, but he had come up with no better plan.

Nedda preceded Charles as he quit the interview room, slamming the door behind him, loud as a gunshot. Mallory, his unintended target, tensed every muscle in her body. She turned to face Riker, but he looked away, not wanting to meet her eyes anymore. These small things, the slam of a door, the turn of Riker's head – they would remain with her for the rest of the day as a portent of things to come.

She was always losing people.

Edward Slope strolled up to the SoHo police station, and a uniformed officer rushed to open the door for him, though the younger man had no reason to recognize the chief medical examiner, a rare visitor in this precinct. Dr Slope's austere presence and excellent suit always commanded instant respect.

As he approached the front desk, he wore his eyeglasses riding low on the bridge of his nose, not caring that his vision was blurred. The doctor had finished a morning's *pro bono* work at the free clinic two blocks away, and he had seen quite enough for one day – homeless people dying of old age in their thirties and forties.

Impaired vision or not, he could never have missed the physically imposing figure of Charles Butler – no more than he could fail to notice a Kodiak bear in his shower stall. The man stood on the other side of the wide room, a head above the police officers gathered here and there in loose groups of twos and threes. Charles was deep in conversation with a tall white-haired woman and a child with pointed ears.

Well, *that* was interesting.

Dr Slope raised his spectacles the better to see the latter as a more mundane person, a very small woman with a pixie haircut and ears that were disappointingly normal.

Ah, and now he had attracted Charles Butler's attention. Dr Slope had never before seen this man angry. Charles had always impressed him as the most congenial of oversized humans, one who seemed embarrassed when he dwarfed other people. Well, this *was* a sight to behold, the wide-shouldered giant marching toward him with such grim resolution, hands curled into fists – and all the surrounding policemen seemed to agree. Their heads were turning, sensing trouble. So impressive was Charles that, all about the room, hands were lightly resting on guns.

SEVEN

When Riker followed his partner into Lieutenant Coffey's office, the chief medical examiner was waiting for them. The pathologist was not a happy man, and neither was their lieutenant.

Dr Slope fixed his eye on Mallory, reprimanding her with a cold stare, and Riker had to crack a smile. This was a reminder of her kiddy days when the doctor had suspected her of some new criminal act each time they met. Slope's worst grievance against her was cheating at poker on those nights when Lou Markowitz had been on midget duty and taken his foster child along to the weekly penny-ante game. By Lou Markowitz's account, his daughter had regularly cleaned out the doctor's pockets, and this had set the tone for Slope's relationship with Mallory down through the years.

'So, Kathy,' said the doctor, absolutely fearless in this forbidden use of her first name, 'what have you done to Charles Butler?' Predicting her trademark line, *I didn't do it*, he gave her no time to answer. 'I saw Charles downstairs a few minutes ago. He all but slammed me up against a wall and demanded a prescription for Valium. And so, of course . . . I thought of you.'

Mallory's only response was to fold her arms, shutting him out and making it clear that she was not going to play games with him today.

Slope's expression was more suspicious than usual, and he was puzzled, too, as if he knew he had caught her at something; though, as yet, the doctor could have no idea what her most recent wrongdoing might be. 'Nothing to say for yourself, Kathy?'

'Mallory,' she said, correcting him as she always did, and her eyes were promising payback for breaking this rule.

Did the doctor care? Not at all.

Slope handed an envelope to Riker. 'That's the report on your corpse. Are we still calling him a John Doe burglar?'

'Yeah,' said the senior detective. 'We can't afford any leaks to the media.'

'I can keep Willy Roy Boyd in paperwork limbo indefinitely,' said Slope. 'But it's just a matter of time before somebody recognizes the corpse as Mallory's lady-killer. I examined the wound to his heart. The sewing shears masked everything but the tip of another object, something sharper, narrower. It wouldn't be inconsistent with an ice pick.'

'And what about the comparisons?'

'To Stick Man?' The doctor took a bundle of yellowed papers from his medical bag. 'Here – your grandfather's notes. I must compliment him on that signature strike. Superb police work. I also read his summaries on the other autopsies. However, in this case, there was so much damage done by the scissors, there's no way to find any sign of it on Boyd's corpse. And nothing stood out in the old autopsy reports on the Winter House Massacre. Of course, with an exhumation, the absence of any chips to the bone would—'

'No way,' said Jack Coffey. 'I'm not spending money to dig up people who died back in the forties.' He looked up at his senior detective. 'I can't believe you expected a Stick Man signature on Mallory's perp.'

'I did,' said Riker, 'for about six minutes. But now I think Nedda was—'

'Nedda *Winter*?' Slope stared at Riker. 'That was the name Charles wanted on the Valium prescription.' The doctor turned to Mallory with a fresh accusation on his face, though he could not name it – not yet.

Riker wished he could call his words back. So little got by Edward Slope. He could tell that the doctor was putting it all together now:

the passage of time, a recent murder in Winter House, the old massacre investigation, an elderly woman he had met downstairs, someone with Mallory's interrogation footprints all over her face and the doctor's best guess at that woman's age – Red Winter's age.

'Oh, my God. You found her.'

Charles Butler's mood had improved, perhaps due to drugs. After filling the Valium prescription at the pharmacy, Nedda Winter had insisted upon sharing it with him, rightly suspecting that his morning had been nearly as bad as hers.

He had already begun the work of undoing Mallory's damage while collecting Nedda's belongings at Winter House, and now he had provided a safe refuge for the woman so that she could do further mending. And, in part, he supposed that Mallory's doomsday warning had spooked him. And Nedda, too? It had come as a surprise when she had accepted his offer of sanctuary so readily. He set her suitcase down inside the door of his guest room, and, upon turning around, noticed that his houseguest had been misplaced. He walked down the hallway calling out, 'Nedda?'

'In here,' she said.

He entered the library and found her seated in the circle of new club chairs. She seemed quite at home in this setting, but then, by her account, she had spent most of her life inside of books – a secondhand life she had called it.

'Is this where you do group therapy?'

'No,' he said, 'I've never had a patient practice. This is where I play poker.' Charles sat down beside her and stretched out his long legs. 'Now, in this big empty space, try to imagine a gaming table made in 1839.'

'Should I imagine the cards as well?'

'No, I'm not *that* far gone. I gave away my old card table so I'd have room for one I bought at an auction. The very next day, the antique table was destroyed in a warehouse fire.'

'An antique. You take your poker seriously.'

'And I always lose, but I love the game – and the company. When my friend Louis Markowitz died, I inherited his chair in a floating weekly poker game. Tonight will be the first time it's ever been canceled.'

'Because of me?'

'Oh, no. I wasn't the one who canceled the game.'

Nedda smiled. 'Well, not to waste these wonderful chairs – if you can't find the right table, you might open up a private practice. You're a natural. I'm something of an expert in therapists, and I say you've got the gift.' She looked around at the other chairs, which did indeed resemble a therapy group arrangement. 'This was my life for decades, one hospital after another and more doctors than I care to remember.'

'Could've fooled me,' he said. 'You don't strike me as someone who's been institutionalized. But then, I suppose it makes a difference that you were never insane.'

'As I said, you have the gift.'

And now he picked up the threads of their earlier conversation. 'So you believed that you could never go home again. But then you did.'

'Thanks to my niece. But now I think it would've been better if I'd never come back.'

'Well, a few criminal intrusions, a violent death – that's quite a bit of trauma. But that's not what you meant, is it?'

'No. You're a good listener, Charles. You can hear things between the words. I meant that it would've been better if my brother and sister never had to set eyes on me again. I'm the intruder at Winter House.'

In this unguarded moment, there was more sadness in her eyes than he could bear.

Empathy was his strength and his weakness; it was what suited him to a therapist's role and what prevented him from ever treating a patient. He would never be able to affect the professional detachment so key to the well-being of a therapist's own mind. He was already dying by degrees, imagining every shock that Nedda Winter had borne, the cost of every death – all the pain that she was feeling now and her terrible sense of isolation. And then he pulled back, emotionally and even physically. He rose from his chair and unconsciously rubbed his hands together, as if in the act of washing them clean of this woman. 'Well, what you need now is rest.'

This was what he also told himself – this lie. In reality, he had just shut her down and shut her out. He knew it, and she knew it.

Nedda was all alone again.

Mallory sat in the front room of Winter House, sipping coffee and becoming acquainted with Nedda's siblings. Riker had begged off on this interview, and she had only thought about his possible reasons in every other minute. And now she made her final judgment on her partner: he was losing the stomach for this case – and for her company.

'I don't understand,' said Cleo Winter-Smyth. 'Why should Nedda be staying at Charles Butler's house?'

'Was that your doing?' asked Lionel Winter.

'No.' Mallory put down the teacup. The time for good manners was fast passing. 'It was Dr Butler's idea. He didn't say why. Do you think he might have some reason to believe that Nedda wouldn't be safe in this house?'

Brother and sister looked to one another for answers.

And now that she had knocked them off balance, Mallory continued, addressing Cleo. 'Maybe it was something your daughter said to him? Is she here?'

'She's not at home,' said Lionel Winter.

Mallory understood his meaning. His niece was not at home to the police.

The detective pulled out a small notebook. 'A few questions came up in our investigation. You had a younger sister who survived the massacre.' She looked down at the notebook page. There was nothing written there. 'Sally? Was that her name? I understand that she ran away from home.'

Cleo wore a frozen smile. 'Oh, the dinner party. That's what set Charles Butler off – all those stories.' She spoke to Mallory, but would not look at her anymore. 'Lionel and I were away at school when Sally left.'

'Yes,' said the detective, 'you're always away when things happen in this house.' She studied more blank pages in her notebook, then faced Lionel. 'You fired Sally's nurse shortly before the girl ran away?'

He nodded.

Mallory waited for him to fill in the silence with nervous explanations, but soon realized that this was not going to happen. He was simply tolerating her presence in the house. She went for the soft spot, moving her chair closer to his sister. She leaned toward Cleo Winter-Smyth. 'But, ma'am, you said you weren't here. Are you *sure* that Sally ran away? Who was looking after her if the nurse—'

'Our guardian.' Lionel raised his voice. 'He was looking after Sally that day. And yes, we're quite sure that she ran away.'

While sister and brother were silently communing with one another, Mallory caught sight of Bitty Smyth's reflection in a mirror that angled toward the grand staircase. The tiny woman was gripping the banister and shaking her head. Mallory pressed on with Cleo and Lionel. 'So there must've been a report filed with Missing Persons. What year was that?'

Brother and sister were having identical reactions, and Mallory knew they were doing the math in their heads. This was the response of teenagers forced by a bartender to recall the date of a fictional birth on a fake driver's license.

So much pressure counting backward.

Cleo fielded this one. 'It was maybe fifty years ago.' She turned to her brother. 'Lionel?'

'Give or take a few years,' he said. 'Our guardian would have filed the report with the police.'

The detective appreciated guile. Prescient Lionel Winter had looked ahead to the next problem. When the police came back to tell him that no missing-person report had been found, then that bit of negligence could be blamed on a dead man, Uncle James.

Mallory added Sally Winter to the body count for Winter House. 'That clears up most of my loose ends.' She produced a yellow pad, the format for a murderer's confession on a typical day in Special Crimes Unit. 'If you could just write out the details and the dates in your own words. Then sign it – both of you.'

She waited out the minutes it took for Lionel's terse written account of Sally Winter's disappearance. Glancing at the mirror again, she caught sight of Bitty crouched below the banister rail on the second-floor landing – odd behavior for a lawyer. That little woman should be rushing down the stairs to caution her mother and her uncle against signing anything for the police.

Too late.

Lionel was done committing this small crime, the falsification of a police statement, and both signatures were on the page. Mallory read the carefully printed words. The faint erasure of numbers was barely visible in the margin. He had finally worked out a year that would match up with the dinner party conversation. 'There's something odd about this date. If Sally Winter ran away forty-eight years ago, she would've been just under ten years old. Now that's odd. Most runaways are teenagers. I've never—'

'Sally might've wandered off,' said Cleo. And she continued on in this classic mistake of explaining too much. 'Our uncle wasn't very good with children.' The woman looked down at her folded hands, and the tone of her voice was more wistful now. 'I had always hoped that some good Samaritan had found Sally – lost, maybe hurt. And maybe—'

Lionel Winter silenced his sister with one look.

'Right,' said Mallory, not bothering to disguise a tone of disbelief. However, Cleo's last words had the ring of something true. 'Well, I'll check it out with Missing Persons.'

The detective stood up and walked to the foot of the stairs, pretending to admire a large painting hanging high above her on the second-floor landing. Below it, Bitty Smyth was crouching behind the rail. Startled, the little woman slowly rose to a stand. Though there was an ocean of air between them, with Mallory's every step forward, Bitty stepped back. In this fashion, the smaller woman was driven to the wall. She edged slowly toward the door of an open room and disappeared. The door closed softly.

How much had the little eavesdropper learned over all the years of growing up in this house? Was this how Bitty knew where to look for Nedda, a woman who had disappeared long before she was born? What other conversations had she overheard this way?

Mallory turned her attention to another large oil painting, as if she had needed this closer inspection of the two young men posed there. Charles Butler had described this portrait of the Winter brothers as a cartoon. She turned to face the curious stares of Cleo and Lionel, and then walked back to them, killing their hopes of a quick end to this interview. 'Let's talk about the day of the massacre.'

Lionel was the first to recover from that little bomb. 'There's no possible relevance to—'

'I'll decide that. I don't have much to work with. I can put in a request for the file and the evidence boxes, but the more I dig, the more chance of a leak to the news media. You want the reporters to know that Red Winter came home?'

A suddenly alarmed Cleo reached out to her brother, stopping just short of physical contact. On some level, a silent conversation was going on between them, for now Lionel nodded in agreement with some unvoiced pact, and his sister lost that frightened look in her eyes.

'Of course,' said Lionel, addressing the detective, 'we'll do whatever we can to avoid publicity. When we were children, we couldn't go anywhere without reporters chasing us. Once, Cleo was nearly trampled in the street. After that, we were sent away to school, and all our summers were spent in the Hamptons. It was years before my sister could live in this house without nightmares.'

Good.

Mallory was satisfied that, under the threat of headlines, they would not be insulating themselves with a battery of lawyers. 'You survived the massacre, so I'm guessing you two weren't in the house that day.' She sat down again, crossing her legs, leaning back and making it clear that she had all day long to hurt them. 'As I said before, you're never home – when things happen here.'

Cleo stood up and crossed the room, heading for the stairs and moving in the manner of one who has lost her sight, hands gripping the furniture until she found the banister. She climbed the stairs as slowly as an invalid.

Mallory gripped the arms of her chair, as if preparing to pursue the woman, but this was only a threat of body language.

'Please let her go,' said Lionel. 'My sister was only five years old. She can't remember the details of that day.' He looked down at his folded hands. 'And I can't forget them. It was a pure accident that Cleo and I survived. We didn't plan to be gone that Sunday. I had a fight with my father and stormed out of the house. I'd only walked a few blocks before I realized that little Cleo was following me. She was crying. My father's temper always had that effect on her. I took her to the park for a Punch and Judy show. You know – the puppets? Then I hired a rowboat, and we drifted around the lake for another hour or so. Neither of us wanted to go home.'

'Were there any outsiders in the house when you left? I don't mean the nanny or the housekeeper.'

'I suppose it's possible. Sometimes we'd wake up and find strangers asleep on the couches, people who'd passed out at some party the night before. But I don't remember seeing anyone else in the house that day. Cleo and I were away for a few hours, two or three.'

'And Nedda? Where was she?'

'She left the house before we did. She went to a brunch with the Smyth family. Sheldon may remember that. He would've been twelve years old then. I saw Nedda leave in the Smyths' car late that morning, and I never saw her again. By the time Cleo and I came back to the house, it was all over. The baby was crying in the upstairs nursery. I remember that.'

He fell silent for a few moments, and Mallory waited him out.

'Cleo ran through the house, shaking all the bodies,' he said. 'She doesn't remember that – or she doesn't want to. She came back downstairs crying. She had the baby in her arms. Everyone was asleep, she said, and maybe sick like Mommy and Daddy. Then she tried to wake up our parents. I yelled at her, this tiny little girl. They're not asleep, I yelled. They're dead! And then, I just stood there. I couldn't move. It was Cleo who called the police that day. And then she rocked Sally in her arms until they arrived. The policemen couldn't get the baby away from her. I remember the officers taking them out the door. I can still see them. Little Cleo, a baby with a baby in her arms.'

'You thought Nedda killed them all, didn't you?'

This had no startling effect on him, but he did not answer her.

Mallory let herself out.

Though there were lots of chairs around the garden, Riker, a confirmed stoop-sitter, preferred his perch on the back steps of this mansion across the park from Winter House. The trees gave him shade from the sun of high noon. He reached into his deli bag and took out the last of his lunch, another cold bottle, and he handed it to Sheldon Smyth, who claimed to prize the detective's cheap brand of beer above all the costly wines in his cellar.

What bullshit.

Smyth was playing the quintessential gentleman and putting the common man, Riker, at ease. But the old fart did it so well. And now that the day had warmed a bit, the lawyer removed his jacket and tie, following his guest's example.

So far, Riker had learned that, despite Sheldon Smyth's profession and a pansy tolerance for beer, they had one thing in common. And now they played another round of I Hate Divorce Lawyers.

'I should've tried harder to get custody of Bitty.' Smyth slurred his words.

'Bet it cost you a bundle in child support and alimony.'

'The settlement was staggering.' Smyth upended the last bottle. 'Oh, dear,' he said, unable to extract another drop. The old man banged on the back door until a woman appeared in a maid's uniform. He stood up, none too steady on his feet, to pull a wallet from his pocket. Upon opening it, he stared at the money inside, as if currency were a mystery to him.

Riker smiled. This man had no idea what beer would cost.

Handing a wad of bills to his maid, Smyth sent her out for replacement bottles. The man was under the impression that he had drunk only half the beer in the exhausted carton, never suspecting the detective's great talent for nursing one drink indefinitely. They were on a first name basis now – Sheldon and Detective.

'Sounds pretty cold,' said Riker, 'the way your ex-wife treated your kid.'

'Bitty's adopted. I suppose that made a difference. But, at least my daughter didn't inherit any of the Winter genes. My father disowned me, you know, when I married into that family. Cut me off. No job, no money. I had to live at Winter House for a while.'

'What was your old man's problem with the Winters?'

'Oh, it dated back to Cleo's father, Quentin, and his brother, James. Very disreputable, both of them. Neither one was worth anything, financially or otherwise. They broke their trust fund after their parents died. Spent all the money, and so fast. This is my father's account, you understand. Winter House was in foreclosure when the younger brother, James, left town with a slew of debts. The older boy, Quentin, was a dilettante who fancied himself a great artist.'

The word *dilettante* had to be repeated twice: first because Riker could not understand the man's beer soaked speech, and the second time because it amused the detective to hear a lawyer stumble this way.

'Quentin solved the money problem by marrying a wealthy woman. That was Nedda's mother, Edwina.'

As the old man rambled on, Riker learned that Quentin Winter had been livid when he discovered the terms of his late wife's will. According to Sheldon's father, Edwina had changed her will once a month, following fights with her husband. In the last version, all the money had been tied up in trust for Nedda and her siblings. Edwina Winter had been pregnant with twins when she died – hence the sibling clause. Within a month of his first wife's death, Quentin Winter had married his favorite model, Alice, who was already pregnant with Lionel.

'No money,' said Smyth, 'but Alice was a very fertile girl. She produced eight siblings for Nedda. All those children ever meant to Quentin was an increase in his guardian allotments.'

'Bastard,' said Riker. 'So Cleo and Lionel take after their dad?'

'Oh, no, nothing like him. The two of them are money-making machines. They're worth millions, but you'd think they'd spent their childhood as starving orphans. Rather mean-spirited about money.'

'And that's why you give your daughter an allowance?'

'Yes. Bitty's not up to working just now, but Cleo and Lionel probably think she's malingering. Might've been more human if they'd inherited something of their father's spirit in spending. And they're not exactly warm people. Poor Bitty.'

'But you knew all the quirks when you married into that family, right?'

'And I didn't care. If you'd only seen Cleo when she was young – what a beauty. What put me off was the way she treated Bitty from the moment I brought that baby into the house. Not a maternal bone in my ex-wife's body. The only thing that stirs Cleo is a rise in the stock market.'

'What about Quentin's brother, James Winter? What did he do for money?'

'No idea. I only know that he never did an honest day's work in his life. That's what my father said. He liked to gamble, but the man had no real profession.'

Riker had begun to wonder if Sheldon was truly as drunk as he seemed. Was the man sharing or *feeding* information? Even lawyers stoned on cocaine were not so generous with the dark side of client histories.

'Did the police ever suspect James in the massacre?' The detective already knew the answer to this one, but he was hoping to catch this man in a lie.

'The police cleared James almost immediately. He had nothing to gain from the murders. Since the trust fund was entailed to a charity, he could never inherit. And James was doing quite well in those days. He lived in a suite at the Plaza Hotel.'

'But you said Lionel caught him stealing from the trust.'

'Yes. I assume, in later years, James had a reversal of fortune. The theft only amounted to housekeeping money, fudging the figures and so on. Nothing major.'

'When did James Winter leave town?'

'I think it was the year Lionel turned twenty-one. Yes, the boy was preparing to take over the trust allotments when he noticed a few irregularities. That's when his uncle James ran off. Probably wanted to avoid prosecution.'

Riker smiled to hide his deep disappointment. So James Winter was still alive years after Humboldt had been stabbed to death in a little town in Maine. A pity. Uncle James had been such a great candidate for a hitman, lots of cash but no visible means of support.

Their fresh beer had arrived via the maid at the back door. And when Smyth had finished two more bottles, Riker decided to take his best shot – before the attorney passed out. 'I hate to bring this up, sir, but my partner still wants to see the trust documents. You think—'

'I *told* you – or was it your partner? No matter. No documents without a warrant.'

'But you're the executor. The city attorney says that you can—'

'Can, but won't. Matter of principle.'

Riker well understood the problem. 'So it wouldn't look good for the firm.'

'Damn right it wouldn't,' said Smyth. 'For over a hundred years, we've been known for absolute discretion.'

And yet, the detective had just completed a tutorial on the Winter family faults.

'Okay,' said Riker. 'You got my word on this. We won't tell anybody that your dad mismanaged the Winter children's trust fund.'

The expression on Sheldon Smyth's face could only be read as guilty surprise, and, in the absence of hot denial, Riker knew he was on to something.

'Hey, I'm a homicide cop. What do I care who diddled what? And the statute of limitations is on your side. But you don't want a gang of cops at the door. I understand. You want discretion? You got it. How's this. You like Charles Butler, don't you? You trust him, right? Instead of us getting a warrant to haul everything downtown, suppose we look over the documents at his place, neutral ground?'

However drunken the man might be, when he smiled, the lucid face of the lawyer made a brief appearance, just popping out long enough to say, 'If you could talk a judge into giving you that warrant, you'd have it by now. No deal.'

Sheldon Smyth's eyes were closing, and Riker left him sitting there amid the litter of empty bottles, one more thing for the maid to clean up.

* * *

The quick rap on his door was somewhat annoying, but hardly loud enough to wake his houseguest. Charles opened the *New York Times*. The rap went on.

Most irritating.

He crushed his newspaper. Even if he had not recognized the impatient knock, almost a signature, he would have known it was Mallory.

Rap, rap, rap.

He glanced at his watch to see that she had allowed him a generous two hours to ply intimate secrets from Nedda, perhaps believing – so insulting – that he would never see through the ruse. Given time for reflection, he had come to understand his true role at the polygraph examination. Riker had as good as confessed, admitting that Charles would have been Mallory's guest if Bitty Smyth had not insisted on his presence.

Rap, rap. Bang!

Eventually, she would go away. She had keys to the offices across the hall, but none to his apartment. Though now he heard the sound of metal on metal.

Oh, fool I.

When had she ever been deterred by the lack of keys?

His intruder was so stealthy, he never heard the door open. Mallory simply appeared at the end of the foyer. Her own surprise was fleeting – there, then gone. He rose from the couch, startled and speechless. Her preemptive strikes could be dazzling. He was stunned that Mallory was the first one to strike a pose of outrage and indignation. Oh, the very idea that she should have to break into his apartment when he was just sitting there all the while. All of this was in her face, deliberately written there for him to read.

Chief Medical Examiner Edward Slope spent his lunch hour on a tree-lined street in suburban Brooklyn, conversing on the freak warmth of October, and lifting his face to the sun. Yes, he agreed with Rabbi

David Kaplan that every day of Indian summer was a gift. They both turned their attention to the mystery crate at the center of Robin Duffy's garage, while they waited for this charter member of the floating weekly poker game to join them.

'One more time, David.' The doctor regarded the crate with grave suspicion. 'It was dropped off the back of an unmarked truck in the dead of night . . . but you don't think Kathy stole it?'

The rabbi shook his head. 'No, and neither do you.'

In Edward Slope's opinion, the rabbi was too gentle to see the worst in others. He also believed that this gentle man regularly beat him at cards by sheer luck and not by the cunning of a born poker player. And, in truth, neither did the doctor believe that Kathy Mallory had stolen the crate, but she might delight in this accusation.

Perverse brat.

And if the truth were fully told, Edward Slope, her principal detractor, loved her unconditionally.

A screen door slammed, and they turned to see a short bulldog of a man walking toward them and grinning widely. 'It's all settled,' he said. 'Charles thinks the game was canceled.'

Edward Slope was still grappling with the concept of a surprise poker game. He faced the open garage, his eyes passing over all the discarded hobbies of Robin Duffy's experiment in retirement from his legal practice. What a failure. The walls were lined with tools for home improvements, a half-finished canoe from the boat-building class and the potted remains of a dead herb garden.

Kathy Mallory was another one who did not deal well with drastic life changes. She had grown up in this neighborhood and lived across the street with her foster parents. The old house had burned down, leaving a messy hole in her landscape until another house had been raised on the same footprint of land. Every fourth week of the poker-game rotation, Edward had remarked on the progress of the builders, and, now that it was done, he could not claim to be shocked.

In the early stages of construction, he had recognized something familiar in the raw timbers, the bones of the house. The completed structure was exactly the same in every maniacal detail. This week, the shrubbery had been added, evergreens shaped the way Helen Markowitz had always pruned them. The young tree recently planted in the yard was different, of course – or was it? No, that tree was the same size when Kathy was a little girl. He recalled the night when Louis had come home with a birthday present for Helen, a genuine baby felon caught in the act of robbing a car. What a surprise. And the following week Edward had helped Louis to dig a hole and put a sapling into that same ground. This had long been the custom of the Markowitz family, planting a tree when a child was born – or snatched off the street during the commission of a felony.

Robin stood beside him now, admiring Kathy's handiwork, as if what she had done was a normal thing. 'The mailbox is the original. She saved it from the ashes.'

'What about . . . inside the house?'

'Just a few things,' said Robin, 'but the kid's still working on it. Took her months to find Helen's wallpaper pattern. The company went out of business, but she tracked down some rolls to a hardware store in Montana. The furniture's a problem, too – all family heirlooms. Some of it dated back to the twenties. What a perfectionist, huh? Every piece has to be *exactly* the same. So she goes to estate sales on her days off.' He glanced back at the crate in his garage. 'That's how she knew where to find the table.' Robin entered the garage and selected a crowbar from the tools on the wall. 'She says we can uncrate it to fit it through Charles's door, but we can't unwrap it yet. I think she's afraid we'll ding up the wood.'

Edward Slope had lost all interest in the surprise poker game. He continued to stare at the house across the street. He tried to imagine Kathy in there, restoring the furnishings of the dead to make her ghosts feel more at home. Or was it an act of pure defiance – creating this illusion that death had never come to her house? Either way, it was quite mad, but also tender, and this argued well for a human heart.

'Confidential?' Mallory was outraged – genuinely this time – as Charles dragged her by the arm, and they moved inexorably down the hall to the elevator. 'You don't *have* patients!' she yelled. '*No* practice! You *can't* claim protected status!'

'Yes, I can.' Unperturbed, he pushed the button to bring the elevator. He was so calm, as if forcibly dragging women around were an everyday thing with him. He would not release her arm while he waited for the elevator doors to open. 'Nedda's my patient,' he said. 'Anything she tells me is in confidence.'

'You're making this up,' said Mallory. 'You don't treat people. That's not your line of work.'

'It is today.' His head lifted to watch the lights of the elevator. 'I think it might be my true calling. Who knows?'

'No, it's just a stunt. You're holding out on me – obstructing justice.'

'Well, that's too bad.'

Something had gone very wrong with her day. Charles was turning against her, and Nedda Winter was responsible for this. Yes, it was Nedda's fault, and he would see that once she had time to explain, to make up some new lie that he could believe in.

Mallory's anger shut down, as if a switch had been thrown, a circuit closed. Charles's hand was lightly covering hers, enclosing it in warmth. His grip tightened as he pulled her into the elevator with him, and she did not mind this. Human contact, flesh to flesh, was so rare in her life. She did nothing to encourage it, but when it came her way, her eyes closed to the slits of a purring cat. The elevator hummed with mechanical clicks and whirrs – her own song of the machine.

And the doors opened too soon.

He pulled her along toward the street door, maybe heading for a quiet café down the block. They would talk, and he—

'Next time you drop by the office,' he said, 'you might give me a call first. I can't have you running into my patient in the hallway.' He let go of her hand, opened the door and put her out in the street – like a cat.

The door slammed.

She looked upward at the sky, and her lips parted with nothing to say. A car pulled up behind her and Riker derailed her thoughts of abandonment.

'Hey, Mallory!'

She turned to see a police cruiser with a uniform behind the wheel and her partner at the rear window, grinning, saying, 'It's a raid, kid. You wanna come?' He opened the door in invitation, then waved a folded sheet of paper. 'I got a warrant for the Winter family trust – all the documents we can carry.'

Behind the cruiser were a police van and two more vehicles driven by uniforms. The cherry lights were all spinning, engines revving up to tell her that it was time to take this road show uptown; they had lawyers to menace, files to pillage, a mess to make, real carnage – what a party.

Nedda was standing at the stove, adjusting the gas flame, when Charles walked into the kitchen, lured there by the aroma of Colombian coffee.

'You know,' he said, 'you and I might be the only people in town who know how to brew coffee in a percolator.'

'I've never made it any other way.'

And with those words, this woman, thirty years his senior, had won his heart. He had not lied to Mallory. Nedda would be his patient, and every fear of subsequent damage to himself was put aside. She had inspired him to be a braver man – a better one. And so he picked up their cups and led her back to the library. Over the next hour, her eyes brimmed with tears, and *he* felt the anguish. He also took over her sense of isolation, and her great fear of being alone. And when she told him of her plan to find a place of her own, he could not bear the idea. He was drowning in Nedda's loneliness.

'Tell me how you got that warrant,' Mallory demanded. 'I went to three judges, and they stopped short of spitting on me.'

'You didn't pick the right one, kid.' And, fortunately, Riker was not a graduate of the Kathy Mallory Charm School. He turned to watch the cityscape flying by his window, then looked back to see his own personal caravan cutting through traffic and ignoring red lights. 'I've been saving this judge for a rainy day. He used to be a civil-rights attorney. Loves the poor, hates the rich. God bless his liberal, left-wing ass.'

No, I don't think so, said the look on her face – smart kid – there had to be more to it than that.

'This judge,' said Riker, 'he's a real *old* fart. Should've retired years ago. He remembers when this town was turned upside down looking for Red Winter, and he's been waiting fifty-eight years for the end of that story.'

'You *told* him who Nedda was?' Unspoken were the words *You idiot.*

Riker let this slide, still flush with the win of his warrant. He had pulled off the perfect marriage of Mallory's love for money motives and his own bone-deep distrust of lawyers.

'Yeah, I told him everything – laid it all out, but don't worry. This judge hates reporters more than cops. Now go back to the other day at the Harvard Club. You told Sheldon Smyth his daughter's life was on the line, and he still wouldn't give you a look at those trust documents. That was cold. Lawyers are almost human when it comes to their kids, but not old Sheldon. So today I got him smashed in his own backyard. Turns out he's a flyweight drinker. I sort of accused his law firm of embezzlement. Now that should've pissed him off, right? But no. Drunk as he is, he says to me, "No warrant, no documents." And that's when I know he's got something to hide.'

Mallory's eyes rolled up, searching the skies outside her window for winged pigs, flights of angels and other miracles. 'And the judge thought that was enough for a warrant?'

'No. Can I finish my story now? So I'm in the judge's chambers when he phones Sheldon Smyth. Figures it's just a misunderstanding. Maybe we can settle this without a warrant. Well, the lawyer's still drunk when he takes the judge's call. His Honor never gets out a word about the trust fund. Something on Smyth's end of the phone pissed him off. The judge says to him, "Suck your what?" And *that* was enough for a warrant.'

'I recommend more rest,' said Charles. 'A nap in the middle of the day is the world's most underrated pleasure.'

'You're right. I haven't had much sleep lately.' Nedda lifted the pan so he could admire the golden brown texture of her omelet. 'And tonight I plan to have it out with Cleo and Lionel.'

'Why the rush?'

'It's time – long past time.' She turned off the stove burner and carried her masterpiece to the kitchen table. 'And I'll have a better chance with them if we're not sharing the same roof.'

Ah, back to her plan for apartment hunting – one of the most stressful activities in New York City. Nedda would fail to thrive in any solitary existence, for profound depression would surely follow such a move.

'Well, fortunately, I own this apartment building.' He pulled down plates from the cupboard and laid them out on the kitchen table. 'And I have a vacant apartment. I think you'd like it here. But take my guest room for a few days. If things work out well with Cleo and Lionel, you may not need a place of your own.'

When they were seated, Charles agreed that, yes, steak sauce was an interesting accent for the omelet. And Nedda asked if he had forgiven Bitty for that little shrine in her bedroom. 'My favorite is the shot of your birthday party. You must've made quite an impression on her that day.'

'Yes and no,' said Charles. 'Bitty would've been ten when that picture was taken. She has obvious issues with self-esteem. So she picked the one person she might approach without fear of ridicule, someone so foolish in her eyes that she could be certain I wouldn't reject her. Then, so as not to risk this certainty, she never even spoke to me that day. If she had, I would've remembered her.'

'Do you mind another theory? You were taller than all the other children in that picture. And even then you had the body of a young god. I think my niece latched onto the idea of you as a protector. And then, on the worst night of her life, you showed up. That must have been quite magical for Bitty. I saw you talking to her. It did her a world of good – your kindness. You were her hero that night. And this morning, you were mine.'

Before therapist and patient could complete this colossal blunder of trading places, Charles picked up his napkin and laid it on the table as his white flag.

Bitty Smyth had retired to her room. Hours had passed by since she had spoken to her aunt on the phone. The cockatiel entertained her by walking about in circles and reciting his entire vocabulary.

Rags only knew one word. 'What?'

The bird had learned this from her. She rarely slept through the night, always rising at some point, sitting up in bed to say that word with each sound that roused her from sleep.

She knelt down beside the cage on the floor and filled the bird's water cup. After pouring him some fresh seed, she realized that she was also hungry. Sensing no one at home anymore, Bitty ventured out to forage for food. She made her way down the stairs, creaking in all the places that made her believe the staircase was always only minutes from falling down.

The front door opened. Bitty grabbed the rail and held it white-knuckle tight.

Oh, it was only the housekeeper with her grocery bags. What was her name? There had been so many of them, none of them lasting for more than a week or so. The new hire tapped in the code to disable the security alarm, then proceeded across the wide front room.

Bitty called down her late lunch order. 'And could you bring it upstairs?'

The woman scowled at this with good reason. It was a chore and a half just to climb to the second floor, and she had already made this trip too many times in one day.

Of late, Bitty had developed a backbone, and now she insisted that a meal be delivered to her room. She had no plans to be caught downstairs when her mother and uncle came home.

Retreating to her room, she passed the time with the old family albums retrieved from storage in the north attic. The bird clawed his way up the weave of the bedspread to join her in examining the photographs, tasting the pages and tearing off the corners. Bitty absently stroked the comb of yellow feathers, and Rags's tiny eyes soon closed in sleep.

The photography had ended the year of the massacre. In the yearly portraits of the Winters and their brood, all the children were gathered on Nedda's side of the photograph. Cleo clung to her eldest sister, and Lionel played with her hair. The others were seated at Nedda's feet.

A loud knock on the door awakened the bird with a start. 'What?' Rags flapped his useless wings and dropped off the edge of the bed, hitting the floor with a dull thud. 'What?'

Bitty rose to answer the heavy-handed knocking. This could only be the resentful housekeeper with her lunch. Upon opening the door, she was faced with her worst fear for the evening. Her mother pushed past her to enter the room.

'Why is Nedda staying with Dr Butler? Tell me,' Cleo demanded. 'What happened at that police station?'

'Don't be difficult,' said Uncle Lionel, as he also entered into the bedroom uninvited.

'Aunt Nedda thought you didn't want her here.'

Uncle Lionel was not surprised by this. 'Did Neddy say why?'

'No, but she'll be back around dinnertime.'

'I know that,' said Lionel, holding up a folded piece of paper. 'The housekeeper took a message from her. She asked if we could both stay at home this evening. She wants to talk to us. Do you know what this is about?'

Behind her uncle's back, the bird was climbing up the lace curtain, his claws leaving holes and tatters in his wake. He gained a perch on the curtain rod, then spread his wings, stepped off into thin air – and dropped like a stone. Bitty watched the stunned creature stumble about in a circle. Lame for decades, old Rags persisted in the idea that he could fly.

Well, this was fun.

Riker counted eight men and women, the partners of this venerable law firm, and they were almost gasping for breath. The air was not so rarified on the lower floor of their holdings. In this nether region, accountants and clerks were caged alongside a storage area for files that dated back a hundred and twenty years. Riker doubted that the attorneys had ever visited this land of the underpaid, though it was only three flights below their penthouse offices.

The firm was obviously a family business, for he could see traces of Sheldon Smyth among the assembled faces, a replicated nose or chin, a pair of snake eyes here and there. Their ages ranged from the twenties to the sixties, and yet they had lined up like children in a fire drill, all eyes on the drill instructor.

His partner had quickly adjusted all of their attitudes, and Mallory had done this without the necessity of shooting one of them as an example to the rest. They listened to her very attentively as she recited the parameters of the warrant. Two of the lawyers seemed on the verge of projectile vomit. Paul Smyth, son of Sheldon, went pale when Mallory said, 'The seizure of documents covers every file even remotely connected to the Winter family trust. That includes the firm's financials.' She tossed this last phrase off as an afterthought, leaving them all with the impression that it was true, and she was not expecting any arguments.

Riker held his breath for a moment, then realized that she was going to get away with this. Amazing. These people all held their own copies of exactly the same warrant.

The two detectives watched in silence while the storage room was gutted by uniformed officers carrying cartons, stacking them in the waiting freight elevator and returning for more. Not satisfied with this staggering plunder of hard copy, Mallory slipped her own disc into the firm's computer, startling the partners anew, saying, 'This is federal software. It's coded to pick up only transactions for the Winter family. Everything else is disregarded as inviolate material.'

Riker knew she was lying, but the eldest lawyer, no doubt left behind by the age of computers, was actually nodding, as if he had heard of this magical, mythical software of hers. The others, perhaps a little more savvy, were hemorrhaging as she copied their entire database. This was a major gamble. Riker knew one elderly judge who would have a heart attack if Mallory's fairy tale on the financials ever got back to him.

And now Sheldon Smyth had arrived. His white head poked out of an elevator, uncertain of his bearings in this strange new world of badly dressed underlings. The knot of his tie was crooked, and he weaved a bit as he sauntered out, puffing up his chest in a prelude to voicing something lawyerly.

Riker put up one hand to ward off Mallory, then picked up the warrant and flashed it. Faster than he could fire off a bullet, this had the effect of deflating the old man, who bent at the waist and plopped down in the nearest chair.

'It's all going to come out.' Mallory's eyes were cast down to the computer keyboard as she spoke to the old man. 'If you want to cut a deal, now's the time.' She raised her face and graced Sheldon Smyth with a smile designed to make him wet his pants. 'I know what you did.'

It was not the petulant housekeeper, but Bitty's mother who fetched the tray of food upstairs. 'Here, eat something. We'll discuss your aunt later on.'

Bitty had lost all interest in food, but her mother prodded her and stood over her until the plate was cleaned and the teacup emptied.

'I'm going to call your father. Sheldon will know what to do.'

Before the food could march back up Bitty's throat, her mother lifted the tray and opened the door. 'Lionel? Coming?'

Of course he was. Brother and sister went everywhere together. They were like twins joined by a shared brain. Uncle Lionel walked toward the door, then paused a moment to turn and stare at his niece. It was that look he usually gave to her mother while they were silently communing. He shook his head, unable to read Bitty's thoughts. No, his niece was from some other planet.

Bitty called it Earth.

Outside the raised window sash, a siren was growing in volume. Rags rushed out of his cage, running across the floor and screaming in concert with the fire engine, believing it to be a giant bird coming to mate with him and bear him away, to change his life and set him free.

Her bird was in love with a big red truck.

The siren faded off down the street. Rags fell silent. He walked back into his cage, tail dragging behind him. He tucked his head under one wing and squatted in a huddle of fluffed feathers. This was a sign of deep depression in Birdworld and Bitty's world as well. She curled into a ball.

EIGHT

Charles Butler cracked the door to his apartment and watched the heavy foot traffic of policemen marching down the hall, their arms laden with boxes. Last in line, Riker set down his own carton to say, 'Hello,' and, 'Sorry about the commotion. We got the trust documents.'

'So I see.'

'But we couldn't cart them back to Special Crimes,' said Riker. 'The boss would've freaked.'

Mallory walked by with a carton. She never turned her head in their direction, and Charles gave no indication that he had even seen her. He nodded his goodbye to Riker, then closed the door – and locked it. Riker heard the sound of a second deadbolt, and then a chain guard falling into place. And Mallory heard this, too. She turned back to the door, as if the sound of three locks might be a message just for her.

Trouble? Oh, absolutely.

Riker would never have believed that Charles Butler had the will-power to hold a grudge for six minutes, and that would be a feud with a total stranger. With Mallory, the poor bastard had no shot at all.

Until today.

The uniformed officers were making their escape to the elevator when Riker carried the last of the haul into Mallory's private office at the back of Butler and Company. He set it down at her feet, saying, 'What are the odds Charles is gonna give us a hand with this? You got another speed reader in your pocket?'

'Better than that,' she said. 'I've got a lawyer on the way.'

'Oh, well that's just *great*. Lawyers read at two hundred dollars an hour – real slow.' He turned to the cork wall. It had been cleared in preparation for their autopsy on a trust fund.

'We don't need Charles.' Mallory opened a folder and held up a sheet with columns of words and numbers. 'The documents are indexed, and all the boxes are clearly marked.' She pinned up the first page of her document list in perfect alignment with the walls. *Two* pushpins.

Riker could see their first problem in the making. Was his little neatness freak even capable of doing this without her usual time-consuming perfection? He decided to experiment. Taking a handful of sheets from her index folder, he plopped them on the cork wall in haphazard fashion, one pin a piece and every sheet dangling at a different angle. One glance over his shoulder told him that it actually hurt her to look at his mess.

'Mallory, we don't have *years* for this.' He walked off to the reception room to answer a knock. When he reached the end of the hall, the door was flung open, and he was assaulted by a little man with the jowls of a bulldog. Riker was forced to endure a bear hug from the only lawyer he could abide.

Robin Duffy had lived across the street from Lou and Helen Markowitz since forever. And now, in his retirement years with both his old friends in the ground, Robin looked upon every connection to them as his extended family. He released his hold on the detective and stepped back. His eyes were lit up and manic. He was just so happy to be here. 'Where's my Kathy?'

The old lawyer was in that small circle of friends allowed to address his partner by her given name and get away with it unscarred.

Bitty Smyth's eyelids weighed ten pounds each. She sat bolt upright on the bed to keep from falling asleep.

When would Aunt Nedda come home?

She poured another glass of water from the pitcher by her bed. The edge of the glass blurred as she lifted it to her lips. She returned the glass to the night table and knocked the alarm clock to the floor, leaving the time of day a mystery.

Or was it night?

She fumbled in the pockets of her skirt and found the business card that Charles Butler had given her. Fortunately, she had memorized the office number, for it would have been difficult to focus on the small print of the card.

Bitty stared at the telephone, as if the large numbers on the dial might be equally difficult. No, she would not call, not yet. She would give it a few more hours. Aunt Nedda would surely come home for dinner without any prompting. She had promised.

It was such a fight to stay awake.

Robin Duffy stood among the cartons, trying to make sense of the numbers stenciled on the cardboard. Lowering his reading glasses, he said, 'Give it up, Kathy. The document index has no relationship to the documents. All I can tell you at this point is that Smyth's firm is hiding something.' His eyes traveled over the towers of boxes, each containing thousands of documents. 'This is an old lawyer's trick – bury the sins in a ton of paperwork.' He glanced at his wristwatch. 'It's time to get Charles.'

Riker listened for the sound of the reception room door closing on the lawyer. He stepped up behind his partner. 'We're never gonna find the will without Charles. You think he'll come?'

Mallory sat at her computer, checking financial data she had raided from the law firm, still following the money. Riker was at the point of repeating himself when she said, 'He'll come . . . for Robin.'

From his turtleneck jersey to his formal evening shoes, Rabbi David Kaplan had dressed all in black. This was the proper attire in his understanding of the criminal underworld. This evening, he played the role of lookout man and loved it. He leaned into the hallway, then quickly withdrew to the elevator and spoke to Edward Slope in a stage whisper. 'Charles is leaving with Robin.' He poked his head out again. 'Now they're going into the office across the hall. The coast is clear.'

'You've been waiting all day to say that line, haven't you?'

'Please, Edward, no noise.'

Together, the chief medical examiner and the rabbi moved their heavy burden along on its rolling pallet, out of the elevator and down the hallway, as Edward Slope said once again, 'There's no such thing as a surprise poker game.'

'Shhh.' The rabbi was reveling in this crime of backward burglary. He turned the knob of the door to Charles Butler's apartment. As promised, it opened easily. Pointing to a piece of tape that covered the bolt, he said, 'Robin's idea.'

And that made this crime of breaking and entering a conspiracy of three. The doctor and the rabbi wheeled the game table in the door, snagging its padded cover on a hinge and tearing it. Had the table not been turned on its side, it would never have fit through the door frame.

At the end of the foyer, they stopped in heart-clutching guilty surprise, as if they had been caught in the act of removing something instead of depositing a gift. Before them stood a tall, stately woman rubbing sleep from her eyes. Her hair was snow white, and her smile was bemused. She clearly recognized Edward Slope as the doctor who had written her Valium prescription earlier in the day. She studied the bulky object on the pallet.

'It's a table,' said Edward Slope, as if the furniture padding might have disguised that fact.

'Ah,' she said. 'I know just the place for it.'

Following Nedda Winter, they wheeled the table into the library. With no mention of the Winter House Massacre and the lady's celebrity status, introductions were made to Rabbi Kaplan as the two men shifted the table off the pallet and placed it in the center of a ring of club chairs. And now the rabbi began to explain what had happened to Charles Butler's last table.

'Burned in a warehouse fire,' said Nedda. 'Yes, I know. But I've never heard of a surprise poker game.'

The doctor consulted his watch. 'Should we unwrap it now or wait for Robin?'

'You dropped something,' said Nedda. 'It fell out of that tear in the padding.'

David Kaplan bent down and retrieved the paper. 'Oh, it's the provenance. Kathy mentioned that it was an antique.' The rabbi scanned the text, then abruptly sank into a club chair. 'Edward, you won't believe where this table has been.'

The job in Mallory's office did not actually require a speed reader. It had taken Charles Butler only a few minutes to break the index code – childishly simple – a few minutes more to locate the correct carton, the correct folder and to hand over the original will to Robin Duffy.

'It's really quite easy.' Charles looked down at the file inventory in his hand. 'The last three digits of the listed items correspond to the first three digits on the cartons. For the actual documents listed in the index, disregard the first and last two digits of the index number, and everything in the middle will match up with the numbers on the file holders.' He never saw their startled faces. His head was deep in a carton as he fished out the folder that gave up the basic structure of the Winter family trust fund. Done with this chore, he asked, 'What else am I looking for?'

'Something incriminating,' said Riker.

'Well, I've got that right here.' Robin Duffy sat behind Mallory's steel desk, poring over papers covered with handwritten lines of faded blue ink. 'I'm not surprised that you couldn't find a copy of this will in the public record. Back in the thirties, you could buy off a clerk for pocket change. And I can tell you right now that Sheldon Smyth's father bought a judge. That's the only way he could've rammed this will through probate.'

Mallory stood behind Robin's chair and read over his shoulder. 'So it's a fake?'

'Worse than that. It's what I call *hysteric form*, confused and flawed. Edwina Winter was angry when she wrote this, and she wasn't thinking straight. Her husband was cut off. That's like an invitation to contest a will. Everything was left to Nedda and her siblings, but the kids only get a draw from a family trust. And there's nothing here to say that Nedda's siblings have to be Edwina's children. Any sibling can benefit from the trust.'

'Well,' said Riker, 'I guess the lady didn't count on Quentin having eight more kids with another wife.'

'But here's the catch,' said Robin. 'She writes, "When my last child is dead, the trust passes on to the New York Historical Society."'

'Sounds smart to me,' said Mallory. 'According to Bitty Smyth, Edwina's husband was the one who killed her. Maybe she saw it coming. She wanted to take the money motive out of murdering her children to inherit.'

'Makes sense,' said Riker. 'That's why Nedda could never be legally declared dead.'

Charles thought of a more likely scenario: Edwina was preventing her husband from spending the money before the children were properly launched into the world, but he kept this to himself.

'With this wording,' said Robin, 'any judge would know it wasn't Edwina's intention to support another woman's children by a future marriage. But that's a moot point. The trust should never have been drawn up in the first place. It was created from the instructions of a flawed will. An honest judge would've set the will aside and divided the money between the infant Nedda and her father, Quentin Winter.' He looked up at Charles. 'I need to see the previous will.'

Charles flipped through the document index. 'Sorry. There's only one.'

'Then the law firm destroyed a preexisting will,' said Robin Duffy. 'Once you get past the hysterics, the rest of it, codicils, gifts to friends and servants, things like that, it's all in correct legal form. She must've copied it from her earlier will.'

'Then we got 'em,' said Riker. 'The old man told me that Edwina changed her will every time she had a fight with her husband.'

'In that case,' said Robin, pausing to look over the mass of cartons, 'the earlier wills were misplaced. You won't find them on the index. You won't find them at all. But they're here.'

Charles Butler stood at the center of the room, sifting through another carton. 'Why didn't Quentin Winter hire a lawyer to break the will?'

'That's an easy one,' said Riker. 'The Winter family's lawyers have always been Smyths. Now I got a question. Why would the law firm keep all this stuff. If it incriminates them, why not destroy it?'

'Lessons of Nixon,' said Robin. 'The cover-up is always worse than the crime. They'd rather look incompetent than go to jail for fraud.' He waved one hand to include every carton in the room. 'I don't have to look at their financials. I know you'll find a penny-perfect accounting for every fee and payout. It might not be honest, but it'll look good on paper and it'll pass an audit.'

'All right,' said Mallory. 'So the firm had to convince Quentin Winter that it wasn't in his best interests to contest the will.'

'Right,' said Robin. 'If they couldn't create the trust from the will instructions, then they'd lose a huge administration fee.'

'And it's not like Quentin was left out in the cold.' Charles placed a folder on the desk. 'That's a summary sheet for payouts in the first year. He had more income than he could spend. There's a generous housekeeping allowance, a maintenance allotment for each child and a guardian's draw.'

Robin studied the file, then nodded. 'The firm padded out his monthly draw. My God, this trust fund was worth twenty-five million dollars. You know what that is in today's dollars? Maybe a quarter-billion.'

'More,' said Mallory, whose gift was calculation.

Walking had become a great effort for Bitty Smyth.

When was Aunt Nedda coming home?

She undid the bolt and slumped to the floor. One ear pressed against the door, she listened to the loud conversation downstairs. Her father's voice joined the cacophony of invectives and blame flying back and forth across the wide front room below. Sheldon Smyth was slurring his words. She knew her aunt had not yet arrived. Aunt Nedda would not be privy to this conversation of family matters. On hands and knees, Bitty crawled back toward her bed and pulled the telephone off the nightstand by its cord.

Rags awoke with a start and flapped his wings. 'What?' He came out of his cage on the run and squawking. Even the bird could see that something was wrong with his mistress.

Charles Butler and Robin Duffy had retired to the more comfortable furnishings of the private office across the hall, where the furniture was not made of cold steel, where a humidor was stocked with Havanas and the whiskey was single malt.

When Riker returned with a take-out meal, his partner was standing before her cork wall, studying the yellowed papers of financials from an era of filing cabinets.

'For the first twelve years, the trust fund outlay should never have exceeded the interest earnings.' She glanced back at her glowing monitor screen and its display of more recent data. 'Today the trust is only worth forty thousand dollars.'

Riker lit a cigarette and took a long contemplative drag. He did his best thinking when he smoked. 'Figure cost-of-living increases, more money for each new kid, and you still can't spend it all, not with a cap on the draw.' And now he dealt with the greater problem of finding something to pass for an ashtray. He settled on a metal cup, dumping its stash of paper clips out on the desk blotter. Experimentally, he dropped in his burnt match, and his partner did not hurt him.

He exhaled.

Mallory walked half the length of the wall, then stopped to tap one sheet of pinned-up paper. 'Here, right after the massacre. This is when it starts.' She moved on down the wall, then paused again. 'Twenty per cent of the money was drained in a period of two years. The firm wrote it off as poor investment of capital.'

'You mean they stole it. I'm betting the guardian helped with that,' said Riker. 'Good old Uncle James. I say he hired Stick Man for the massacre.'

'Him or Sheldon Smyth's father. My guess is collusion. Nedda went to brunch with the Smyth family on the day of the massacre – conveniently out of harm's way.' Mallory walked back to her computer and tapped the keys to change the document on the monitor's screen. 'I found the money, only now it's well over a hundred million, all in personal brokerage accounts for Cleo and Lionel.' She printed out a sheet. 'This is their investment history. They took a bath in the nineties and again with the tech-stock fiasco. Now their holdings are zero risk, hardly any growth. But they show a deposit income of one million a year that doesn't derive from stocks and bonds. And I know where it came from.' She split her screens to pick up an item she had flagged on the law firm's financial data. 'The law firm has a payout of one million every year. It's listed under client settlements.'

'Lawyers paying clients?'

'Not that simple.' Mallory spent a few quiet minutes following the money through cyberspace, switching screens, diddling keys, and robbing banks via their databases. 'I've got a memo to purchase bearer bonds. The dates and the amounts add up on both sides. Lionel and Cleo cashed in those bonds to make their yearly deposits.'

The screen changed again, and Riker turned away the moment he saw the logo for Mallory's latest invasion, bypassing lockouts to enter

Internal Revenue files. It always made him uncomfortable to witness a crime in progress.

'They don't pay any taxes on the yearly million,' said Mallory. 'The tax is paid to the IRS by a check drawn on an offshore account for a bogus corporation.'

'I feel a headache coming on,' said Riker. 'Who's doing who?'

'Best guess? It looks like Lionel and Cleo busted the Smyth firm for embezzlement. But simple restitution wouldn't require money laundering on this scale. What if they nailed Sheldon Smyth's father for hiring a mass murder?'

Bitty had left the bolt undone, and it had taken some time for this little horror to settle in. Her mind was slipping.

So sleepy.

And her limbs felt like cement. She struggled to make the short trip from her bed to the door, shuffling, unable to lift her heavy feet from the carpet. She slid the bolt home so no one would intrude upon her, not until her aunt returned. Bitty sat on the floor, her back propped up against the door, listening, waiting for rescue. Aunt Nedda should have been here by now. She must come very soon. She must. Bitty called Charles Butler's office number again.

Mallory continued to scroll down the lists of investments. Riker watched her run calculations of large figures on a split screen. She was so good with the math of money motives. The assistance of a forensic accountant would only have slowed her down.

'I can access trades back to the early eighties,' she said. 'Allowing for dividends paid out and reinvested, market booms and dives, I'd say this stock portfolio was built up from the law firm's yearly payouts over at least forty years. The Smyth firm is paying back the stolen money, but not to the trust fund. It all goes into Lionel and Cleo's personal accounts.'

'Proof of embezzlement,' said Riker, 'motive for a massacre. And people ask me why I hate lawyers. I guess murder runs in the family, first the father and now the son. Sheldon's gotta be the one who hired Willy Roy Boyd. He had to kill Nedda before she started asking questions about the trust fund.' The detective crushed out his cigarette. 'I love this case more and more every minute.'

'This financial arrangement works better for Lionel and Cleo. Instead of a lifetime draw on the trust fund, they have access to all of the money. And now, they're part of the embezzlement. The restitution money should've gone back into the trust.'

'If Nedda dies, they get to keep it.' And now he understood the elaborate money laundering. 'Those two still don't know that the will and the trust were never valid.'

Mallory nodded. 'Because the Winters' attorneys have always been Smyths.'

Charles poured a drink for Robin Duffy and ignored the telephone on his office desk. One of Mallory's machines would pick up the call at the reception desk. Before entering into a business partnership with her, he had never been an answering-machine sort of person. If calls had gone astray, he had always assumed that people would call back. So simple. And, in case of emergency, they would send a telegram to the door. Should he be out of town when people called, well, that was their hard luck and one less hassle to deal with.

Now he could not escape his callers. The machine seemed to work for their convenience and not his own. Machines were always conspiring to strip all the charm from his life. Once, he had tried to disconnect the device, and all of the phones had gone dead. Mallory's wiring was not to be trifled with. He had never attempted another such insurrection.

The phone stopped ringing.

Riker sat on the floor with the emptied-out contents of another carton, searching for a lost child among the papers. 'You're right, Mallory.

221

Sally Winter never attended a private school, either. No tuition payments.'

'I don't think she lived long enough for kindergarten,' said Mallory, leafing through her own stack of files. 'There's no record of payouts for nannies after the toddler years. Lots of medical bills. There was a live-in nurse. After Sally Winter turned four, the nurse's paychecks stopped.'

'So the kid was sick,' said Riker. 'Maybe she died of natural causes. I can't see any motive to kill Sally.'

'Then why would Lionel say she'd run away when she was ten years old? You know that was a lie. And why isn't there a death certificate on file with the city?'

'Sally could've died somewhere else. Maybe it was a case of neglect. Uncle James wouldn't want anyone to know he was an unfit guardian, not before he'd finished milking his cut from the trust fund.' Riker turned to the open doorway to see Charles and Robin walking down the hall toward the reception room. A moment later, that distant door opened and closed. He guessed that they were making a deli run for food and wondered if they would remember to bring him a beer.

Mallory was sifting through the smallest carton, the one that had belonged to his grandfather. She began to pin the old man's diagrams of the massacre to the wall.

'Hey,' said Riker, 'you don't want Charles and Robin to see that stuff.'

'They won't be back. They'll be playing poker all night.'

Charles Butler entered his apartment behind Robin Duffy, who headed straight for the library, and now he heard Edward Slope call out, 'It's about time!'

Upon entering the book-lined room, he could hardly fail to notice an old gaming table surrounded by his new club chairs, and three of those chairs were filled by the charter members of the weekly floating poker game.

'Oh, it's a beauty,' said Robin, admiring the ornate carving and the touches of gilt and inlays.

Indeed, it was a good piece of furniture, in the sense of being solid and made of good hardwood, but it was too ornate, not the graceful antique of Charles's dreams. This table had obviously been constructed in the twentieth century, and one might even call it gaudy.

'The provenance,' said Edward, handing a sheet of paper to Robin, whose eyes went round. The doctor turned to Charles, saying, 'It's a gift from Mallory. It once belonged to Bugsy Siegel.'

A mobster and a brutal killer, but Charles let this slide, for it was so rare to receive a present from Mallory that did not require an electronics manual to operate.

'Oh, Bugsy.' Robin Duffy ran one hand over the tabletop, caressing it with real love in his eyes. 'Bugsy Siegel, the man who invented Las Vegas. It just doesn't get any better than this.'

Indeed, there were smiles all around the room. Even the rabbi approved. And now Charles realized that the other table, the one linked to a former president, would never have made them so happy. Mallory had found the magic that he had been searching for, a history of smoke-filled rooms and high-stakes players, a table with a provenance on the wild side.

He sat down in a chair and smiled at this company of friends. He had inherited all of them from Kathy Mallory's foster father. Charles's other bequest, a seat in this poker game, was also an ongoing treasure. But the game had represented so much more to the late Louis Markowitz, that crafty, manipulative good man – that stellar card shark.

Charles had heard all the players' war stories of watching Kathy Mallory grow up in the Markowitz household, and he had heard all the theories for why Louis Markowitz had taken a young child to the weekly poker game. Edward Slope had once espoused the idea that Louis was teaching his semi-reformed street thief to steal in a more socially acceptable manner – rather than going straight for a victim's wallet or ripping off cars. David Kaplan had been closest to the truth with the theory of playtime, for young Kathy had never had friends her own age. She had always frightened normal children.

But these three men had never understood how truly devious their late, great friend had been. The policeman's profession was prone to sudden death, and Louis had been a farsighted man. He had forced these men to love his only child over the years when she was learning to cheat them and beat them all at cards.

And they loved her still.

Though she had long ago outgrown their company and deserted their game of penny-ante stakes and wild cards, these men would never desert Kathy Mallory. They were family now.

Canny Louis.

'Lionel and Cleo were in the park that day.' Mallory had pinned up all the old diagrams of Winter House. 'But Stick Man didn't know they were missing. I think the original plan was to kill everyone in the house but the baby and Nedda. It had to look like a psycho on a killing spree instead of a hired murder.'

'But, as long as they had Nedda, why would they need the baby?'

'The draw on the fortune goes to Nedda and her siblings. That's a lot of money to ride on the life of one child. Suppose they always planned to stash Nedda somewhere else?'

'Like an asylum?'

'Right. They can produce her if they have to. But, even if she dies in a hospital under an assumed name, the lawyers can still keep her alive on paper, and the money rolls on. But James Winter has to be established as the legal guardian of a surviving child. This was what I got from the DA's office. They say the court would've assumed guardianship for a missing child, and the court could've declared Nedda dead after seven years. So this is the only way that James can get his share of the money. Even if he'd had the brains to contest the original will—'

'He would've been a murder suspect with a huge money motive,' said Riker. 'Okay, but Sally was a bad choice. The kid was sick.'

'She was a baby, no friends, no school connections. If Sally had been the only survivor, they probably would've replaced her with another kid when she died. I don't think anyone minded that Cleo and Lionel weren't in the house that day. That was an accidental bonus. Two spares.'

Nedda Winter carried a plate of sandwiches into the library and set them on the game table amid the beer bottles and ashtrays filled with smoking cigars. Charles held a chair for her. 'You'll play, of course.'

'I might watch for a while, but I'm not much good at card games.'

'Good.' Edward Slope opened a fresh deck. 'At last, Charles has someone he can beat at poker.'

'You're one to talk,' said Robin Duffy. 'When Kathy was eleven years old, she cleaned you out once a week.' He turned his wide smile on Nedda. 'Poor little kid. She used to list to one side with the weight of all of Edward's money in her pockets. And Lou laughed so hard he cried.'

The doctor ignored this. 'Charles, did you know that Nedda's father saw the shoot-out between the cops and Two-Gun Crowly on West Ninetieth Street?'

'My father and thousands of other West Siders,' said Nedda. 'My grandfather was with him that day. He said the shoot-out went on for three hours. When Two-Gun Crowly gave up the fight, he still had a pistol stuffed in each sock.'

Rabbi Kaplan picked up the deck and dealt out the cards. 'My father only took me to baseball games. I had no idea the Upper West Side could be so exciting.'

Nedda, Charles, Edward and Robin fell silent.

'What if the massacre started at the top of Winter House?'

'That's not the way the cops figured it at the time.' Riker stepped back from the cork wall to take in the reconstruction of his grandfather's work. 'But I think they got a lot of things wrong.'

He added more pages from the old man's files. 'Check this out. Granddad made these notes in an interview with the lead detective. This was right before Fitzgerald died of cancer. Now this was maybe ten, fifteen years after the murders. It helps if you know that Fitzgerald ruled out murder for hire. The lawyers told him that the uncle knew the terms of Edwina's will twelve years before the massacre. James Winter always knew that he could never inherit. Well, that killed the only money motive. If there's no adult who stands to gain, then who hired the hitman? That's why the cops settled for a lunatic on a killing spree. Fitzgerald figured it this way. Stick Man starts on the first floor and works his way up. Then he runs out of steam when he gets to the nursery. Or maybe something scares him off before he can finish the job and kill the baby.'

'But your grandfather always figured it was a pro. Why?'

'Fitzgerald's theory hung on what the lawyers said. They're the ones who killed the money motive. But Granddad never trusted lawyers.'

'Nine people. That's a lot of killing, a lot of risk. Maybe Stick Man wasn't working alone. Three generations of hitmen. What if there was a fourth – an up-and-comer?'

'A fledgling killer?'

Most of the poker chips were in neat stacks in front of Nedda Winter. 'This is so embarrassing.'

Her comment was met with a chorus of encouragement. The other players had been so eager to teach her the game that they had helped her to beat them at every hand. Eventually she did manage to lose all the money back to them, but she had to fight them for the privilege.

The telephone rang, and Nedda glanced at her watch. 'I'll get it. I'm sure it's for me.'

Four gentlemen rose to their feet as she left the room.

David Kaplan turned to Charles. 'She's a charming woman. How did you meet?'

Charles made a slight stumble in his mind. So many confidences to keep. 'She sat next to me at a dinner party.' That was the truth, was it not? Well, no. And now, he could feel the heat rising to his face, and how would the rabbi read this sudden blush?

David Kaplan's head tilted to one side. He must find it odd and disconcerting to catch a friend in a lie. His beard framed a sweet smile, and his eyes were both forgiving and more, telling his host that he could only believe the best of him. David, the master of cryptic logic, had apparently deduced that honor must lie in the direction of falsehood – and the new player was not what she seemed.

Nedda returned to the table, saying with regret, 'I have a hired car waiting for me downstairs. I'll have to say good night. And thank you all. This was the most fun I've had in years.'

'Send the car away,' said Charles, rising from his chair. 'I'll take you home.'

'No, no. You stay right where you are. I'll be fine. We always use this driver. My niece has a car service.'

'Then I can at least walk you down to the street. I insist.'

When the apartment door had closed behind them, Charles said, 'Maybe it's unwise right now. I mean – hashing this out with your brother and sister. After what you've been through in the past few days—'

'I should've done this the day I came home. Don't worry about me.'

Charles opened the door to the waiting car and handed Nedda into the backseat. And then he gave her a set of his house keys. 'Promise you'll come back tonight – no matter how late.'

He watched the taillights of the car disappear as it rounded the corner onto Houston, then turned back to see Mallory in shadow, leaning against the wall of the building.

'This is getting out of hand, Charles. Suppose you gave your house keys to a mass murderer?'

'You don't expect me to believe that,' he said. 'You don't.'

'I know she's killed before.'

'Self-defense,' he said. 'And that man was a serial killer.'

'Nedda didn't know that. And he wasn't holding a weapon when he died. Could you stab an unarmed man in the heart? Could you even imagine it? I don't think you could ever kill another human being. You're just not made that way.' She followed him inside the building, close on his heels, saying, 'What's Nedda made of? Don't you wonder? Imagine her sticking that ice pick into a man's chest. She'd have to be fast – no hesitation, one clean strike. No fear.'

'That's enough.' He walked past the elevator and opened the door to the stairwell.

'And she did it in the dark.' Mallory climbed the stairs behind him, chasing words with pictures she planted in his head. 'He never saw her coming for him.' She followed him through the stairwell door and down the hall to his apartment. 'And what about that man in the park last night? What if she'd killed him, too? Would we still be talking about self-defense?' They stopped outside his door, but the poisoning went on relentlessly. 'When we found her in the park, she had an ice pick in her pocket. Remember that, Charles.'

How could he forget – ever?

'Nedda will always be welcome in my house.'

Mallory looked as if he had struck her. 'And I'm not. I'm just annoying you.'

Oh, no, on the contrary. He could never encounter Mallory without feeling a sudden lightness of the head, a fullness of the heart and a gang of birds fluttering inside his rib cage. He reached out to touch her, but his hand dropped back to his side. Never did they truly connect, and they never would, for his nature had made him incapable of two things for a certainty: he could never kill a human being, and he could not tell this woman that he would love her until he died.

How sad was that?

The door to his apartment opened.

'Finally!' A grinning Robin Duffy took Mallory by the arm and pulled her inside. 'Edward's winning streak is back. You have to stop him, Kathy. He's murdering us.'

Lying on the floor, her head pressed to the wood, Bitty awakened to a shrill sound from the telephone receiver, an alarm to remind her that the phone was off the hook. Rags was running about in circles, shrieking to hold up his end of the conversation with this mechanical noise.

Bitty struggled to raise herself up to a sitting position, then cracked the bedroom door to listen for the sound of Aunt Nedda's voice, but she was not there, not home yet. The other voices were growing more distant, fading off to another room with a door they could close for privacy.

Aunt Nedda, where are you?

Any more delay could cost dearly. If she closed her eyes one more time, she might never wake again.

Robin Duffy had found the only flaw in Mallory's gift, a hole in one of the struts that branched out from the table's pedestal. It had been drilled by the previous owner, a ship's captain, so he could run a chain through the wood and secure the table in rough weather.

However, given the original owner, a renowned gangster, Robin had hopes of a more exciting explanation. His eyes were wide with great expectation. 'Is that a bullet hole?'

'Yes,' said Mallory, 'that's exactly what it is.' She dealt the cards out all around. 'And away we go. The name of the game is five card stud. No wild cards. No nickels and dimes in the pot. Sky's the limit. This is not your grandmother's poker game.'

Four men mentally fastened their seat belts.

She had to smile at Charles. He was looking down at the best hand he had ever held, and she knew he was pondering a problem of ethics, one he could not solve. If his cards had been dealt from the bottom of the deck, a little gift from herself, it would not be right to play the hand, and he should fold. What a gentleman.

It was too easy for her to read his thoughts.

Now he was worried. Since she knew he held a world-class hand, if he folded his cards instead of playing them, it would be like accusing her of cheating. Oh, but if he won and had to show his hand, then everyone would know she had cheated. The hand was that good.

She should know.

Kathy Mallory was not only a master of palming cards; she could also tie a fair Gordian knot. This one had been designed with no possibility of an honest resolution. He would have to settle for the least damage – just as she did every day.

Charles played the hand he was dealt. She knew he would. Fortunately for him, he could never run a bluff. The other players read victory all over his giveaway face and they folded. No one called him on his hand and asked to see his cards. Of course, she had predicted that outcome – just as he had. His winning pot was small, but so was his guilt.

Mallory fell a bit short of tradition by not taking all of the medical examiner's money within half an hour of play. She had left him a short stack, and Edward Slope eyed his dwindled chips with ill-disguised dismay. She folded her own cards, and that seemed to give him a glimmer of hope. The doctor won this hand, but that was pure mercy on her part.

'I've got a problem,' she said, addressing the doctor. 'How does a man move through a mansion, killing floor by floor, stabbing nine people with an ice pick, and there's not one scream to give him away?'

While Edward Slope was pondering this, Mallory watched the rabbi. David Kaplan had that look of trying to recall an elusive dream. The nightmare of the Winter House Massacre? And now he let it go and looked down at his cards. This settled her mind on the problem of the other players keeping her confidences.

The doctor sipped his beer, then leaned back in his chair. 'If the murderer had chased his victims through the house, there would've been lots of noise. So, obviously, it didn't happen that way. More than likely, the victims weren't expecting to be stabbed.'

Like Nedda's dead burglar. Are you listening, Charles?

Edward Slope studied the hand she had dealt him. 'The first reaction would be stunned surprise. The heart is shredded, blood draining. Shock sets in. I'll take two cards.'

She dealt them out, and they were good ones.

Happier now, the doctor continued. 'Next, the sensation of cold is followed by sudden weakness throughout the body, then loss of consciousness. A quiet death.'

Charles would be wondering if Nedda's burglar had died quietly. And now he must realize that she had never needed to ask these questions of the doctor. Who knew more about violent death than she did? Yes, at last, he understood that she was maligning Nedda Winter for his own sake.

Their eyes met across the table. Almost imperceptibly, he moved his head from side to side to tell her that this was not working.

The rabbi folded his cards, saying, 'I'm out.' He then went off to the kitchen in search of another cold beer.

Mallory leaned toward the medical examiner, saying, 'So the hitman wasn't a stranger to that family.'

'And that narrows it down,' said Charles, 'to a hundred gangland types who attended parties at Winter House.'

'Yeah,' said Robin. 'Nedda told us that Lucky Luciano came to dinner one night. Can you imagine that? But you can cross that bum off the list. His murders were messy.'

Mallory was thinking about a little boy, just four years old, and his drawing of a stick figure. She pictured a bit of blood and one tiny hole where the ice pick had pierced the paper and a child's heart in one strike. There was only one scenario. In the moment before his death, the boy had been holding up that drawing, showing it to someone he knew, maybe someone he loved, saying a child's ritual line, 'Look what I did.'

The front windows were dark as Nedda climbed the stairs to the front door of Winter House.

Her hopes died.

Lionel and Cleo had no doubt bolted for the summer house in the Hamptons. There would be no family gathering, no reconciliation tonight.

She unlocked the door and opened it onto a dark foyer, calling out, 'Bitty? Are you home?'

Upon crossing the threshold, she saw a dim light coming from the hallway that led to the kitchen, but the front room was pitch black. She was turning round with the intention of finding the wall switch for the chandelier when she heard the sound of footsteps rushing up behind her.

She could hear the voice of Uncle James coming from a long ways off and many years ago, yelling, 'Nedda, drop the ice pick! Drop it *now*!'

NINE

The front room flooded with light from the chandelier. Lionel ran past her to the front door. Nedda had forgotten to turn off the alarm. She murmured apologies to her brother as he madly tapped the button pad on the foyer wall, entering the code that would prevent it from going off.

Crisis over.

And now that they were spared another visit from the NYPD, he said, 'Neddy, we couldn't reach Dr Butler. We thought you might've gone back to the police station – possibly under arrest. We couldn't get anything out of Bitty.'

Arrest? For which of her crimes? Did he mean the stabbing to death of a man in this same room or the other man she had planned to kill in the park? Or was her brother alluding to the mass murder of their family members?

She turned to the sound of more footsteps. Cleo entered the front room, followed closely by her ex-husband. Sheldon was no doubt here by design; her brother and sister had no wish to be alone with her tonight. She was wondering where her niece might be hiding when a weak voice called down from the staircase, 'Here. Up here.'

Four heads were turning, lifting to the sight of Bitty dragging herself to the edge of the stairs. In a childish gesture, one small hand raised slowly, as if to wave bye bye, and then she laid her head down on the floor and closed her eyes. Nedda was the first to reach her. None of them could wake her.

* * *

Charles was holding a rather mediocre hand of cards when he answered the knock at his door. His unexpected visitor was a stout woman from a more Luddite-friendly century. An old-fashioned carpetbag sat on the floor at her feet.

O pioneer.

She had the well-muscled arms of a woman who labored hard for her living, and the iron gray hair was bound in braids. Her walking shoes were sturdy, and the blue dress had great integrity, so plain and serviceable. He half expected her to produce a pitchfork or some other farm implement. She stared him down with great sensible brown eyes, then extended a hand to greet him, albeit somewhat reluctantly. The calluses on her palms fitted so well with the social slot he had created for her.

Later, he would learn that the hobby of her retirement years was rock climbing, hence the good muscle tone and calluses; that she hailed from a large city in the state of Maine, so much for the farm life; that she held advanced degrees in library science and was a denizen of cyberspace.

'Susan McReedy,' she began, not one for unnecessary pronouns and verbs of introduction. 'I don't take you for a sneak, Mr Butler, and I'll tell you why. When I asked you blunt questions on the phone, you didn't lie to me. You wouldn't tell me the truth, Lord knows, but you wouldn't lie. And I suspect that goes against the grain with you. So tell me straight out. Is she still alive?'

After escorting their new interview subject into Charles Butler's private office, Riker sat down in an armchair beside the librarian from Maine. Mallory regretted agreeing to second chair in this interview. Out in the hallway, her partner had argued that little old ladies were his forte, that they loved him on sight. This might well be true, but Susan McReedy was not little, nor did she look all that old, and she could probably take Riker down in two falls out of three.

Riker began with small talk and offers of coffee or tea. The woman from Maine tapped one shoe, barely tolerating this waste of her time. Off his game today, he had missed the other signs of her fidgeting fingers and lips pressed tight. He compounded his error by pausing a beat too long to allow her the full impact of his widest smile. Miss McReedy did not respond in kind. Her mouth dipped down on one side, and now both shoes tapped the floor with irritation. This baffled him. He must wonder what foot he had put wrong.

So obvious.

'You're sure I can't get you a cup of coffee?'

The woman only glared at him, finding him suspicious because of his engaging grin – too quick and easy, too *professionally* charming.

Mallory had a cure for excess charm.

She rose from the couch and moved into that narrow area between their chairs, too close to allow this woman any personal space – and closer. She put her hands on the arms of Miss McReedy's chair and bent low until their eyes were level. Closer. 'So your father was a cop? Was he a *lousy* cop? Didn't he raise you right?' Every inflection dropped out of her tone, and each word had equal weight when she said, 'I – am – the – law. I don't have time to mess with you. Start talking.'

Though Susan McReedy never twitched or blinked, she did smile in approval. 'You want the whole story, or just the salient points?'

Riker stood up, conceding his chair to the new champion of senior-citizen interviews, and Mallory sat down, saying, 'I want everything you've got on the red-haired girl. Don't leave anything out.'

'All right. The girl's hair wasn't red the first time I saw her. It was shoe-polish black – dyed and cut real short.' Miss McReedy had lost her edge, almost mellowing as she described the night, fifty-eight years ago, when two local boys had seen the yellow stalks of headlights beaming up beyond the rim of a bottomless quarry pool. 'The car was hung up on an outcrop of rocks twenty feet below the rim, just hanging there, smashed to bits, all turned around and ready to fall another fifty feet to the water. When Dad and the neighbors got to the lip of the quarry, it looked like it was going down any second. There were six flashlights altogether, all aiming straight down through a broken windshield, and they could see the girl plain as day. So much blood. The twisted metal pinned her down on the passenger side. It was a sheer drop between the edge of the rock face and that car.'

Riker interrupted her, leaning in, asking, 'How did your dad read the scene that night? Did he take it for an accident?'

Susan McReedy turned to Mallory with a raised eyebrow to ask if this interruption was necessary. Mallory only stared at her in silence, and the woman took this for an affirmative.

'My father had two different theories, two years apart. That night, he figured it for an accident. The quarry pool was a good place to lose a car – a body, too – but leaving the headlights on would defeat that purpose, wouldn't it? Now the door on the driver side hung open and angled down toward the water. So he figured the driver – Dad was guessing a teenage boy – ten wrecks out of ten were teenagers – well, he thought the driver must've dropped into the pool and drowned. That was assuming the crash didn't kill him first. You could expect a corpse to bloat up with gas and rise to the surface after a while, but that one never did.'

Mallory made a rolling motion with one hand to move the story back on track.

'Well, a sheer drop like that one, you'd need a rope to get down to where the car was. Dad and my uncle were rock-climbing fools. They had all the gear in the trunks of their cars, and pretty soon, both of them were rappelling down that rock wall by the light of the neighbors' flashlights. They worked for hours to free the girl from that car. One wrong move, the car would drop and the girl would be lost. Nothing has ever come out of that pool – except bloated dead bodies, animals mostly, and a few suicide jumpers.

'All the while they worked, they did a balancing act to keep the car from teetering off that outcrop of rock. Hooked their own lifelines onto the metal. They could've died that night. They didn't care. They were going to carry that girl out if it killed them both to do it.

'So the ambulance crew lowered the stretcher, then Dad and Uncle Henry strapped her in. After they hauled her up, the ambulance driver took one look at that poor broken girl and told my dad she'd never make it. Well, Dad climbed into that ambulance and rode with her to the hospital, talking to her all the while, *demanding* that she survive. And she did. But it was a few years before she was mended. It was one operation after another. She was real brave – all that pain – years of it.'

Riker asked, 'What about the car?'

'It fell into the quarry pool. Dad and his brother were on the way up when the car went down. It was that close.'

'So your dad never traced the car?'

'No need. He knew whose car it was while he was still up on the rim. It was stolen from my uncle's parking lot. Uncle Henry had a little restaurant, the only one for miles around.'

Riker exchanged looks with Mallory.

'I know what you're thinking,' said Miss McReedy, 'but you're getting ahead of the story. You said every detail, right? Well, Dad figured the girl was at least eighteen if not older, full grown. She was a tall one. So that's what he put in his report. If the doctors thought different they never said, or maybe they just couldn't tell. She was so smashed up, poor thing. No part of her was whole. And she could never tell Dad anything helpful, not her name or who the driver was, nothing at all. The hospital called her Jane Doe. We called her our Jane. She lived at our house between hospital stays. Dad could never quite let go of that girl until the day he died, and his brother felt the same way. The three of them were forever tied together in a way that wasn't quite like family. In some ways, it was a closer bond. I know that sounds odd.'

'I understand it,' said Riker.

Mallory knew she had missed something important here, but she let it slide away, for it had nothing to do with her case.

Susan McReedy was less annoyed with Riker when he asked about her father's second theory. 'I'm getting to that,' she said. 'The poor girl had gone through four operations before she was off the crutches for good. Then she wanted to earn her own keep. Two years had gone by. We thought she was at least twenty years old by then.'

The woman reached down and pulled a paperback book from the carpetbag at her feet. 'But I guess we all know better now. She was only twelve when we found her. Isn't that right?' Miss McReedy turned from Mallory to Riker. Her expression was almost a challenge to contradict her. She was satisfied by their silence and continued. 'So she was just fourteen years old when my uncle gave her that little apartment over the restaurant. I wish that we had known she was just a little girl.'

The woman stared at her shoes, overcome by sadness. Mallory and Riker kept their silence.

'Everyone admired our Jane for working in the restaurant – so public and all. Customers tended to stare at her in all the wounded places that showed, but she soldiered on. Looked them all right in the eye as if her face were normal, good as theirs. That's when we came to believe she was really on the mend.'

Mallory stared at the cover illustration of the book in the woman's hand. It was a reproduction of the *Red Winter* painting. A store receipt stood for a bookmark. This woman had only recently worked it all out.

'I guess,' said Susan McReedy, 'I can put one thing and another together pretty well. First that New York author calls me a few years back. And then Mr Butler – the same questions.' The librarian held up the book when she said, 'I'm sure you guessed – our Jane didn't look anything like this on the night of the accident – or anytime after that. Her face was broken, nose, cheekbones, her jaw – and that child's legs. Oh, Lord. They rebuilt her with steel pins and sewing needles.'

Susan McReedy paused, but not to any dramatic effect. She was having difficulty going on with her story, and she had not yet come to the most important part. Riker was leaning forward to interrupt one more time. Mallory glared at him to warn him off.

'So one day, all of us were going up to Bangor to see my grandma. But Jane wanted to stay behind. Well, my uncle closed the restaurant that weekend, and he guessed the girl wanted to spend her free time reading. Always had her nose in a book, that one – a habit she picked up in the hospital, I guess.

'Two days later, we came home and found her in that little apartment over the restaurant. She was sitting on her bedroom floor beside a dead body – a man with an ice pick in his chest. Flies everywhere, but our Jane didn't seem to notice them – or him, either. She'd gone all the way crazy. Just rocking back and forth. I don't think she could hear us when we spoke to her.'

It was all too clear that Miss McReedy was seeing that tableau again, fresh as yesterday's blood and blowflies.

'And your dad,' said Riker, 'how did he read that crime scene?'

'It was obvious. The man she'd killed – he'd broken into her place. No doubt about it. He broke down the bedroom door to get at her. It was off its damn hinge. She must've been so frightened.'

'And,' said Mallory, 'she just happened to keep an ice pick in her bedroom.'

'Yes, and that was the saddest part. That nearly killed my father. And that's how he put the whole thing together.' She fell silent for a moment.

'So that's when he worked out his second theory,' said Riker, gently prompting her.

Susan McReedy nodded. 'It was an old ice pick he found in the dead man's chest. The painted handle was flaking. It used to be in Uncle Henry's restaurant. He told Dad he tossed it out just after our Jane moved in upstairs. The girl must have found it in the trash and kept it all that time. Dad saw flakes of that same color paint on the underside of her pillowcase. And that's how he knew, for all that time, she'd gone to sleep every night with that pick underneath her pillow. All that time she'd been waiting for that man, the one who'd left her for dead at the quarry. She'd been waiting for him to come back and finish her off.'

The retired librarian looked down at her hands as she folded the paperback book into a fat cylinder. 'And then came the second theory of what happened at the quarry pool. Dad figured our Jane was the only one in the car when it went over the rim that night. So that was no accident. It was attempted murder. Dad didn't see the driver as a local man, nobody who lived in walking distance. He'd stolen that car because he'd be needing his own car to make a getaway. So he was a stranger, just like our Jane.

'After she killed that man with the ice pick – if Dad had only known – how young she was. Well, if he'd known, then I don't think he would've let them take her to the hospital that day or any other day. From there she went to a state asylum. That made Dad and my uncle so crazy. They tried, time after time, to get her out of there and bring her home. But every time they got a new sanity hearing, she'd do something to mess it up. Once she slashed her wrists. Another time it was her throat. Finally, Dad had to let go of her. He came to understand—' Susan McReedy's hands were clasped tightly around her paperback and squeezing it. 'This really hurt him – but he realized that our Jane felt safer in that place than home with us. He didn't protect her when she needed him most. My father went to visit her every weekend until he died. Then the asylum was closed down for Medicare fraud, and the patients were scattered all over creation. Years later, I tracked one Jane Doe to a nursing home north of Auburn – but it wasn't our Jane.'

'All right,' said Mallory, moving on, 'your father must've traced the dead man's fingerprints.'

'Yes, he did. It took a while. No national data base in those days. The dead man had a record in three southern states, con games and stealing. Never killed anybody that we knew of. He was jailed under a slew of names, but never for any great length of time.'

'What about Humboldt,' said Riker, 'remember that one?'

'And all his other names.' She bent down to the carpetbag at her feet and pulled out a thick envelope. Opening it, she emptied the file folders onto the coffee table.

Mallory leafed through the decades of yellowed documents, one man's search for a red-haired girl's past, an ongoing inquiry that had lasted another twenty years after Nedda had killed Stick Man. And now she was staring at the original cards bearing the dead man's fingerprints.

'So,' said Susan McReedy, regaining her poise, 'you think that man, Humboldt, killed her family. You think that's why our Jane took him down with an ice pick.' She held tight to the paperback book with the painted image of a naked child, Red Winter, her Jane. 'So she saw that – her family murdered. Twelve years old and she—' Words had failed the woman from Maine.

'Yeah,' said Riker. 'If the reporters get hold of this story . . .' He knew that he would not have to finish that thought for her.

The woman was nodding, saying, 'I understand. We never talked, and I was never here.' She turned to Mallory. 'But could I see her – just a picture of her?'

Mallory held up one finger to tell the woman to remain where she was, then rose from her chair and left the room – taking the files of Jane Doe along with her. When she returned, she held out a crime-scene photo, and not the one that pictured Nedda Winter seated near a more recent corpse. It was a simple shot of the old woman standing before the grand staircase, majestic, her face and body no longer broken as they were in Miss McReedy's memories. 'Here, take it. Keep it.'

'Thank you.' The woman stared at the image of her Jane grown old. 'She looks good, doesn't she? I never saw her face after—' She looked up at Mallory, smiling at a sudden recollection. 'My father paid for that, you know – after she was committed to the asylum. Three more operations with a plastic surgeon, and it cost the moon to do it. But Dad just had to finish putting her back together again.' Miss McReedy became lost in the photograph once more. 'Oh, what a pretty robe she's wearing. And that looks like a real fine house.'

'Yeah,' said Riker, 'a mansion.'

The woman looked up from this treasure that marked the end of her own family quest. 'This story doesn't have a happy ending, does it?'

'No,' said Mallory. 'Don't expect that.'

And now that Susan McReedy's usefulness was over, the young detective turned her back and left the room and went to her own office, where she began to pin the contents of the Maine file to her cork wall. Fifteen minutes had passed, and she was not yet done marrying these pages to those in the file made by Riker's grandfather when her partner sang out, 'Hey, Mallory! You gotta hear this.'

She walked into the reception room to find Robin Duffy and Riker bent over the answering machine. They were playing back the messages from Bitty Smyth slurring her words more with each call and asking when her aunt was coming back home.

'Nedda's gone,' said Robin. 'And so is Charles. A little while ago, Nedda called him on the phone in his apartment. He was off like a shot. Going to the hospital, he said. Something about an overdose of pills.'

Cleo Winter-Smyth, her brother and her ex-husband were seated in the hospital lounge, and all three heads were slowly turning to follow the progress of Charles Butler's march from the street door to the front desk. A nurse assured him that, yes, he was on the restricted list of visitors.

He could feel three pairs of eyes on his back as he walked to the elevator. Apparently these family members had not made the cut.

Curious.

Riker folded his cell phone. 'They're all at the hospital. The whole family came in together. Sheldon Smyth's there, too.'

'Good.' Mallory double-parked her car in front of Winter House. 'Then there's nobody home to mess with the crime scene.'

According to Riker's source at the hospital, the only crime had been an attempted suicide, but his partner loosely translated this to an attempted murder that would give them free access to the house without the tedium of chasing down a warrant.

They climbed the short flight of stone steps to the front door. Mallory was unwrapping the small velvet pouch that held her favorite lock picks.

'Hold it.' Riker turned the knob. The door opened. 'I'd say that speaks well for the family.' He entered the foyer and looked around. 'Nobody home. They were in such a hurry to get Bitty to the hospital, they forgot to lock up.'

'Not quite. One of them stopped to set the alarm.' She punched in the numbers and the glowing light went out.

'How'd you know the code?' He held up both hands. 'Never mind, I never asked.'

A door was closing on the floor above them.

'There's someone in the house.' Mallory raced up the stairs and reached Bitty Smyth's bedroom in time to hear the toilet flush and smell the vomit beneath a layer of cleaning solvent. The evidence was now swirling down the drain.

A woman in a shapeless dress, hired help by the looks of her, emerged from the private bathroom to see Mallory standing there, angry.

And the woman screamed.

'You cleaned up after Bitty Smyth,' said Mallory, unperturbed by the high-pitched wailing. 'Who told you to do that?'

'Police!' the woman screamed. 'Help! Police!'

Riker was in the doorway, panting and reaching into his back pocket for the badge that would shut this woman up. He could not yet speak. Heavy breathing was all that he could manage.

The woman screamed again, louder this time.

243

* * *

Bitty had been drifting in and out of consciousness. When she was fully awake, the hospital's resident psychiatrist ordered the room cleared. The two visitors retreated, going off in search of the cafeteria.

Nedda relied on Charles to follow the signs and arrows that would lead them to hot coffee. He guided her into a brightly lit room of Formica tables, sparsely populated with people in street clothes, some sitting alone, others huddled in twos and threes. Only matters of life and death could account for the laymen gathered here at this late hour.

Charles seated his companion at a secluded island table close to the wall and far from eavesdroppers. When he returned with their coffee in paper cups, he picked up the conversation begun in the corridor. 'So you're quite sure it was a suicide attempt?'

She nodded. 'Bitty's not a strong person. I remember when I was drowning in despair. I know all the signs. My own suicide attempt took years. I used to swallow pills that other patients spit out on the floor.'

'But your niece has a prescription for sleeping pills. No chance of an accidental overdose?'

'None. Bitty also has a phobia. She can't swallow tablets. They have to be crushed in water before she can get them down. You see how unlikely it is that she could lose track of them.'

'Did you mention that to—'

'The psychiatrist? Yes. Bitty gave my name as next of kin. I'm sure my sister didn't appreciate that.'

And consequently this would not be the time for any family meeting with the object of reconciliation.

'What triggered the attempt? Any ideas?'

'My fault,' said Nedda. 'Looking at this through Bitty's eyes, I blame myself. She worked so hard to do this wonderful thing for Cleo and Lionel. She found their lost sister. It should have been a magnificent present. Poor Bitty. She couldn't know that I was the last person they would ever want to see.'

'Why such animosity?'

'Because of the murders – their parents, their brothers and sisters. Every time they look at me, it hurts them more than knives cutting into their eyes.'

When Charles and Nedda returned to Bitty's hospital room, her attending physician was waiting for them, saying, 'It's all settled. She'll be with us for a few days.'

'And there'll be a cop posted on the door,' said Mallory, striding into the room. She glared at the tiny woman on the bed as if this attempt at suicide had been a ploy simply to annoy her.

Charles could tell that Bitty was only feigning sleep this time, but he said nothing to give her away.

Mallory turned her attention to Nedda. 'You should've called the police first. Now it's too late. All the evidence is gone. No one told those idiots in the emergency room to save the stomach contents.'

The doctor was about to take offense at this, for she was referring to *his* idiots. But now, thinking better of that, with perhaps a keen eye for disturbing personalities who carried guns, he was edging away from Mallory and toward the door, then gone.

'There's no mystery about her stomach contents,' said Nedda. 'Prescription sleeping pills. My niece took an accidental overdose.' She lied nearly as well as her opponent. 'Calling the police never entered my mind.'

That much was certainly true.

Oh, no.

Mallory was leaning over Bitty for a closer look, saying, 'She's faking. She's awake.'

'That's enough,' said Nedda. 'My niece needs rest, and you need to leave this room.'

The young detective was squaring off against the older woman when Charles appeared at Nedda's side, lending support to the idea that Mallory should leave, and right now. It was an unsettling moment. Charles looked into Mallory's eyes and roughly guessed her thoughts. She was wondering if he would humiliate her, if he would physically move her out of this room, laying hands on her for the second time in one day. And, no, he would not have the heart for that. But she chose not to give him the benefit of that doubt in her mind. She turned and left the room.

Mallory could commit any sort of bad act and depend upon *him* to feel the guilt.

How did she do that?

Riker sat with the family members in the reception area of the hospital.

His pen moved across the page of his notebook, taking down their statements on Bitty's overdose. 'Any idea how many pills she took?'

'No, we never thought to ask,' said Bitty's mother. 'It was quite a scene. Nedda was jamming her fingers down my daughter's throat to induce vomiting. I was—'

'On the phone,' said Lionel, finishing the sentence, 'calling for an ambulance.'

Sheldon Smyth was being unusually quiet for a lawyer. Riker wanted to stick a knife in the old man by asking exactly when Cleo and Lionel had discovered that the law firm was ripping off their trust fund, but Mallory would shoot him for tipping their hand too soon.

He looked up to see his partner marching across the lobby, heading toward this little family with all the deadly resolution of a train on the way to a wreck. He turned back to Cleo, resident of a planet where people communicated via telepathy. The woman was staring at her brother. Something passed between them, and they were of one mind, Riker was sure of that, before their heads turned in unison to stare at Mallory.

These people were creeping him out.

* * *

This time, Bitty was not faking. She had fallen into a natural state of sleep, and there was no conversation between Charles and Nedda, neither of them wanting to disturb her rest.

But now the patient stirred, eyes opening to smile at her aunt. 'I knew you'd come.'

'To the rescue?' said Charles. 'So you knew you were in trouble tonight.'

'I must have taken too many sleeping pills.' All the signs of a lie were there, eyes shifting away from his, fingers fidgeting on the blanket, so uncomfortable in this falsehood.

'You're not sure?' He smiled to say never mind. 'I heard your messages on my machine. 'It seems like you knew what was happening, but you waited for Nedda. Why not call an ambulance yourself?'

'I wasn't thinking very clearly?'

Perhaps she had not believed that her family would have opened the door to an ambulance. That was one possibility, the one that Kathy Mallory would have liked best.

Mallory sat in the hospital lounge, facing Cleo and Lionel with the clear understanding that they were a unit. What they had suffered as children might have formed that weird bond. Or it might have developed while they were murdering their little sister, the only Winter child still unaccounted for. Bitty Smyth's near death had expanded the possible scenarios for Sally Winter's disappearance.

Where would two children hide a little corpse? Not in the hat closet that had so intrigued Mrs Ortega. Children did not wall up bodies. They buried them as they buried family pets. The dead girl would have taken up no more ground than a good-size dog.

Child's play.

Brother and sister sat together with the same body language, arms folded, eyes level and calm, meeting her gaze and awaiting the inevitable interrogation. She let them wait. Sheldon Smyth seemed sober now. The old lawyer was tensing, also bracing for an onslaught of questions. His brow was lightly filmed with sweat, though the hospital lounge was cool and dry.

This old man was going to be so easy to break.

She could watch the works of his brain churning behind his eyes, trying to anticipate her first question, heart racing. All three of them were waiting for her, wondering when she would begin the inquisition. The three of them were leaning slightly forward, expectant crows on a wire.

Mallory stood up and turned her back on the trio, then crossed the lobby in tandem with her partner – and without a single word spoken.

The documents raided from the Smyth firm gave Mallory's private office at Butler and Company the look of a temporary warehouse, but one located in that other dimension where Chinese puzzle blocks were born. She was stacking cartons of varied sizes to form an enormous cardboard cube at the center of the room.

While she explained that the outer shell was made with as-yet unread documents, Riker admired the walls of her structure from all sides. It was a maniacally efficient use of space, and very disturbing to a man who tossed discarded beer cartons into the corners of his apartment so he could readily discern the empties from the partially emptied.

Riker wrecked her perfect symmetry by dragging a carton out of formation.

An hour later, he was sitting on the floor, almost done, gently laying out the last of the brittle pieces of paper from the middle years of the previous century. These canceled checks bore the signature of the guardian, James Winter, and they were arranged in the order of their dates. 'If Sally Winter didn't die of natural causes, we can rule out Uncle James for the killer.' He looked up at his partner. She was engrossed in Pinwitty's book and paying no attention to him. 'Aren't you going to ask me why?'

'Hmm.' Mallory turned another page.

Riker had finished working backward in time to lay out the last check. 'It looks like James skipped town before Sally died. All the signatures in this group were traced. Every one of them exactly the same. I guess the Smyth firm didn't want to break in a new guardian so they kept him around on paper. But these forged checks are still making payouts for doctor's visits and home nursing for the kid.'

'I never thought James Winter killed Sally.' Mallory held her place, marking the page with one finger as she closed the book. 'This text is unreadable, but the pictures are interesting. Were there any prints on Stick Man's ice pick? There's nothing about it in this book or your grandfather's notes.'

'Who knows? I told you, all the evidence boxes were robbed, gutted for souvenirs. That ice pick disappeared fifty years ago.'

One long red fingernail tapped the book cover. 'So how did Pinwitty get a photograph of the pick?'

'What? There aren't any photographs in that book.'

'Then Charles's copy must be a revised edition.' Mallory opened the volume and showed him the clear picture of an ice pick in an evidence bag. 'You can even read the detective's signature on the label.'

Upon their second visit to Martin Pinwitty's one-room apartment, the first thing the detectives noticed was an elaborate profusion of flowers, exotic blooms well beyond the author's purse.

'It's a sympathy bouquet. My mother died yesterday.' Pinwitty rushed to the stove and began a lame attempt at hospitality, lighting a flame under his teakettle.

This time, the detectives did not feel obliged to eat stale pastries and drink cheap swill. Riker turned off the gas burner. 'Just give us the ice pick, and we'll go.'

Pinwitty's lips parted as if to scream.

Riker was holding up the book, and it was opened to the picture of the murder weapon in an evidence bag. '*This* pick.'

'I bought that photograph. I never actually had the—'

'No,' said Riker, 'you don't wanna lie to a cop.' He flipped through the pages of the picture section. 'You took all these shots yourself. Cheaper that way, right? Your publishers even gave you a photographer's credit.'

'I don't have the pick anymore.'

'Yeah, you do,' said Riker. 'The Winter House Massacre is your whole life. Once you had that pick, you'd never let it go.'

'My mother's illness was very costly. I had to sell off a lot of things.'

Riker shook his head to let the man know that he was not buying this excuse. 'You would've sold your mother for medical experiments before you sold that pick.'

Pinwitty was backing away, when he made eye contact with Mallory. He turned back to face Riker, finding him less threatening – a mistake – and now the author made a little stand of sorts. He straightened what passed for a spine and thrust out his chin, what there was of it. 'The pick is mine. I bought and paid for it.'

'Well,' said Riker, 'that makes my job a lot easier. You just admitted to buying stolen goods. Give me the pick or we tack on a few more charges.'

'Statute of limitations,' said the author. 'I bought it more than seven years ago.'

'You got me there, pal. I can see that I just don't watch enough cop shows on television. So I guess all we've got on you is concealing evidence in an ongoing case. No, wait a minute. If you broke the seal on the bag, we can add tampering with evidence. And then there's my personal favorite, obstruction of a homicide investigation.' He stepped toward Pinwitty, and the man fell back into a chair, startled to be suddenly sitting down and looking up at the detective's angry face. Riker put his hands on the padded arms of the chair and leaned into the author's face as he explained the worst of this man's crimes. 'And you're pissing off my partner.'

Riker pointed to Mallory, who was seated in a chair next to the sympathy bouquet, idly ripping the heads off of flowers.

The chief of Forensics personally returned the ice pick to Mallory and Riker. More accurately, he dropped the pick on his desk blotter and threw the paperwork in Riker's direction. The big man leaned forward, voice icy, saying, 'You told my people this was a rush . . . for a fifty-eight-year-old homicide. You *bastards*. I'm up to my eye-balls in work, and you come in here with this crap.'

Riker was mentally digging himself a foxhole underneath his chair.

'So,' said Mallory, so casually, as if she were not in deep trouble for lying to Heller's staff, 'you got a match on the fingerprints?'

And now it was her turn to receive a flying object – the small white card with Nedda Winter's elimination prints from a more recent crime scene. It sailed across the desk and landed in her lap.

Riker regarded Finnegan's Bar as the front room for his upstairs apartment. It saved him the trouble of picking up his dirty socks when company came calling. And now he greeted his first guest of the evening and waved the man to an empty bar stool reserved in his honor. 'Hey, thanks for coming.'

Charles Butler had been to Finnegan's before, but he still turned heads with the regulars, men and women with guns. He stood a head above the rest, broader in the shoulders and entirely too well dressed for this dive and this company of wall-to-wall police. 'When will they release Nedda?'

'She's not a prisoner.' Riker held up one hand to flag down the bartender. Two fingers in the air netted him a nod and a promise of two beers. 'She can walk out any time she likes. This wasn't Mallory's idea. Nedda wanted to do it. I'll get a call when it's over. You're sure the lady doesn't want police protection tonight?'

'No, she was adamant about that. She's positive that her niece attempted suicide. And I agree with her. Maybe it was a cry for help, but not attempted murder.'

'So Nedda's moving in with you?'

'For a few days.' Charles accepted a beer from the bartender. 'Maybe longer.'

'You didn't discuss any of the evidence with her, did you? I mean the will, the trust fund.'

'No, it never came up in the conversation. And I don't think she gives a damn about money. That's Mallory's fixation, not Nedda's.' Charles sipped his beer, not inclined to volunteer any more.

'So I'm guessing you and Mallory are at odds right now. I'm guessing 'cause the kid never tells me anything.'

'I suppose I question her methods.'

'Yeah, she does things that you'd never do.' Riker drained his glass. 'And a few things I wouldn't do, either. That's what makes her a great cop. Now, if she was working for the opposition, I'd lose sleep at night. Did you have any time to look at my file?'

Charles laid the ancient folder on the bar. It contained more of Pinwitty's collection, pictures recently acquired for the next revision of his book. The old crime-scene photographs showed all the dead bodies of the massacre, some large and some painfully small. 'I agree with you. It fits better with a murder for hire. Not the work of a lunatic or someone with anger issues.' He lowered his head and spoke to his glass. 'You know what's most disturbing about the massacre at Winter House? Oddly enough, it's the lack of rage. Assembly-line carnage. How do you profile a killer like that? Someone sane who kills for the money?'

'Well, Charles, you don't. You know why? These people don't drop in from another planet. They don't start out as psychos. They're us.' He could see that Charles was resisting this idea. 'I can tell you how it's done, how they're made. You take a youngster out in the woods. The boy's first kill is all set up for him. The victim is kneeling on the ground, hands tied behind his back. All the kid has to do is put the gun to the back of this man's skull and squeeze the trigger. But the victim is begging for his life and crying. There's maybe two, three other men watching the kid. They're all junkyard dogs, but they wear silk suits. They drive nice cars. And the boy looks up to them. He can't back down, can he? Naw, too humiliating. Plus, he's scared shitless. He's either one of them or he's a liability. Hell of a choice he's got. So he does it. It's a small thing, they tell him. Just squeeze the trigger, kid, they say. And that's what the kid does. He blows a human being away and gets sick all over his shoes. He's crossed a line, and he can't get back. The next time is easier. Soon it's just his job. He wasn't born to do this. I guess that's why the mob would call him a *made man*. He'll spend most of his life in prison, but the boy doesn't know that yet. You can make a hitman out of almost anybody, but it's better if you get 'em young.'

Riker nodded toward the window. Beyond the glass, a twelve-year-old boy stood on the sidewalk talking to a girl, his flawless face growing pinker by the second. He was falling in love for the first time, his whole shining life ahead of him. 'That kid would do.'

Charles turned his face to the window and the youngster on the sidewalk, so innocent, the raw makings of evil. 'What about Mallory – when she was younger?'

'Naw. She wasn't the best scratch material.' Did that sound reassuring? Would Charles buy a lie? 'When she was ten years old, she was a full-blown person.' He smiled at this memory of a wildly talented street thief with the chilling eyes of a small stone killer. 'And she hasn't changed all that much.'

Charles seemed genuinely relieved. What a gift for denial. Poor bastard, he was always seeking evidence of a beating heart and a bit of a soul, never appreciating the true marvel of Mallory – that she functioned so well without them.

TEN

Lieutenant Coffey was in the dark, and he was in awe. On the other side of the one-way glass, Nedda Winter was seated at the long table, passively watching a police aide, who laid out the polygraph equipment, the rubber tubes, the clips and their wires.

'So that's Red Winter.' Jack Coffey's words were as soft as whispers in church. 'When the lady came in, she told the desk sergeant that your polygraph exam was never finished.'

The lady?

Nedda Winter's supporters were legion now.

'This was her idea, not mine.' Mallory sat down beside the lieutenant.

'But no pressure, right?' He kept his eyes on the woman in the next room. 'I know her niece attempted suicide tonight. You didn't make any threats against Bitty Smyth, did you?'

Even Bitty had champions.

When the police aide had departed from the interview room, Nedda Winter reached out for the transducer and attached this cardio device to her thumb. Next the woman bound herself with the rubber tubes that would record her breathing, and last she attached the clips to her fingers. Dragging her wires with her, she moved her chair back to the wall. After removing both her shoes, she sat there, very still, staring at the one-way mirror, the window for the two police sitting side by side – watching.

'All the years I've been on this job,' said Jack Coffey, 'I've never seen anybody do that before.' He turned his eyes to Mallory. Unspoken was the question *What did you do to that woman?* He could never voice his suspicions. Contrary to policy, Mallory had failed to tape the previous polygraph examination. Now he was assuming the worst of her and only grateful that there was no proof.

Mallory's hands curled into fists under cover of darkness.

Rising from his chair, the lieutenant said, 'Lock up this room before you go in there. I don't want anyone to see this.' And he would not watch either, no stomach for it.

'Wait,' said Mallory. 'You think I'm a monster, right? So why don't *you* take over?' Her tone was pure acid. 'Go on. Fix the old lady a nice cup of tea. Be her new best friend. See if she tells you *anything* useful – anything at all.'

Jack Coffey's hand rested on the doorknob. He would not turn around, and he could not leave.

'But first,' said Mallory, 'you can take my badge.' She rose from her chair and stepped closer to the window on the interview room, then leaned her forehead against the glass. 'I'm so tired of everybody lining up behind Nedda Winter. What's the point of me showing up for work anymore?' Mallory reached into her back pocket and pulled out the leather folder that held her gold shield. 'The old woman's holding out on me, and that'll get her killed. But what the hell. If she dies, she dies, right? And nobody cares who massacred her family. And Sally Winter – more old history. Who cares if that little girl's body was stuffed in a hole like a dead dog? Not me – not you.'

Jack Coffey turned around to face his detective. 'I know you'll never let go of that badge, Mallory. You're better at this than your old man when he was in his prime.' He quit the room, closing the door softly, just to let her know that, though she had cut him at the knees, there were no hard feelings.

And now that she had beaten Coffey, she glanced at the window on the interrogation room. One down and one to go.

She looked over her handiwork, this barefoot woman wired to a machine, every muscle tensing, bracing. They stared at one another. Nedda was blind to Mallory, but well aware that she was being watched from the other side of the mirror. The woman was waiting so patiently for the game to begin. She raised her head, as if to ask the young detective – *When?*

Kathy Mallory left the observation room, locking the door behind her, not out of deference to Jack Coffey's wishes, but for the sake of privacy alone. She entered the brightly lit interview room, and Nedda Winter looked up with no reproach for what was about to happen to her.

Mallory knelt down on bended knee and lifted Nedda's right foot in her hand, noting its fragile, paper-thin skin and the raised blue veins that came with age and a hard life. She gently slipped one shoe back on the woman's foot and carefully tied the laces, not too loose, not too tight. When she had done the second shoe, she raised her face to Nedda's. 'The night you killed Willy Roy Boyd – you didn't find that ice pick on the bar – in the dark. You had it under your pillow, didn't you?'

Nedda nodded between wariness and surprise.

Mallory removed the metal clips and unfastened the tubes that bound the woman's breast. 'You never feel safe anymore, do you?'

'No. Not for a long time.'

'Not since you left the last hospital.' Mallory walked back to the table and pulled out an ordinary wooden chair that had no wires. 'Sit here.' Fumbling with her list of rules for a life, she added the word '*Please*'. When Nedda had joined her at the table, the detective said, 'Suppose we just talk.'

And Nedda did.

She began with the morning of the massacre, counting up the dead. 'All those bodies. When I got to the top of the house and saw the nanny on the floor, I couldn't go into that nursery. I didn't want to see Sally's body. I couldn't find Cleo and Lionel, but I'd only searched the rooms upstairs.'

Returning to the staircase, she had stopped awhile by her step-mother's corpse. 'She was a silly, flighty woman, but I loved her so much. She was the only mother I ever knew. Then I sat down on the steps beside my father's body.'

James Winter had entered the house as she was pulling the ice pick from her father's chest. 'Uncle James bundled me into the car, and we drove to a dingy little building in Greenwich Village. He left me there for days and days. Said he had to go back for the ice pick because my fingerprints were on it. When I saw him again, he told me it was no good. The police got to the house before he did, and they had the ice pick. He said they'd found the bodies of all the children, Cleo and Lionel too. And the baby was dead. They were hunting for me, he said. He cut off my hair and dyed it with shoe black. I stayed in that room for a long time. I don't know how many days. I lost count. An old woman brought my food. Clothes, too – I think they were hers. She was very kind to me.'

'She's the one who taught you to read the tarot cards,' said Mallory.

'How did you know that?'

'I know almost everything. Just a few more loose ends. Go on.'

'One night, the street outside my window was full of police. I thought they'd come for me. The old woman came upstairs. She said we had to clean the place right away, and then I'd have to leave. If the police found any trace of me, she'd go to jail. We worked all night into morning, washing down the walls, the floor, the furniture. While she was downstairs, getting a suitcase for me, the police came and took her away. Later that day, Uncle James came back. We waited for dark, and then we drove up to Maine. He said he had a summer cabin there. When we crossed the state line, he stole a car from a restaurant parking lot and left his own car in its place. I remember a road into the woods. After that, all I have are missing pieces of memory – like Uncle James turning off the headlights. I thought that was queer. The road was so narrow, and the woods were pitch dark.

We were driving blind. The last thing I recall was the car's inside light coming on. I don't remember the crash. When I woke up, I was in the dark, and the car was rocking. I was in so much pain. I turned on the headlights. They pointed straight up at the sky, and below me there was nothing but black space. I screamed.'

'A cop named Walter McReedy rescued you.'

'Yes. Later, he told me that the driver had drowned in the quarry pool.'

'You never told McReedy who the driver was?'

'I thought Uncle James was dead. Walter said the body would float up eventually, but it never did. And he never mentioned finding my uncle's abandoned car in the restaurant parking lot. I could never ask him about it. I told him I couldn't remember anything.'

'And that's how you knew your uncle meant to kill you that night.'

'Yes. Uncle James must have jumped from the car just before it went over the edge. That's why the inside light came on. And the police never found his car because he'd used it to drive back to New York. So I knew he'd tried to kill me. And he was still alive.'

'You couldn't tell Walter McReedy the truth.'

'No, and I couldn't go home again. I didn't know that there was anyone alive to come back to. And the police had my fingerprints on the ice pick.'

'This pick.' Mallory reached into her knapsack and pulled out a plastic bag containing the murder weapon. 'There were only two fingerprints on the handle. That's how the police ruled you out as a suspect. Thumb and index finger, the prints you left when you pulled the pick out of your father's body. There's no other scenario for the way they appeared on the weapon. Otherwise the pick was clean. So the lead detective figured the killer had the presence of mind to wipe that pick after using it to murder nine people – so why leave two clear prints behind on a murder weapon? The fingerprints cleared you. Those cops only wanted to find you and bring you home.'

Nedda bowed her head. 'If I had known that Cleo and Lionel were still alive, I would've told Walter McReedy everything. But I believed Uncle James when he told me that their bodies were found in the kitchen. I never got to that room.'

Mallory leaned toward her, one hand resting on her arm. 'You spent two years with the McReedy family.'

'Off and on – between surgeries. Most of the time was spent in the hospital.'

'The McReedys never talked about the Winter House Massacre? That was national news.'

Nedda almost smiled. 'Once, there was life before television. You can't imagine that, can you? But we had radio on a clear night, one station from Bangor that played gospel music.'

'You were famous.'

'But I wasn't the Lindbergh baby – just the debris of a crime that happened somewhere else. The local paper was a two-page weekly newsletter. And the biggest news in that small town was the story of the McReedy brothers rescuing me and risking their lives to do it. Now you see why my uncle took me there to die.'

Mallory nodded. 'And all that time you spent with the McReedy family, you were waiting for James Winter to come back and kill you.'

'Yes. Twice I thought he was dead, and I was wrong both times. When I was fourteen, I thought I was being watched. No – I *knew* he was watching me.'

'Your uncle James.'

'Yes. I found cigarette butts at the edge of the yard, and sometimes I'd see them glowing in the dark from my window. I didn't want Uncle James to come after me while I was living with the McReedys. I couldn't lose my second family that way. So . . . when the family left town to visit relatives . . . I stayed behind.'

'You set yourself up as bait to draw him out.'

'I loved the McReedys.' Nedda looked down at her folded hands. 'The man came for me in the dark. He broke down my bedroom

259

door. But I was ready for him. I'd been ready for two years.'

'You stabbed him with an ice pick you kept under your pillow.'

'Yes, but it wasn't Uncle James. I sat next to the corpse all night long. When morning came, I never looked at the man's face. I couldn't bear to see him. I was still afraid of him – even then. Can you understand that?'

No, Mallory could not, but she nodded, saying, 'You were only a little girl.'

'When the McReedys found me there with the body, I was sent to a hospital. They said I was in shock. I couldn't speak for days. It took a long time for Walter McReedy to identify the corpse. He visited me in the hospital and told me that I'd killed a small-time criminal named Humboldt. I asked him over and over if that could be a mistake, and he said no, that was impossible. Fingerprints never lied.'

'So you stayed in the hospital to keep that family safe. You figured James Winter was always out there, waiting for another chance to kill you.' This also explained the death of Willy Roy Boyd and the near-death experience of the private investigator in the park. It was Nedda Winter's job in life, all her life, to protect the people she loved.

The detective laid two sets of fingerprint cards on the table. One had been found in Pinwitty's stash of stolen evidence, souvenirs of a massacre. 'These are your uncle's elimination prints. The police took them on the day of the massacre. They wanted to rule out family members.' The second set of prints had come from the New Orleans police; this was the fruit of Riker's grandfather and his lifelong search for Red Winter. 'This set of prints belonged to the man you stabbed in Maine. They're a perfect match for James Winter.'

'That's impossible.' Nedda shook her head. 'My uncle was alive for *years* after I stabbed Humboldt.'

'No, that's the story you got from your family. And the real story? After two years as guardian, James Winter's signatures were forged on all his checks. He was dead. You stabbed him to death when you were fourteen years old. He died in Maine the night he came back to kill you.' She held up both sets of cards. 'Walter McReedy was right. Fingerprints can't lie. Your uncle and Humboldt were the same man.'

Mallory waited out a long silence in something close to pity or mercy – as close as she could come to these qualities. She had just told this woman that her life in hiding had been for nothing – that she could have gone home to grow up in her own house with Cleo and Lionel – her family. And now the truth was slowly, quietly killing Nedda Winter.

'If you like . . . I could get you a cup of tea,' said Mallory, as if she had not just destroyed this woman.

Nedda reached out for the detective's hand, but she must have sensed that her touch would be unwelcome, and she withdrew.

'These are just copies.' Mallory slid the fingerprint cards across the table, making a little bridge to Nedda Winter with these sorry bits of paper. 'You can keep them . . . if you like.'

The woman's mouth opened wide to emit a strangled cry. She doubled over as if her great pain were physical and her wounds mortal. And then came the tears.

And now Mallory knew what she must do.

She left the room to fetch a cup of tea. The magical properties of this drink were writ large in her inherited rule book for life in Copland. Tea was a detective's official bandage for grief and tears – so said her foster father. Coffee made people jittery, Lou Markowitz would say, and soda's just as bad. Oh, but a cup of tea could soothe all the bloodless wounds, the killer pain that came with the worst news of life and death in New York City. Mallory had simply accepted this arcane lore and gave it equal credence with her store of instructions for the best way to bag blood-soaked clothing and the meaning of maggots in a ripe corpse.

Tea would fix Nedda Winter.

The three of them silently advanced down the hospital corridor, but Cleo and Lionel were not part of Sheldon Smyth's united front. They

Carol O'Connell

had reservations, and Sheldon must have sensed this for he turned to his ex-wife, saying, 'Cleo, we simply can't leave Bitty here.'

'Why not?'

'It doesn't matter now,' said Lionel Winter. 'The decision's been made for us. Bitty isn't going anywhere.' He pointed to the end of the corridor and the police guard posted outside of his niece's room.

'He won't be a problem,' said Sheldon. 'I can get a court order if it comes to that. I'm not without friends in this town.'

'And family,' said Cleo. Indeed, there were Smyth connections to all the major fortunes of New York City. They were prolific with their seed, all but sterile Sheldon. He had been forced to adopt his family's bastards, Paul and Bitty, the cuckoo's eggs planted in other people's bloodlines.

'Bitty will be in my custody,' said Sheldon.

'We'll see,' countered his ex-wife. Lionel stood at her side to form a little wall of two that would brook no resistance. Cleo left her ex-husband to the chore of cowing the young policeman while, against the officer's protests, she and Lionel walked into Bitty's hospital room.

Charles Butler entered the interrogation room to find Nedda with her eyes red and swollen. Her face was wet with tears.

He held his arm out and she took it, allowing him to raise her from the table. As they moved toward the door, she did an odd thing, considering whom she was dealing with tonight. Nedda rested one hand on Mallory's shoulder and lightly kissed her hair. The young detective never moved. She only sat there, rigid, unyielding – alone.

Charles and his elder companion strolled arm-in-arm out of the police station and down the narrow SoHo street, heading in the direction of his apartment building.

She corrected his premature judgment on her weeping. 'Mallory has given me the greatest gift. I've never been so happy.'

Charles struggled with the image of Mallory as a bringer of gifts

262

and joy. However, it was hard to argue with the evidence of this smiling woman at his side.

She pressed the precious fingerprint cards to her breast. 'You know it was Bitty who told me that they were alive – my brother and sister. I had something to live for, someone to come home to. You can't know how badly I wanted my family back.' She paused in a pool of lamplight and studied her cards. 'Now, thanks to Mallory, I can prove that I was innocent, and that I never abandoned them or stopped loving them.'

An hour later, Charles was still coming to terms with the gift, terrible and wonderful, that Nedda had received at the police station. Oh, the waste of all those years. Tonight, this woman glowed by candlelight that softened the evidence of age, and he could see what her alternate life might have been: far from the narrow confinement of hospitals, her intelligence and grace, wealth and beauty would have laid open the entire world for Nedda Winter. He found her lack of bitterness remarkable, and so he was the one who felt the profound sense of loss. They sat at the kitchen table, sharing a late evening repast of wine, a wide selection of cheeses and a generous assortment of oven-warm croissants stuffed with sweetmeats. Charles fobbed this off as snack therapy.

Stuffed with his good intentions of excess food, his houseguest pushed back from the table. 'This is so charming – a psychologist who holds sessions in the kitchen. How wise. So cozy and secure.'

'Good,' he said, 'I'm glad you approve. The next session is breakfast.'

Nedda glanced at her watch. 'I wonder if Bitty's asleep. I suppose it's too late to call her at the hospital.'

'No need to worry about her. I think it'll do Bitty good to be out of that house for a night. And you, too.' He had made up the spare room and intended to bar Mallory from the door indefinitely, even if it meant laying his body down across the threshold. 'Tomorrow night, we'll have your brother and sister over here for dinner.'

'And that, of course, means group therapy.'

'And down the road, we'll include your niece when she's ready.'

'Charles, did you find it odd that Bitty never wanted to move out of Winter House and get a place of her own?'

'No, not at all. I don't think she'll be able to leave until she has her mother's approval. I assume that's the reason she went looking for you – to finally please her mother.'

'She got no thanks for that. With just a few words, Uncle James made me believe that I was the prime suspect. I'm sure he had an easier time convincing two younger children.'

'You're quite sure he did that?'

'Yes. It was pretty obvious the first time I saw them at the hospice. Horrible, isn't it? For Lionel and Cleo, I mean. No wonder they spent all their time at the summer house. And poor Bitty. Not the response she expected from them, but she couldn't take back her gift. And now – this suicide attempt. I've been such a disappointment to her.'

Bitty Smyth stepped out of the Rolls-Royce. Her father and mother held her arms as they supported her – *imprisoned* her, and Uncle Lionel drove off to the parking garage with his precious car. Bitty looked up at the only home she had ever known and its dark parlor windows so like dispassionate eyes. Winter House did not care what transpired within tonight, not because it was inanimate, but because it had grown accustomed to the lack of love and the plethora of death.

ELEVEN

Cleo Winter-Smyth fumbled in her purse for her own prescription sedatives. She handed the pharmacy bottle to her ex-husband. 'Sheldon, you'll have to crush these in water.'

'Why?'

'Because your daughter could *never* swallow pills.'

Bitty watched him amble off toward the kitchen. She was always startled by each reminder that her father knew less about her than strangers did. But now this pain was put aside. Uncle Lionel would be back from the garage soon, and this was rare and precious time, a few minutes alone with her mother. 'I want to show you something.' She retreated to the foyer closet, flung open the door and swept three hats from a lower shelf.

'No, Bitty, don't do that.' Cleo had the tone of one reprimanding a four-year-old as she came up behind her daughter and bent low to collect the fallen haberdashery. But now the hats dropped to the floor as her hands flew up to cover her face. 'My God. It's a *mouse* hole. But the house *hates* mice. How could this—'

'No, Mother. I drilled that hole myself. See how shallow the closet is? And the back wall isn't cedar. All the other closets in the house—'

'Well, of course it's shallow. It's a hat closet. It's always been a hat closet.'

'There's no such thing. Aunt Nedda said this was a normal closet when she was a little girl. She said coats were kept in here.'

'Well, the house was rented out when we were children. One of the tenants must have changed it into a hat closet.'

'No, it's a *normal* closet with a false wall. If you look through the hole—'

'Not a *mouse* hole,' said Cleo. 'Well, that's a relief.' Her eyes traveled over the exposed section of the wall. 'You're right. It's not cedar. Looks cheap. I can't believe I've never noticed that before. But then, it's always been full of hats. There was a time when everyone wore them. So it made sense, you see, to have a place to—'

'It's *not* a *hat* closet!' This was Bitty's attempt at yelling, but it came out as an impatient squeak. 'It's a hiding place.' She hunkered down in front of the drilled hole. With more composure, she said, 'If you shine a light in there, you can see a trunk. It's just like the trunks in the attic. Did you ever count them, Mother? One for every dead Winter – except for Sally. Didn't you ever wonder about Sally's trunk?'

'The south attic? We never go up there. Why would we? Why would you? I don't think I want to – Oh, no. Bitty, I *asked* you *not* to do that.'

Hats were in flight once more as Bitty cleared one shelf and then another. Cleo ran about the foyer rescuing hats on the fly and yelling, 'Bitty, stop! Stop it this instant!' She reached high in the air to catch one with a wide brim sailing by like a Frisbee.

Bitty lifted one board from its moorings and then the next. She never heard the door open, but now Uncle Lionel was behind her asking, 'What's going on? Bitty, have you lost your mind?'

Bitty was laughing, though not hysterically. This was genuinely funny. She might be the only one in the house who could pass a psychological evaluation.

Cleo's arms were wrapping round her daughter as she yelled, 'You're not well! You don't know what you're doing! This has to *stop*!'

Oh, yes – the terrible insanity of skimming hats across the foyer.

Bitty wrestled free. She ran through the doorway and across the front room, aiming herself at the kitchen like a missile. She collided with her father. A glass of water fell from his hand and crashed to the floor. She circled round him, ducking his hand and almost slipping in the wide puddle. Upon entering the kitchen, she pulled open the glass cabinet that housed the fire extinguisher and the ax.

Bitty returned to the front room to enjoy one shining moment as the center of attention. The three of them were agape and staring at the fire ax in her hand. Her father was shaking his head, trying to make sense of this sight – his daughter armed with a lethal weapon. Ah, and now she discovered a new side effect as she walked toward them and they moved back.

Power.

She entered the foyer to stand before the closet. It was now bare of every shelf within her reach. She took one mighty swing of the ax to crack open the brittle plaster wall. Her second swing was too high, slicing through one of her mother's hats and trapping the blade in the cut of the high shelf.

Braver now, the trio entered the foyer, hands reaching out.

'Don't you dare!' Bitty pulled the ax free and turned on them.

Her mother held up her hands like a mugging victim. 'It's all right, dear. Everything is going to be all right.'

Bitty swung the ax again, putting another hole in the thin board of the closet's back wall and raising a small cloud of white plaster dust.

'That's enough,' said her mother, sternly now, as if her forty-year-old child were merely acting up in front of company.

Bitty made another swing, wielding the ax with all her might. The wall cracked inward. She used the ax as a hammer to drive the shards of the wall back into a hollow space.

'That's enough!' said Cleo. 'Stop it!'

Completing her very first act of open rebellion, Bitty pulled loose other sections of the ruined wall, working like a dervish to expose the small trunk on the floor behind it. As she gripped a brass handle and dragged it out, it became wedged in the opening. With one hard tug, the trunk came loose and flew backward with Bitty into the room, landing on its side and falling open to spill its contents at her mother's feet.

A rotted nightgown, a yellow braid – a tiny skeleton.

If a doll had bones.

Lieutenant Coffey had been almost flattered – almost – when District Attorney Buchanan deigned to visit Special Crimes Unit at this late hour, having left a dinner party and one royally pissed-off campaign contributor during an election year. The dapper little weasel had come accompanied by an honor guard of five minions, all of them dressed in tuxedos and shiny shoes. There were rarely any of the female assistant DAs in his traveling entourage; they were much too tall in high heels. Buchanan liked to surround himself with small men, following the principle that no head should be higher than the king's.

For the past ten minutes, the lieutenant had endured the protocol of ascending and descending speech. He was always called Jack, and Buchanan was addressed as sir or *Mister* District Attorney. And now Buchanan had run out of breath in a rather one-sided argument, or perhaps he had simply exhausted his store of insults.

The lieutenant picked his next words with care. 'Well, sir, it's the kind of case that comes along once in a career.'

'That's no excuse. I told your detectives to stay clear of that law firm. They completely disregarded my direct order. And now I understand that they're harassing one of Sheldon Smyth's clients – a seventy-year-old woman, for God's sake. She's being watched around the clock.'

'Yes, sir. We have a plainclothes detail guarding Nedda Winter.' Coffey sat down behind his desk and picked up a pen.

'Well, Jack, you can forget that court order for protective custody. I blocked it.'

'Yes, I know.' Jack Coffey's grin was wide and impolitic as he finished scribbling his note, and now he passed it to the district attorney, who read the single line.

'Oh, Jesus Christ.' The note dropped to the floor as Buchanan stood up and cleared the room, waving his ADAs out the door, yelling, 'Move – now!' When his entourage had fled the office, the district attorney lowered his voice to a conspirator's whisper. 'Red Winter? You plan to implicate the Smyths in the Winter House Massacre? Do you want me to have a heart attack, right *here*, right *now*?'

Oh, yes, and if there was a God—

'No fucking way, Jack. The lawsuit potential is staggering. Now listen carefully. This is *another* direct order from me to Mallory and Riker. From now on, your detectives stay away from the Smyth firm and Nedda Winter.'

'In that case, screw it. You don't get to order my detectives around. That's my job. And, if you're not gonna help them, then stay the hell out of their way.'

Buchanan's mouth was moving, but no words were coming out. This was almost an assault, these words of insurrection. And now it must occur to him that the lieutenant had a bomb in his pocket.

He did.

'I smell conflict of interest,' said Coffey, and this was a roundhouse punch of words. 'Hell, you're going out of your way to *advertise* it.' He walked around his desk to loom over the shorter man, and Buchanan lowered himself into the chair. The lieutenant bent down, working his way into the man's personal space, and the DA had nowhere to go. 'I'm betting that law firm turns up on your A-list for campaign contributions. You like the Smyths so much? Fine. Then you go down with them.' Heady words in an election year.

Mallory appeared out of nowhere. Neither man had heard her coming. She laid a copy of Sheldon Smyth's canceled check in the DA's lap to back up the lieutenant's charge of conflict of interest. Buchanan was a long time staring at that check, as if he were counting the many zeros of his purchase price.

As if Mallory only wanted change for a dollar, she said, 'I need a court order to force Nedda Winter into protective custody. No judge will sign off on that until they get a call from you.'

The man's eyes were little gray pinballs as he considered his options. And now, Buchanan the Weasel was back, eyes sly and calculating. He crushed the photocopy in one white-knuckled fist, perhaps with the idea that women were easier to intimidate. 'Is this your idea of—'

'A gift?' Mallory dusted imaginary lint from the shoulder of her blazer. 'Yes, that's exactly what it is. You'll want to return that campaign contribution before we make the arrest.'

Mallory was now dead to the district attorney. He turned his angry face on the lieutenant. 'All right, Jack. You'll get custody of the old lady – but that's all you get.' He held up the photocopied check. 'Down the road, you *don't* get to use this crap on me again.'

'Deal.' And Coffey would abide by it. The favor bank of cops, politicians and other felons depended upon the principle of honor among extortionists.

Cleo Winter-Smyth made a break with manikin demeanor. She was so much softer now. Leaning down to the trunk, she wiped ages of dust from the small brass plaque to read the name of her youngest sister, 'Sally.' The woman sank to the floor and knelt before the spilled remains of a dead child. There was no flesh on the bones. A hole had been gnawed in the trunk, and that could only be the work of hungry rats.

So much for the theory that it was the house and not the exterminator that killed the vermin and other pests.

The rodents had left behind a long corn-silk braid. Cleo caressed it with a trembling hand. 'Baby Sally. That's what we called her.' She picked up a tiny shoe, brittle with age. The laces had rotted away. In a stutter of tears, she said, 'We were a family, Sally, Lionel and me.'

Bitty was stunned. Mother instinct had been there once, but it had been exhausted on a little girl who had died so long ago.

Mother? Can you see me? I'm standing here right beside you. I'm alive. Look at me. Look at me!

This was the lament of a child, and it had never worked. Bitty stared at the ax in her hand and the destruction of the closet wall. She was still invisible for all of this.

'Baby Sally,' echoed Lionel with more feeling than Bitty would have thought possible. Suddenly, the bizarre little family reunion with a skeleton was done. Feelings spent, brother and sister donned their masks again and turned in unison to face Sheldon Smyth.

Lionel stepped toward the man, as if to strike him. 'Your father told us she died in the hospital. But Sally never made it that far.'

'What are you saying?' The lawyer was backing away.

'Uncle James was long gone,' said Cleo. 'Sally didn't have a guardian to authorize hospital care. Did that worry your father, Sheldon?'

'Maybe,' said Lionel, 'he was afraid the authorities would ask too many questions. They might find out that our guardian had abandoned us.'

Cleo seamlessly continued her brother's thought. 'The court would've appointed another guardian and asked a lot of questions. But the Smyth firm wasn't finished draining our trust fund.'

Lionel pointed to the bones at his feet. 'So it was Sally's bad luck to get between the lawyers and the money.'

'You can't believe my father would have any part in murdering a small—'

'No, I don't,' said Cleo. 'Sally was dying from the day she was born. But I think her death was damned inconvenient for him.'

'And when she *was* dead,' said Lionel, 'your father put her inside that wall. If she was ever found, then Uncle James could take the blame – if he ever came back.'

'If Uncle James ever demanded the rest of his cut,' said Cleo.

'There's no other explanation for keeping Sally's body in the house. Or did your father intend to blame it on us?'

Lionel Winter turned to his niece with mild surprise, as if noticing Bitty for the first time. 'Your mother and I were only children – so easy to intimidate. Uncle James disappeared after a few years, and the three of us were left with a nanny and Sally's nurse. If the authorities found out what our situation was, they would've split us up and put us in foster care. That's what the lawyers told us. They said we were penniless. Sheldon's father moved the three of us into the summer house. He said the cost of taking care of us was out of his own pocket – his *generosity*, *his* money.'

'He told us we were worse than penniless,' said Cleo. 'He said this house would have to be rented out to pay down the family debts.'

'One day, your mother and I came back from school, and the nurse told us our little sister had been taken to the hospital. We never saw Sally again.'

'She was here all that time.' Cleo glared at her ex-husband.

If the ax were in her mother's hand—

'I'd like to know,' said Lionel, 'was Sally dying or dead when the nurse called your father out to the summer house to collect her?'

'No, Sheldon,' said Cleo, 'don't shake your head – don't pretend that you don't know all the details. I know your father would've warned you about a little body walled up in this house.'

'The Smyths are long-term planners,' said Lionel.

Cleo looked down at her daughter, another Smyth. 'Didn't you ever wonder why your father never wanted custody of you? The Smyths plan ahead for generations.' Bitty turned to her father, but he was looking elsewhere. All her life she had been told of a custody battle that had never taken place. And all this time, she had been her father's tie to the Winter family fortune, a tie that could not be undone until a day when all the money would flow back again the other way – generational planning.

The lawyer in Sheldon Smyth was smiling at his ex-wife. 'If this is made public, Cleo, you and your brother lose everything back to the trust fund. When Nedda dies, it all goes to the Historical Society. You'll be dead broke, the both of you, and lucky if you don't wind up in jail.'

'But we didn't do anything wrong,' said Cleo. 'We were the victims.'

'I don't think the district attorney will see it that way,' said Sheldon. 'It all depends on what sort of a deal I make for myself – if it comes to that – if you push me to it. You two became co-conspirators when you had the trust fund money repaid to your personal accounts. You were originally intended to have a lifetime draw, but you wanted *all* the money. Those were *your* terms.'

'That was so long ago,' said Lionel. 'Surely the statute of limitations—'

'It doesn't apply here. Ask my daughter. She's a lawyer. The yearly reparations installments – oh, let's call it extortion – that makes it an ongoing crime.'

Lionel and Cleo turned to Bitty, silently asking if this was true.

It was an interesting moment for a legal consultation. Bitty loosened her grip on the ax, then idly shifted it from hand to hand, giving this problem actual consideration. 'Did either of you sign anything to get those yearly payments?'

'Damn right, they did,' said Sheldon. 'That money is trust fund restitution. It can't be disguised as any other form of compensation. If the firm goes down, so do they.'

'Sorry.' Bitty shrugged. 'That's how Daddy's firm ensured your silence. They made you part of the crime.' She looked down at the tiny skeleton at her feet. 'Two crimes.'

'And no statute of limitations,' said Sheldon, who was enjoying this just too much. 'You see, the trust was never entirely drained. The theft of the restitution money is a crime in progress – conspiracy grand theft.' He nudged Sally Winter's trunk with the toe of his shoe. 'And, may I point out, that you're the ones in possession of a dead child. The fact that the body was hidden — well, that guarantees a homicide investigation. Reporters camped out on the doorstep, television people and their cameras following you everywhere you go. You find that appealing?'

No, they did not. Cleo was holding on to Lionel's arm for support.

'So,' said Sheldon, 'it appears that we have a lot to talk about. And then we have to put Sally back in the wall.' He turned to his daughter. 'Bitty, my love, you're also a part of this now.' He gave her his most radiant smile, then turned back to his ex-wife. 'Cleo, suppose you put on a pot of coffee. We'll all sit down together and—'

'Bitty,' said Cleo, 'go up to your room. I'll call you down when we've agreed on something.' She reached out and plucked the ax from her daughter's hand as if this deadly weapon were no more than a disallowed sweet that might ruin Bitty's dinner. 'Go on now.'

Defenseless, Bitty climbed the stairs. When she turned back, she saw her uncle picking up the bones of his little sister and gently, reverently placing them in the trunk.

Nedda was drinking Courvoisier in Charles's front room when she began to beep. She pulled the pager from her pocket. 'Bitty made me take this when we were at the hospital.'

'Horrible invention,' said Charles. 'I'd never own one. Pagers and cell phones. Those gadgets don't make life easier for people. They simply make escape impossible.'

She looked at the glowing display of digits on the face of the pager. 'And, of course, this number is Bitty's cell phone.'

'Then I'll give you some privacy,' said Charles. 'I have some work to do in my office across the hall. I might be a while, so don't wait up. Sleep well. See you in the morning.'

Nedda waited until he was gone, then rang Bitty's number, charmed by the old-fashioned rotary dial on the antique telephone. She held the receiver to her ear and only counted one ring, before she heard Bitty's voice. 'Hello, dear. How are you feeling . . . What? . . .

Calm down . . . Yes, dear, but why did you leave the hospital? . . .
Why would they . . . Don't upset yourself . . . No, of course I don't
mind . . . We'll sort this out when I get there.'

Nedda found paper and a fountain pen in the drawer of a small
writing desk. She left a note for Charles, explaining that Bitty needed
her and that she might be gone for a few hours. Her next call was to
the car service.

An unmarked police car stopped beside a recently vacated stretch of
curb outside of Charles Butler's apartment building. The watchers
were changing shifts, and all the attention of the man behind the
wheel was devoted to the task of parallel parking. His partner stood
on the sidewalk, directing the stop and starts of squeezing the car into
a tight parking space. That done – a perfect job – they settled in for
the last tour of duty on this plainclothes detail. When the custody
order arrived, the old woman would be taken away by police from
another division. It was going to be an early night, and they were
both thinking ahead to cold beers and hot slices from Ray's Pizza as
the taillights of Nedda Winter's limousine disappeared around the
corner.

Harry Bell, the desk sergeant in the SoHo station house, looked up to
see a rookie standing before him, though he should not have seen the
youngster's face for another five hours. The cop was supposed to
be sitting in a chair outside of Bitty Smyth's hospital room, an
unauthorized posting that had drained the bank of favors owed to
Detective Mallory.

'Peterson,' said the sergeant, 'you should be uptown. Guard duty
at the hospital? Is it all coming back to you now?'

'I was relieved of duty,' said Peterson, tacking on a belated '*sir*'.

'Now that's funny, kid, 'cause I don't remember calling you back
here. So whose idea was—'

'It was the family. They relieved me.'

'The Mafia? *That* family? Was gunplay involved?'

'No, sir.' The boy made the mistake of smiling at his sergeant's little joke instead of running for his life. 'It was Sheldon Smyth. He's the lady's father – and he's a lawyer.'

'Oh, well, that makes it okay.' Sergeant Bell knew he could shoot this boy right now for just cause and get away with it. 'I guess they changed the line of command. Now it's lawyers giving orders to the uniforms – instead of their sergeants. Well, somebody should've told me.'

Harry Bell's smile grew wide and wicked as the young cop's face quickly reddened. The torture of raw recruits passed for sport on a slow night. That was what rookies were for. That was why God had made so many of them. 'Tell you what, kid, why don't you go upstairs and explain all of this to Detective Mallory? No, go ahead. She'll understand. Ever met her?'

'No, sir.'

Perfect.

'Well, she looks like a babe, real pretty, but don't let that fool you. Down deep, she's a motherly type.'

Harry Bell watched the rookie drag his feet climbing the stairs to Special Crimes Unit. If the sergeant had been wearing a hat, he would have removed it and whistled a funeral hymn.

Winter House was dark when Nedda opened the front door. By the dim glow filtering in from the street, she could see the floor strewn with haberdashery and bits of plaster. Her niece's frightened ramble on the telephone seemed more coherent to her now.

The wall switch would not work, but the security alarm still glowed. She tapped in the code to disable it, then crossed the threshold into the front room, moving toward the staircase in total darkness. Her only weapon was beneath the pillow in her bedroom. She looked up at the sound of her name whispered from the second-floor landing. By the light of a candle, Bitty drifted down the stairs, pausing halfway with a finger pressed to her lips to caution silence. She lifted the candle high to light Nedda's way as they climbed slow and stealthy toward Bitty's bedroom.

Once they were behind a closed door, her niece said, 'I called the police. They're not coming. Maybe I put it badly. I might have seemed hysterical. I told them I was afraid to leave my room. The lights wouldn't work. They already think I'm crazy. They said I should call an electrician.'

Scores of candles were alight on every surface and wavering with the drafts of the house. Nedda picked up a candlestick and walked back to the door. 'I'll go down to the cellar. I know where the fuse box is.' But first she would go to her bedroom to fetch the ice pick.

'No!' Bitty grabbed her aunt's arm, pulled her away from the door, then slid the thick bolt safe home. 'They're all downstairs in the kitchen. They'll see you.'

'They?'

'Uncle Lionel and my parents.'

'Why does that—'

'Please, Aunt Nedda.'

This was probably not the time for a rational conversation. She only wanted to end Bitty's fear. 'All right, dear. If that worries you, I'll use the garden door to the cellar.'

'But one of *them* pulled out the fuses!'

'So I'll put in new ones. There's a big supply of them on top of the fuse box, a flashlight, too.' Nedda put one hand on the doorknob.

'Don't leave me alone.' The look on Bitty's face was pure anguish.

Nedda was wondering how much of this could be put down to hysteria, and then Bitty described the trunk of Sally Winter and its sad contents.

Hard news – as though her youngest sister had died only this moment, and the grief was new.

Sally, my Sally.

So the house, truly sickened, was coughing up its dead tonight.

'I know why the house has gone dark,' said Bitty. 'I'm supposed to have an accident on the stairs.'

The desk sergeant noted every head in the station house turning toward the stairs, and it was no surprise to see Kathy Mallory flying back to earth, her feet touching down on every third step. Apparently, young Peterson had confessed.

With eyes cast down, Sergeant Bell feigned interest in his paperwork. As the detective sped by his desk, he inquired after the health of his young rookie. 'Did you kill him?'

He looked up to see the back of Mallory pushing through the door and into the street.

'I'll take you back to Charles's place in SoHo.' Nedda looked through her purse by the light of a dozen candles, finally emptying it out on the bed to search for a scrap of paper with a phone number for the car service. 'Here, I found it.' She picked up the telephone receiver and listened to a dial tone. 'Well, the phone is still working.'

Bitty screamed and grabbed her aunt's arm.

Nedda whirled around. On the far side of the room, the wastebasket was in flames. The fire climbed the curtains with astonishing speed, eating the lace, flames licking the ceiling and spreading along the wallpaper. Bitty was yelling and waving her arms. The bird ran from its cage, wings flapping in a fair imitation of his mistress. Nedda scooped up the bird and crammed it into a deep coat pocket, then grabbed her niece by the arm. 'We have to go, Bitty. We have to get everyone out of the house.'

Nedda slid back the bolt and dragged her niece into the hall, closing the door as the bedcovers burst into flames. They were at the edge of the stairs when she saw a march of three candle flames below and the glow of three disembodied heads floating in the dark. The small procession of Cleo, Lionel and Sheldon moved toward the staircase.

Smoke seeped out from under the door and, rising in a draft, drifted across Bitty's face. 'Oh, God!' She broke free of her aunt's grasp and ran up the stairs to the next landing.

'No, Bitty! Come back!' Nedda gave chase as the little troop of candles had dwindled to two and climbed the stairs.

Bitty's face was a picture of abject horror as she looked back toward her room. The smoke was escaping through the wide crack beneath the door and winding upward, following her up the stairs. Nedda caught up to her niece, but failed to get hold of her. Bitty's hands were windmills to fend off all comers as she ran upward. The smoke went with her, rising in her wake. She stumbled and would have tumbled back, but Nedda was behind her to break the fall. A gray cloud was forming below and billowing toward them, obscuring the stairs.

'Bitty, we have to go back through the smoke. Hold your breath.'

'No! No!'

Nedda warded off the swats from her niece's flailing hands. Below her, she heard the bedroom door being opened. 'No!' she screamed. 'Close that door! I've got Bitty. I'll get her out. Save yourselves.' The smoke was spreading and thickening, blotting out the landing below. She dragged her niece down into the smoke, the only way out. It cost her precious air to scream, 'Cleo, Lionel! Get out! Get out of the house!'

Beloved faces were emerging from the black cloud, coughing, choking, hands reaching out. Bitty was loose again, running upstairs to where the air was still breathable.

'Fire!' The homeless man banged on the glass door of the apartment building. He was in tears. 'Fire! People are dying! Don't you believe me?'

No, probably not. It was one of those upscale places where tenants walked toy dogs that ran on batteries for all he knew. The rich were a different species, and he had never suspected them of sanity or humanity. The doorman, with his white gloves and fake gold buttons, had been among these people too long. When he turned to the glass, he did not see the shabby madman crying outside in the cold, banging the door in frustration, trying to save a few lives. No, this man looked right through the bum, then turned his back, well insulated from the sounds of the street, the chill of the night air – the smell of derelicts and smoke.

'Bastard!'

The temperature was dropping, and the homeless man pulled up the collar of his threadbare coat as he ran back to the house next door. The tiny woman sprawled on the steps was rolling on her side. A cell phone fell from the pocket of her dress and clattered to the steps. The derelict grabbed it up to punch in the emergency number that would bring out the fire engines.

And *now* he was believed.

A small tan car pulled up in front of the house with a screech of brakes, followed by the slam of a door. A long-legged, green-eyed blonde was bearing down on him.

Oh, lady, what cold eyes you have.

In a split second, he identified her as a cop. For so many years he had been kicked awake by cops while huddled in doorways uptown and down, and, no mistake, this woman was one of them.

Big trouble.

He knew what an odd sight he was, a raggedy bum with a cell phone. He held out the phone to surrender it, yelling, 'I didn't steal it, okay? It fell out of her pocket.' And this was followed closely by a silent prayer that he would not be hurt.

The cop was staring at the dark front windows. No flames were visible, but the reek of smoke was strong. And now she looked at him, actually *saw* him – *spoke* to him. 'You called nine-one-one?'

'Yeah.' He looked down at the woman who lay at his feet. 'There's more people in there. An old lady carried this one out, and then she ran back inside. She said to tell the firemen they were all upstairs. Don't know how many—'

He watched the cop pull a penlight from the pocket of her blazer as she marched up the stairs to the door. A puny penlight. He knew it would be useless where she was going.

He called after her. 'I tried to stop the old lady. Then I closed the door behind her. You never wanna feed oxygen to a fire.'

A fireman had told him that.

And now he watched the cop's back as she disappeared into the house, and he gave her up for dead. He knew the odds against her ever finding her way back. It was the smoke that killed and not the flames. He had learned this the hard way in a flophouse fire, barely escaping with his life, but not all of his hair and skin.

Another smoke alarm went off – loud and piercing mechanical shrieks. Calling out to survivors would be a waste of air and effort. Mallory pulled her T-shirt up to cover her nose and mouth. She entered the dark front room on the run, heading for the staircase, guided by the thin beam of a penlight that lit up a stream of gray fog on the lower floor. She aimed her light at the top of the stairs. The pathetic beam could not penetrate the thicker smoke flooding the second floor; it only bounced off a roiling, black, boiling upside-down sea, and she was going into it. Eyes tearing, shut tight, she pocketed the penlight and gained the second-floor landing as air exploded from her lungs. She hit the floor and sipped from the inch of air above the floor, then crawled along the carpet. She found the first body by touch, a man by the feel of him, and he was dead. Like a sack of sand, the corpse lacked the yield of an unconscious victim. This flesh was only a bag for meat and bone. And Mallory moved on.

How many survivors? How many rooms in this house?

Lungs bursting, she ducked her head to sip more air from the floor, strained through her silk T-shirt. The smoke alarms were deafening. More of them were going off in sequence as the smoke climbed upward through the house.

And this was happening in seconds that were hours long.

She would never find the others. The alarms were maddening her with their screaming urgency. She wished – they – would – just – *stop*!

And they did.

The smoke alarms were shutting down one by one. Were their plastic covers melting in the heat? Now she could hear the flames, the crack and dull roar, but not see them. Above her, there was a shriek that was not mechanical – not human.

The pet bird.

That creature could not have lasted six seconds in this lethal atmosphere. Someone had to be sheltering it from the poisoned air. Mallory crawled toward the sound of the screaming cockatiel, and her groping hands met the next flight of stairs. Coughing, choking, she rose to a stand, found the rail and took the stairs three at a time, stone blind, to the next landing. Back down to the floor, crawling again, drinking air from the ground and finding it poisoned. Coughing, coughing. On her right side, a door opened into the hall, slamming into her shoulder, and two bodies tumbled out. Mallory sucked better air from the closet floor as her hands passed over the two women wrapped in one another's arms – one living, Nedda by the long braid, and one dead, Cleo. Mallory pulled the sisters apart, then yanked up Nedda's coat to shelter the woman's face from the smoke. Crawling on all fours, she dragged the unconscious Nedda, feeling her way, following the margin of wood floor between the carpet and the railing.

Which way? Was she turned around? Where was the dead man's body?

Down below, where the music was.

Someone had turned on a radio. She heard the slurry static of changing channels, and now a saxophone was calling her down, luscious siren notes. She moved away from the rail, dragging her burden with her, and found the first stair. Rising, she lifted Nedda onto her back in a fireman's carry and made her way down, falling, kneeling at the last step on the second floor. Diving down to the ground again for air, all smoke now, coughing, coughing, choking, starved for air, muscles weakening, then shot. The music swelled up all around her, the stab and jab of horns rising to the high notes. Wake up! Get up! Get *up*! On hands and knees, she crawled with Nedda on her back. Moving toward the music, she found the landmark of the dead man's body.

She put her mouth to the carpet and sipped all the oxygen there was, then pulled back the sheltering coat and covered Nedda's mouth with her own. She kissed her with a breath of air, then rose to stand, lifting the woman again, so heavy – too heavy. Mallory fell, and Nedda rolled off of her and away. The heat was sapping strength from arms and legs.

It would be over soon. She was already half dead.

The single notes of a clarinet were falling down the scale, laughing, taunting. Trumpets screamed high, and the slap of a bass beat with the rhythm of her heart. A sly trombone sang, *Go, girl!* The sax was back, luring her away from the heat. This way. Then a shout of horns. This way out! This was the sound of adrenaline. She was rising, lifting Nedda onto her back. Down the stairs. So many stairs. The fire was behind her. She could hear it spit and crack. The heat was at her back. Pitching forward now, and falling. One wild hand found the railing, and she leaned all of her weight against it. This eased the heavy burden on her back. Down-stepping, now, half sliding.

Only seconds going by.

Hours of stairs.

She lost the precious air in her lungs before she touched down on level ground. She fell on her knees, and the sharp pain revived her. The music was loudest here. The most lethal air was above her, but she was drinking smoke from the ground, coughing, choking, lungs on fire. She could not get up one more time. Music all around her, *no* direction. Up was down, and there was no longer a concept of forward or back. The way out was lost. The door was on the moon. She opened her eyes, stinging, burning, hoping for a sliver of street light from the front windows to orient her position in the room. Instead, she saw the glow of flames, a small fire that lit up the brass knob of the door. A signal fire to light her way? Yes, and she was up on all fours, crawling toward it, the heavy weight on her back pressing her kneecaps down on knife points. Paying dearly for every foot of ground.

Someone turned off the radio.

Seconds passing, listening for footsteps.

The door flew open. Clean air rushed in – and life itself – with the sound of heavy boots pounding toward her, flashlights blinding her. Eyes closing again, her body collapsed. Hands were lifting Nedda's body off her back, then helping Mallory to rise, feet off the ground, strong arms enfolding her, carrying her out. She looked down to see the small fire by the door. It was nested in a hubcap. Another pair of boots sent it flying.

Outside, gulping air, lungs burning, searing, eyes opening, almost blind for the stinging tears. A fireman set her down on the sidewalk, yelling, 'Where the hell is that ambulance?'

More firemen were dropping from the truck and running toward the house. And one carried Nedda Winter to the ambulance as it screamed up to the curb. No one but Mallory saw the small ball of feathers drop from the old woman's coat pocket. The bird thudded to the sidewalk, weakly fluttering its wings. It rolled off the curb and into the gutter.

Slowly, Mallory was bending down to this lame creature, reaching for it, when a fireman gripped her by the shoulders. Unable to speak, she pointed upward toward the door, then found the words, coughing, wheezing, to tell him there was someone else alive in there. Someone had turned off the radio. He shook his head, not making any sense of this, then let her go. Her knees buckled, and more hands were reaching out, breaking her fall, as she slumped to the ground and lay on her side. She opened her eyes to see the bird a few feet away from her face. It was struggling to breathe.

She watched it die.

Mallory was rolled onto her back, and her face was covered with a plastic mask attached to a tank of oxygen.

A raggedy man knelt on the ground beside her. 'Sorry about your hubcap,' he said, as a paramedic covered his shoulders with a blanket.

She recognized him as the derelict who had used Bitty Smyth's cell phone to call out the fire engines. Beneath the blanket, he was shivering in shirt-sleeves. To fuel his little signal fire, he had burned his coat.

The corridor was filled with detectives from Special Crimes Unit. Riker knew that most of them had already pulled a double shift, yet they were pumped, jazzed on coffee and busy hammering firemen and paramedics, doctors and nurses for information, taking statements, doing paperwork and biting down on stale sandwiches from the hospital canteen. They were tying up loose ends and taking care of business – all for Mallory – one of their own. Every single one of those beautiful bastards had responded to the call of an officer down.

But she would not *stay* down.

Dirty and tired and stinking of smoke, Mallory was still working her case. Detective Janos, a brutal-looking man the size and shape of a refrigerator carton, hovered near her, sometimes stealing up behind her to gingerly replace the blanket around her shoulders each time she shook it off. The rest of the squad was giving her a wide berth. Had she been any other cop, they would be slapping her on the back, swallowing her up in bear hugs, and there would be a disgraceful exhibition of tears in the eyes of grown men. This scene of human warmth, tears and joy, was what Riker had wanted for Mallory.

What a fantasy that was.

One, she had no use for human contact; and, *two*, she was busy.

The case was all but wrapped. The only enduring mystery of the night was a skinny little bum who roamed the halls, carrying soda cans and bags of potato chips – and wearing Mallory's leather coat. He never strayed far from her, his only source of change for the vending machines. The bum approached her now, and she mechanically dipped into her pockets to give him more quarters.

Her face was a bare inch from the glass window in the door to the intensive-care unit. Riker joined her there. Together, they watched Charles Butler bow down to the patient on the bed, holding Nedda's hand so gently as he strained to catch her words. A doctor and two nurses were also in attendance and showing grave concern.

Detective Mallory was persona non grata among these tender caregivers. Never mind that she had walked through fire to save this woman's life.

That's my Kathy.

She was always on the outside looking in, but she never whined about her lot, and he had to love her more for that.

In one hand she clutched a paper bag. Mallory called its contents evidence – Riker called it a dead bird. The kid was clearly not herself tonight. She was entirely too patient as she waited her turn at the elderly patient on the other side of the glass.

She faced Riker, asking, 'What's the body count?'

'One less than we figured. Bitty's father was there all right, but he didn't die inside the house. Looks like old Sheldon was the first one out the door. What a man, huh? A couple of patrol cops found him a few blocks away. He was dead. Looks like a heart attack.' Riker held up a yellow pad lined with fountain-pen dollops of ink amid the flourishes of a witness's old-fashioned penmanship. 'We got this statement from an eighty-year-old priest. You'll like it. It really classes up our paperwork for the night.'

For this special occasion of wrapping a case, he donned the reading glasses that he never wore in public and read the priest's observations on the death of Sheldon Smyth. '"The poor man was terrified, as if the devil himself was after him. And he even smelled of smoke. Chilled me, it did. So he was running to beat the devil, all in a sweat from hellfire, when he clutched at his chest. His eyes rolled back to solid whites. Blind he was – and dead. I'm sure of it. That was the moment. Yes, it was. And here it gets strange. I swear to you, he was still running – stone dead – maybe three steps before he dropped to the ground."'

Riker quickly pocketed his spectacles. 'It's enough to make the fire a mitigating factor in his death. So, if you like Sheldon for hiring Willy Roy Boyd, we're done. We've got three dead. Four if we count that little skeleton in the trunk. Bitty loses both her parents and her uncle in one night. I wonder what she'll do now?'

'Maybe she'll grow,' said Mallory.

Riker shrugged. It was a good thing that Lieutenant Coffey had broken the news to Bitty Smyth. Mallory was no good at this part of the job, whether the newly made orphans were forty years old or four.

'There was someone else in that house,' she said. 'You know who it was?'

'No, kid. Everybody's accounted for. The body count squares with what Bitty told us. Nobody else was in that house.'

'Then who turned on the radio?'

Oh, back to that again. 'The firemen never found—'

The ICU door opened, and Charles stepped out into the corridor. One look at his eyes and anyone could see that he was destroyed. Riker turned away. Charles's strong personal attachment to Nedda was something he had never foreseen.

And the damage of this night just went on and on.

'Mallory,' said Charles, 'she wants to see you. But before you go in . . . she doesn't know about Lionel and Cleo. That was my decision. So, please . . . you can't tell her they're dead. It's just too much, too cruel. Nedda's already in a world of pain. And I think she knows that she's dying. She won't take the morphine until she's spoken to you.'

Mallory did not have all night to wait for him to finish. The ICU door was closing on her back.

Lieutenant Coffey made room for Charles Butler on the bench by the nurses' station, then turned back to the chore of editing his senior detective's report. He drew thick black lines through all the passages that incriminated – damned to hell – District Attorney Buchanan, who had dragged his heels on the protection order for Nedda Winter. The woman was not expected to live through the night; but Riker's career was ongoing, and Jack Coffey planned to keep it that way. One more line was crossed out, and Detective Riker's pension was saved.

Mallory's statement posed a different problem. The arson team had already interviewed her, and so he could not erase the passage about the radio. He added a line about oxygen deprivation. That would fix it.

The lieutenant laid his pencil down on the clipboard and turned to the sorry-looking man beside him. 'Charles, you look like hell.'

'I've been there.' The man leaned far forward, elbows propped on his knees, and buried his face in both hands. 'Mallory only told me six times that Nedda was in grave danger. I should never have been trusted to look after her.'

'Hey, Charles, if it makes you feel any better, Mallory *never* trusted you to look after that woman.'

The man's hands fell away from his face, and Jack Coffey could only describe this naked expression in terms of a slaughterhouse steer stunned with a bat and awaiting the blade that would slit his throat.

The lieutenant rushed his words to explain all the failures of the night, naming the names in Riker's original, unedited report and describing the precautions taken. 'It was *our* job to keep Nedda Winter alive, not yours.' He ended this litany with the officer who bungled the last watch. 'Bad timing all around tonight, and everybody gets a piece of the blame – except you.'

Nothing said had undone the damage to Charles Butler, for he was hearing none of this. The psychologist's eyes were fixed on the window of the intensive-care unit, where Nedda, his only patient, lay dying.

* * *

The old woman seemed so frail, so tired and older now by at least a decade. And, once more, she had been invaded by high technology. Wires ran from the bandages that taped electrodes to her flesh and connected her to monitors perched on a pole by the bed. Wavy lines charted every function of her body. Tubes ran in and out of her, carrying fluid to the veins of her bruised arm, and other liquids were carried away and emptied into plastic bags. Her eyes opened and closed in long slow blinks.

As Mallory approached the bedside, Nedda asked, 'Did the fire destroy the house?'

'No, it's still standing. Lots of smoke damage everywhere, but the fire was contained on the second floor.'

'Poor house.' She turned her eyes to the detective. 'That night in the park – I always wondered – why did you return my ice pick?'

'I thought you might need it.'

'So you didn't think I was paranoid, just a crazy old woman.'

Oh, yes, Mallory had believed that this woman had been driven insane long ago, but now she said, 'No.'

'You've seen the trunk with Sally's bones?'

Mallory nodded.

'You risked your life to save me tonight,' said Nedda. 'It's greedy, I know . . . but I have a favor to ask.'

'Name it.'

'Mercy for Lionel and Cleo.' Her words were more labored now. 'See them as I do . . . as they were . . . children with no one to love them. All they ever had was each other. I promise you . . . they didn't kill Sally . . . They could never—' She coughed up a bit of blood, but stayed Mallory's hand as the detective reached for the nurse's call button. 'Please, listen . . . Those three children shared a bond of abandonment . . . and loss. Can you understand that?'

Mallory understood it too well. She was always losing people. 'All right. I'll never go near them. I promise. I'll leave them in peace.'

'No, Mallory . . . I want you to talk to them. Tell them about the massacre . . . what really happened. And tell them . . . I didn't know they survived it.'

The old woman faltered, drawing breath and creasing her face with deepening lines of great pain. What was it costing her to say these words?

She reached out for Mallory's hand and wound her weak fingers around it. 'There's a metal suitcase under my bed . . . Maybe it survived the fire. Find it. It'll help you . . . make them understand that I never abandoned them . . . never stopped loving them.' Her fingers tightened on the detective's hand. 'They'll believe it . . . if it comes from you.'

Mallory nodded. Of course they would. She was the one person who would never stand accused of insincere platitudes and lies of kindness. Nedda had chosen her messenger well – but too late. 'I promise. I'll tell them everything.' The words sounded awkward and false, and she credited this to her lack of practice in her attempt to lie with good intention – to be kind.

And yet she was believed.

Nedda Winter's mouth twisted between a smile and a grimace. 'At least, at the end, I was there for Bitty . . . My life wasn't really wasted. And I understand Walter McReedy so much better now . . . If saving Bitty was all that I had ever done with my time on earth . . . it's enough. I finally found out what I was made of . . . and I was better than I knew.'

The eyes closed, and the muscles of the face relaxed in the absence of pain, years fading off with the loss of agony lines. The lines of life signs on two of the bedside monitors went flat, and a third continued on with its recording of a body function displayed in electric-orange waves of light. But Mallory knew that the technology lied. There was no mistaking death for even the deepest sleep. It was the unnatural stillness that gave it away, that frozen quality of a bird photographed in flight.

Good night, Red Winter.

Mallory's left hand was slowly rising, closing to a fist – a hammer. She rammed it into the wall above the bed, wanting the pain.

This was not *right*! It was not *fair*!

Again and again, she attacked and cracked the plaster as she counted up all of the dead on her watch. She was bleeding when the doctors came to take her away and to mend her broken hand.

TWELVE

Sleepless, Charles Butler had taken to barefoot wanderings at all hours. It was five o'clock in the morning when he padded down the narrow hall of Butler and Company to the office in the rear.

Mallory's computer monitors were all aglow, and her knapsack lay on the desk alongside the remains of a take-out meal. The half-filled coffee cup was still warm. He faced her cork wall and the penultimate symptom of a neat-freak spiraling out of control – a violent sprawl of paperwork. Her case elements were pinned in a horizontal splatter pattern. How many hours had she spent on this? All night long? Yes, her loss of sleep was apparent in the abandonment of perfect alignments. The wall was so messy that, at first, he thought this must be Riker's work. But no – there *was* a rudimentary order in the chaos. However primitive, this linear progression was very un-Riker-like and all Mallory. Her signature ruthlessness survived in the single-minded march of data across the wall.

When would she ever let it go?

When would he?

Charles sat down at the desk and covered his face with both hands, somewhat surprised to discover that he had grown a three-day stubble of beard. And how many days had he worn this bathrobe?

Grief and profound depression were exhausting him. Guilt was even more tiring, and he was not yet done second-guessing his time with Nedda Winter. That was the horror of hindsight: there were always a hundred different paths that one might have taken to a different outcome. What truly drove him mad was that he had not listened to Mallory. How many times had she warned him that Nedda might die? Accidental death or not, if he had only kept Nedda close, she would be alive.

At odd moments, tears streamed down his face. He had no control over them. Before him, there was always a picture of Nedda happy in the realization of a simple little dream, Nedda free of sorrow and pain – what might have been. He laid his head on the desk. He would never take on another patient.

Her burden was more difficult, more death than he was accountable for. Unaccustomed to failure, Mallory had never acquired the emotional muscles necessary to pick herself up when she tripped and fell from grace. How well he could empathize with that, but he could not help her. Spliced together, he doubted that he and she would make one complete and healthy human. The other impediment was their friendship. Friends did not call attention to one another's bloodstained souls and psyches.

Half the contents of her knapsack had been spilled across the desk blotter. He picked up a bottle with the hospital's pharmacy label. It was filled with pain medication prescribed for her broken hand. There was no need to count out the tablets; he knew that she had taken none of them. Mallory would not want to dull her beautiful brain, not while she was obsessing over all the details of one terrible night gone awry. However, he was also assured that she was not suffering, not likely to pay much attention to the aching throb of broken bones and damaged muscle. To paraphrase an old song from his youth, she did not have time for the pain.

And so – *he* felt the pain.

Thus crippled, he picked up her pen and passed an hour writing letters to Mallory, long sorry lines of apology, taking all the blame for Nedda's death. And then he had the good sense to lay down the pen. How unfair to burden her with his own obsession. Charles smashed the pages into the pockets of his robe, then rose from the chair to stretch his legs. He walked the length of the giant bulletin board, a disaster zone on several levels.

Well . . . maybe not.

At first, her pushpin style had been perfect in every alignment of paper, and then, as she had continued down the wall, pinning up new documents, they hung increasingly askew, as if she had become more and more agitated in her rush from one end of the wall to the other. The new configurations of diagrams and photographs, text and sundry bits of paper were laid out like a jigsaw puzzle without any helpful irregularities in the pieces. He had only the gist of the thing: neither of them could quite let go of Nedda Winter. And, truly, it seemed impossible that such a person could be removed from the planet by a freak accident. Mallory's linear paper storm relentlessly moved on down the wall toward that same conclusion.

At the very end of the wall, a report from the fire marshal knocked everything else out of his head. This was not possible. He read it twice. There were no portable radios in Winter House, none that would work without current, and the antique radio in the front room had not been in working condition for many years.

Oh, no. Madness was a recent thing with him, and there was *nothing* wrong with his memory.

Charles returned to the desk, took up pen and paper once more, then left a note pinned over the technical report. The bold lines of red marking pen stood out from all the rest, and this bit of tampering with her wall could not fail to annoy her the moment she walked in the door. It was a simple message – Mallory loved brevity – only three words writ large, *This is wrong*.

It was late afternoon when Bitty Smyth approached her own home like a thief, stealing through the park, keeping to the elongating shadows of rock formations and evergreens. The police vehicles were no longer parked in front of Winter House. The reporters were long gone, and there was a sense of emptiness about the place.

And desolation. As Aunt Nedda would say, 'Poor house.'

Bitty eased herself over the low stone wall and sprinted across the wide boulevard, dodging traffic, her fugitive brown eyes darting left and right. She raced up the front steps and faltered with the keys, dropping them twice before she could undo the locks. Finally, she opened the door to an acrid smell of stale smoke and mildew. Three days later, the air was still dank from the water hoses. Fearing an electrical fire, she hesitated to turn on the foyer light. Fear of the dark finally weighted her decision to flip the wall switch. The lights flickered on and off.

And Bitty sucked in her breath.

Vandals.

The smoke-stained walls of the foyer had suffered fresh damage. They were cracked by huge nails driven into the plaster with great force. Each nail staked a sheet of paper.

Senseless violence.

As she scanned the papers, Bitty fancied that she could hear the echo of every nail hammered in anger: BANG! – a fire marshal's diagram of her bedroom, the point of origin for the blaze; BANG! – another diagram showing the location of the cellar fuse box; BANG! – an official finding of arson.

Impossible.

The fire had been the pure accident of a candle falling into a wastebasket. Neither she nor Aunt Nedda had been near the candlestick when it had fallen off the bureau.

BANG! – a drawing of the cellar that marked the place where the pulled-out fuses and the spares had been hidden; BANG! – a forensic report on a flashlight recovered from the ashes of a bedroom closet; its round head matched to paint chips and a circular pattern of dust on the fuse box in the cellar.

BANG, BANG, BANG! A score of documents led to the end of the wall and turned a corner.

Bitty screamed.

295

No, no, no!

Rags. This was too cruel. Her pet cockatiel had been staked to the next wall, one nail for each tattered wing, and, for a few moments, the flickering lights gave the dead bird the illusion of flapping feathers and flight.

BANG! – beside Rags's tiny carcass was Mallory's witness statement. The detective had found three prone victims trapped above the fire's point of origin. Most damning were the final words: *The only survivor will inherit millions.*

BANG! – an application to freeze the assets of the Winter fortune in probate limbo.

Though the house was utterly silent, absent all but imaginary hammers, Bitty's hands rose up to cover her ears.

And then she held her breath – the better to listen.

She heard no voice or footfall, yet Bitty knew that she was not alone in the house. Creeping toward the threshold of the front room, her eyes were slowly adapting to the soft remains of sunlight slanting through the parted drapes and falling from the skylight dome at the top of the house. Now she could see every detail of a workman's scaffolding inside the curve of the blackened staircase. It was a network of wooden planks and buttressing metal rods swirling upward.

Mallory, dressed in dusty blue jeans, a T-shirt and a gun, hung there in midair.

Bitty blinked.

No, the detective stood on a high platform at the center of this giant skeleton of wood and steel, a suitcase resting at her feet, so like a woman waiting for a train or a bus to pass by high in the air. And so patiently – as though Mallory had been waiting there all this time, days and days. One crippled hand in a plaster cast dangled at her left side. Her hair and clothes bore a darker dust of ashes that had come down from the second floor with the metal suitcase, the one that Aunt Nedda had kept under her bed.

Always locked.

The detective picked up the suitcase, held it high over her head and sent it crashing to the floor below. It fell open, disgorging leather-bound journals, the sort that came with small locks and keys – decades of diaries.

'I like money motives,' said Mallory. 'And now . . . you have one.'

Bitty was shocked into a calmer state than she could otherwise have managed. She moved farther into the room, drawn along, as people are drawn to accident scenes. The lawyer in her was surfacing, and *it* wanted a look at those diaries. At last, she stood before the scaffolding, believing that there was hardly any fear in her voice when she forced a smile and looked upward, saying, 'What a droll sense of humor.'

'I'm not known for that.'

Still smiling, Bitty splayed her hands. 'But I haven't committed any crimes.'

'No?' Mallory bent down to pick up two electrical cords. 'Let's count them.' In a sleight of her one good hand, she joined the cords together, plug and socket. The room flooded with light from all quarters, brilliant spotlights, a dozen or more white-hot suns perched atop high poles. Bitty covered her face with both hands and closed her blinded eyes.

When she could see again, she turned in the direction that every light was focused upon. All the mirrors had been taken down from one wall. It was covered over with hundreds of papers and nails and cracks running jagged down the plaster. After a full minute of stunned silence, she looked back over one shoulder. The detective had not changed her stance, but was she at least one platform lower – closer?

'How did you get these trust documents?' Bitty strived to convey a suspicion of theft. 'No judge would ever sign a warrant to raid a law firm for—'

'Your father didn't tell you? Why doesn't that surprise me?'

Mallory stepped off the narrow wooden plank and dropped to the wider platform below. This time, her running shoes made noise with contact. 'Old Sheldon didn't like you much, did he? Well, maybe you pissed him off when you tried to blackmail his law firm.'

'You can't be—'

'You threatened him with a very old crime.' Mallory pointed to the wall. 'Right below the trust documents, you'll find the warrant for your father's safety-deposit box. That's where I found the restitution agreement for the embezzled trust fund. It proves that the law firm stole money from the Winter children. That was my partner's favorite piece of evidence – proof of lawyers robbing orphans.'

Bitty turned to face the scaffold, one hand shading her eyes from the bright lights. 'I swear to you, I never—'

'You *knew*. When you worked in your father's firm, you had lots of time to study the trust fund documents. I also found a copy of his will. Two years ago, he cut you off without a cent. That's how I know you didn't leave on sabbatical. He fired you. I've seen the firm's financials – yours, too. He paid you hush money – your *allowance*. That's what *he* called it – ten percent of your old salary. You actually made less money as a blackmailer.' The detective's smile was derisive. 'You just couldn't stand up to him, could you? He called your bluff, and you folded. You crept away with a few pathetic crumbs like a good little mouse.'

Mallory stepped to the edge of the platform.

Bitty's head snapped left toward the distraction of a faulty pole light blinking on and off. When she turned back to the scaffold, Mallory was gone, and this silent piece of work was more alarming than the sound of the crashing suitcase. Could Mallory have dropped to earth from such a high place without making the slightest noise?

Or could she fly?

'I know everything now,' said Mallory.

Bitty jumped. Her heart banged. Her eyes went everywhere. Where had—

'When blackmail didn't work, you came up with a new swindle.'

Bitty slowly revolved, her eyes alternately squinting at bright lights and peering into shadows. 'I have no idea what you're—'

'I *know* how you found your aunt.' The detective stood under a spotlight at one end of the wall, as if she had simply materialized there. 'It was a job that generations of good cops couldn't do. That bothered me from the beginning.'

'If you had only asked—' Bitty's hands joined tightly, fingers interlaced, but not in prayer. 'I would've told you about the investigator.'

'Joshua Addison?'

'Yes, my private investigator.'

'No, he's mine now.' Mallory ripped a sheaf of papers from the wall. 'This is his statement – all your requirements for the job.'

Bitty nodded unconsciously. She knew this list by heart: find an old woman approximately seventy years of age, tall and fair and blue of eye, a woman without documents or memories of family and home.

'It was a shopping list for a doppelgänger,' said Mallory. 'You weren't even *looking* for your aunt. Any old woman would do, as long as Cleo and Lionel believed she was their sister. You didn't even have to worry about a DNA test. By the time—'

'I wanted to please them.'

'No, you didn't. They were horrified. That's the way Nedda put it in her last diary, the one she started in the hospice. She mentioned you, too – in detail. It was her impression that you weren't all that surprised by the reception she got from Cleo and Lionel. Now back to your PI's shopping list. Addison told me you were only interested in nursing homes. Good hunting grounds for old women who can't even remember their names.'

Bitty eased herself down to the floor, fearing that if she did not sit down, she might fall on weakening knees. Mallory had erred on one point. Not just any old woman would do to separate her family from their money. It had taken years and all of her savings to find just the right one, a senile old crone with a resemblance to the Winter family. How astonished she had been to discover that the best candidate of the lot was the genuine article.

'I even know why you picked the state of Maine.' Mallory was moving across the room, and it seemed to Bitty that the detective would walk over her or through her, but the young woman stopped suddenly, as a train would stop just short of collision. 'Maine was close enough to keep tabs on your search,' said Mallory. 'But it was far enough from New York City so you wouldn't have to worry about the Smyth name being linked to the Winter family. The PI was pretty lame, and I'm guessing that's why you picked him. But he finally made that connection.'

Bitty was always looking up at people, and suddenly she tired of this. She fixed her eyes on a middle ground, and her voice was insistent when she said, 'I didn't break any laws. I never—'

'Your plan was too complicated.' Mallory hunkered down to Bitty's eye-level. 'That's why so many things went wrong. You had to improvise too much. But, in every new game plan, Nedda was meant to die. Your mother and your uncle would take the blame. You supplied them with a motive. Their uncle James planted the idea, but you're the one who convinced them that Nedda murdered their family.'

As Bitty formed the idea that Mallory was using pure guesswork, the detective was shaking her head, saying, 'I *know* how you poisoned them against Nedda. So you planned a revenge motive for Cleo and Lionel. They do everything together, don't they? Get one, you get two. With them in prison, you'd control all the money.' Mallory held a sheet of paper within an inch of the other woman's face. 'Now you get nothing.'

Pulling back, Bitty recognized the page torn from a book on New York State law. The underscored passage mandated that felons could not profit from a crime. She watched the paper drift to the floor. In one fluid motion, Mallory was risen, then gone, and Bitty was left to stare at the fallen page washed in bright light. 'I didn't commit any felonies. There's no proof of—'

'Let's start with Willy Roy Boyd, the scum you hired to kill Nedda.' The detective ripped a newspaper clipping from the wall and held it up for Bitty to see. The headline recounted the capture of a serial killer. 'This was your idea of the help-wanted pages. It cost you a lot of money to get him out on bail with that new hearing. He'd need lots more to keep his pricey lawyer. He would've killed a battalion of women for you.' She let go of the clipping, and it drifted to the floor.

Bitty turned away. 'You can't seriously—'

'I'm *dead* serious.' Mallory's voice came from behind, and Bitty could feel the breath on her neck. 'I talked to Boyd's lawyer.' Another piece of paper rattled close by Bitty's ear. 'I have the letter you sent with the payoff money.'

Bitty raised her head with new hope. 'In my handwriting? I don't think so.' The letter had been typed on a computer.

'Don't even try to run a bluff on me.' Mallory's face appeared in front of her, blotting out everything else in the world. 'Your bedroom was the only one with locks, two heavy-duty bolts – *recently* installed. You were afraid that Boyd might get carried away and kill you, too. He never knew that you were the one who hired him.'

'No, there was an attempted break-in the previous week. You *know* that.'

'Right. I always wondered if that one inspired the second try, or did you arrange both of them? Was Boyd your fallback plan? Heavy guns, Bitty – a serial killer. But at least he was a proven commodity. He'd already killed three women. Must've been a shock when Nedda brought him down with an ice pick. You never imagined that, did you? Well, some plans only work on paper.' Mallory stood up, suddenly impatient, and walked back to the wall. 'Willy Roy Boyd died during the commission of a felony. You hired him to kill your aunt. By law, his death belongs to you.'

'That's absurd.'

'Oh, really? Did you sleep through every class on criminal law? The next charge is conspiracy in attempted murder for hire. Pecuniary gain raises the ante on the penalty. Look it up.'

Bitty rallied and lifted her head, feeling braver when speaking to the younger woman's back. 'You have nothing to link me with that man.'

'You're right.' Mallory's smile was a chilling piece of work. 'In your original plan, Nedda would die and Boyd would survive. So you'd never give him anything that would lead the police back to you. But I'm sure you fed him enough detail to implicate your aunt and uncle.'

'Supposition.'

'Yes, it's a very weak case. Lucky I have you for multiple murders.'

'No,' said Bitty, head slowly shaking from side to side. 'What are you—'

'Every death by arson is murder. I only have to prove one and the jury will throw in all the rest for free – including Willy Roy Boyd.' The detective padded toward the scaffolding and knelt down by the open suitcase and its spilled contents. She picked up one of the diaries and flipped through the pages until she found an entry that she liked. 'Listen to this. It begins, "Love me again." She means Cleo and Lionel. All Nedda wanted was a reconciliation with her brother and sister.' The detective turned ahead a few pages. 'For a while, she was making progress. Then it went sour after Nedda stabbed Boyd. That was your work, Bitty.' She held up the book. 'It's all here. Oh, one more thing – I know what you did with the videotape, the one that went missing that night.'

'All right, I burned it to protect Aunt Nedda. I thought she'd killed an unarmed burglar.'

'Nice touch, Bitty. Always a good idea to work a little truth into the lie. I believe you burned the tape, but that's not what I meant. Your car service logged the trip to the summer house the next morning – a very early ride. You showed that videotape to Cleo and Lionel, didn't you? You wanted them to see Nedda's handiwork with an ice pick – the same kind of weapon that slaughtered their family. It must've destroyed them to watch that film. Too bad you don't have the tape anymore. It might've come in handy at your trial. The state will say you burned incriminating evidence. Boyd was dead before the lights came on, but maybe the tape showed you pulling out the ice pick and driving a pair of shears into his corpse.'

'I didn't do that.'

'Bitty, I never thought you *could* do it. But will the *jury* believe you? Now – just take it a little further. The autopsy proves two strikes and two different weapons – maybe two killers. Maybe Boyd wasn't quite dead when he was stabbed the second time. The prosecutor might argue that you were afraid Boyd could identify you as the one who hired him.'

'That's not true.'

Mallory arched one eyebrow. 'So?' She looked down at the journals in her hands. 'When the jury reads these diaries – Nedda's little dream – they're going to hate you, Bitty. They're going to kill you, too. On the night before the fire, Nedda called you from SoHo. She was planning another attempt to reconcile with her brother and sister. That would've ruined all your hard work shoring up the revenge motive. So, you staged a suicide, and you cut it close, but then you expected Nedda home for dinner hours earlier. Charles Butler's fault. He invited her to a poker game.'

The detective busied herself with picking up all the spilled diaries and putting them back into the suitcase. 'Let's see. More crimes. Oh, right – the night of the fire? You turned out the lights at the basement fuse box. There was an old flashlight kept on that box. The arson investigator found it in your closet. Did you think you'd have time to plant the flashlight in someone else's room after your aunt died?'

'The fire was accidental.'

'I know. So what were you planning for Nedda that night? A fall

303

down the stairs? No, too uncertain. Most people survive that sort of tumble. You were the one who pointed that out on the night of the dinner party.' Mallory reached back into the suitcase and pulled out a diary. 'It's all here. Your aunt was a great one for detail. You planned to push Nedda over the banister, right? According to you, that's the way Edwina Winter died, a tried-and-true method.' She opened the diary and turned the pages. 'Here it is. Nedda describes you rushing Charles Butler at the banister. For a minute there, she thought he'd go over the rail. That was your dress rehearsal, Bitty. For the real thing, you had to pull the fuses – turn off every light. It's the only way you could do a murder – behind the back and in the dark. The prime suspects would be Cleo and Lionel. But now that they're dead, you inherit everything. Good motive for arson.'

'But you *know* it was an accident.'

'The fire was where it all went wrong, wasn't it? The smoke and flames. You panicked. You ran up the stairs instead of down. Yes, I believe it was an accident. You'd never take that kind of risk. But, once again, Bitty, will the *jury* believe you?'

Mallory paced the floor, snapping her fingers. 'Stay with me, Bitty. Do the math. Willy Roy Boyd counts as the first murder charge. When the arson investigation is finished, the body count will stand at five.' She ripped a sheet from the wall. 'This is the autopsy report on your father. It links the trauma of the fire to a fatal heart attack. Every death by arson is murder.'

'It was an accident!'

The detective smiled, and Bitty grasped the irony before it was voiced.

'After years of planning and scheming, you'll get tripped up by something you didn't do. But you *did* pull out the fuses and hide the spares. You lit the candles that set the house on fire – and those people died. Do you think I care if you only planned to kill *one* of them?' Mallory's voice was calm and all one note, almost bored as she walked along the wall, tearing off more sheets in quick succession. 'So now

I've got you for patricide, matricide, the murders of your aunt and uncle and Willy Roy Boyd. Too bad you couldn't commit mass murder in another borough. Now the Queens DA won't kill anybody, not even cop killers. But the Manhattan DA *loves* the death penalty.'

The wave of Mallory's hand encompassed all the chaos of the wall and the suitcase of diaries. 'Now you might remember this from a law class you *didn't* sleep through. The DA calls it a preponderance of evidence. The sheer weight of it is enough to crush you to death. And there's more. Juries love things they can hold in their hands, like the fuses and the spares you hid by the garden door. That's what really sealed the arson finding. Then there's the pack of diaries.'

'Aunt Nedda was insane. She had a history of—'

'No, according to Dr Butler, all those diaries were written by a perfectly sane woman. So – things the jury can hold on to. There's the flashlight – and the fire ax with your fingerprints on it.'

'You know why my prints are on the ax. I used it to—'

'Yeah, *right*. Little Sally Winter's bones. That was another nice touch, Bitty. Some malicious slander to paint Cleo and Lionel as the kind of people who could murder a child. Why not Nedda? What you don't know is that your mother was on the phone with my partner before the fire broke out. She was making plans to surrender the trunk to the coroner's office in the morning. Cleo and Lionel only wanted to know how long it would be before the family could bury that little girl's remains. That was all they cared about. Finally – a proper burial for Sally Winter.'

'You know I used that ax to get Sally's trunk out of the closet.'

'Right, that's what you said in your statement, but we only have your word on that. Your mother never mentioned you. So the DA will argue that you used that ax to keep those frightened people from escaping a burning house.'

'No, there was a witness who saw Nedda carry me out. I was unconscious. I couldn't have stopped anyone from leaving if—'

'A witness? You mean the homeless man who called in the fire?

The arson team went looking for him. Turns out someone bought him a train ticket to a warmer climate. Now where was I? Oh, right – the prosecutor's closing remarks. He'll paint a picture of you swinging that ax, scaring those poor people, driving them up the stairs and then setting the fire to trap them there. When he's done with the jury, they'll want to climb out of their box and kill you with their hands.'

'Is that what you'd like to do?'

'No.' Mallory shrugged. 'It's all the same to me – nothing personal, just a job.' She handed Bitty a small white card. 'This has your Miranda rights. You're under arrest. Read the card fast, Bitty. We have to go.'

'I know what you're doing, Detective. So transparent. You want to scare me into a plea bargain – a guaranteed conviction instead of risking a lost trial.'

'No, I've never known a lawyer to confess to anything. And I'm counting on that. So is the district attorney.'

'You expect me to believe that all this – this spectacle – and what you did to my bird, nailing him to a wall – that was just *fun* for you?'

'Yes,' said Mallory, 'that's exactly what it was.'

Bitty wished that this young woman would not smile. It was so unsettling. And those eyes. It crossed her mind that the detective might be seriously disturbed. Or was this calculated – just another part of the show?

'Now,' said Mallory, 'I'll tell you what's going to happen to you, and that'll be fun, too. The courts might unfreeze just enough money for a reasonable criminal defense. They will *not* give you millions of dollars to buy legal talent. When your cut-rate attorney sees the trial going sour, he'll try to plead you out on the weaker case, the murder for hire, one death – Willy Roy Boyd. You'd be Nedda's age when you got out of prison, but you'd be alive. Here's the snag. Once the trial has started and all the facts are out, the DA can't accept a plea on a lesser charge. He's a political animal – it's an election year – the voters would crucify him. You see the beauty of it, Bitty? You won't plea-bargain until your case is sinking. But the DA can't settle for less than mass murder and the death penalty, not if he's winning. And – he – can't – lose.'

The detective slung a coat over one arm, then picked up the suitcase of diaries. 'We have to go now.' She consulted a pocket watch. 'You'll be arraigned tonight. What's your plea?'

This was the showdown or at least a countdown of sorts, for Bitty was tensing her body as Mallory tapped off the passing seconds with the toe of one shoe.

'Time's up.'

The electric lights went out, leaving only the illumination from the skylight dome. Bright motes of dust swirled around Mallory, catching light and endowing her with a cylindrical aura. As the detective moved forward, Bitty backed out of the room, slowly retreating to the foyer, where the body of the dead bird was staked to the wall, but all she could see was the detective crossing the front room, coming closer and growing in height and mass with each footfall.

Oddly enough, a stone weight was rising from Bitty's breast. Her nerves had calmed, and she could breathe more easily. She called out to Mallory, almost defiant, 'You *lied* to me! This case *was* personal, wasn't it?'

Mallory had been all too right about one thing: Bitty had no intention of pleading guilty to any charge. Done with hysterics, she was coolly plotting the destruction of the case against her, all circumstantial evidence. And, if she could not win at trial, she would win on appeal. If she confessed, all was lost. Her last thought was that the detective could read her mind and sense the rebirth of hope.

The suitcase dropped from Mallory's hand to the floor.

Bitty knew this moment would be burned into memory until the day she died. Years from now, she might recall the angry young avenger standing there with a great sword in her right hand. And perhaps that peculiar fantasy would arise from a glint of gunmetal in the shoulder holster – *that* coupled with this stunning sight of Mallory with eyes burning bright and hair disheveled, as if she had just stepped from the whirlwind.

Only now, as the last few steps between them were closing, did Bitty understand that this case was indeed a personal matter to Mallory, that some great harm had been done to this young woman, deep damage beyond the evidence of her broken left hand. Oh, her eyes – that fixed stare, a cat's dare for the mouse to move, even to twitch. And the gun in her right hand was on the rise.

BANG!

THIRTEEN

Lieutenant Coffey sat in a cop bar on Greene Street, downing straight shots of bourbon with his senior detective. The mood was not celebratory, though Riker believed that Mallory would never be punished for what she had done.

The lieutenant lifted his head to pose a question, one that could only be asked at that point of inebriation where he had hopes of forgetting the answer by the time his hangover kicked in. 'What the hell happened? The *real* story?'

'What'd Buchanan tell you?'

'I never asked for his version. I want *yours*.'

'Okay.' Since the lieutenant was buying, Riker ordered another round. 'That morning, we laid it all out for the district attorney, more evidence than he's ever seen for one case – a *ton* of documentation. Buchanan didn't care. He refused to prosecute Bitty Smyth. Little coward. He was actually afraid to risk losing the biggest case of his career – in an election year. Can you beat that? After all this work, what does he say to us? He says it's all circumstantial.'

'He was right,' said Coffey.

Riker ignored this because it was true. 'So Mallory says the whole package is enough to bury Bitty Smyth. Buchanan says no. He says juries are too stupid to follow her evidence. It would be a fight just to keep 'em awake long enough to present the case.'

'The man's right again,' said Coffey.

'So Mallory asks him, point blank, "What's it gonna take?" Then

Buchanan says, "Bring me a full confession."' Riker slammed the flat of his hand on the bar. 'And that's *exactly* what she did. That afternoon, we went to Winter House to wire the place for sound.'

'I don't remember listening to any tapes, Riker.'

'Never got a chance to plant the mikes. Bitty showed up as soon as the last cop car pulled away from the house.' In other words, *no* tape was better than an *edited* tape. He did not hold with the idea of tampering with evidence.

After a go-around with Bitty Smyth, the detectives had returned to the DA's office and handed the woman's confession to Buchanan along with the terms of a plea bargain.

'And then,' said Riker, 'Buchanan really pushed his luck. He told us he wouldn't accept the confession. Said it was probably obtained under duress. That pompous little weasel never even talked to Bitty Smyth. He didn't know squat.'

'Was he right?'

Riker was selective in his deafness. Timing was so important tonight. 'Well, the DA went back on a solid deal.' The detective leaned toward his commanding officer. 'This is just between us, right?'

Jack Coffey nodded his understanding, and this was his promise, his seal of silence.

Half of the battle for Mallory's job security was won.

'Good,' said Riker. 'So Mallory staked the confession to the DA's desk with an ice pick.' He averted his eyes from the lieutenant's startled face as he added, on a point of historical interest, 'It was the same pick that was used in the Winter House Massacre.' Now he turned back to Coffey and smiled. 'It was a gift.'

In a sudden change of heart – inspiration of cowardice – District Attorney Buchanan had accepted the confession, electing to follow that time-honored credo: never make an enemy of a psycho cop. And, bonus, the little man had wet his pants, further guaranteeing that what had happened in that room would never leave that room. Riker had not enjoyed any of this. Mallory had scared the hell out of him, too, and he had almost felt sorry for a lawyer. Sometimes, in unguarded moments, he forgot that she was always dangerous – and more so now that she was wounded. The cast on her hand broke his heart.

How much more should he disclose to Jack Coffey before he requested a long leave of absence for his partner? And which one of them would take Mallory's gun away from her?

'Wait, Riker. Back up. How did Mallory *get* that confession? You skipped over that part.'

Stalling for time and just the right words, Riker checked his watch. A police transport would be en route to the women's prison by now. The case had ended without a trial, only Bitty's anticlimactic confession in open court. She had pleaded guilty to a charge of murder for hire and four counts of manslaughter, all sentences to run concurrently. The only proviso of the plea bargain had been that Mallory not be present during the proceedings. 'Bitty Smyth got a better deal than she deserved.'

'That may be,' said Coffey, 'but why did she waive her right to a trial? No, wait – I got a better question. What did Mallory *do* to that woman?'

'Nothing.' Riker was feigning indignation, and he must be doing it badly; the boss was still waiting on his answer. How should he put this? As if he had just recalled some minor detail, he said, 'Well, she shot the head off a dead bird.' Riker was quick to raise his right arm in the gesture of an oath. 'My hand to God, that's all she did. The kid never even yelled at Bitty Smyth.'

'So Mallory spent a bullet. Where'd it go?'

'It's not in the wall anymore. You can't even tell where the hole was.'

'And the headless bird?'

'It went to swim with the fishes in the East River.' Of course, that would depend on the vagaries of plumbing and sewage routes; Mallory had flushed the bird down a toilet.

* * *

This evening, Charles Butler was dressed and showered, but not shaved; his cleaning woman had hidden the razor.

Mrs Ortega watched her employer pulling volumes from his library shelves. He called them guidebooks for the road.

'Where ya goin'?'

'Not every journey involves leaving the house,' he said.

She perused a volume by Hermann Hesse, but found the print too dense for her taste. 'Me, I like a good fast read,' she said, 'with lots of white space on the page.'

He ran one finger down a row of titles on a lower shelf, plucked out three novels and handed them to her. 'Here, gifts, first-edition Hemingways. I think you'll like them.'

She set them on top of her cleaning cart, then turned back to his own short stack. 'I don't get it. If you've already read them, what good are they?'

Mrs Ortega could wait all day for an answer to that one. Charles Butler's eyes had gone all strange as he focused on some point above her head and behind her. She turned around to see Mallory standing just inside the door.

Spooky kid – quiet as a cat.

One icy glance from Mallory told the cleaning woman that she was dismissed from this babysitting job, and Mrs Ortega was glad to go. She was sometimes afflicted with magical thinking from the Irish side of her family; over a passage of days, she had sensed a change in the very air of this apartment; it was thickening with sadness, and she could hardly breathe.

Charles Butler sat beside Mallory as she drove along Central Park West. She had not yet convinced him that he was not responsible for Nedda Winter's death, but she had finally succeeded in getting him out of the house.

They were going on a field trip to see the radio.

Shock therapy.

The man was badly broken. His eyes had a shattered look, and other fracture lines were showing in his face and in his rambling speech. Somehow she must put him back together again without any helpful manuals on human frailty. His world was more fragile than she knew.

Charles's luck with parking spaces was riding with her tonight. She pulled up to the curb in front of Winter House. He was still going on and on about the radio when they climbed the steps to the front door. Why did he have to pick that one thing to obsess about?

Mallory led the way into the house. He was beside her in the foyer as she trained her flashlight on the two silver control panels by the door. 'This one is for the security alarm. And this one is for the sound system. There's a panel just like it in every room. It works the same way yours does.' She tapped the built-in speaker. 'The music you heard after the dinner party – when you and Nedda were sitting outside on the steps? It came from here.'

'No, I *told* you – Nedda couldn't work this thing, and neither could I. She played the old radio in the front room.'

'All right, let's have a look.' Mallory took him by the hand and led him across the foyer threshold, preceded by the beam of her flashlight. She pulled the smoke-stained drapes aside, allowing the light of streetlamps into the room, and she opened the front windows to cut the smell of mildew with clean, cold air.

Charles was staring at the old-fashioned radio.

Mallory pulled it away from the front wall and turned it around to expose a rotted backing with holes in it. Charles moved closer as she used a metal nail file to undo the screws. She removed the back panel to expose the innards: another century's technology of cracked glass tubes, frayed wires and loose connections. There were also cobwebs made by generations of spiders spinning their homes inside this antique box. The bones and skull of a long-dead mouse completed the evidence of a nonworking radio.

And now Mallory deconstructed this tiny crime scene for Charles. 'Twenty or thirty years ago, this mouse took a hit of current from an exposed wire. It made him wild. He batted around in the dark and broke these tubes. Probably bled out on the broken glass. You see? This radio has been useless for a very long time. The one in Nedda's room is in worse shape. It doesn't even have a cord.'

'No, it's a trick. This is a different radio.'

Mallory shook her head, and waited for his good mind to kick back into gear, to shake out the dust of deep depression and function logically once more.

'But *you* heard a radio the night of the fire,' said Charles, 'and no one has questioned *your* sanity.'

'Well, I know it wasn't this one. Even if this radio had been in working condition, Bitty pulled out all the fuses that night – no electricity. What I heard was probably a small portable. It must've been destroyed in the fire.'

He seemed so suspicious now. Did he know she was lying? No, there was also doubt in his face. Her lie was making sense to him. Apparently, Charles did believe in the rules governing electricity.

In truth, if a battery-operated radio had been in the house – even if it had been near the fire's point of origin – the investigators would have found residue materials, but there were none. And because it was so important to account for everyone in the house on that night, the arson team had gone looking for signs of Mallory's radio operator, the one who had turned the music on and off. They had even run tests for music seeping in from neighboring buildings – all negative. Yet, like Charles, Mallory could not admit to imaginary songs. She never would. He *must*.

'I saw her play this radio twice,' he said, insistent. 'The first time was at the crime scene. And I've got a lot of witnesses for that performance.'

She nodded. 'I heard music that night, but the built-in sound system—'

'And I heard it again,' said Charles, angry now. 'The night of the dinner party. It was a warm night. Nedda opened the front windows. We sat outside on the stoop. We drank wine and listened to this radio for hours.'

'When Nedda thought she was disabling the alarm, she probably hit the control panel for the stereo system. I'm sure Nedda believed the music came from the radio, but she was insane.'

'No, she wasn't. I never had a conversation with her that wasn't perfectly lucid.' He turned his back on Mallory and left the house. She followed him as far as the open front door and watched him sit down on the steps.

After a few minutes of scavenging, she had found a wine cabinet behind the bar, and the rubber seal on its door was still intact. She selected a good sturdy merlot, the only wine that had a prayer of surviving the heat of the fire on the upper floor. With the wine and two glasses in hand, Mallory joined Charles outside on the steps. Indian summer was long gone, but he did not seem to feel the cold night air of fall.

'All right,' she said, 'we'll restage what happened that night.' She held up the bottle for his inspection, and he examined the label.

'This was served at the dinner party. I always wondered how Sheldon Smyth knew the vintner of my private stock. Do you have any idea what these bottles cost?'

'Not a problem, Charles. You're receiving stolen goods from a police officer.' She uncorked the wine and set the bottle down on the steps to let it breathe. He would consider it a worse crime if she simply filled their glasses before the wine had time to mellow. And Mallory had brought some reading material to pass the time. She opened her knapsack and withdrew a small leather-bound book. 'This is Nedda's last diary. I used it to run a bluff on Bitty Smyth. Open it.'

He did.

Every line was the same, the same words written over and over: *Crazy people make sane people crazy*. Charles flipped through page after page, incredulous. He turned his stricken face to hers.

'I have a whole suitcase full of them,' she said, 'all exactly alike. I believe Nedda was sane when she went into the first asylum – but not when she came out of the last one. That would be expecting too much from her. You know why? These lines are true, Charles. Any cop will tell you that. We deal with crazy all the time. And it rubs off. It gets into your head and your gut. It drives you crazy. Nedda wanted me to have her diaries. She asked me to show them to Cleo and Lionel. Maybe she thought she'd written something else on those pages. And I'm sure that Nedda believed she heard music on the radio.'

'Totally mad.' He continued to turn the pages. 'And I didn't see it. How could I have failed this woman so badly?'

'After a few therapy sessions? You said all her conversation with you was lucid, and I'm sure it was. Trust me, she was a strong lady, very good at holding things together in situations . . . where all the sane people crack up.' Mallory took the diary from his hand and looked down at the pages, lines of madness, lines of truth. 'Not your fault, Charles. She seemed sane enough to me, too. Nedda was probably using all her energy to keep her mind together for a while. She had unfinished business with her brother and sister.'

He nodded. 'If Cleo and Lionel had seen the diaries, the relationship would have been quite different.'

'They would've taken better care of her,' said Mallory. 'So if Nedda listened to a radio that never worked—'

'But *I'm* not insane.' He hung his head, suddenly recognizing that this was now open to debate. 'The night you called me to the crime scene, I saw her play that radio. She raised the volume and turned it off with the dial.'

'The whole face of the radio would've lit up when it played. Did you see that?'

'Yes.' Less sure of himself, he added, 'I think so.'

'You're no worse than the average eyewitness. People see what they expect to see.' She reached into her coat pocket and pulled out a sheaf of papers. 'This is the play list for all the radio stations. The night of the dinner party, Nedda told you her station only played jazz from the forties. That's wrong. There's only one that plays jazz that time of night. But it's a mix of contemporary and—'

'I *know* what I heard.'

'Do you? Your sound system only plays classical music. When I programmed the channels, those were the only ones you wanted to hear, remember? Nedda was the expert on jazz. I don't know what tunes you were listening to that night, but she only heard what she wanted to hear.'

'I know jazz when I—'

'Listen to me. One more time, all right? Before Nedda came outside with the wine, she probably tried to disable the alarm. I'm betting it wasn't even turned on. So she tapped the control buttons for the sound system by mistake. That was the music *you* heard, a local station that plays—'

'No, that's not it. Her sister had that system programmed for popular music, rather crass – *and*, I promise you, nothing as elegant as Duke Ellington.'

'You know how easy it is to mess up the programming.' She had reset the channels on his own sound system many times before painting the on/off switch with nail polish and forbidding him to touch any other buttons. 'You wouldn't know the dates of every piece you heard that night. Nedda would, but she was listening to music inside her head – no songs older than the Winter House Massacre.'

'So first,' said Charles, still the skeptic, 'she mistook the stereo panel for the alarm. Then she just got lucky with all those buttons and called up the one jazz station out of all—'

'What, at core, do you believe in? Coincidence and luck – or a haunted radio?'

Her solution had trumped his ghost story. She could see that he was defeated. At least, he had ceased to resist her take-no-prisoners logic. A graceful loser, Charles smiled, but not in the usual inadvertent manner of a happy loon. He had learned a new expression, more sardonic, and Mallory knew that he would never be the same; the cost of closing her cases had become too damned high.

She poured the wine, the medicine, into their glasses, then lifted hers in a toast. 'To the lady who loved jazz.'

Charles clinked his glass with Mallory's, and they sat very close together in the chill night air, sharing wine and a bit of body heat and the illusion that life had not been forever changed by a death too many.

Nearby was a burst of static, and a radio began to play an old Count Basie tune. Mallory drummed her fingers to the same rhythm.

Charles did not.

If he heard the music, he never acknowledged it, not by the tap of his foot or a nod in time to the beat. No, of course not. He was stable now and smiling as he looked up at the stars – the silent stars. All was right on Charles Butler's planet.

Mallory's fingernails dug deep into her palms, making red crescent wounds in the flesh, as if pain could drown the low notes of a string bass thrumming close to the earth – the ripple of piano keys that flew over the trees and up to the sky.

Crazy people make sane people crazy.

She looked back at the open windows of Winter House, expecting to detect a faint glow from the dial of an old-fashioned radio.

COMING NEXT ...

If you've enjoyed this episode in the Detective Kathy Mallory series, turn the page for a preview of her next case.

SHARK MUSIC

PROLOGUE

The haunt of Grand Central Station was a small girl with matted hair and dirty clothes. She appeared only in the commuter hours, morning and evening, when the child believed that she could go invisibly among the throng of travelers in crisscrossing foot traffic, as if that incredible face could go anywhere without attracting stares. Concessionaires reached for their phones to call the number on a policeman's card and say, 'She's back.'

The girl always stood beneath the great arch, pinning her hopes on a tip from a panhandler: Everyone in the world would pass by – so said the smelly old bum – if she could only wait long enough. The child patiently stared into a thousand faces, waiting for a man she had never met. She was certain to know him by his eyes, the same rare color as her own, and he would recognize young Kathy's face as a small copy of her mother's. Her father would be so happy to see her; this belief was unshakable, for she was a little zealot in the faith of the bastard child.

He never came. Months passed by. She never learned.

Toward the close of this day, the child had a tired, hungry look about her. Hands clenched into fists, she raged against the panhandler, whose fairy tale had trapped her here in the long wait.

At the top of rush hour, she spotted a familiar face, but it was the wrong one. The fat detective was seen in thin slices between the bodies of travelers. Though he was on the far side of the mezzanine,

Kathy fancied that she could hear him huffing and wheezing as he ran toward her. And she waited.

Crouching.

One second, two seconds, three.

When he came within grabbing distance, the game was on – all that passed for sport in the life of a homeless child. She ran for the grand staircase, shooting past him and making the fat man spin. Sneakers streaking, slapping stone, the little blond bullet in blue jeans gained the stairs, feet flying, only alighting on every third step.

Laughing, *laughing*.

At the top of the stairs, she turned around to see that the chase was done – and so early this time. Her pursuer had reached the bottom step and could not climb another. The fat man was in some pain and out of breath. One hand went to his chest, as if he could stop a heart attack that way.

The little girl mouthed the words, *Die, old man.*

They locked eyes. His were pleading, hers were hard. And she gave him her famous *Gotcha* smile.

One day, she would become his prisoner – but not today – and Louis Markowitz would become her foster father. Years later and long after they had learned to care for one another, each time Kathy Mallory gave him this smile, he would check his back pocket to see if his wallet was still there.

ONE

It appeared that the woman had died by her own hand in this Upper West Side apartment. It was less apparent that anyone had ever lived here.

The decor was a cold scheme of sharp corners, hard edges of glass and steel, with extremes of black leather and bare white walls. Though fully furnished, a feeling of emptiness prevailed. And the place had been recently abandoned – unless one counted the stranger, the corpse left behind in Kathy Mallory's front room.

The gunshot to the victim's heart made more sense after reading the handwritten words on a slip of paper that might pass for a suicide note: *Love is the death of me.*

'If only she'd signed the damn thing,' said Dr Slope.

The homicide detective nodded.

Chief Medical Examiner Edward Slope had turned out for this special occasion of sudden death at a cop's address. If not for a personal interest in this case, the remains might have been shipped to his morgue on a city bus for all the doctor cared. A house call was not in his job description; that was the province of an on-call pathologist. But tonight Dr Slope had departed from protocol and forgotten his socks. And, though he wore a pajama top beneath his suit jacket, he was still the best-dressed man in the room.

By contrast, Detective Sergeant Riker had the rumpled look of one who had gone to bed in his street clothes. His face also had a slept-in effect, creased with the imprint of a wadded cocktail napkin.

Drunk or sober, Riker's nature was easygoing, but his hooded eyes gave him a constant air of suspicion. He could not help it, and he could not hide it tonight of all nights. The gunshot victim had been found in his partner's apartment, and now he awaited the official coin toss of homicide or suicide.

Because the medical examiner had known Detective Mallory in her puppy days, the older man was only mildly suspicious, only a *little* sarcastic when he asked, 'And where is Kathy tonight?'

Riker shrugged this off, as if to say that he had no idea. Untrue. By a trace of credit card activity, he knew that Mallory had filled her gas tank in the states of Pennsylvania and Ohio. But he thought it best not to mention that his young partner was on the run, for the medical examiner had not yet signed off on a cause of death. The detective looked down at the dead woman, who appeared close to his own age of fifty-five. If not for the bullet hole in her chest, Savannah Sirus might be asleep. She looked all in, exhausted by her life.

Dr Slope knelt beside the corpse. 'Well, I can understand why you'd want a second opinion.'

Oh, yeah.

And Detective Riker needed this opinion from someone in the tiny circle of people who cared for his young partner, though she did nothing to encourage affection. Both men had been forbidden to call her Kathy since her graduation from the police academy; she so liked that frosty distance of her surname. However, the doctor had found it hard to break a habit formed in Mallory's childhood, and so she was always Kathy to him. Brave man, he even called her that to her face.

Dr Slope continued his observation of the corpse. 'Not the usual way for a woman to kill herself.' Women were self-poisoners and wrist slashers. Their suicides were rarely this violent.

'Yeah,' said Riker, 'but it happens. This looks like a typical vanity shot to me.' That much was true; men were inclined to eat their guns, but the ladies seldom messed up their faces with headshots. He saw the victim's chest wound as a small blessing in Mallory's favor.

'There's no evidence that Miss Sirus held the muzzle to her breast,' said Dr Slope, raising a point on the debit side.

Absent was the gunshot residue, the smoky halo of point-blank range, and this had set off alarm bells for the first officer on the scene tonight. This wound more closely resembled a conversational range between victim and shooter. Rather than turn another cop over to Internal Affairs, the West Side detectives had shifted this case to the SoHo precinct where Mallory worked. Riker could still make a case for suicide if the woman had held the gun at arm's length – and that scenario spoke to fear of firearms. Perhaps Savannah Sirus had even closed her eyes before she pulled the trigger.

Or maybe Mallory shot her.

After the corpse had been rolled over, Dr Slope pulled a thermometer from his black bag. Riker, who was old school, averted his eyes as the medical examiner raised the lady's skirt and pulled her panties down. The detective moved to the couch to wait out the findings on the body temperature.

Alongside the Polaroid shots he had taken of the dead body, a cheap handbag lay on the coffee table. It could only belong to the victim, for this was nothing that his partner would carry. Mallory's taste ran upscale; even her blue jeans were tailored, and squad-room gossip had it that the studs were made of gold. Perverse kid, she did what she could to encourage rumors of illegal income. This was her idea of fun: Catch me if you can.

Hard rain beat down upon a speeding car that was far from home. The small vehicle was deceptive in its styling, for this was not a model rumored to eat up the road, and yet it raced at wild, outlaw speeds.

Nearing the western edge of rainy Ohio, a lone patrolman blinked rapidly to clear his tired eyes, but there was no mistake of blurred vision. His engine was powerful, pushed to the limit on this wet road – and the Volkswagen Beetle was leaving him behind.

Impossible.

His aunt owned a car like that one, and he knew the speedometer topped out at one-forty, though he considered that to be a private joke on the part of the manufacturer.

The convertible's color scheme of silver body and black ragtop was all too popular, and the lack of a visible license plate further complicated the problem of identification. It was a short chase — hardly a race. The other car was not speeding up, nor was there any wobble or weave to signify that the driver was in any way alarmed by the spinning red light and screaming siren. The trooper's radar clocked the VW's cruising speed at a constant one hundred and eighty miles an hour.

Oh, fool!

What was he thinking?

He banged his fist on the dashboard. Damned equipment never worked right. Rain-slick road or dry pavement, that speed was an impossible feat for the little ragtop Beetle. But then, he had never met the driver.

And he never would.

At the subtle rise of road ahead, he could swear that he saw bright streaks of forked lightning under the wheels; the silver car had left the ground, flying, hydroplaning on the water.

The silver Beetle was out of sight when the trooper's car stopped well short of the Ohio state line — beaten. There would be no official report on his patrol car being humiliated by, of all things, a Volkswagen, for this would be akin to reporting alien spacecraft. And so, without a single speeding ticket, the small convertible would run Route 80 through the neighboring state of Indiana and across another border into Illinois. The driver's destination was the Chicago intersection of Adams Street and Michigan Avenue — the eye of the storm.

Behind his back, Riker heard the snap of the doctor's latex gloves. The examination of Savannah Sirus was done.

The detective asked, oh so casually, as if there were not a great deal riding on the answer, 'So, Doc, what do I put down for the time of death?'

'Your absolute faith in rectal thermometers is really quite touching,' said Dr Slope. 'I don't suppose a helpful neighbor heard the shot while he was looking at his wristwatch?'

The detective looked over one shoulder and smiled at the older man to say, *No such luck.* The neighbors had heard gunfire from this apartment on other occasions, and, good New Yorkers all, they had become selectively deaf to what Mallory was doing in here.

'Well, then,' said Slope, 'just put down today's date for now. Rigor mortis is always a crapshoot, and I've got too many variables to call a time of death with body temperature. An open window on a cold night – dried sweat stains on her blouse. For all I know, the woman had a raging fever when she died.' He circled the couch to stand before the detective. 'So what've *you* got?'

Riker upended Savannah Sirus's purse and spilled her possessions across the glass coffee table. There were two clusters of house keys. He recognized a silver fob on the set that would open the door to this apartment. 'Looks like the lady was Mallory's houseguest.' Another item from the purse was an airplane ticket from Chicago to New York. 'I don't think we'll be calling out a crime-scene unit for this one.' He was testing the waters here, for the medical examiner had not yet made a pronouncement of suicide.

Dr Slope turned to face his minions waiting in the hallway beyond the open door. He gave them a curt nod. The two men wheeled a gurney through the front door and set to work on bagging the victim's remains. When they had cleared the room, taking the late Savannah Sirus with them, the doctor sank down on the couch beside Riker. 'You think your partner knows what happened here tonight?'

Rather than lie, the detective said, 'Well, you tell me.' One wave of his right hand included the leftovers of a takeout dinner, an empty wineglass and a saucer full of cigarette butts. 'Point taken?'

The medical examiner nodded. He was well acquainted with

Mallory's freakish neatness. The young homicide detective would never tolerate anything out of place in her apartment. She was the sort who compulsively straightened picture frames in other people's houses. Ergo, the mess had been made after her departure. Dr Slope stared at the open window. 'Riker? You think our victim originally planned to jump, then changed her mind and shot herself?'

'No.' But he understood the other man's reasoning. This was the only open window on a cold spring night – and the screen had been raised. 'The woman knew Mallory reasonably well. She's been staying here awhile.' He held up the plane ticket. 'Got here three weeks ago.' He neglected to mention that the ticket was round-trip; Mallory's houseguest had no thoughts of dying in New York City – not on the day she arrived. 'Savannah Sirus didn't know much about guns and ammo. Now this is the way I see it. She thought the bullet might pass through her body and mess up a wall. Well, Mallory wouldn't like that, would she?'

The doctor was shaking his head in accord with this.

Riker continued. 'So the lady opened that window and pulled up the screen. That's where she was standing when she shot herself. And it looks like she's been planning this for a while.' He pointed to the gun on the floor. 'You didn't think that was Mallory's, did you?'

'No,' said Dr Slope. 'I suppose not.'

The weapon on the carpet was a lightweight twenty-two, a lady's gun. Kathy Mallory was no lady; she carried a cannon, a Smith & Wesson .357 with a bigger kick and better stopping, maiming, killing power.

However, Riker knew that this gun on the floor did indeed belong to Mallory. She collected all kinds of firearms, none of them registered, and a twenty-two had its uses. But the matter of gun ownership might interfere with the doctor's finding of suicide.

The detective slouched deep into the leather upholstery as he pondered where his partner was headed tonight. And why had she stopped showing up for work?

Mallory, what did you do with the time – all your crazy days of downtime?

Rising from the black leather couch, Riker forced a yawn, as if he needed to affect a blasé attitude about violent death. In fact, he had been born to it, a true son of New York City. 'I'm gonna check out the other rooms.'

He passed by the guestroom and caught a glimpse of rumpled sheets and a blanket used by Savannah Sirus. Farther down the hall, another open door gave him a view of Mallory's own bedding. There was not a single wrinkle in the coverlet, as if no one had ever slept there, and this lent credence to a theory that she never slept at all. Mallory the Machine – that was what other cops called her.

Dr Slope was walking behind him when Riker entered another room of spotless good order, his partner's den, where no dust mote dared to land. Some people had dogs; Mallory kept computers, and they sat in a neat row of three, their Cyclops eyes facing the door, waiting for her to come home. Even her technical manuals were well trained, each one perched on the precise edge of a bookcase shelf. The back wall was lined with cork, and Riker was puzzled by what, at first glance, had passed for striped wallpaper. He turned his head to catch a look of profound shock in the medical examiner's eyes.

And that was puzzling, too.

From ceiling molding to baseboards, the cork wall was covered with sheets of paper, each one filled with columns of figures. Riker guessed that these were telephone numbers by the separation spaces for area codes and prefixes. Though reading glasses rested in his breast pocket, he preferred to squint, and now he noticed that six of the numerals were arranged in random combinations, but one floating sequence of four remained the same in every line. So this was what she had been doing with the time since he had seen her last – apart from pumping bullets into her walls, blowing bugs to kingdom come when she could not find a fly swatter. And, given a dead body in the front room, he suspected her of worse behavior. Thankfully, in some saner moment, she had patched the holes in the plaster.

Dr Slope's eyes widened as he took in the thousands of numbers on the cork wall. Most had red lines drawn though them, all perfectly straight in machine precision. He moved closer to the wall, the better to see with his bifocals. 'Oh, my God. She *drew* these lines with a pen.'

And those hand-drawn lines could only indicate telephone numbers that had not panned out for Mallory. The detective gripped the medical examiner's arm and turned the man around to face him. 'You've seen this before.' Riker's tone slipped into interrogation mode, close to accusation when he said, 'You know what this is all about. Talk to me.'

The doctor nodded, taking no offense. 'I saw something like this a long time ago – on the Markowitzes' old phone bills. As I recall, it was that first month after Kathy came to live with them. So she was eleven years old.'

Yeah, sure she was.

Louis Markowitz, a late great cop, and his wife, Helen, had raised the girl as their own, but never would Kathy Mallory talk to them about her origins. She would not even give up her right age. At first, she had insisted on being twelve, and Lou had bargained her down by one year, though she might have been a ten-year-old or a child as young as nine.

The medical examiner stood at the center of the room, wiping the lenses of his bifocals with a handkerchief. 'Lou showed me his phone bills, line after line of long-distance calls. Kathy made all of them.' The doctor stepped closer to the wall, nodding now. 'Yes, it's the same. You see, when she was a child, she was prone to nightmares. Lou thought the bad dreams might've triggered those calls. Sometimes he'd come downstairs late at night and catch her with the telephone. She made hundreds of these calls that first month. This wall reminds me of the Markowitzes' phone bill. In every long-distance telephone number, four of the numerals were always the same, and the others just seemed random. She wouldn't tell Lou anything helpful, but he worked out a good theory. He knew there was someone out there, some connection to her early life, but she could only remember part of a telephone number.'

'So Lou called the numbers on his phone bill.'

'Yes, all of them. And he found an odd pattern. Every call was made at some obscene hour of the night – so even the men were inclined to remember them. You see, when a man answered, she hung up the phone. But if a woman answered, she'd always say, "It's Kathy, I'm lost." '

'That must've driven the women *nuts*.'

'Yes, it touched their soft spots and their panic buttons.' The doctor turned his face to a high-rise window on the dark city. 'According to Lou, all of the women begged Kathy to tell them who she was – and where could they *find* her? But the child would just hang up on them. Lou figured that Kathy never got the response she wanted. Those women didn't know who she was. So then she'd dial the next combination of numbers . . . trying to make a connection to someone who would recognize her.'

'A woman.' Riker fished through his pockets and pulled out a piece of paper given to him by the first officer on the scene. This note listed sketchy vitals of victim identification, including a home telephone for the late Savannah Sirus. One sequence of four numbers matched the ones repeated on the cork wall. 'I guess the kid finally made her connection.'

Eight hundred miles away, another corpse had been found.

Hours after the windows of shops and offices had gone dark, an umbrella was snatched up by a gust of wet wind. Tearing and twirling, it scraped across the broad steps of the Chicago Art Institute. The only watchers were two great cats, standing lions made of bronze and blind to this broken trophy from the battle against horizontal rain.

Their green patinas were altered by strikes of lightning and red flashes from the spinning lights of police vehicles. Cars and vans converged upon the construction site at the other side of Michigan Avenue.

Two homicide detectives were soaked through and through. They surrendered, throwing up their hands and then jamming them into coat pockets. Grim and helpless, they watched the heavy rain come down on their forensic evidence and carry it away. There it went, the body fluids, stray hairs and fibers, all flowing off down the gutter. The corpse, washed clean, could tell them nothing beyond the cause of death – extreme cruelty. There had never been a crime scene quite like this one in the history of Chicago, Illinois, nothing as shocking, nothing as sad.

The religious detective made the sign of the cross. The other one closed his eyes.

The dead man at their feet was pointing the way down Adams Street, also known as Route 66, a road of many names. Steinbeck had called it a road of flight.

The rainstorm had abated, but the owner of the gas station had no plans to do any legal business at this late hour. Locked behind the wide door of his garage was one happy crew of gambling men in the grand slam of Chicago crap games, high rollers only, beer flowing, dice clicking and folding money slapping the cement floor.

Big night.

A fortune was in play amid clouds of cigar smoke when the silver Volkswagen's driver, a young woman in need of gas, had come softly rapping at the door. Then she had banged on the heavy metal with both fists and kicked it a few times, calling way too much attention to the activities inside.

Stop the music!

And now he stood beside her under the bright lights of his gas pumps – and the crap game was forgotten.

'Is that what I think it is?' The man gazed lovingly upon her engine. 'Oh, yeah.' He looked up at her with a wide grin. 'Girl, what have you done? A Porsche engine in a Volkswagen Beetle?'

And *how* had she done it?

Even if he had been cold sober, this problem would have given him a headache. It *might* have been possible to modify an old model with the engine in the rear, but this was a new Beetle with front-wheel drive, built for an engine under the *hood*. No kind of engine could work in the damned *trunk*. Yet there it was.

He had to take three paces back to see how this magic trick was worked. The silhouette of the car was slightly off, elongated, but otherwise a perfect job. The girl had fabricated a VW Beetle onto the frame of the 911 Twin Turbo Porsche. Before he stopped to wonder why she had done such a thing, he had already moved on to the problem of the convertible's roof: that tall hump of a ragtop might cut into the speed, but not by much. Now how would this counterfeit body affect the Porsche's performance in cornering?

'Hey, girl? If you take a curve too fast, you'll roll this car. You know that, right?'

Advice and gasoline were all that he could offer her. The tall blonde preferred to work alone. By frosty glare and body language, she had taught him to keep his greasy hands off her immaculate engine.

'You got some time?' he asked. 'I could put on a roll bar.'

The girl shook her head. No sale. She selected another tool from a lambskin pouch and worked on the mounting for a wiring harness. He guessed there was a rattle that annoyed her. Well, it would never do that again. She made it that tight, stopping just shy of stripping the screws.

'Girl, you might wanna think it over. If not here, then get one somewhere else.' It was not her money he was after; he only wanted to keep this youngster alive. She appeared to be the same age as his daughter. 'With a roll bar, you'd have a sporting chance to keep your pretty head if the car flips over.'

And damned pretty she was with her milk-white skin, her cat's eyes and those long red fingernails. The girl in blue jeans was downright unnatural; real people never looked this good at close quarters. And so he guessed that she was not from his part of the world, but maybe from someplace straight up and past the moon. Hers were the greenest eyes he had ever seen. If asked, he would not be able to describe their color in terms of any living thing. Electric, he would say. Yeah, electric green and bright like a dashboard light – not human at all. And he thought she might be carrying a gun beneath her denim jacket.

His gaze had lingered too long on that bulge where a shoulder holster might be. Her eyes were on him now – so cold. She seemed to be looking at him across the distance between a cat and a mouse, and he knew that this was all the warning she would ever give him. He had his choice of two creatures: she might be a stone killer, and then there was his own kind. 'You're a cop, right?' The mechanic pulled a wallet from the pocket of his grimy coveralls, and he did this slowly – no sudden movements to set her off. He showed her the identification of a retired Chicago police officer.

Her face gave away nothing, not her next move, not anything at all. The situation could go sour at any second. If he had guessed wrong about her, he might wind up dead. In his sixtieth year, his reflexes had slowed. But now, as a sign of trust, she ignored him once more and turned back to a perusal of her engine.

He began to breathe again.

'I was on the job for thirty-five years.' He faced the bastardized car, and his voice carried just a touch of sarcasm. 'Thought I'd seen it all.' Still attempting to make conversation, he said, 'Nobody would ever figure you for a Volkswagen type. Not your style, girl. It's a car for people my age, burnout rock 'n' rollers who could never get past the sixties. Hell, this should've been *my* car.'

The Porsche beneath the fabricated shell explained a lot – on several levels. A true VW convertible was a happy little vehicle with no hard edges, a cartoon of a car, and it got a smile everywhere it went. He took the young blonde's measure again. Cosmetics – like this fake car body hiding a killer engine – could never so neatly disguise what *she* was. And if this young cop believed that she could work undercover, she was dead wrong. But he could think of no other explanation for a civil servant driving a car with an engine that cost the moon and the stars – unless the kid was on the take.

Her dashboard had another modification that never came from the factory. He made another foray to draw her out for a chance at shoptalk, and he meant *cop*shop. 'Well, I see you got a police scanner. Me, too.'

She studied her engine, forgetting that he was alive.

He tried again. 'So . . . you know about the murder on Adams Street? . . . No?' Did silence mean *no* on her planet? 'They found the body right in the middle of the damn road. Real piece of work. I heard the cop chatter on my scanner.'

'Adams Street and what?'

'Michigan Avenue.' He had a gut feeling that she already knew this address, but his guts had lied to him before, and a bullet fired when his back was turned had forced his retirement from the Chicago Police Department.

Casually, as if opining on the weather, the girl said, 'And there's something peculiar about the crime scene.'

Though she had not asked him a question, he gave her a slow nod to say, *Oh, yeah. This one's about as peculiar as it ever gets.* Aloud, he said, 'I bet that's why you turned out tonight. Am I right?' Force of habit from the old days, he would always chain one odd thing to another: this strange young cop, this bastard car with New York plates – this crime. 'A serial killer, right? And New York's got an interest?'

Oh, how he missed the Job, his old religion of Copland.

The young blonde packed up her tool pouch and closed the trunk on that fabulous engine. The fuel pump rang its bell – the gas tank was full. She handed him a platinum credit card, giving him second thoughts about her status as underpaid police. She waited in silence for her receipt.

As she was driving off, though he had no hope of being heard, he called after her, 'You be careful out there!' His eyes traveled over darkened buildings where innocent people lay sleeping. 'And the rest of you stay the hell out of her way,' he warned them in a lower voice – in case he had guessed wrong about – what was she called? He looked down at his copy of the credit card receipt and read only one name. 'Well, don't that beat all?'

American Express called her Mallory – just Mallory.

The mighty storm front, born in Chicago, had cut a sodden path eastward. It rained on a patch of the Jersey coast, and then, like many another tourist, it crossed the George Washington Bridge, entered New York City – and died.

Only a few drops of water pocked the windshield of a sleek black sedan as it rolled out of a SoHo garage and pulled into the narrow street. The traffic was light, and this was good, because Detective Riker was hardly paying attention to the other cars as he rode out of town.

After another check on Mallory's credit cards, he learned that she had bought a late supper in South Bend, Indiana, still traveling west on Route 80, and leaving no doubt that Chicago was her destination. With one cellphone call, Riker had activated the anti-theft device installed in her car. And then he had bartered his soul to the Favor Bank to bury the paperwork on her surveillance. Given her straight route and likely point of entry, her LoJack's signal had been picked up when the car crossed the state line into Illinois. And, thanks to a police car tracker in Chicago, Riker knew that his partner had stopped awhile at a gas station in that city – even before she had used her credit card to pay for fuel. Though she was definitely in flight, he took some comfort in her use of traceable credit instead of cash. And she knowingly drove a car equipped with a LoJack device; this alone spoke well for the theory that she had not murdered Savannah Sirus.

And everything else argued against innocence.

In his request for covert assistance from Chicago, the New York detective had traded on his reputation as a shabby dresser with a low bank balance; these hallmarks of a dead-honest cop made his badge shine in the dark. There were even rookies in the state of Illinois who had heard of Riker. And he planned to destroy the best part of himself – for Mallory's sake.

He stopped for a red light and closed his eyes. More frightening than the corpse in Mallory's front room was the wall of telephone numbers in her den. If nightmares had triggered her childhood calls, then Riker had to wonder, *Kid, what are your dreams like now?*

Have you read every case in the Kathy Mallory series?

Mallory's Oracle

Crime brought them together. A killer tears them apart.

Book 1 in the Kathy Mallory series.

When NYPD Sergeant Kathy Mallory was an eleven-year-old street kid, she got caught stealing. The detective who found her was Louis Markowitz. He should have arrested her. Instead he raised her as his own, in the best tradition of New York's finest.

Now Markowitz is dead, and Mallory the first officer on the scene. She knows any criminal who could outsmart her father is no ordinary human. This is a ruthless serial killer, a freak from the night-side of the mind.

And one question troubles her more than any other: why did he go in there alone?

The Man Who Lied to Women

Some lies can get you killed.

Book 2 in the Kathy Mallory series.

No one in New York's Special Crimes section knows much about Sergeant Kathy Mallory's origins. They only know that she can bewitch the most complex computer systems, can slip into the minds of killers with disturbing ease.

When a woman is murdered in Central Park, it appears to be a case of mistaken identity. Mallory goes hunting the killer, armed with under-the-skin knowledge of the man's mind and the bare clue of a lie.

Mallory holds on to the truth: everybody lies, and some lies lead to death. And she knows that, to trap the killer, she must put her own life at risk.

Killing Critics

When art imitates death.

Book 3 in the Kathy Mallory series.

An artist is murdered, in a stylish, surprising and deadly act of performance art. The murder almost goes unnoticed, but it reminds NYPD detective Kathy Mallory of an older, more brutal crime investigated years before by Mallory's now dead adoptive father.

As soon as Mallory starts to work on the new crime, old ghosts rise up, and the word comes down from on high to close her down, to shut her out the case.

But for Mallory, rules exist only to be shattered . . .

Flight of the Stone Angel

Revenge is a reason for living.

Book 4 in the Kathy Mallory series.

Seventeen years ago, a six-year-old girl disappeared from the small town of Dayborn, Louisiana.

She vanished the day of her mother's murder, and all assumed that she, too, was dead.

Now, Kathy Mallory has returned home. She has left her badge and her police issue revolver behind in New York City. She is no longer a cop. Just a daughter in search of a very personal revenge.

Shell Game

There's a shooter in the crowd.

Book 5 in the Kathy Mallory series.

At a sell-out festival of magicians in Manhattan, in front of a live audience and eight million television viewers, a death-defying trick goes tragically wrong.

NYPD detective Kathy Mallory has learned the hard way that things are rarely what they seem. But she is the only cop who believes the death is not an accident.

Hiding behind the smoke and mirrors is a ruthless killer who will soon strike again.

Crime School

Some people never learn.

Book 6 in the Kathy Mallory series.

Fifteen years have passed since a junkie whore and a police informer, known simply as Sparrow, cared for a feral child when she was lost and alone.

Now, on a hot August afternoon, in an East Side apartment, a woman is found hanged. Carefully placed red candles and an enormous quantity of dead flies suggest a bizarre ritual. NYPD detective Kathy Mallory does not recognise her immediately. But soon finds that she is staring her bitter past in the face, as she pursues a case which also has its origin in an unsolved murder committed years ago.

Dead Famous

How fast can you run?

Book 7 in the Kathy Mallory series.

It's the highest profile acquittal in recent history – and when a serial killer starts taking justice into his own hands, interest hits fever pitch.

NYPD detective Kathy Mallory finds herself in a race against time to save the remaining three members of the jury before the Reaper gets to them first.

And before the radio shock-jock Ian Zachary plays the next round in his deadly ratings-grabbing game of 'hunt the juror'.

Shark Music

They search the highway of death.

Book 9 in the Kathy Mallory series.

The mutilated body is found lying on the ground in Chicago, a dead hand pointing down Adams Street, also known as Route 66, a road of many names. And now of many deaths.

A silent caravan of cars drives down the road, each passenger bearing a photograph, but none of them the same. They are the parents of missing children, brought together by the word that children's gravesites are being discovered along with the Mother Road.

Detective Kathy Mallory drives with them.

The Chalk Girl

A child covered in blood. A body in the trees.

Book 10 in the Kathy Mallory series.

She appeared in Central Park: red-haired, blue-eyed, smiling, perfect – except for the blood. It fell from the sky, she said, while she was looking for her uncle, who turned into a tree. Poor child, people thought. And then they found the body in the tree.

For NYPD detective Kathy Mallory, there is something about the girl that she understands. And she will lead to a story of extraordinary crimes; murders stretching back years, blackmail and complicity and a particular cruelty that only someone with Mallory's history could fully recognise.

In the next few weeks, Kathy Mallory will deal with them all . . . in her own way.

It Happens in the Dark

Forty seconds from alive to dead.

Book 11 in the Kathy Mallory series.

The killer had just forty seconds to act, in total darkness, surrounded by a theatre full of people.

NYPD detective Kathy Mallory knows that even the most impossible of crimes have an explanation, if only you look in the right place. And after three deaths in three nights, she needs to find that place soon.

But when everything about the scene of crime is rigged for dramatic effect, and the suspects are actors, judging the difference between appearances and reality can be deadly . . .

You can buy any of these other bestselling
books by **Carol O'Connell** from your
bookshop or *direct from her publisher*.

FREE P&P AND UK DELIVERY
(Overseas and Ireland £3.50 per book)

Kathy Mallory series

Mallory's Oracle	£7.99
The Man Who Lied to Women	£8.99
Killing Critics	£8.99
Flight of the Stone Angel	£8.99
Shell Game	£8.99
Crime School	£8.99
Dead Famous	£8.99
Winter House	£8.99
Shark Music	£8.99
The Chalk Girl	£8.99
It Happens in the Dark	£8.99

Stand-alone novels

Bone by Bone	£6.99
Judas Child	£8.99

TO ORDER SIMPLY CALL THIS NUMBER

01235 400 414

or visit our website: www.headline.co.uk

Prices and availability subject to change without notice